Praise for Larry B...

"Larry Brown writes like a force of natu... seems lived in, authentic, and on the m...

"He has an ear for the way people talk, an eye for their habits and manners, a heart for their frailties and foibles, and a love for their struggles and triumphs." **–JOHN GRISHAM**

"He is blunt and abrasive about subjects that tend to cause flinching. He tells stories in plain language." **–The New Yorker**

"He knows things . . . you didn't think would get found out until Judgment Day." **–JACK BUTLER**

"He is a master." **–BARRY HANNAH**

"[He] writes as if he owns—legitimately and without challenge, mind you—the entire grief-stricken, joy-ridden world, and a few things beyond it." **–BOB SHACOCHIS**

"Direct, powerful, and singularly honest." **–WILLIE MORRIS**

"Clear, simple and powerful." **–Time**

Praise for *Facing the Music*

"A stunning debut." **–The Atlanta Journal-Constitution**

"One of our finest writers." **–CHARLES FRAZIER**

"Larry Brown . . . is a choir of Southern voices, all by himself."
–The Dallas Morning News

Praise for *Big Bad Love*

"Invested with stunning presence and complexity."
—*The New York Times Book Review*

"Big, bad and wonderful . . . A stunning collection of stories about real people and real life." —*The Atlanta Journal-Constitution*

"Rather like some perfect object one has come across in a wilderness, these are stories of affirmation . . . Human, compassionate and compelling." —HARRY CREWS, *Los Angeles Times*

"A voice as true as a gun rack, unpretentious and uncorrupted. [In] a surprising combination of sharp wit and great sorrow . . . comes a sure sense of a compassionate writer deeply in touch with the sorrowful rhythms of not just Southern, but human, life."
—*The Philadelphia Inquirer*

Praise for *Joe*

"Brilliant . . . Larry Brown has slapped his own fresh tattoo on the big right arm of Southern Lit."
—*The Washington Post Book World*

"The novel, written in a luminescent prose tempered by wit, moves gracefully forward by tracking the independent movements of its three artfully conceived and skillfully balanced principals. As their lives mesh, the novel's momentum, and its rewards, build. A fourth major role may be said to belong to the terrain itself, a Mississippi so vividly sketched you can all but mount it on your wall." —*The New York Times Book Review*

"Sinewy and lyrical." —*Los Angeles Times*

"Larry Brown has an ear for the way people talk, an eye for their habits and manners, a heart for the frailties and foibles, and a love for their struggles and triumphs. His fireman's diary is a wonderful book." **—JOHN GRISHAM**

"Larry Brown is never romantic about danger . . . In this book he goes through his life with the same meticulous attention with which Thoreau circled the woods around Walden Pond."
—*The New York Times Book Review*

"Clear, simple, and powerful, and great rowdy fun to read."
—*Time*

Praise for *Father and Son*

"Larry Brown will cause you to be disappointed with every other novel you may pick up this year." **—THOM JONES**

"His most wise, humane and haunting work to date." **—*Publishers Weekly*** **(starred review)**

"Riveting." **—*Kirkus Reviews*** **(starred review)**

"This is a novel that will live with you day and night."
—KAYE GIBBONS

"A powerful tale of love and betrayal, family ties and brutal revenge."
—*The Atlanta Journal-Constitution*

"The model is Faulkner, but his influence has been absorbed and transcended." **—*The New York Times Book Review***

"So vividly written it is almost cinematic."
—*The Orlando Sentinel*

"It reads like a stud poker game of life, tension growing with the turning of each card." —*The Dallas Morning News*

"Cancel the competition for suspense thriller of the year. Larry Brown has already won it with *Father and Son*."
—*St. Louis Post-Dispatch*

Praise for *Fay*

"Larry Brown is a true original, and *Fay* is among his best works. Follow Fay past the kudzu-draped woods and cinderblock bars and sunburned fields of Brown's imagination. It's a journey you won't regret." —*Chicago Tribune*

"For years, Larry Brown has been known and respected as a writer's writer. But now, with *Fay*, this profoundly southern novelist may win the broad readership he so richly deserves . . . Spellbinding."
—*People*

"A well-oiled machine . . . More ambitious than any of Brown's previous novels, *Fay* might just be his best work yet."
—*The Denver Post*

"A novel of the first order. . . . Gripping and virtually seamless . . . The writing, the characters, and the plot are so compelling that you can't help but stay with the book until its conclusion."
—*The Washington Post Book World*

Praise for *Billy Ray's Farm*

"Brown is the real thing." *—The Washington Post*

"Brown makes us care about these rural days and nights—and the people who pass through them." *—Southern Living*

"Brown's muscular sentences hold us in the intensity of the moment . . . forceful description with unexpected tenderness."
—The Atlanta Journal-Constitution

"Equal parts Henry David Thoreau and long-suffering Job."
—Minneapolis Star Tribune

"Like his novels, Brown's essays are built out of small, often raw details." *—USA Toda*y

"Read this book. Read it for its emotional honesty and humor."
—The Roanoke Times

TINY LOVE

ALSO BY LARRY BROWN

Facing the Music, stories

Dirty Work, a novel

Big Bad Love, stories

Joe, a novel

On Fire, essays

Father and Son, a novel

Fay, a novel

Billy Ray's Farm: Essays from a Place Called Tula, essays

A Miracle of Catfish, a novel

TINY LOVE

The Complete Stories
of Larry Brown

WITH A FOREWORD BY JONATHAN MILES

ALGONQUIN BOOKS OF CHAPEL HILL   2019

Published by
ALGONQUIN BOOKS OF CHAPEL HILL
Post Office Box 2225
Chapel Hill, North Carolina 27515-2225

a division of
WORKMAN PUBLISHING
225 Varick Street
New York, New York 10014

"Plant Growin' Problems" originally appeared in *Easyriders* (June 1982). "Nightmare"
originally appeared in *Rod Serling's The Twilight Zone Magazine* (January/February 1985).
"The Crying" and "And Another Thing" originally appeared in *Reb Fiction '90*, edited by
Barry Hannah (Southern Reader Books, 1990). "Tiny Love" originally appeared in
Writer's Harvest, edited by William H. Shore (Mariner Books, 1994). "A Birthday Party"
originally appeared in the *Southern Review* (Autumn 1992). "A Roadside Resurrection"
originally appeared in the *Paris Review* (Fall 1991). *Facing the Music* © 1984, 1985, 1986,
1988 by the estate of Larry Brown, published by Algonquin Books of Chapel Hill in 1989.
Big Bad Love © 1990 by the estate of Larry Brown, published by Algonquin Books of
Chapel Hill in 1990.

This is a work of fiction. While, as in all fiction, the literary perceptions and
insights are based on experience, all names, characters, places, and incidents
either are products of the author's imagination or are used fictitiously.

LIBRARY OF CONGRESS CATALOGING-IN-PUBLICATION DATA

Names: Brown, Larry, 1951–2004, author. | Miles, Jonathan, writer of foreword.
Title: Tiny love : the complete stories of Larry Brown / with a Foreword by Jonathan Miles.
Other titles: Short stories
Description: First edition. | Chapel Hill, North Carolina : Algonquin Books of Chapel Hill,
    2019. | Includes bibliographical references.
Identifiers: LCCN 2019008852 | ISBN 9781616209759 (trade paperback : alk. paper)
Subjects: LCSH: Short stories, American.
Classification: LCC PS3552.R6927 A6 2019 | DDC 813/.54—dc23
LC record available at https://lccn.loc.gov/2019008852

10 9 8 7 6 5 4 3 2 1

First Edition

CONTENTS

Foreword
by Jonathan Miles   vii

Plant Growin' Problems   1

Nightmare   12

FACING THE MUSIC

Facing the Music   19

Kubuku Rides (This Is It)   27

The Rich   45

Old Frank and Jesus   52

Boy and Dog   66

Julie: A Memory   77

Samaritans   90

Night Life   102

Leaving Town   125

The End of Romance   149

The Crying   157

And Another Thing   173

Tiny Love   179

A Birthday Party   204

BIG BAD LOVE

Part I

    Falling Out of Love   219

    The Apprentice   229

    Wild Thing   241

    Big Bad Love   254

    Gold Nuggets   267

    Waiting for the Ladies   280

    Old Soldiers   290

    Sleep   302

Part II

    Discipline   311

Part III

    92 Days   339

A Roadside Resurrection   415

FOREWORD

Larry hated me telling this story. But Larry also understood that the most natural place to begin is at the beginning, and this was ours.

Late in 1992 I was sitting at the upstairs bar at the City Grocery in Oxford, Mississippi, when a man approached me. He was older than me by a couple decades: neither tall nor short, sparely built, with doleful-looking eyes and a narrow face etched in worry lines. Shyly, in a smoky, murmury drawl, he asked if I was the one who'd written the short story in that week's issue of *South Vine*, a local alt-weekly. I told him I was. "My name's Larry Brown," he said, and while this should've knocked me back, it didn't. Larry had published four books by then, the covers of which I'd seen down the block at Square Books, but I'd yet to read any of them. The writers I was reading then were all long dead; literature, I guess I thought, was the handiwork of ghosts. I was too young and too dumb, in other words, to feel any weight in the moment; I certainly didn't sense the gears of my life shifting.

He said a few generous words about the story, and, softened, I admitted it was the first piece of fiction I'd ever published. This triggered something in him—a flash of a grin, a gleam in his expression—that

I'd only understand later. "My wife and I are headed downstairs to eat some quail," he said, pointing behind him to a woman who stood waiting with a look of tender exasperation. "Why don't you come on down with us and we'll celebrate?"

I need to be honest here: My stomach hollered yes before the rest of me did. On that night, like many before and after, I had about eight dollars to my name—enough for a few beers and, if any bills remained, a half-pint of chicken salad from James Food Center. (Mary Annie, Larry's wife, would later say that's why she put up with him inviting some random kid to dinner with them—I was clearly starving.) The City Grocery, now a Mississippi dining landmark, was brand-new that year. While the upstairs bar was humble and rowdy, with drinks served in plastic cups and a rack of Zapp's potato chips behind the bar, the downstairs restaurant was urbane and elegant—what back then we called fancy. Candlelight shimmered across white cotton tablecloths. Servers carried expensive bottles of wine as gently as they would infant children. The green beans called themselves haricots verts.

We drank and ate and smoked and talked: about writing, some, but more about reading. Larry talked about writers the way other folks talk about athletes: staggered by their prowess and feats, quoting lines and scenes as excitedly as one might recount a game-buzzer three-pointer. We talked about music, too: another subject that always brought a glow to him. But something was gnawing at him. Every now and again, sipping a Crown and Coke, he'd glance darkly at a neighboring table, and then at Mary Annie, who'd shake her head no. Tracking his glance, I saw two couples at the table: two gray-haired men, wearing suits, with two women glinting with jewels. They had easeful laughs that, at a certain volume level, caused Larry to tighten. The more he drank, the more he kept glancing.

Finally he stubbed out a cigarette, wadded his napkin onto the table, and stood up. These were quick angry gestures, but Larry was smiling: an inscrutable, boyish smile. He walked over to the table, placed the toe of his cowboy boot on the edge of one of the men's chair, hopped onto the table, and started—dancing. Dancing, yes: a slow tabletop version of the twist, his boot heel stirring a plate of shrimp and grits, Larry swiveling his hips and pistoning his elbows and all the while wearing a look of profound satisfaction. The restaurant, of course, froze; even the servers stopped mid-stride. The only sounds were the music, and the clinking of plates and flatware under Larry's shuffling boots. The two couples at the table stared down into their laps. Mary Annie rolled her eyes and hid her face. But I kept staring, enthralled, even mesmerized, until the song ended, when Larry descended from the table, took his seat again, and, as though nothing had happened, lit a fresh cigarette and resumed what he'd been saying about Flannery O'Connor.

I didn't know then why he'd done it. (One of the men, a local banker, had refused Larry a loan—insultingly, I suspect—when he was trying to quit his job at the fire department to write full-time.) I didn't know about his long and tortured struggle to make himself into a writer, the infinite rejections he'd endured (from dozens of editors and at least one banker), the faith to which he'd clung when almost everyone and everything suggested he quit, the singular literary vision that emerged only after he'd typed his millionth midnight sentence on Mary Annie's old Smith-Corona typewriter, the deep roar of his artistry. All I knew, in that moment, was that I wanted to hang out with this guy forever.

LARRY BROWN, AS you're about to see, wrote about human frailties. He wrote about people whose lives have come to feel stunted, or unmoored, and who find themselves unable or unwilling to resist perilous impulses: for sex, for alcohol, for violence, for numbness, for the kind of crazed love that doubles as a wrecking ball, even for art. He wrote about people in dire straits—emotional, financial, romantic, existential—who often choose, with varying levels of awareness, to make things more dire: to burn it all down, in some cases; in others, just to feel a new kind of heat. Among Larry's many strengths as a writer, maybe foremost, was a kind of negative capability: He never flinched. His characters flowed onto the page without dilution or filtering, their defects left intact—their confusions, bigotries, lusts, fears, cruelties, all the sediment of their weaknesses. That's one reason, aside from deadline glibness, that reviewers sometimes likened his stories' effects to moonshine's: they burn, they bite, they leave a scalded sensation in your chest. Larry never sought for us to admire his characters, or even to side with them; but he refused to let us scorn or pity them either. What he asked us to afford them was the same thing he applied, rigorously, to their creation: unsparing empathy. The source of his achievement, I think, is this very empathy—his clear and tender regard for human frailties, his adherence to Samuel Taylor Coleridge's assertion that both good and bad people are invariably less so than they seem. It also happens to be the one thing he didn't have to teach himself when, in the autumn of 1980, he decided to become a writer.

Not that he set out to write about the broad spectrum of human frailties in Lafayette County, Mississippi—not at first, anyway, and not at second either. No, after lugging Mary Annie's old typewriter into their bedroom that autumn, Larry Brown set out to write about a man-eating bear terrorizing Yellowstone National Park. The ambition, then, was merely to earn some extra money, but with his mind instead of his hands.

He was twenty-nine years old, and the father of three young children. (A fourth, Delinah, died shortly after her birth in 1977.) For seven years he'd been working as a firefighter in Oxford, the county seat. Before that, and also on his offdays from the fire department, he'd worked as a grocery sacker, housepainter, hay hauler, pulpwood cutter and hand-loader, fence builder, bricklayer's helper, carpenter, carpet cleaner, truck driver, forklift driver, dockworker, pine-tree planter, timber deadener, surveyor's helper, plumber, and answering-service employee. The cumulative weight of these jobs was sapping him; his own life, as thirty loomed, was beginning to feel stunted. His father had worked as a sharecropper then a factory worker before dying at the age of forty-six, a destiny Larry didn't wish to inherit. "I didn't want to work with my back for the rest of my life," he later told an interviewer. "I didn't want to remain poor. I wanted my children to have better opportunities than what I had. I wanted to work for myself. I saw people work their whole lives in factories, standing on concrete forty hours a week, and I didn't want that life. I wanted more than that from life."

The means to that end, he thought, might be writing. As Larry would later concede, this scheme of his was, at first, almost tragicomically naïve. Merit of the work notwithstanding, fiction pays dividends the way slot machines do: lavishly for some, meagerly for others, none for most. The Man Booker Prize, as I write this, has just been awarded to the northern Irish novelist Anna Burns, for her third novel; she relied on food banks to sustain her during its writing. But Larry had more than just these structural odds stacked against him. Aside from school assignments, he'd never written before: not as a child, not as a teen, not ever—he was starting from scratch. The last piece of writing he'd done, a senior term paper about deer hunting, earned him an F, derailing his high-school graduation. Hence Mary Annie's dry, muted response when Larry announced his intention to write: "Oh yeah?" A shrug. "Well . . . okay."

The killer bear novel—all 327 single-spaced pages of it ("I didn't even know about double-spacing," he'd later say)—came bouncing back from publishers, as did the next four novels he wrote. (As with first loves, however, Larry never quite forgot that first novel; you'll see it affectionately lampooned in his story "The Apprentice.") The short stories he wrote suffered the same boomerang fate. "I know I'm ignorant of things like theme and mood, grammar in places, the basic things," he wrote to the editor Gordon Lish in 1983, upon receipt of a rejection. "You're talking to a twelfth-grade flunkout here."

Yet Larry Brown's ascent, from his humble, almost impetuous start to his eventual rank among the vanguard of American realists, wasn't quite so improbable as some observers have characterized it. The idea of fiction writers as trained professionals—all but licensed by the nation's guild of MFA programs—is a relatively recent one. The writers with whom Larry was most familiar in 1980—Jack London, Zane Grey, Stephen King, even William Faulkner—had essentially done what he was setting out to do: taught themselves to write while supporting themselves with other jobs, channeling their imaginations into words, and, consequently, themselves into a new and more vivid life. "I had one burning thought that I believed was true," he later wrote. "If I wrote long enough and hard enough, I'd eventually learn how."

This is where, in the cinema version, you'd see the writer at his desk. Fingers clacking typewriter keys. Wadded-up paper overflowing a trash can, cigarette butts clumped in an ashtray. (Larry's editor, Shannon Ravenel, once told me she could tell immediately when a manuscript of Larry's entered her office—the smell of Marlboro smoke, even through the envelope, would herald its delivery.) Through a window you'd glimpse the seasons passing: the steel-colored Mississippi winter morphing into the yellowy-green dog days of summer. Maybe a calendar on the wall, its pages blowing off as in old-timey films.

But the typewriter, in that scene, as in Larry's life, wouldn't ever stop clacking.

Larry wrote ghost stories, Westerns, Civil War stories, African hunting tales, and detective stories. He wrote tongue-in-cheek outdoors instruction (under the pen name Uncle Whitney) and essays about gun safety, coon hunting, and lingerie. In the meantime he tried enrolling, as a special student, in a one-semester writing class at the University of Mississippi. When the instructor, the novelist Ellen Douglas, asked if he'd written anything before, he said yes ma'am—three novels and about a hundred short stories. ("Come to class," she told him.) Through Douglas he discovered Dostoyevsky, Conrad, Ambrose Bierce, and Flannery O'Connor—and also the existence of a bookstore on the Oxford town square, which he'd somehow failed to notice. Its owner, Richard Howorth, added Raymond Carver and Harry Crews and Cormac McCarthy to Larry's self-styled syllabus. Season by season, book by book, the scope of Larry's ambition began broadening, his determination hardening all the while. "Know this," he wrote to Lish. "I pump a fire truck ten days a month but that ain't my life's work. Writing is. And nothing has happened yet to make me change my mind."

The only thing that came close to deterring him was the walk from the mailbox. It stood on the side of Highway 334, about eighty yards from Mary Annie's mother's house, where they were living in the early eighties and where Larry's eldest son lives now. (Larry would build another house on the property, in 1986, and move the family there.) He'd walk out there every afternoon, on days when he wasn't at the firehouse. Mary Annie grew to hate watching him return, carrying a deadening stack of manila envelopes: his stories, all of them returned to him affixed with form rejection notes, some stories clocking ten, twelve rejections. It sank him every time. He'd walk back slowly, as though studying the gravel.

Until one day he didn't. One day Larry got an envelope—letter-sized, the right kind—and this time he came up the driveway fast. *Easyriders*, a magazine for Harley-Davidson riders (and the breast-baring women who love them), was publishing a story of his. First publication carried, for him, an intense and specific type of joy—the ecstasy of validation, as though his passport had been stamped for entry into a new and greener land. (His memory of it, I think, was the source for the grin he gave me, and the dinner invitation, when I revealed I'd just published my own first story: the headwaters of our friendship.)

When the story appeared, in the June 1982 issue, Larry's mother, Leona, went seeking a copy at an Oxford newsstand. The salesclerk hesitated to hand it to her. One imagines the clerk anxiously scanning the cover, with its pouting, crimped-hair model, the words "evil, wicked, mean, nasty" printed on her tank top, a cover line beside her hip promising "Lotsa Motorcycle Women!" Finally he said: "Mrs. Brown, you're a nice lady. Why're you buying this magazine?" I never heard what Leona said back to him, but I suspect it was the same thing the writer Lewis Nordan's mother exclaimed when she went seeking a story of his in an unfamiliar-to-her magazine called *Playgirl*: "My son's in there!" Leona Brown, it bears noting, was a spectacularly proud mother, and Larry often said his mother's reading habits—family legend says she read every book in the Oxford library—were the seeds of his own. In 1991, he inscribed his second novel, *Joe*, to her as follows: "For Mama, the most important one . . . It was a long time coming, but the world sees it now. I know some laughed at my dream but you never did. Thank you for my life. Your loving son, Larry."

THAT *EASYRIDERS* STORY, "Plant Growin' Problems," kicks off this collection. The spiraling tale of a marijuana-growing biker's encounter with a seedy Georgia sheriff, it belongs to a mostly extinct species of male adventure stories, the kind Elmore Leonard and Mickey Spillane used to write for pulp magazines in the mid-twentieth century. It operates, then, within a much narrower compass than Larry's later stories do. Yet we can already see certain hallmarks of Larry's style fixed in place, like surveyor's flags. The universe he sketches, for instance, is characteristically devoid of moral clarity, with the sheriff both a user and distributor of the marijuana at the story's locus. The vernacular is gutty and fresh ("I wouldn't try that shit, boy," the sheriff warns the biker. "Not 'less you want the undertaker packin' your asshole fulla cotton 'bout dark"). Spurts of humor shoot from unexpected places (as when the sheriff ambushes the biker with an Ed McMahon bellow: "Heeeeeeeeeere's Cecil!"). Most significantly, perhaps, there's the moral dilemma with which Larry saddles his biker protagonist: "Against his better judgment, against the nagging little voice of his conscience" is how Larry framed the character's pivotal action. That's trademark Larry Brown: the not wanting to do good, but doing good anyway; the not wanting to do bad, likewise.

I'll note here, as an aside, that Larry did own a motorcycle in the eighties. I asked him about it once, after noticing a bike leaning against the back side of the house, mummified with rust and all but hidden beneath a tangle of vines and scrub. It used to be his, he explained, but he'd sold it to a guy who'd paid him $400 then said he'd be back shortly with a trailer to haul it off. He was still holding it for the guy, he told me. "How long've you been waiting for him?" I asked, hiking an eyebrow at the weeds enshrouding it. Larry thought about this for a while. "I guess it's four years now," he said. In the intervening years he hadn't so much as touched the bike, in case the guy finally did return for it. Larry, after all, had gone and spent the four hundred bucks, and a deal's a deal. That was trademark Larry Brown, too.

Once the thrill subsided, it became clear to Larry that first publication was just that: first. More than a year of unremitting rejections followed. If he ever feared that his single publication might've been an aberration, a fluke, he wasn't alone. Barry Hannah, the South's analog to Samuel Beckett, had recently arrived in Oxford as the university's writer-in-residence. Larry pressed enough stories on him—"Brown's early badness," Barry called them—that Barry took to ducking out the back of the bar, as he'd later write, "when I saw [Larry] coming down the walk with the inevitable manila envelope." When "Plant Growin' Problems" appeared, "I cheered but secretly believed he'd peaked out." (Barry confessed these doubts, I should note, for the sole purpose of eating them, crow-style, years later. "Passion begat brilliance" is how he summarized Larry's career.)

It's this period of Larry's apprenticeship I find most interesting, because at some point therein Larry moved the goalposts for himself. The ambition was no longer to earn extra money, or to merely see his work in print; the ambition, as great as it gets, was to make Art. You see glints of this in the next two stories—far more dazzlingly in the latter—that he published: "Nightmare," which the horror writer and editor T. E. D. Klein ran in *Twilight Zone* magazine in 1985, and "Boy and Dog," which appeared in *Fiction International* a few months earlier (and later took a slot in *Facing the Music*, Larry's debut collection). "Nightmare" is a brief, bilious fever dream chronicling a man's passage into the afterlife, with a wretched caucus of ghosts attending to his destiny. It's a horror story, down to its (exposed) bones, but note the way Larry heaped adjectives and gerunds at the front of his sentences, as if to sustain a funereal drumbeat through the story. He was playing with language now, using it less as a tool than an instrument. In "Boy and Dog" he took a much further leap, close to quantum. On one level it's a formalist exercise, a late-night self-dare: 293 five-word sentences, stacked as evenly as coins. Yet the story it relates—a Butterfly Effect–maelstrom resulting from a car running over a dog—is wrenching and complex, with deadpan humor woven into deadpan tragedy, the constraints of the story's form somehow magnifying its unsettling effects. With his depiction of firefighters (ineptly) battling a car fire, moreover, Larry was now drawing from firsthand experience and observation, grounding his fiction in his native soil. He was applying what he'd learned to what he'd already known.

A stray line from "Nightmare," in retrospect, begs for repurposing: "And finally he found his voice, found that indeed he did have a voice." Passion had started begetting brilliance.

AMONG LARRY'S PASTIMES, lowriding was the favorite. That's what he called it, anyway, and what it meant was driving around, most often alone but sometimes with a friend, without any errand or destination, in the twilit hour of the day he called "the gloam." He'd climb into his truck and from his driveway head right or head left, depending on his mood or his whim or where the big pinkening sky of the Yocona river bottom looked most inviting. The route stuck to back roads, never coming near the bustle of Oxford, about ten miles northwest of his homeplace. He drove slowly—so slowly, in fact, that his own mother used to complain about getting stuck behind him; she'd gun the engine and shake her fist at him as she passed. The truck was always a comfortable mess inside: a scree of cassette tapes on the passenger seat and floorboards, empty cigarette packs atop the dash, a book or two wedged somewhere. Sometimes he'd throw a small cooler of beer in the truck bed; at other times he'd stash a half-pint of schnapps up front. If he was alone, he'd ride around and think, engaging in a kind of county-road meditation, chewing his mental cud until the sun petered out.

If he wasn't alone, of course, he'd spend the ride talking. It was the best kind of talking, because unlike at the bar, or even back at the house, there were no interruptions or competing voices. There wasn't any rush, no need to get to the point; you weren't going anywhere to begin with. He'd talk about his writing, his reading, his family, the letters he'd received that day, the bushhogging he'd done or needed to do. He'd play new music he'd bought or been sent (musicians were always sending him their albums). He'd spy a coyote in someone's field and stop the truck to gawk at it, as excited as if he'd discovered a new species. But always, at least with me, he'd narrate the landscape. Larry always expected me to move out that way, when and if I ever settled down, so occasionally his narration was like that of a Realtor: pointing out land and houses that could be had for cheap, quiet-looking places where one could write unbothered. But mostly he just told stories about passing landmarks, essentially dropping narrative pins on a private map of Lafayette County. The Dumpster on Delay Road where some dude used to jump out and expose himself. The bend on Old Taylor Road where a car chase once paused so that a sleeping dog in the road could rise, stretch, and dodder off, the sheriff's deputy and his quarry resuming the chase the moment the dog was clear. The stretch of road, skid marks long faded, where two boys in a car doing ninety hit a tractor-trailer broadside, where it'd been up to Larry's fire crew to extract their almost-decapitated bodies. The abandoned house on a scraggly pine ridge that he bequeathed to his fictional Jones family, in the novel *Joe*, so they'd have somewhere to squat.

Larry didn't navigate the way other people might, on a relaxed joyride. He didn't take a road to see where it led. He knew where every road led. He knew where to slow down because certain dogs had a thing for chasing cars. He knew whose fence it was that had a break in it, and that he ought to call him later to make sure his cattle hadn't escaped. He knew, for the most part, who lived in the houses and trailers he'd pass, and more important, he knew their stories: what they'd done and had done to them. And he let those stories go drifting into his.

Larry never regarded the people he wrote about the way reviewers did: as (and I'm quoting here) poor whites, the underclass, lumpen, rednecks, trailer trash, white trash. (When one magazine crowned him the "King of White Trash," Larry slyly told Leanne, his daughter, that this made her the Princess of White Trash.) These were economic and classist designations, and economics and class—and for that matter categories—never interested Larry. The models for his characters were individuals, not types: the people he'd grown up with, that he'd worked beside, that he'd get talking to at bars, that he'd rescued from crushed vehicles, that he'd listened to trading stories and gossip at the little country store he ran for a while in the eighties, that he'd see walking shoeless on the roadside with no easy destination he could imagine for them. What interested him was what their hearts contained: love, grief, meanness, longing, fear, hurt. Not the frailties that came from being poor, but rather those that came from being human.

A FEW MORE NOTES, before you turn to the good stuff. There are four stories wedged between those that were collected, respectively, in *Facing the Music* and *Big Bad Love*: "And Another Thing," "The Crying," "Tiny Love," and "A Birthday Party." Larry published the first two in *Reb Fiction '90*, a locally published anthology that Barry Hannah edited in 1990. "Twenty-Three Short Stories from Barry Hannah's Writing Class" was the subtitle, but as Barry intimated in his preface, the correct number should have been twenty-one. "I've taught everyone in these pages except Larry Brown, who never needed the school," he wrote, "and whose name stands for the real condition of the Rebel, as rebellious against the system, the preposterous deal that life puts on us."

Larry worked sporadically on "Tiny Love" over the course of several years, before publishing it, in 1994, in an anthology entitled *Writer's Harvest*. It's a tragicomic romp about the limits of love, the carrying capacity of devotion, that ends with a startlingly dark swerve, the photonegative of an O. Henry twist. With a fingerpicked guitar accompaniment, it could be one of the John Prine ballads Larry so loved: desolate, droll, stoical, cockeyed, prickly, lovelorn.

The fourth, "A Birthday Party," appeared in the *Southern Review* in 1992. It's my least favorite of his stories, I'll confess—partly because I catch a whiff of secondhand smoke in it, drifting over from Charles Bukowski's ashtray, but mostly because there's a sourness to it that, to my ear, Larry didn't fully calibrate. He had his own misgivings about the story, which he originally wrote to give to the friends who'd attended his fortieth birthday party, worrying that it was "too maudlin and nasty." Maybe. It goes without saying that one shouldn't ever infer alignments between a fiction writer's work and his life, even when the writer appears to yoke them (as Larry occasionally did), so I'm not going to inventory the myriad ways in which Leon Barlow (our narrator here, and also in the more fully realized "92 Days") was unlike Larry Brown.

Except one: Larry, unlike the crotchety Barlow of "A Birthday Party," was unfailingly generous to would-be writers (I know because I was one of them), even the hopeless ones (because he understood that's what he'd been considered, once upon a time). Permit me two anecdotes about that. Once, when Larry and I were fishing at his pond, he got to grousing—uncharacteristically—about a novel he was reading, a seven-hundred-page cinder block of some of the worst writing he'd ever encountered. What's worse, he told me, was that he was still three hundred pages shy of finishing. I asked the name of the book, but it wasn't a book; it was a manuscript some guy had mailed him from Idaho. (He got a lot of those in the mailbox, too, in addition to the albums.) When I noted that he wasn't under any obligation to, y'know, finish it, Larry flashed me an appalled and shaming look. "He sent it to me," he said, "all the way from Idaho." A deal was a deal, apparently, even when, y'know, it wasn't really a deal. I have no doubt Larry sent the guy a frank but gentle letter about his novel. I'm sure he told him he had more and harder work to do. But I guarantee you he told him he could do it, and believed it. "If you want to hurt bad enough for something," goes the best line in "A Birthday Party," "you can have it."

Second story: Sometime in the mid-nineties a young poet made a pilgrimage to Larry's house. From Iowa, I think. Larry put him up in the living room where the poet wrote poems while maintaining a staggering blood-alcohol level that sometimes led to howling. Days passed, then weeks. Leanne would step over him and his empty beer cans on her way out the door for school in the mornings. Finally Mary Annie couldn't take it any longer; she told Larry he had to evict the poet. "I can't," protested Larry, softhearted to a fault. "He says he's got something wrong with the brakes on his car." Sympathy long exhausted, Mary Annie glared at him and said: "He doesn't need brakes to *leave*, Larry."

Larry Brown was the first fiction writer I knew, so for many years I thought the reactions his work inspired—the pilgrimages to his front door, the flood of letters and manuscripts from prisons and college campuses and all points between, the late-night phone calls from strangers that forced the Browns to change their phone number more than once—were normal, the standard repercussions of art. They weren't. Nor were they limited to what we might call civilians. Writing in the *Los Angeles Times Book Review*, Harry Crews wrote of his first encounter with *Facing the Music*: "In twenty-five years of writing, it was the first time I picked up the phone and tried to call the author." Why? Our responses to art are always particular and peculiar, so it's dicey to generalize; but I did see a common thread over the years. Larry never came across, as many writers do, as a kind of lifeguard to his characters, monitoring them from a high, dry perch. No, Larry was always down in the water with them, no matter how deep and churning, so that when the rip tides came, the panics and struggle felt immediate and real. The word *authentic* often got bandied about, in praise of Larry, but that word has always seemed freighted to me, a marketer's term. What *authentic* got at, but didn't fully elucidate, was the fidelity in Larry's work, both textural and psychological; the way he rendered life without distortion, without gloss, without sentiment; the way his stories reflected the human condition not as he wanted it to be—or the bleak flip side, how he feared it to be—but rather how it was, and how it felt. Even in "A Roadside Resurrection"—this collection's final story, and Larry's most parodic (and berserk) offering—he's channeling something real: the grotesque dimensions of faith, the burning desire for transcendence. Dig a shovel into his stories, in short, and you'll pull up clay; cut his characters and they'll bleed. "It may be going too far," wrote Eudora Welty, "to say that the exactness and concreteness and solidity of the real world achieved in a story correspond to the intensity of feeling in the author's mind and to the very turn of his heart; but there lies the secret of our confidence in him." Our confidence, and perhaps our urge to call him in the dark of the night: to commiserate with a fellow traveler who hasn't just witnessed life's burdens but, based on the stooped shoulders of his prose, must've surely also strained and faltered beneath them.

It's been fifteen years since Larry died—in his sleep, at the age of fifty-three, like his father in one regard (dying young) but unlike him in all the ways Larry wanted. The last words he spoke, to Mary Annie at bedtime, were, "Life is good, isn't it, M.A.?" And it was. He helped raise three children who have proven constitutionally incapable of foregoing or abandoning their dreams. In the twenty-four years he spent writing, Larry published six novels, a memoir, a book of essays, and all the stories awaiting you, carving his name, indelibly, onto the thick tree trunk of American literature. He strained and he faltered, yes, but he never lost faith. "What do you have going for you?" he asked himself in a 1982 journal entry. "Nothing but desire, no talent, and a love of the written word." But, he added, "that last should be enough to overcome the other two." And it was.

—JONATHAN MILES
Milford, New Jersey

TINY LOVE

Plant Growin' Problems

Jerry Barlow eased the '67 Sportster to the edge of the sand road and shut off the motor. He listened closely to the silence of the woods. Aside from the voices of a few mockingbirds and blue jays crouched in the leaves of blackjack oak and scrub pine, nothing could be heard except the ticking of his hot motor. He got off and unstrapped the short-handled hoe and the gallon jug of liquid plant food from the chrome sissy bar.

He knew Bacon County, Georgia, was a dangerous place to be doing what he was doing, but he was sure he wouldn't get caught. He lit a cigarette and listened carefully for a few more minutes. Hearing nothing, no approaching vehicle, he picked up the hoe and the jug and stepped off the road. He had fifteen healthy female plants not four hundred yards off the road, and it was time to water them and hoe the weeds from between the stalks.

There was a fairly worn trail leading from the road beside his bike to his small patch of grass, and he didn't look down and see the tracks made by somebody's heavily booted feet. He slung the hoe over his shoulder and walked through the warm August woods, carefully watching ahead for snakes. There were rattlesnakes in these woods, and some of them were as thick as a man's wrist.

Ahead of him by a few hundred yards, Sheriff Cecil Taylor lay on his enormous gut and wiped away the streams of sweat running down under his sunglasses. His cruiser was backed up and carefully hidden down the road a piece, as it had been for the last three days in a row. He could have sent some of his deputies to do this job, but he wanted to catch Jerry Barlow with the grass himself. He liked to get these drug addicts under his thumb, especially when they were bikers like Barlow.

Sheriff Taylor had carefully estimated the yield on these fifteen plants, and by the time fall got here and they were fully matured, he was pretty sure he could make a really big bundle by selling the stuff to his brother-in-law, who also happened to own the finest whiskey still in this part of the state. But that wasn't the whole story, not at all. Sheriff Taylor knew this particular patch of weed would probably be good enough to save back a couple of pounds for his own personal stash. He loved a good buzz as much as the next man.

He watched Jerry crest the last ridge, coming into the small clearing where the dirt was dark and sandy. He had to hand it to Barlow: he'd picked a very good spot for his weed. The soil here was just right, just loose enough for a good root system and rich enough to furnish the plants with the nutrients they needed. And there damned sure wouldn't be anybody wandering around Rattler's Roost in the summertime, not unless he wanted a fast, fatal case of snakebite. But Barlow had parked his bike in the same spot once too often, and Taylor had found his patch.

He had hoped the Barlow boy wouldn't do anything stupid like trying to run or fight. He'd hate to have to shoot the shit out of him, because then he wouldn't be able to keep the grass for himself. There'd be an investigation and some of those damned DEA boys would be in here and they'd confiscate the grass and keep it for themselves like they always did. Even so, he reached back and unholstered the heavy .357 Mark III Trooper and assumed the prone firing position.

From his hiding place under the low foliage of a small patch of honeysuckle vines, he was sure Barlow wouldn't see him until he was ready for him to. He lay back and watched the young man as he eased carefully up to the clearing and looked all around. Sheriff Taylor chuckled to himself as Jerry laid the hoe down and began pouring the blue liquid plant food around each plant. Abruptly, the fat man hollered, "Heeeeeeeere's Cecil!" and laughed out loud when Jerry spun to face him, his expression one of shocked surprise. Sheriff Taylor was a pretty sorry old sonofabitch, but he had a great sense of humor.

Jerry was in a low crouch, looking almost as if he meant to try and run for it, but he stopped when he heard the hammer come back on the big pistol. A drop of sweat ran down his nose and hung on the end, suspended in the hot dusty silence between them.

"I wouldn't try that shit, boy," Taylor said. "Not 'less you want the undertaker packin' your asshole fulla cotton 'bout dark."

Jerry relaxed and eased his lanky six-foot frame to the ground. He sat cross-legged, watching the red-faced sheriff get up off the ground, still holding the cannon in front of him.

"You can put the gun away, man. I ain't goin' nowhere."

"Oh yeah, boy, you goin' somewhere." The pot-bellied officer dusted off the front of his pants and shirt but didn't put the gun away. His tone was almost jovial, and the speech was well rehearsed.

"Definitely goin' somewhere. Prob'ly up to Reidsville for a goodly portion of your life. Either that or out to the farm for a while."

Jerry knew what he was talking about. The county ran a small correction unit for the lesser criminals, a condition forced onto many county law enforcement agencies by the overcrowding of the prisons and the ever-increasing numbers of felons. He'd heard some bad things about that place. He'd talked to a boy who had spent fifteen months out there for passing a bad check, and the boy had told Jerry he'd leave the country before he'd let them put him back in that rathole. The inmates were forced to work twelve-hour days in the truck patches raising vegetables, and he told Jerry that most of the money from the sale of the produce went right into Cecil Taylor's back pocket. The boy also hinted that there were some people who went inside and never came back out. At least, not alive. He thought about all this as Taylor crossed the small patch of ground between them and stopped in front of him.

"Stand up!" The words came up from his pot gut in a wheeze. He wore a small, thin smile on his cruel lips.

Jerry stood up slowly and waited while Taylor walked in a small circle around him. His mind raced as he tried to figure a way out of this. The only chance he had was to get away right now—hit the sheriff with his fist or get the gun away from him. If the cop ever got him to the jail it would be all over. He didn't even want to think about spending the next few years in Reidsville.

"You fuckin' bikers think you can just do like you please, don't you?"

Jerry didn't answer.

"Dirty, greasy scum." The words made the blood rush up Jerry's neck and turn his face red. It was now or never. He whirled and threw

his fist, but the fat man had already anticipated it. He stepped aside
with a practiced motion and let the punch go over his shoulder, bringing the barrel of the gun down on top of Jerry's skull. A light flashed
inside his head and his brain shorted out. He didn't even feel it when
he hit the ground.

He couldn't tell how much time had passed when he
woke up, but the sun hung low in the blue Georgia sky. He was alone.
Mosquitos had bitten him all over his arms and face and they buzzed
around his head in a maddening swarm. He couldn't bat them away
because his wrists were firmly held by a pair of bright chrome handcuffs. Jerry jerked them apart, but the cold steel only cut into the flesh
of his wrists. There was no way to break them or get them off. But
maybe he could make it back to the road. He didn't know why the
sheriff had left him alone like this, but he wasn't about to wait around
for him to come back.

He got up on one knee and almost passed out again from the pain
throbbing through his head. It felt as if somebody had his head between
two ball peen hammers, batting it back and forth. He had to let several
minutes pass by before he could get to his feet. The pounding in his
temples sent jolts of agony racing through him with every step he took,
but he didn't take very many. He stopped when he saw Sheriff Taylor
blocking the trail. The fat man had been watching him all the time. And
in his hands he was holding a very large diamond-back rattler. It was on
the end of a stick with a wire loop drawing tightly around its neck. The
bulk of its thick body moved and swayed in the air below the head. The
forked tongue flickered and tested the air. Jerry froze where he stood.
He was about to be murdered; there was no doubt in his mind.

"Interestin' thing about these snakes," the sheriff said. "Catch 'em
any time you want to. All you got to have's a little piece a garden

hose and a teaspoon of gas. Just stick the hose down his hole and pour in the gas. It runs 'em out every time. They'll probably find your body sometime this winter, after deer season opens. Won't be nobody around till then. I 'preciate you leavin' me the dope, though." Then he came after Jerry.

Jerry tried to run, but the pain was bad. The fat man was laughing and wheezing as he closed in on him. Jerry turned and tried to get closer to the road, but he knew he'd never make it, not while he was still hurt like this. If the situation hadn't been so deadly it would have been ridiculous. Jerry was running and stumbling and trying to jump the clumps of palmetto and sawbriar, and the sheriff was whooping and chasing him like a fun-loving schoolboy after a little girl with pigtails, only there was no teacher for Jerry to run to. Taylor was about to catch him.

Jerry risked one glance behind him just as he got up close to a huge pin oak, and he saw an amazing thing happen. Sheriff Taylor was so intent on catching Jerry that he forgot about watching the handle of the stick, and it got tangled between his fat thighs. He tripped and landed facedown on his flabby belly. His jowls hung slack with horror as he sat up and Jerry ducked behind the tree. The sheriff squealed at the top of his lungs like a stuck pig when he saw the snake hanging from his arm, the fangs sunk to the roof of its mouth. The jaws were stretched wide, chewing and working, injecting the venom deep into his bloodstream.

He screamed while he clawed at the holster with his free hand, blubbering like a baby until he got the pistol out. There was mad panic in his eyes as he looked from Jerry to the snake and started begging him for help.

"Oh, Jesus God, help me! He bit me! He bit me! Oh, God, the sonofabitch is in my arm!"

Then he cocked the pistol, stuck the muzzle against the smooth white scales of the snake's belly, and blew it apart with one thunderous blast. Little pieces of pink meat and snake guts splattered against his face, some of it landing on his lips. He laid the gun down, and Jerry watched in fascination from behind the tree as the sheriff grabbed the pulpy, writhing body and pulled the head and fangs out of his arm with an awful groan. Clear liquid oozed from the twin punctures on his forearm. The holes were red and puffy and he could feel a tingle starting in his fingertips. He screamed for help again.

"You gotta help me, you gotta help me! Please, you gotta cut me! Oh, lord, you gotta cut me!" Then his voice trailed off to a weak whimper as his head sagged down on his chest.

"You throw me the gun, man," Jerry called. He didn't intend to step out and help, and then get a hole blown through him for his trouble. "I got a knife. I'll cut it, but you got to throw me the gun."

Sheriff Taylor was shaking and a rigor went through his body. His heart was pounding and he knew each second that passed and each beat of his heart would send the venom closer and closer to the big muscle. But instead of throwing the gun he snatched it up and screamed. "You sonofabitch!"

Jerry ducked back behind the tree as four deafening blasts rocked the woods around him. The soft-nosed slugs tore into the trunk of the tree, and he pressed his face flat to the ground and trembled as shock after shock ran through the wood. Then he heard the dull click of the hammer striking on spent cartridges and looked up. The sheriff's face was a pasty white color, drained of blood: the man realized that he was about to die a slow and horrible death here in these woods where the maggots and buzzards would strip his rotting carcass. He was crying now. The pistol fell from his stiff fingers and dropped to the dusty ground. Jerry got up immediately and walked toward the fallen man, holding the cuffs in front of him.

"Open 'em quick if you want me to help you."

He knelt in front of Taylor and the fat man fumbled for the key on his belt. His hands were shaking but he found the tiny hole in the cuffs and they clicked open.

"Cut it—you gotta cut it quick!"

Jerry dug in his pocket and found his knife, a three-bladed Case that would shave the hair on his leg. He didn't waste any time telling Taylor how bad it was going to hurt: he just grabbed the sweaty arm and made two deep, slashing cuts across the fang marks. The skin and meat peeled apart like overripe fruit as the blade bit deep. Blood jumped out in two gushing streams but Taylor didn't seem to feel the fiery bite of the knife. A look of relief washed across his face.

"Okay," Jerry said, "that oughta hold you till you can get to the hospital if you hurry. I don't think he hit a vein or you'd be having a heart attack by now."

Taylor got to his feet and swayed dizzily. He clutched at Jerry with his bloody hands and begged him for help.

"You got to walk me to my car. It's parked right up here about two, three hundred yards away."

Jerry pushed his hands away and backed up.

"No way, man. I did all I'm gonna do for you. I'm gettin' the hell outta here."

"You can't leave me! I can't make it out! Help me to my car!"

Jerry had started to walk away, but he turned back because the fat man was crying in the most pitiful voice he had ever heard. It was stupid even to consider helping him. As soon as he got to his car, he'd get on the radio and call for help, and more than likely for some deputies to come after Jerry. One part of him said "leave him," but he didn't think he'd be able to live with himself if he did that. He didn't want to be responsible for the man's death, even after what had just happened. All he wanted was to get away.

Against his better judgment, against the nagging little voice of his conscience, he slipped the sheriff's arm around his neck and said, "Come on."

The bitten arm was swelling rapidly now. Already the fingers were puffed up so bad he could barely move them.

"Which way's your car, man?"

Jerry was having a hard time holding up the fat man. Sweat poured off both of them.

"Straight up the hill . . . over to . . . the left . . . buncha . . . pine trees."

Jerry staggered under the dying man's weight and the pounding pain still racing through his head. After five minutes of all-out effort, he came out on the road below the car. He was so tired he could hardly stand. Taylor sank down slowly to his knees. His arm was turning purple, and every vein stood outlined against the skin. His flesh looked as if it was about to burst.

"Can't go . . . no further," he panted. "You got to . . . drive the car . . . down . . . here. Get me to . . . a . . . hospital. Keys . . . under the seat."

Jerry sagged against a tree and looked down at him. The sheriff had lost his hat somewhere back in the bushes and his graying hair hung in his eyes. The man appeared near death. Jerry closed his eyes briefly against the sweat stinging them, then turned and ran in a shuffling, head-jarring trot.

He almost ran past the tan cruiser, hidden in a thicket of pine trees. The keys were right where the sheriff had said they would be. Jerry cranked it quickly, then pulled out and backed down the road until he saw Taylor. The sheriff was sinking fast. Jerry couldn't tell that the fat man was watching him carefully from under slitted eyes. He allowed Jerry to pull him to his feet and help him under the wheel. Then, with a practiced fluid movement, he reached and pulled a double-barreled shotgun from under the seat. The barrels were sawed off six inches ahead of the chambers. The spit dried in Jerry's mouth when he found himself staring into the twin black holes.

He wondered what it was going to feel like to be shot in the face. When he heard the hammers come back, he knew there would be nothing but a roar and then blackness forever. He couldn't hold his words back.

"Is this how you pay me back, you fat sonofabitch? You'da died if it hadn't been for me. I shoulda left your fat ass back there."

Taylor's lips and face were swollen and he couldn't speak plainly. He drooled a little. It was hard for him to hold his head up straight. Jerry had trouble understanding his words.

"You damn bikers . . . ain't got . . . nobody fooled . . . not me . . . I . . . know . . . I . . . know."

A great pain seized the sheriff's chest, causing him to sag back against the seat. It felt like a huge fist holding his heart and squeezing the blood out of it. His tongue went up into the roof of his mouth. The barrel swung away from Jerry as he fell back, holding his flabby tit with the hideous black hand, three times its normal size. Jerry moved fast without thinking. His foot lashed out and struck the shotgun, pushing it up into the air. It went off, both barrels going at the same time, blowing a shower of pine cones and needles down through the tree limbs. Jerry didn't wait to see anything else. He took off running, hearing the car behind him, and didn't stop until he got to his bike. The cruiser came roaring out of the dirt road, sliding sideways with a madman behind the wheel.

The tires were churning and bucking across the dusty ground, throwing a curtain of dirt and sand into the hot air. Taylor had the transmitter of the radio in his puffy hand, howling and screeching orders and instructions that were never heard because his fingers were too thick to depress the transmit button. The Harley coughed once and roared to thundering life as Jerry put all his weight into the kick-starter. Even over the rumble of his own motor, he could hear the carburetor of the Plymouth engine sucking in a great gust of air as Taylor laid his dying foot into it.

Jerry kicked the bike into first and goosed it, popped the clutch and laid it over, spinning in a tight circle in the sand, the swingarm bouncing and jarring until he pulled it back up and flew down the road behind the tan cruiser, eating dust but determined to see the end of it. The car pulled out of sight quickly, then he was riding blind in a cloud of dust. He rode through a hundred yards of it until suddenly the cloud stopped in a sharp curve.

Jerry's foot came down hard on the rear brake and he stopped with the sound of his motor beating loud in his ear. The big pine tree was still shaking from the impact of 6,000 pounds of airborne car hitting it at sixty plus. Sheriff Taylor was lying partway out on the hood in a pool of shattered safety glass and spewing blood.

As Jerry spun out of the sand and hit second gear, he laid the bike low into the next curve and started picking up some speed. He glanced over his shoulder, and it seemed to him that the dead man was waving good-bye with his puffy black hand.

Nightmare

Sleeping, he had a vision. Cold, he shivered and turned. The walls pressed around him in his dark sickroom and he saw that strange visitors had arrived to torment him in his dreams. They did not touch him. Snoring, he slumbered awake.

Bad things had come to haunt him; fingers forced through rotting wood had come to seek him.

Look at us, they said, and bones bore out their testimony. Have we gone to a better place? Their hair had fallen away in patches; their skulls were damp and mildewed, gray with age.

You've got it good here, they said. Up here on the hill. You should try it a while down in the bottom where we stay. You think this is bad? Try sleeping on wet sheets.

But he was afraid and would not answer. Chilled, he quaked and turned in his raiments.

Polyester, they said, fingering the material. Look at this. Hey, Fred, come here and look at this. They don't use silk anymore?

He did not understand. Confused, he shut his eyes and ears. What nightmare came with consciousness?

You're new here, they said, aren't you? We thought so. We feel their shovels. The vibrations carry. Even their footsteps. Was it nice? Did many shed tears for you?

Betrayed, he clasped his hands. Weeping, he felt no pulse. Eviscerated, he had no heart.

The faces settled around him, chieftains gathered about a council fire. Some shot through the head. Others burst open at Belleau Wood. Here one fell at Shiloh. See his missing arm.

This one said: You might be interested to know that in 1866 45 percent of the public funds collected by the state of Mississippi were spent on artificial limbs. No? Then how about his? Fred here was walking down a road in 1942 on his way to join the army when he was run over by a family of people of German descent. They were sausage makers. Isn't that a riot? Four of them in a '39 Packard. The old man's the only one left alive. He's got some grandkids on dope in Los Angeles, but he's never seen them. He's hooked up to a respirator in Panama City and he's been screaming every night for the last forty-two years. Fred's been holding a grudge against him.

He flailed soundlessly against the sweaty material, and it seemed that a weight had settled on his chest. When he opened his eyes a small rotted child was sitting there.

No ice cream, it said. Its skull had been halved and one mad orb leaned out on a red strand like the eye of a broken doll.

No ice cream. Puppies I could have had. Swimming in creeks and touching girls at fourteen.

But it was not his fault. None of it. Silent, he screeched and tried to gag. Labored. Fought with his knotted fists what had no shape or existence. Struck mightily but without progress.

Panting, he lay composed. Thin beads of sweat never formed.

A nightmare, he said. I am having a nightmare again.

They smiled to see his logical mind, all the ordered facts to explain his embalmment, the varnished casket beginning to mold.

One in tattered rags lay upon him. Stretched out, full and cold. Feet to feet. Hip to hip. Toe to toe.

You can just stop all this foolishness right now, it said. You might as well get used to it. We're here to help you.

And finally he found his voice, found that indeed he did have a voice.

I am sick, he said. I am a very sick man. I need my rest.

The faces watched. Gray, all gray. They had seen it before.

And kids, he said. Two in high school. One plays the guitar. He's good on Hank Williams stuff. When I'm well we sit out on the porch and he plays for me.

They watched him. Somnolent, ravished of emotion, sleepwalkers. One yawned. Gristles hinged on a cusp of bone.

And this is just a nightmare. The medicine. I've had them before. Nurse? Would you come in here, please?

Something wet and dark came inside the circle of faces, a leprous, glistening thing that hissed and touched him with shards of heat. Small fires danced in his ribs. They bared their teeth and it howled and vanished, smoke left in its trail. He felt the cold take him again.

And my poor wife, he said. She worries about me so. She can't sleep at night.

Reconciled, they let him talk on. Wise, they waited. Old, they gripped their tattered rags about themselves and leaned forward to speak of dreams and demons and faded plastic flowers.

Dead, he heard weeping high above him, and finally understood.

FACING THE MUSIC

Facing the Music

I cut my eyes sideways because I know what's coming. "You want the light off, honey?" she says. Very quietly.

I can see as well with it as without it. It's an old movie I'm watching, Ray Milland in *The Lost Weekend*. This character he's playing, this guy will do anything to get a drink. He'd sell children, probably, to get a drink. That's the kind of person Ray's playing.

Sometimes I have trouble resting at night, so I watch the movies until I get sleepy. They show them—all-night movies—on these stations from Memphis and Tupelo. There are probably a lot of people like me, unable to sleep, lying around watching them with me. I've got remote control so I can turn it on or off and change channels. She's stirring around the bedroom, doing things, doing something—I don't know what. She has to stay busy. Our children moved away and we don't have any pets.

We used to have a dog, a little brown one, but I accidentally killed it. Backed over its head with the station wagon one morning. She used to feed it in the kitchen, right after she came home from the hospital. But I told her, no more. It hurts too much to lose one.

"It doesn't matter," I say, finally, which is not what I'm thinking.

"That's Ray Milland," she says. "Wasn't he young then." Wistful like.

So he was. I was too once. So was she. So was everybody. But this movie is forty years old.

"You going to finish watching this?" she says. She sits on the bed right beside me. I'm propped up on the TV pillow. It's blue corduroy and I got it for Christmas last year. She said I was spending so much time in the bed, I might as well be comfortable. She also said it could be used for other things, too. I said what things?

I don't know why I have to be so mean to her, like it's her fault. She asks me if I want some more ice. I'm drinking whiskey. She knows it helps me. I'm not so much of a bastard that I don't know she loves me.

Actually, it's worse than that. I don't mean anything against God by saying this, but sometimes I think she worships me.

"I'm okay," I say. Ray has his booze hanging out the window on a string—hiding it from these booze-thieves he's trying to get away from—and before long he'll have to face the music. Ray can never find a good place to hide his booze. He gets so drunk he can't remember where he hid it when he sobers up.

Later on, he's going to try to write a novel, pecking the title and his name out with two fingers. But he's going to have a hard time. Ray is crazy about that booze, and doesn't even know how to type.

She may start rubbing on me. That's what I have to watch out for. That's what she does. She gets in bed with me when I'm watching a movie and she starts rubbing on me. I can't stand it. I especially can't stand for the light to be on when she does it. If the light's on when she does it, she winds up crying in the bathroom. That's the kind of husband I am.

But everything's okay, so far. She's not rubbing on me yet. I go ahead and mix myself another drink. I've got a whole bottle beside the bed. We had our Christmas party at the fire station the other night and everybody got a fifth. My wife didn't attend. She said every person in there would look at her. I told her they wouldn't, but I didn't argue much. I was on duty anyway and couldn't drink anything. All I could do was eat my steak and look around, go get another cup of coffee.

"I could do something for you," she says. She's teasing but she means it. I have to smile. One of those frozen ones. I feel like shooting both of us because she's fixed her hair up nice and she's got on a new nightgown.

"I could turn the lamp off," she says.

I have to be very careful. If I say the wrong thing, she'll take it the wrong way. She'll wind up crying in the bathroom if I say the wrong thing. I don't know what to say. Ray's just met this good-looking chick—Jane Wyman?—and I know he's going to steal a lady's purse later on; I don't want to miss it.

I could do the things Ray Milland is doing in this movie and worse. Boy. Could I. But she's right over here beside my face wanting an answer. Now. She's smiling at me. She's licking her lips. I don't want to give in. Giving in leads to other things, other givings.

I have to say something. But I don't say anything.

She gets up and goes back over to her dressing table. She picks up her brush. I can hear her raking and tearing it through her hair. It sounds like she's ripping it out by the roots. I have to stay here and listen to it. I can understand why people jump off bridges.

"You want a drink?" I say. "I can mix you up a little bourbon and Coke."

"I've got some," she says, and she lifts her can to show me. Diet Coke. At least a six-pack a day. The refrigerator's crammed full of them. I can hardly get to my beer for them. I think they're only one calorie or something. She thinks she's fat and that's the reason I don't pay enough attention to her, but it isn't.

She's been hurt. I know she has. You can lie around the house all your life and think you're safe. But you're not. Something from outside or inside can reach out and get you. You can get sick and have to go to the hospital. Some nut could walk into the station one night and kill us all in our beds. You can read about things like that in the paper any morning you want to. I try not to think about it. I just do my job and then come home and try to stay in the house with her. But sometimes I can't.

Last week, I was in this bar in town. I'd gone down there with some of these boys we're breaking in, rookies. Just young boys, nineteen or twenty. They'd passed probation and wanted to celebrate, so a few of us older guys went with them. We drank a few pitchers and listened to the band. It was a pretty good band. They did a lot of Willie and Waylon stuff. I'm thinking about all this while she's getting up and moving around the room, looking out the windows.

I don't go looking for things—I don't—but later on, well, there was this woman in there. Not a young woman. Younger than me. About forty. She was sitting by herself. I was in no hurry to go home. All the boys had gone, Bradshaw, too. I was the only one of the group left. So I said what the hell. I went up to the bar and bought two drinks and carried them over to her table. I sat down with them and I smiled at her. And she smiled back. In an hour we were over at her house.

I don't know why I did it. I'd never done anything like that before. She had some money. You could tell it from her house and things. I was a little drunk, but I know that's no excuse. She took me into her bedroom and she put a record on, some nice slow orchestra or something. I was lying on the bed the whole time, knowing my wife was at home waiting up on me. This woman stood up in the middle of the room and started turning. She had her arms over her head. She had white hair piled up high. When she took off her jacket, I could tell she had something nice underneath. She took off her shirt, and her breasts were like something you'd see in a movie, deep long things you might only glimpse in a swimming suit. Before I knew it, she was on the bed with me, putting one of them in my mouth.

"You sure you don't want a drink?" I say.

"I want you," she says, and I don't know what to say. She's not looking at me. She's looking out the window. Ray's coming out of the bathroom now with the lady's purse under his arm. But I know they're all going to be waiting for him, the whole club. I know what he's going to feel. Everybody's going to be looking at him.

When this woman got on top of me, the only thing I could think was: God.

"What are we going to do?" my wife says.

"Nothing," I say. But I don't know what I'm saying. I've got these big soft nipples in my mouth and I can't think of anything else. I'm trying to remember exactly how it was.

I thought I'd be different somehow, changed. I thought she'd know what I'd done just by looking at me. But she didn't. She didn't even notice.

I look at her and her shoulders are jerking under the little green gown. I'm always making her cry and I don't mean to. Here's the kind of bastard I am: my wife's crying because she wants me, and I'm lying here watching Ray Milland, and drinking whiskey, and thinking about putting another woman's breasts in my mouth. She was on top of me and they were hanging right over my face. It was so wonderful, but now it seems so awful I can hardly stand to think about it.

"I understand how you feel," she says. "But how do you think I feel?"

She's not talking to me; she's talking to the window and Ray is staggering down the street in the hot sunshine, looking for a pawnshop so he can hock the typewriter he was going to use to write his novel.

A commercial comes on, a man selling dog food. I can't just sit here and not say anything. I have to say something. But, God, it hurts to.

"I know," I say. It's almost the same as saying nothing. It doesn't mean anything.

We've been married for twenty-three years.

"You don't know," she says. "You don't know the things that go through my mind."

I know what she's going to say. I know the things going through her mind. She's seeing me on top of her with her legs over my shoulders, her legs locked around my back. But she won't take her gown off anymore. She'll just push it up. She never takes her gown off, doesn't want me to see. I know what will happen. I can't do anything about it. Before long she'll be over here rubbing on me, and if I don't start, she'll stop and wind up crying in the bathroom.

"Why don't you have a drink?" I say. I wish she'd have a drink. Or go to sleep. Or just watch the movie with me. Why can't she just watch the movie with me?

"I should have just died," she says. "Then you could have gotten you somebody else."

I guess maybe she means somebody like the friendly woman with the nice house and the nice nipples.

I don't know. I can't find a comfortable place for my neck.

"You shouldn't say that."

"Well it's true. I'm not a whole woman anymore. I'm just a burden on you."

"You're not."

"Well you don't want me since the operation."

She's always saying that. She wants me to admit it. And I don't want to lie anymore, I don't want to spare her feelings anymore, I want her to know I've got feelings too and it's hurt me almost as bad as it has her. But that's not what I say. I can't say that.

"I do want you," I say. I have to say it. She makes me say it.

"Then prove it," she says. She comes close to the bed and she leans over me. She's painted her brows with black stuff and her face is made up to where I can hardly believe it.

"You've got too much makeup on," I whisper.

She leaves. She's in the bathroom scrubbing. I can hear the water running. Ray's got the blind staggers. Everybody's hiding his whiskey from him and he can't get a drink. He's got it bad. He's on his way to the nuthouse.

Don't feel like a lone ranger, Ray.

The water stops running. She cuts the light off in there and then she steps out. I don't look around. I'm watching a hardware store commercial. Hammers and Skilsaws are on the wall. They always have this pretty girl with large breasts selling their hardware. The big special this week is garden hose. You can buy a hundred feet, she says, for less than four dollars.

The TV is just a dim gray spot between my socks. She's getting on the bed, setting one knee down and pulling up the hem of her gown. She can't wait. I'm thinking of it again, how the woman's breasts looked, how she looked in her shirt before she took it off, how I could tell she had something nice underneath, and how wonderful it was to be drunk in that moment when I knew what she was going to do.

It's time now. She's touching me. Her hands are moving, sliding all over me. Everywhere. Ray is typing with two fingers somewhere, just the title and his name. I can hear the pecking of his keys. That old boy, he's trying to do what he knows he should. He has responsibilities to people who love him and need him; he can't let them down. But he's scared to death. He doesn't know where to start.

"You going to keep watching this?" she says, but dreamy-like, kissing me, as if she doesn't care one way or the other.

I don't say anything when I cut the TV off. I can't speak. I'm thinking of how it was on our honeymoon, in that little room at Hattiesburg, when she bent her arms behind her back and slumped her shoulders forward, how the cups loosened and fell as the straps slid off her arms. I'm thinking that your first love is your best love, that you'll never find any better. The way she did it was like she was saying, here I am, I'm all yours, all of me, forever. Nothing's changed. She turns the light off, and we reach to find each other in the darkness like people who are blind.

Kubuku Rides

(This Is It)

Angel hear the back door slam. It Alan, in from work. She start to hide the glass and then she don't hide the glass, he got a nose like a bloodhound and gonna smell it anyway, so she just keep sitting on the couch. She gonna act like nothing happening, like everything cool. Little boy in the yard playing, he don't know nothing. He think Mama in here watching Andy Griffith. Cooking supper. She better now anyway. Just wine, beer, no whiskey, no vodka. No gin. She getting well, she gonna make it. He have to be patient with her. She trying. He no rose garden himself anyway.

She start to get up and then she don't, it better if she stay down like nothing going on. She nervous, though. She know he looking, trying to catch her messing up. He watch her like a hawk, like somebody with eyes in the back of they head. He don't miss much. He come into

the room and he see her. She smile, try to, but it wrong, she know it
wrong, she guilty. He see it. He been out loading lumber or something
all day long, he tired and ready for supper. But ain't no supper yet. She
know all this and ain't said nothing. She scared to speak because she
so guilty. But she mad over having to *feel* guilty, because some of this
guilt *his* fault. Not all his fault. But some of it. Maybe half. Maybe less.
This thing been going on a while. This thing nothing new.

"Hey honey," she say.

"I done unloaded two tons of two-by-fours today," he say.

"You poor baby," she say. "Come on and have a little drink with
Mama." That the wrong thing to say.

"What?" he say. "You drinkin again? I done told you and told you
and told you."

"It's just wine," she say.

"Well woman how many you done had?"

"This just my first one," she say, but she lying. She done had five
and ain't even took nothing out the deep freeze. Wind up having a
turkey pot pie or something. Something don't nobody want. She can't
cook while she trying to figure out what to do. Don't know what to
do. Ain't gonna drink nothing at all when she get up. Worries all day
about drinking, then in the evening she done worried so much over
not drinking she starts *in* drinking. She in one of them vicious circles.
She done even thought about doing away with herself, but she hate to
leave her husband and her little boy alone in the world. Probably mess
her little boy up for the rest of his life. She don't want to die anyway.
Angel ain't but about thirty years old. She still good-looking, too. And
love her husband like God love Jesus. Ain't no answer, that's it.

"Where that bottle?" he say.

Now she gonna act like she don't know what he talking about.
"What bottle?" she say.

"Hell, woman. Bottle you drinkin from. What you mean what bottle?"

She scared now, frightened of his wrath. He don't usually go off. But he go off on her drinking in a minute. He put up with anything but her drinking.

"It's in the fridge," she say.

He run in there. She hear him open the door. He going to bust it in a million pieces. She get up and go after him, wobbly. She grabbing for doors and stuff, trying to get in there. He done took her money away, she can't have no more. He don't let her write no checks. He holding the bottle up where she can see it good. The contents of that bottle done trashed.

He say, "First glass my ass."

"Oh, Alan," she say. "That a old bottle."

"Old bottle? That what you say, old bottle?"

"I found it," she say.

"Lyin!" he say.

She shake her head no no no no no. She wanting that last drink because everything else hid.

"What you mean goin out buying some more?" he say. He got veins standing up in his neck. He mad, he madder than she ever seen him.

"Oh, Alan, please," she say. She hate herself begging like this. She ready to get down on her knees if she have to, though.

"I found it," she say.

"You been to the liquor store. Come on, now," he say. "You been to the liquor store, ain't you?"

Angel start to say something, start to scream something, but she see Randy come in from the front yard. He stop behind his daddy. Mama fixing to get down in the floor for that bottle. Daddy yelling stuff. Ain't no good time to come in. He eight year old but he know what going on. He tiptoe back out.

"Don't pour it out," she say. "Just let me finish it and I'll quit. Start supper," she say.

"Lie to me," he say. "Lie to me and take money and promise. How many times you promised?"

She go to him. He put the bottle behind his back, saying, "Don't, now, baby." He moaning, like.

"Alan *please*," she say. She put one arm around his waist and try for that bottle. He stronger than her. It ain't fair! They stumble around in the kitchen. She trying for the bottle, he heading for the sink, she trying to get it. Done done this before. Ain't no fun no more.

He say, "I done told you what I'm goin to do."

She say, "Just let me finish it, Alan. Don't make me beg," she say. Ain't no way she hold him, he too strong. Lift weights three days a week. Runs. Got muscles like concrete. Know how to box but don't never hit her. She done hit him plenty with her little drunk fists, ain't hurt him, though. He turn away and start taking the cap off the bottle. She grab for it. She got both hands on it. He trying to pull it away. She panting. He pulling the bottle away, down in the sink so he can pour it out. They going to break it. Somebody going to get cut. May be him, may be her. Don't matter who. They tugging, back and forth, up and down. Ain't nobody in they right mind.

"Let go!" she say. She know Randy hearing it. He done run way once. Ain't enough for her. Ought to be but ain't.

He jerk it away and it hit the side of the sink and break. Blood gushing out of his hand. Mixing with the wine. Blood and wine all over the sink. Don't look good. Look bad. Look like maybe somebody have to kill theirself before it all get over with. Can't keep on like this. Done gone on too long.

"Godomightydamn," he say. Done sliced his hand wide open. It bad, she don't know how bad. Angel don't want to see. She run back to the living room for the rest of that glass. She don't drink it, he'll get it. She grab it. Pour it down. Two inches of wine. Then it all gone. She throw the glass into the mirror and everything break. Alan yell something in the kitchen and she run back in there and look. He got a bloody towel wrap around his hand. Done unloaded two tons of wood today and hospital bill gonna be more than he made. Won't take fifteen minutes. Emergency room robbery take longer than plain robbery but don't require no gun.

He shout, "This is it!" He crying and he don't cry. "Can't stand it! Sick of it!"

She sick too. He won't leave her alone. He love her. He done cut his hand wide open because of this love. He crying, little boy terrified. He run off again, somebody liable to snatch him up and they never see him again. Ought to be enough but ain't. Ain't never enough.

SHE FLASHING BACK NOW. She done had a wreck a few weeks ago. She done went out with some friends of hern, Betty and Glynnis and Sue. She done bought clothes for Randy and towels for her mama and cowboy boots for Alan. Pretty ones. Rhino's hide and hippo's toes. She working then, she still have a job then. It a Saturday. Randy and Alan at Randy's Little League game. She think she going over later, but she never make it. She get drunk instead.

They gone have just one little drink, her and Betty and Sue and them. One little drink ain't gone hurt nothing or nobody. Betty telling about her divorce and new men she checking out. She don't give no details, though. They drinking a light white wine but Angel having a double One Fifty-One and Coke. She ain't messing around. This a few weeks ago, she ain't got time for no wine. And she drink hers off real quick and order and get another one before they even get they wines down. She think maybe they won't even notice she done had two, they all so busy listening to Betty telling about these wimps she messing with. But it ain't even interesting and they notice right away. Angel going to the game, though. She definitely going to the game. She done promised everybody in the country. Time done come where she have to be straight. She got to quit breaking these promises. She got to quit all this lying and conniving.

Then before long they start talking about leaving. She ask them to stay, say Please, ya'll just stay and have one more. But naw, they got to go. Glynnis, she claim she got this hot date tonight. She talk like she got a hot date every night. Betty got this new man she going out with and she got to roll her hair and stuff. But Sue now is true. Angel done went to high school with her. They was in school together back when they was wearing hot pants and stuff. This like a old relationship. But Sue know what going on. She just hate to say anything. She just hate to bring it out in the wide open. She got to say something, though. She wait till the rest of them go and then she speak up.

She say, "I thought you goin to the ball game, girl." She look at her watch.

"Yeah," Angel say. "Honey, I'm goin. I wouldn't miss it for the world. But first I got to have me some more One Fifty-One and Coke."

Sue know she lying. She done lied to everybody about everything. This thing a problem can't keep quiet. She done had troubles at work. She done called in late, and sick, done called in and lied like a dog about her physical condition with these hungovers.

Now Angel hurting. She know Sue know the truth but too good to nag. She know Sue one good person she can depend on the rest of her life, but she know too Sue ain't putting up with her killing herself in her midst. She know Sue gone say something, but Sue don't say nothing until she finish her second wine. This after Angel ask her to have a third wine. Somebody got to stop her. She keep on, she be asking to stay for a eighth and a ninth wine. She be asking to stay till the place close down.

So Sue say, "You gone miss that ball game, girl."

She say she already late. She motion for another drink. Sue reach over and put her hand over Angel's glass and say, "Don't do that, girl."

"Late already," she say. "One more won't make no difference."

She know her speech and stuff messed up. It embarrassing, but the barmaid, she bring the drink. And Sue reach out, put her hand over the glass and say, "Don't you give her that shit, woman."

Girl back up and say, "*Ma'am?*" Real nice like.

"Don't you give her that," say Sue.

Girl say, " Yes'm, but ma'am, she order it, ma'am."

Girl look at Angel.

"Thank you, hon," she say. She reach and take the drink and give the girl some money. Then she tip her a dollar and the girl walk away. Angel grab this drink and slosh some of it out on her. She know it but she can't help it. She don't know what went wrong. She shopping and going to the ball game and now this done happened again. She ain't making no ball game. Ball game done shot to hell. She be in perhaps two three in the morning.

Sue now, she tired of this.

"When you goin to admit it?" she say.

"Admit what?"

"Girl, *you* know. Layin drunk. Runnin around here drinkin every night. Stayin out."

She say, "I don't know what you talkin about," like she huffy. She drinking every day. Even Sunday. Especially Sunday. Sunday the worst because ain't nothing open. She don't hit the liquor store Saturday night she climbing the walls Sunday afternoon. She done even got drunk and listened to the services on TV Sunday morning and got all depressed and passed out before dinnertime. Then Alan and Randy have to eat them turkey pot pies again.

"Alan and Randy don't understand me," she say.

"They love you," Sue say.

"And I love them," she say.

"Listen now," Sue tell her, "you gonna lose that baby and that man if you don't stop this messin around."

"Ain't gonna do that no such of a thing," she say, but she know Sue right. She still pouring that rum down, she ain't slacked off. She just have to deny the truth because old truth hurt too much to face.

Sue get up, she got tears in her eye and stuff, she dabbing with Kleenexes. Can't nobody talk sense to this fool.

"Yes you will," she say, and she leave. She ain't gone hang around and watch this self-destruction. Woman done turned into a time bomb ticking. She got to get away from here, so she run out the door. She booking home. Everybody looking.

Angel all alone now. She order two more singles and drink both of them. But she shitfaced time she drink that last one, she done been in the booth a hour and a half. Which has done caused some men to think about hitting on her, they done seen them thin legs and stuff she got. This one wimp done even come over to the table, he just assume she lonesome and want some male company, he think he gonna come over like he Robert Goulet or somebody and just invite himself to sit down. He done seen her wedding ring, but he thinking, Man, this woman horny or something, she wouldn't be sitting here all by her lonesome. And this fool almost sit down in the booth with her, he gonna buy her a drink, talk some trash to her, when he really thinking is he gonna get her in some motel room and take her panties off. But she done recognized his act, she ain't having nothing to do with this fool. She tell him off right quick. Of course he get huffy and leave. That's fine. Ain't asked that fool to sit down with her anyway.

Now she done decided she don't want to have another drink in this place. Old depression setting in. People coming in now to eat seafood with they families, little kids and stuff, grandmamas, she don't need to be hanging around in here no more. Waiters looking at her. She know they wanting her to leave before she give their place a bad name. Plus she taking up room in this booth where some family wanting to eat some filet catfish. She know all this stuff. She know she better leave before they ask her to. She done had embarrassment enough, don't need no more.

Ain't eat nothing yet. Don't want nothing to eat. Don't even eat at home much. Done lost weight, breasts done come down, was fine and full, legs even done got skinny. She know Alan notice it when she undress. She don't even weigh what she weigh on they wedding night when she give herself to Alan. She know he worried sick about her. He get her in the bed and squeeze her so tight he hurt her, but she don't say Let go.

She trying to walk straight when she go out to her car, but she look like somebody afflicted. Bumping into hoods and stuff. She done late already. Ball game over. It after six and Randy and Alan already home by now. Ain't no way she going home right now. She ain't gonna face them crying faces. And, too, she go home, Alan ain't letting her drink another drop. So she decide to get her a bottle and just ride around a while. She gonna ride around and sober up, then she gonna go home. And she need to do this anyway because this give her time to think something up like say the car tore up or something, why she late.

Only thing, she done gone in the liquor store so many times she ashamed to. She see these same people and she know they thinking: Damn, this woman done been in here four times this week. Drinking like a fish. She don't like to look in they eyes. So she hunt her up another store on the other side of town. She don't want to get too drunk, so she just get a sixer of beers and some schnapps. She going to ride around, cruise a little and sober up. That what she thinking.

She driving okay. Hitting them beers occasionally, hitting that peach schnapps every few minutes because it so good and ain't but forty-eight proof. It so weak it ain't gonna make her drunk. Not no half pint. She ain't gonna ride around but a hour. Then she gonna go home.

She afraid to take a drink when anybody behind her. She thinking the police gonna see her and throw them blue lights on her. Then she be in jail calling Alan to come bail her out. Which he already done twice before. She don't want to stay in town. She gonna drive out on the lake road. They not as much traffic out there. So she go off out there, on this blacktop road. She gonna ride out to the boat landing. Ain't nobody out there, it too cold to fish. She curve around through the woods three or four miles. She done finished one of them beers and throwed the bottle out the window. She get her another one and drink some more of that schnapps. That stuff go down so easy and so hard to stop on. Usually when she open a half pint, she throw the cap far as she can.

Angel weaving a little, but she ain't drunk. She just a little tired. She wishing she home in the bed right now. She know they gonna have a big argument when she get home. She dreading that. Alan, he have to fix supper for Randy and his mama ain't taught him nothing about cooking. Only thing he know how to do is warm up a TV dinner, and Randy just sull up when he have to eat one of them. She wishing now she'd just gone on home. Wouldn't have been so bad then. Going to be worse now, much worser than if she'd just gone on home after them double One Fifty-Ones. Way it is, though. Get started, can't stop. Take that first drink, she ain't gonna stop till she pass out or run out. She don't know what it is. She ain't even understand it herself. Didn't start out like this. Didn't use to be this way. Use to be a beer once in a while, little wine at New Year's. Things just get out of hand. Don't mean to be this way. Just can't help it. Alan used to would drink a little beer on weekends and it done turned him flat against it. He don't even want to be around nobody drinking now. Somebody offer him a drink now he tell em to get it out of his face. He done even lost some of his friends over this thing.

Angel get down to the boat ramp, ain't a soul there. Windy out there, water dark, scare her to death just to see it. What would it be to be out in them waves, them black waves closing over your head, ain't nobody around to hear you screaming. Coat be waterlogged and pulling you down. Hurt just a little and that's all. Just a brief pain. Be dead then, won't know nothing. Won't have no hurts. Easy way out. They get over it eventually. Could make it look like an accident. Drive her car right off in the water, everybody think it a mistake. Just a tragedy, that's all, a unfortunate thing. Don't want to hurt nobody. What so wrong with her life she do the things she do? Killing her baby and her man little at a time. And her ownself. But have to have it. Thinking things when she drinking she wouldn't think at all when she not drinking. But now she drinking all the time, and she thinking same way all the time.

She drink some more beer and schnapps, and then she pass out or go to sleep, she don't know which. Same thing. Sleeping she don't have to think no more. Ain't no hurting when she sleeping. Sleeping good, but can't sleep forever. Somebody done woke her up, knocking on the glass. Some boy out there. High school boy. Truck parked beside, some more kids in it. She scared at first, think something bad. But they look all right. Don't look mean or nothing. Just look worried. She get up and roll her window down just a little, just crack it.

"Ma'am?" this boy say. "You all right, ma'am?"

"Yes," she say. "Fine, thank you."

"Seen you settin here," he say. "Thought your car tore up maybe."

"No," Angel say. "Just sleepy," she say. "Leavin now," she say, and she roll the window up. She turn the lights on, car still running, ain't even shut it off. Out in the middle of nowhere asleep, ain't locked the door. Somebody walk up and slit her throat, she not even know it. She crazy. She got to get home. She done been asleep no telling how long.

She afraid they gonna follow her out. They do. She can't stand for nobody to get behind her like that. Make her nervous. She decide she gonna speed up and leave them behind. She get up to about sixty-five. She start to pull away. She sobered up a little while she asleep. Be okay to get another one of them beers out the sack now. Beer sack down in the floor. Have to lean over and take her eyes off the road just a second to get that beer, no problem.

Her face hit the windshield, the seat slam her up. Too quick. Lights shining up against a tree. Don't even know what happened. Windshield broke all to pieces. Smoke coming out the hood. She wiping her face. Interior light on, she got blood all over her hands. Face bleeding. She look in the rearview mirror, she don't know her own self. Look like something in a monster movie. She screaming now. Face cut all to pieces. She black out again. She come to, she out on the ground. People helping her up. She screaming I'm ruint I'm ruint. Lights in her eyes, legs moving in front of her. Kids talking. One of them say she just drive right off the road into that tree. She don't believe it. Road move or something. Tree jump out in front of her. She a good driver. She drive too good for something like this.

COST THREE THOUSAND dollars to fix the car this time. Don't even drive right no more. Alan say the frame bent. Alan say it won't never drive right no more. And ain't even paid for. She don't know about no frame. She just know it jerk going down the road.

She in the hospital a while. She don't remember exactly, three or four days. They done had to sew her face up. People see them scars even through thick makeup the rest of her life. She bruised so bad she don't get out the bed for a week. Alan keep saying they lucky she ain't dead. He keep praising God his wife ain't dead. She know she just gonna have to go through it again now sometime, till a worse one happen. Police done come and talked to her. She lie her way out of it, though. Can't prove nothing. Alan keep saying we lucky.

Ain't lucky. Boss call, want to know when she coming back to work. She hem and haw. Done missed all them Mondays. She can't give no definite answer. He clear his throat. Maybe he should find somebody else for her position since she so vague. Well yessir, she say, yessir, if you think that the best thing.

Alan awful quiet after this happen. He just sit and stare. She touch him out on the porch, he just draw away. Like her hand a bad thing to feel on him. This go on about a week. Then he come home from work one evening and she sitting in the living room with a glass of wine in her hand.

HE BACK NOW from having his hand sewed up. He sitting in the kitchen drinking coffee, he done bought some cigarettes and he smoking one after another. Done been quit two years, say it the hardest thing he ever done. He say he never stop wanting one, that he have to brace himself every day. Now he done started back. She know: This what she done to him.

Angel not drinking anything. Don't mean she don't have nothing. Just can't have it right now. He awake now. Later he be asleep. He think the house clean. House ain't clean. Lots of places to hide things, you want to hide them bad enough. Ain't like Easter eggs, like Christmas presents. Like life and death.

Wouldn't never think on her wedding night it ever be like this. She in the living room by herself, he in the kitchen by himself. TV on, she ain't watching it, some fool on Johnny Carson telling stuff ain't even funny. She ain't got the sound on. Ain't hear nothing, ain't see nothing. She hear him like choke in there once in a while. Randy in the bed asleep. Want so bad to get up and go in there and tell Alan, Baby I promise I will quit. Again. But ain't no use in saying it, she don't mean it. Just words. Don't mean nothing. Done lost trust anyway. Lose trust, a man and wife, done lost everything. Even if she quit now, stay quit, he always be looking over that shoulder, he always be smelling her breath. Lost his trust she won't never get it back.

He come in there where she at finally. He been crying, she tell it by looking at him. He not hurting for himself, he not hurting for his hand. He cut off his hand and throw it away she ask him to. He hurting for her. She know all this, don't nobody have to tell her. Why it don't do no good to talk to her. She know it all already.

"Baby," he say. "I goin to bed. Had a long day today."

His face look like he about sixty years old. He thirty-one. Weigh one sixty-five and bench press two-ninety. "You comin?" he say.

She want to. Morning be soon enough to drink something else. He be gone to work, Randy be gone to school. House be quiet by seven-thirty. She do what she want to then. Whole day be hers to do what she want to. Things be better tomorrow maybe. She cook them something good for supper, she make them a good old pie and have ice cream. She get better. They know she trying. She just weak, she just need some time. This thing not something you throw off like a cold. This thing deep, this thing beat more good people than her.

Angel say, "Not just yet, baby. I going to sit in here in the livin room a while. I so sorry you cut your hand," she say.

"You want to move?" he say. "Another state? Another country? You say the word I quit my job tomorrow. Don't matter. Just a job," he say.

"Don't want to move," she say. She trembling.

"Don't matter what people thinks," he say.

She think he gonna come over and get down on the floor and hug her knees and cry, but he don't. He look like he holding back to keep from doing that. And she glad he don't. He do that, she make them promises again. She promise anything if he just stop.

"Okay," he say. "I goin to bed now." He look beat.

He go. She by herself. It real quiet now. Hear anything. Hear walls pop, hear mice move. They eating something in the cabinet, she need to set some traps.

Time go by so slow. She know he in there listening. He listen for any step she make, which room she move into, which furniture she reach for. She have to wait. It risky now. He think she in here drinking, they gonna have it all over again. One time a night enough. Smart thing is go to bed. Get next to him. That what he want. Ought to be what she want. Use to be she did.

Thirty minutes a long time like this. She holding her breath when she go in there to look at him. He just a lump in the dark. Can't tell if he sleeping or not. Could be laying there looking at her. Too dark to tell. He probably asleep, though. He tired, he give out. He work so hard for them.

Tomorrow be better. Tomorrow she have to try harder. She know she can do it, she got will power. Just need a little time. They have to be patient with her. Ain't built Rome in a day. And she gonna be so good in the future, it ain't gonna hurt nothing to have a few cold beers tonight. Ain't drinking no whiskey now. Liquor store done closed anyway. Big Star still open. She just run down get some beer and then run right back. Don't need to drink what she got hid anyway. Probably won't need none later, she gonna quit anyway, but just in case.

She know where the checkbook laying. She ain't making no noise. If he awake he ain't saying nothing. If he awake he'd be done said something. He won't know she ever been gone. Won't miss no three dollar check no way. Put it in with groceries sometime.

Side door squeak every time. Don't never notice it in daytime. Squeak like hell at night. Porch light on. He always leave it on if she going to be out. Ain't no need to turn it off. She be back in ten minutes. He never know she gone. Car in the driveway. It raining. A little.

Ain't cold. Don't need no coat.

She get in, ease the door to. Trying to be quiet. He so tired, he need his rest. She look at the bedroom window when she turn the key. And the light come on in there.

Caught now. Wasn't even asleep. Trying to just catch her on purpose. Laying in there in the dark just making out like he asleep. Don't trust her. Won't never trust her. It like he making her slip around. Damn him anyway.

Ain't nothing to do but talk to him. He standing on the step in his underwear. She put it in reverse and back on up. She stop beside him and roll down the window. She hate to. Neighbors gonna see him out here in his underwear. What he think he doing anyway, can't leave her alone. Treat her like some baby he can't take his eye off of for five minutes.

"I just goin to the store," she say. "I be right back."

"Don't care for you goin to the store," he say. "Long as you come back. You comin back?"

He got his arms wrapped around him, he shivering in the night air. He look like he been asleep.

"I just goin after some cigarettes," she say. "I be back in ten minutes. Go on back to bed. I be right back. I promise."

He step off the porch and come next the car. He hugging himself and shaking, barefooted. Standing in the driveway getting wet.

"I won't say nothin about you drinkin if you just do it at home," he say. "Go git you somethin to drink. But come back home," he say. "Please," he say.

It hit her now, this enough. This enough to stop anything, anybody, everything. He done give up.

"Baby," he say, "know you ain't gone stop. Done said all I can say. Just don't get out on the road drinkin. Don't care about the car. Just don't hurt yourself."

"I done told you I be back in ten minutes," she say. "I be *back* in ten minutes."

Something cross his face. Can't tell rain from tears in this. But what he shivering from she don't think is cold.

"Okay, baby," he say, "okay," and he turn away. She relieved. Now maybe won't be no argument. Now maybe won't be no dread. She telling the truth anyway. Ain't going nowhere but Big Star. Be back in ten minutes. All this fussing for nothing. Neighbors probably looking out the windows.

He go up on the porch and put his hand on the door. He watching her back out the driveway, she watching him standing there half naked. All this foolishness over a little trip to Big Star. She shake her head while she backing out the driveway. It almost like he ain't even expecting her to come back. She almost laugh at this. Ain't nothing even open this late but bars, and she *ain't* going to none of them, no ma'am. She see him watch her again, and then she see him step inside. What he need to do. Go on back to bed, get him some rest. He got to go to work in the morning. All she got to do is sleep.

She turn the wipers on to see better. The porch light shining out there, yellow light showing rain, it slanting down hard. It shine on the driveway and on Randy's bicycle and on they barbecue grill setting there getting wet. It make her feel good to know this all hers, that she always got this to come back to. This light show her home, this warm place she own that mean everything to her. This light, it always on for her. That what she thinking when it go out.

The Rich

Mr. Pellisher works at the travel agency, and he associates with the rich. Sometimes the rich stop by in the afternoon hours when the working citizens have fled the streets to punch their clocks. The rich are strangers to TUE IN 6:57 OUT 12:01 IN 12:29 OUT 3:30. Mr. Pellisher keeps his punch clock carefully hidden behind stacks of travel folders, as if he's on straight salary. As if he's like the rich, free of the earthly shackles of timekeepers. He keeps a pot of coffee on hot for the rich, in case the rich deign to share a cup with him, even though Mr. Pellisher pays for the coffee himself.

But the rich don't drink coffee in the afternoons. The rich favor Campari and soda, Perrier, and old, old bottles of wine. The rich are impertinent. The rich are impatient. The rich are rich.

Mr. Pellisher can see the rich coming from his office window, where he pores over folders of sunny beaches and waving palms, of cliff divers and oyster divers. The rich arrive in Lincolns white and shimmering, hubcaps glittering like diamonds. They are long and sleek, these cars the rich drive, and clean. No one has ever puked on the floormats of a car belonging to the rich. Empty potato chip bags and candy wrappers are not to be found—along with Coke cans and plastic straws—on the car seats of the rich. If they are, they were dropped there by the rich.

He straightens his tie when he sees the rich coming, and sets out styrofoam cups and sugar cubes. He straightens his desk and pulls out chairs, waiting for the rich. And when the rich push the door open, he springs from his desk, hand offered in offertory handshake. But the handshakes of the rich are limp, without feeling, devoid of emotion. Mr. Pellisher pumps the hands of the rich as if he'd milk the money from their fingers. The fingers of the rich are fat and white, like overgrown grubs. Mr. Pellisher offers the rich a seat. He offers coffee. The rich decline both with one fat wave of their puffy white hands. The rich often wear gold chains around their necks. Most of the rich wear diamond rings. Some of the rich wear gold bones in their noses. A lot of the rich, especially the older rich, have been surgically renovated. The rich can afford tucks and snips. With their rich clothes off, most of the rich are all wrinkles below their chins.

The rich live too richly. The rich are pampered. The rich are spoiled by the poor, who want to be rich. To Mr. Pellisher, who is poor, the rich are symbols to look up to, standards of excellence which must be strived for. The rich, for instance, are always taking vacations.

Mr. Pellisher turns the air-conditioning up a notch in his office, as the rich begin to sweat. He offers coffee again. The rich refuse. The rich have only two minutes to spare. They must lay their plans in the capable hands of Mr. Pellisher and depart to whatever richening schemes the rich pursue. Just one time Mr. Pellisher would like to take a vacation like the rich do, and see the things the rich see, and have sex with the women the rich have sex with. He often wonders about the sex lives of the rich. He speculates upon how the rich procure women. Do the rich advertise? Do the rich seek out the haunts of other rich, in the hope of ferreting out rich nymphomaniacs? Or do the rich hire people to arrange their sex? Just how do the rich make small talk in bars where only strangers abound? Do the rich say, "I'm rich," and let it go at that? Or do the rich glide skillfully into a conversation with talk of stocks and bonds? Are the rich perverted? Do the rich perform unnatural sex acts? Can the rich ever be horny? Do the rich have sex every night? Watch kung-fu quickies? Eat TV dinners? Buy their own beer? Wash their own dishes? Are the rich so different from himself?

He thinks they are not. He knows they are only rich. And if some way, somehow, he could be rich, too, he knows he would be exactly like them. He knows he would be invited to their parties. Summoned to their art exhibits. Called from the dark confines of his own huge monstrous cool castle to sit at the tables of other rich and tell witty anecdotes, of which he has many in great supply. He knows the rich are not different from himself. They are not of another race, another creed, another skin. They do not worship a different God.

Mr. Pellisher has many travel folders. He spreads them before the rich, as a man would fan a deck of cards. He has all the points of the globe at his fingertips, like the rich, and he can make arrangements through a small tan telephone that sits on his desk. He is urgent, ready. He has a Xeroxed copy of international numbers taped beneath the Plexiglas that covers his desk. He can send the rich to any remote or unremote corner of the world with expert flicks of his fingers. He can line up hotels, vistas, visas, Visacards, passports, make reservations, secure hunting licenses, hire guides, Sherpas, serfs, peasants, waiters, cocktail waitresses, gardeners, veterinarians, prostitutes, bookies, make bets, cover point-spreads, confirm weather conditions, reserve yachts, captains, second mates, rods, reels, secure theater tickets, perform transactions, check hostile environments in third-world countries, wire money, locate cocaine, buy condos, close down factories, watch the stock market, buy, sell, trade, steal. With his phone, with the blessing of the rich, he is as the rich. He is their servant, their confidant, their messenger. He is everything anybody rich wants him to be.

But he wonders sometimes if maybe the rich look down on him. He wonders sometimes if maybe the rich think that just possibly they're a little bit *better* than him. The rich are always going to dinner parties and sneak previews. The rich have daughters at Princeton and sons in L.A. He knows the rich have swimming pools and security systems. He wonders what the rich would do if he and Velma knocked on their door one night. Would the rich let them in? Would they open the door wide and invite them in for crab? Or would they sic a slobbering Doberman on them? The rich are unpredictable.

The rich do not compare prices in the grocery stores or cut out coupons. The rich are rich enough to afford someone to do this for them, who, by working for the rich, does not feel at all compelled to check prices. No, the rich have their groceries bought for them by persons whose instructions do not include checking prices.

Mr. Pellisher, poor, lives with the constant thought that leg quarters at forty-nine cents per pound are cheaper than whole chickens at seventy-nine cents per pound, and even though he does not like dark meat, Mr. Pellisher must eat dark meat because he is not like the rich. That is to say that he is not rich. He figures the rich eat only breasts and pulley bones. The rich do not know the price of a can of Campbell's chicken noodle soup. The rich have no use for such knowledge.

How great Mr. Pellisher thinks this must be, to live in a world so high above the everyday human struggles of the race. The rich, for instance, never have to install spark plugs. The rich have never been stranded on the side of the road. The rich have never driven a wheezing '71 Ford Fairlane with a vibrating universal joint. Or put on brake shoes, tried to set points, suffered a burst radiator hose. They have never moaned and cursed on gravel flat on their collective rich backs with large rocks digging into their skin as they twisted greasy bolts into a greasy starter. The rich have it so easy.

The rich are saying something now. The rich are going on vacation again. South of France? Wales? The rich have no conception of money. They have never bought a television or stereo on credit. They owe nothing to Sears. Their debutante daughters' braces were paid for with cash. The rich have unlimited credit which they do not need. In addition, the rich have never dug up septic tanks and seen with their own eyes the horrors contained there.

It appears that the rich are meeting other rich in June at Naples. From there they will fly to Angola. The ducks will darken the sky in late evening. The rich will doubtless shoot them with gold-plated Winchesters. The rich have never fired a Savage single-shot. The rich will go on to Ridder Creek in Alaska, where the salmon turn the water blood-red with their bodies. The rich have never seined minnows to impale upon hooks for pond bass. The rich do not camp out. The rich have never been inside a mobile home.

Mr. Pellisher has dreams of being rich. He plays Super Bingo at Kroger's. He goes inside and makes the minimum purchase twice a week, and gets the tickets. Each one could be the one. This is not the only thing he does. He also buys sweepstakes tickets and enters publishers' clearing house contests. But he never orders the magazines from the publishers. He does not affix the stamps. He has an uneasy feeling that the coupons from people who do not buy the magazines wind up at the bottom of the drawing barrel, but he has no way to prove this. He has no basis for this fear. It is unreasonable for him to think this. It is a phobia that has not yet been named.

The rich wish to have their matters taken care of immediately. They have their priorities in order. The rich have mixed-doubles sets to play. The rich have eighteen holes at two o'clock. Mr. Pellisher has taken to putting on the weekends and acquiring some of the equipment necessary for golfing. He watches the Masters9 Classic and studies their pars and handicaps.

The rich are saying something else now. The rich wish to know which card Mr. Pellisher requires. The rich can produce MasterCharge, etc., upon request. The rich are logged and registered in computers all over the world. The wealth of the rich can be verified in an instant.

Mr. Pellisher has filled out all the needed forms. He has written down all the pertinent information. He has been helpful, courteous, polite, professional, warm, efficient, jovial, indulgent, cordial, ingratiating, familiar, benevolent. He has served the rich in the manner they are accustomed to. There is no outward indication of malice or loathing. But inside, in the deep gray portions of his mind where his secret thoughts lie, he hates the rich. What he'd really like to do is machine-gun the rich. Throttle the rich. He would like to see the great mansions of the rich burned down, their children limned in flame from the high windows. He would like to see the rich downtrodden, humbled, brought to their knees. He'd like to see the rich in rags. He'd like to see the rich on relief, or in prison. Arrested for smuggling cocaine. Fined for driving drunk. He'd like to see the rich suffer everything he ever suffered that all their money could heal.

But he knows it can never be so. He knows that the rich can never be poor, that the poor can never be rich. He hates himself for being so nice to the rich. He knows the rich do not appreciate it. The rich merely expect it. The rich have become accustomed to it. He doubts the rich ever even think about it.

He tells none of this to the rich. He would like to, but he cannot. The rich might become offended. The rich might feel insulted. The rich might stop doing their business with him. Mr. Pellisher feeds off the rich. He sucks their blood, drawing it, little by little unto himself, a few dollars at a time, with never enough to satisfy his lust, slake his thirst.

The rich are leaving now. They are sliding onto their smooth leather seats, turning the keys in ignitions all over the world that set high-compression motors humming like well-fed cats. Their boats are docked and hosed down with fresh water. Their airplanes are getting refueled and restocked with liquor. Their accountants are preparing loopholes. Their lobsters are drowning in hot water, their caviar being chilled on beds of ice.

Mr. Pellisher waves to the rich as they pull away from the curb. But the rich don't look back.

Old Frank and Jesus

Mr. Parker's on the couch, reclining. He's been there all morning, almost, trying to decide what to do.

Things haven't gone like he's planned. They never do.

The picture of his great-grandpa's on the mantel looking down at him, a framed old dead gentleman with a hat and a long beard who just missed the Civil War. The picture's fuzzy and faded, with this thing like a cloud coming up around his neck.

They didn't have good photography back then, Mr. P. thinks. That's why the picture looks like it does.

Out in the yard, his kids are screaming. They're just playing, but to Mr. P. it sounds like somebody's killing them. His wife's gone to the beauty parlor to get her hair fixed. There's a sick cow in his barn, but he hasn't been down to see about her this morning. He was up all

night with her, just about. She's got something white and sticky running out from under her tail, and the vet's already been out three times
without doing her any good. He charges for his visits anyway, though,
twenty-five smacks a whack.

That's . . . seventy-five bucks, he thinks, and the old white stuff's
just pouring out.

Mr. P. clamps his eyes shut and rolls over on the couch, feels it
up. He had cold toast four hours ago. He needs to be up and out
in the cotton patch, trying to pull the last bolls off the stalks, but
the bottom's dropped out because foreign rayon's ruined the market.
He guesses that somewhere across the big pond, little Japanese girls
are sewing pants together and getting off from their jobs and meeting boyfriends for drinks and movies after work, talking about their
supervisors. Maybe they're eating raw fish. They did that on Okinawa
after they captured the place and everything settled down. He was on
Okinawa. Mr. P. got shot on Okinawa.

He reaches down and touches the place, just above his knee. They
were full of shit as a Christmas turkey. Eight hundred yards from the
beach under heavy machine-gun fire. No cover. Wide open. They
could have gotten some sun if they'd just been taking a vacation. They
had palm trees. Sandy beaches. No lotion. No towels, no jamboxes,
no frosty cool brewskies. They waded through water up to their
necks and bullets zipped in the surf around them killing men and
fish. Nobody had any dry cigarettes. Some of their men got run over
by their own carriers and some of the boys behind shot the boys in
front. Mr. P. couldn't tell who was shooting whom. He just shot. He
stayed behind a concrete barrier for a while and saw some Japanese
symbols molded into the cement, but he couldn't read them. Every
once in a while he'd stick his head out from behind the thing and
just shoot.

He hasn't fired a shot in anger in years now, though. But he's thinking seriously about shooting a hole in the screen door with a pistol. Just a little hole.

He knows he needs to get up and go down to the barn and see about that cow, but he just can't face it today. He knows she won't be any better. She'll be just like she was last night, not touching the water he's drawn up in a barrel for her, not eating the hay he's put next to her. That's how it is with a cow when they get down, though. They just stay down. Even the vet knows that. The vet knows no shot he can give her will make her get up, go back on her feed. The vet's been to school. He's studied anatomy, biology. Other things, too. He knows all about animal husbandry and all.

But Mr. P. thinks him not much of a vet. The reason is, last year, Mr. P. had a stud colt he wanted cut, and he had him tied and thrown with a blanket over his head when the vet came out, and Mr. P. did most of the cutting, but the only thing the vet did was dance in and out with advice because he was scared of getting kicked.

The phone rings and Mr. P. stays on the couch and listens to it ring. It's probably somebody calling with bad news. That's about the only thing a phone's good for anyway, Mr. P. thinks, to let somebody get ahold of you with some bad news. He knows people just can't wait to tell bad news. Like if somebody dies, or if a man's cows are out in the road, somebody'll be sure to pick up the nearest phone and call somebody else and tell him or her all about it. And they'll tell other things, too. Personal things. Mr. P. thinks it'd probably be better to just not have a phone. If you didn't have a phone, they'd have to come over to your house personally to give you bad news, either drive over or walk. But with a phone, it's easy to give it to you. All they have to do's just pick it up and call, and there you are.

But on second thought, he thinks, if your house caught on fire and you needed to call up the fire department and report it, and you didn't have a phone, there you'd be again.

Or the vet.

The phone's still ringing. It rings eight or nine times. Just ringing ringing ringing. There's no telling who it is. It could be the FHA. They hold the mortgage on his place. Or, it could be the bank. They could be calling again to get real shitty about the note. He's borrowed money from them for seed and fertilizer and things and they've got a lien. And, it could be the county forester calling to tell him, Yes, Mr. Parker, it's just as we feared: your whole 160-acre tract of pine timber is heavily infested with the Southern pine beetle and you'll have to sell all our wood for stumpage and lose your shirt on the whole deal. It rings again. Mr. P. finally gets up from the couch and goes over to it. He picks it up. "Hello," he says.

"Hello?"

"Yes," Mr. P. says.

"Mr. Marvin Parker," the phone says.

"Speaking," says Mr. P.

"Jim Lyle calling, Mr. Parker. Amalgamated Pulpwood and Benevolent Society? Just checking our records here and see you're a month behind on your premium. Just calling to check on the problem, Marv."

They always want their money, Mr. P. thinks. They don't care about you. They wouldn't give a damn if you got run over by a bush hog. They just want your money. Want you to pay that old premium.

"I paid," Mr. P. says. He can't understand it. "I pay by bank draft every month."

A little cough comes from the phone.

"Well yes," the voice says. "But our draft went through on a day when you were overdrawn, Mr. Parker."

Well kiss my ass, Mr. P. thinks.

Mr. P. can't say anything to this man. He knows what it is. His wife's been writing checks at the Fabric Center again. For material. What happened was, the girls needed dresses for the program at church, capes and wings and things. Plus, they had to spend $146.73 on a new clutch and pressure plate for the tractor. Mr. P. had to do all the mechanical stuff, pull the motor and all. Sometimes he couldn't find the right wrenches and had to hunt around in the dirt for this and that. There was also an unfortunate incident with a throw-out bearing.

Mr. P. closes his eyes and leans against the wall and wants to get back on the couch. Today, he just can't get enough of that couch.

"Can I borrow from the fund?" says Mr. P. He's never borrowed from the fund before.

"Borrow? Why. . . ."

"Would it be all right?" Mr. P. says.

"All right?"

"I mean would everything be fixed up?"

"Fixed up? You mean paid?" says the voice over the phone.

"Yes," says Mr. P. "Paid."

"Paid. Why, I suppose. . . ."

"Don't suppose," says Mr. P. He's not usually this ill with people like Jim Lyle of APABS. But he's sick of staying up with that cow every night. He's sick of his wife writing checks at the Fabric Center. He's sick of a vet who's scared of animals he's sworn to heal. He doesn't want Jim Lyle of APABS to suppose. He wants him to know.

"Well, yes sir, if that's the way. . . ."

"All right, then," Mr. P. says, and he hangs up the phone.

"Goodbye," he says, after he hangs it up. He goes back to the couch and stretches out quick, lets out this little groan. He puts one forearm over his eyes.

The kids are still screaming at the top of their lungs in the yard. He's worried about them being outside. There's been a rabies epidemic: foaming foxes and rabid raccoons running amuck. Even flying squirrels have attacked innocent people. And just last week, Mr. P. had to take his squirrel dog off, a little feist he had named Frank that was white with black spots over both eyes. He got him from a family of black folks down the road and they all swore up and down that his mama was a good one, had treed as many as sixteen in one morning. Mr. P. raised that dog from a puppy, played with him, fed him, let him sleep on his stomach and in front of the fire, and took him out in the summer with a dried squirrel skin and let him trail it all over the yard before he hung it up in a tree and let him tree it. He waited for old Frank to get a little older and then took him out the first frosty morning and shot a squirrel in front of him, didn't kill it on purpose, just wounded it, and let old Frank get ahold of it and get bitten in the nose because he'd heard all his life that doing that would make a squirrel dog every time if the dog had it in him. And old Frank did. He caught that squirrel and fought it all over the ground, squalling, with the squirrel balled up on his nose, bleeding, and finally killed it. After that he hated squirrels so bad he'd tree every squirrel he smelled. They killed nine opening day, one over the limit. Mr. P. was proud of old Frank.

But last week he took old Frank out in the pasture and shot him in the head with a .22 rifle because his wife said the rabies were getting too close to home.

Now why did I do that? Mr. P. wonders. Why did I let her talk me into shooting old Frank? I remember he used to come in here and lay down on my legs while I was watching "Dragnet." I'd pat him on the head and he'd close his eyes and curl up and just seem happy as anything. He'd even go to sleep sometimes, just sleep and sleep. And he wouldn't mess in the house either. Never did. He'd scratch on the door till somebody let him out. Then he'd come back in and hop up here and go to sleep.

Mr. P. feels around under the couch to see if it's still there. It is. He just borrowed it a few days ago, from his neighbor, Hulet Steele. He doesn't even know if it'll work. But he figures it will. He told Hulet he wanted it for rats. He told Hulet he had some rats in his corncrib.

Next thing he knows, somebody's knocking on the front door. Knocking hard, like he can't even see the kids out in the yard and send them in to call him out. He knows who it probably is, though. He knows it's probably Hereford Mullins, another neighbor, about that break in the fence, where his cows are out in the road. Mr. P. knows the fence is down. He knows his cows are out in the road, too. But he just can't seem to face it today. It seems like people just won't leave him alone.

He doesn't much like Hereford Mullins anyway. Never has. Not since that night at the high school basketball game when their team won and Hereford Mullins tried to vault over the railing in front of the seats and landed on both knees on the court, five feet straight down, trying to grin like it didn't hurt.

Mr. P. thinks he might just get up and go out on the front porch and slap the shit out of Hereford Mullins. He gets up and goes out there.

It's Hereford, all right. Mr. P. stops inside the screen door. The kids are still screaming in the yard, getting their school clothes dirty. Any other time they'd be playing with old Frank. But old Frank can't play with them now. Old Frank's busy getting his eyeballs picked out right now probably by some buzzards down in the pasture.

"Ye cows out in the road again," says Hereford Mullins. "Thought I'd come up here and tell ye."

"All right," says Mr. P. "You told me."

"Like to hit em while ago," says Hereford Mullins. "I'd git em outa the road if they's mine."

"I heard you the first time," says Mr. P.

"Feller come along and hit a cow in the road," goes on Hereford Mullins, "he ain't responsible. Cows ain't sposed to be in the road. Sposed to be behind a fence."

"Get off my porch," says Mr. P.

"What?"

"I said get your stupid ass off my porch," Mr. P. says.

Hereford kind of draws up, starts to say something, but leaves the porch huffy. Mr. P. knows he'll be the owner of a dead cow within two minutes. That'll make two dead cows, counting the one in the barn not quite dead yet that he's already out seventy-five simoleans on.

He goes back to the couch.

Now there'll be a lawsuit, probably. Herf'll say his neck's hurt, or his pickup's hurt, or something else. Mr. P. reaches under the couch again and feels it again. It's cold and hard, feels scary.

Mr. P.'s never been much of a drinking man, but he knows there's some whiskey in the kitchen cabinet. Sometimes when the kids get colds or the sore throat, he mixes up a little whiskey and lemon juice and honey and gives it to them in a teaspoon. That and a peppermint stick always helps their throats.

He gets the whiskey, gets a little drink, and then gets another pretty good drink. It's only ten o'clock. He should have had a lot of work done by now. Any other time he'd be out on the tractor or down in the field or up in the woods cutting firewood.

Unless it was summer. If it was summer he'd be out in the garden picking butter beans or sticking tomatoes or cutting hay or fixing fences or working on the barn roof or digging up the septic tank or swinging a joe-blade along the driveway or cultivating the cotton or spraying or trying to borrow some more money to buy some more poison or painting the house or cutting the grass or doing a whole bunch of other things he doesn't want to do anymore at all. All he wants to do now's stay on the couch.

Mr. P. turns over on the couch and sees the picture of Jesus on the wall. It's been hanging up there for years. Old Jesus, he thinks. Mr. P. used to know Jesus. He used to talk to Jesus all the time. There was a time when he could have a little talk with Jesus and everything'd be all right. Four or five years ago he could. Things were better then, though. You could raise cotton and hire people to pick it. They even used to let the kids out of school to pick it. Not no more, though. Only thing kids wanted to do now was grow long hair and listen to the damn Beatles.

Mr. P. knows about hair because he cuts it in his house. People come in at night and sit around the fire in his living room and spit tobacco juice on the hearth and Mr. P. cuts their hair. He talks to them about cotton and cows and shuffles, clockwise and counterclockwise around the chair they're sitting in, in his house shoes and undershirt and overalls and snips here and there.

Most of the time they watch TV, "Gunsmoke" or "Perry Mason." Sometimes they watch Perry Como. And *some*times, they'll get all involved and interested in a show and stay till the show's over.

One of Mr. P.'s customers—this man who lives down the road and doesn't have a TV—comes every Wednesday night to get his haircut. But Mr. P. can't cut much of his hair, having to cut it every week like that. He has to just snip the scissors around on his head some and make out like he's cutting it, comb it a little, walk around his head a few times, to make him think he's getting a real haircut. This man always comes in at 6:45 P.M., just as Mr. P. and his family are getting up from the supper table.

This man always walks up, and old Frank used to bark at him when he'd come up in the yard. It was kind of like a signal that old Frank and Mr. P. had, just between them. But it wasn't a secret code or anything. Mr. P. would be at the supper table, and he'd hear old Frank start barking, and if it was Wednesday night, he'd know to get up from the table and get his scissors. The Hillbillies always come on that night at seven, and it takes Mr. P. about fifteen minutes to cut somebody's hair.

This man starts laughing at the opening credits of the Hillbillies, and shaking his head when it shows old Jed finding his black gold, his Texas tea, just as Mr. P.'s getting through with his head. So by the time he's finished, the Hillbillies have already been on for one or two minutes. And then, when Mr. P. unpins the bedsheet around this man's neck, if there's nobody else sitting in his living room watching TV or waiting for a haircut, this man just stays in the chair, doesn't get up, and says, "I bleve I'll jest set here and watch the Hillbillies with ya'll since they already started if ya'll don't care."

It's every Wednesday night's business.

Mr. P. doesn't have a license or anything, but he actually does more than a regular barber would do. For one thing, he's got some little teenincy scissors he uses to clip hairs out of folks' noses and ears. Plus, Mr. P.'s cheaper than the barbers in town. Mr. P.'ll lower your ears for fifty cents. He doesn't do shaves, though. He's got shaky hands. He couldn't shave a balloon or anything. He could flat shave the damn Beatles though.

Mr. P.'s wondering when the school bus will come along. It's late today. What happened was, Johnny Crawford got it stuck in a ditch about a mile down the road trying to dodge one of Mr. P.'s cows. They've called for the wrecker, though, on Mr. P.'s phone. They gave out that little piece of bad news over his phone, and he thinks he heard the wrecker go down the road a while ago. He knows he needs to get up and go down there and fix that fence, get those cows up, but he doesn't think he will. He thinks he'll just stay right here on the couch and drink a little more of this whiskey.

Mr. P. would rather somebody get him down on the ground and beat his ass like a drum than to have to fix that fence. The main thing is, he doesn't have anybody to help him. His wife has ruined those kids of his, spoiled them, until the oldest boy, fourteen, can't even tie his own shoelaces. Mr. P. can say something to him, tell him to come on and help him go do something for a minute, and he'll act like he's deaf and dumb. And if he does go, he whines and moans and groans and carries on about it until Mr. P. just sends him on back to the house so he won't have to listen to it. Mr. P. can see now that he messed up with his kids a long time ago. He's been too soft on them. They don't even know what work is. It just amazes Mr. P. He wasn't raised like that. He had to work when he was little. And it was rough as an old cob back then. Back then you couldn't sit around on your ass all day long and listen to a bunch of long-haired hippies singing a bunch of rock and roll on the radio.

Mr. P.'s even tried paying his kids to get out and help him work, but they won't do it. They say he doesn't pay enough. Mr. P.'s raised such a rebellious bunch of youngsters with smart mouths that they'll even tell him what the minimum wage is.

Even if his oldest boy would help him with the fence, it'd still be an awful job. First off they'd have to move all the cows to another pasture so they could tear the whole fence down and do it right. And the only other pasture Mr. P.'s got available is forty acres right next to his corn patch. They'd probably push the fence down and eat his corn up while he's across the road putting up the new fence, because his wife won't run cows. Mr. P.'s run cows and run cows and tried to get his wife out there to help him run cows and she won't hardly run cows at all. She's not fast enough to head one off or anything. Plus, she's scared of cows. She's always afraid she's going to stampede them and get run over by a crazed cow. About the only thing Mr. P.'s wife is good for when it comes to running cows is just sort of jumping around, two or three feet in any direction, waving her arms, and hollering, "Shoo!"

Mr. P. can't really think of a whole lot his wife *is* good for except setting his kids against him. It seems like they've fought him at every turn, wanting to buy new cars and drive up to Memphis to shop and getting charge accounts at one place and another and wanting him to loan money to her old drunk brother. Mr. P. doesn't know what the world's coming to. They've got another damn war started now and they'll probably be wanting his boys to go over there in a few more years and get killed or at the very least get their legs blown off. Mr. P. worries about that a good bit. But Mr. P. just worries about everything, really. Just worries all the time. There's probably not a minute that goes by when he's awake that he's not worrying about something. It's kind of like a weight he's carrying around with him that won't get off and can't get off because there's no way for it *to* get off.

The whiskey hasn't done him any good. He hoped it would, but he really knew that it wouldn't. Mr. P. thinks he knows the only thing that'll do him any good, and it won't be good.

He wonders what his wife'll say when she comes in and sees him still on the couch. Just him and Jesus, and grandpa. She's always got something to say about everything. About the only thing she doesn't say too much about is that guy who sells the siding. Mr. P.'s come up out of the pasture on the tractor four or five times and seen that guy coming out of the house after trying to sell some siding to his wife. She won't say much about him, though. She just says he's asking for directions.

Well, there the bus is to get his kids. Mr. P. can hear it pull up and he can hear the doors open. He guesses they got it out of the ditch all right. He could have taken his tractor down there and maybe pulled it out, but he might not have. A man has to be careful on a tractor. Light in the front end like they are, a man has to be careful how he hooks onto something.

Especially something heavy like a school bus. But the school bus is leaving now. Mr. P. can hear it going down the road.

It's quiet in the house now.

Yard's quiet, too.

If old Frank was in here now he'd be wanting out. Old Frank. Good little old dog. Just the happiest little thing you'd ever seen. He'd jump clean off the ground to get a biscuit out of your hand. He'd jump about three feet high. And just wag that stubby tail hard as he could.

Old Frank.

Mr. P. thinks now maybe he should have just shot his wife instead of old Frank when she first started talking about shooting old Frank. Too late now.

Mr. P. gets another drink of the whiskey and sees Jesus looking down at him. He feels sorry for Jesus. Jesus went through a lot to save sinners like him. Mr. P. thinks, Jesus died to save me and sinners like me.

Mr. P. can see how it was that day. He figures it was hot. In a country over there like that, it was probably always hot. And that cross He had to carry was heavy. He wonders if Jesus cried from all the pain they put Him through. Just thinking about anybody being so mean to Jesus that He'd cry is enough to make Mr. P. want to cry. He wishes he could have been there to help Jesus that day. He'd have helped Him, too. If he could have known what he knows now, and could have been there that day, he'd have tried to rescue Jesus. He could have fought some of the soldiers off. But there were probably so many of them, he wouldn't have had a chance. He'd have fought for Him, though. He'd have fought for Jesus harder than he'd ever fought for anything in his life, harder than he fought on the beach at Okinawa. Given his own blood. Maybe he could have gotten his hands on a sword, and kept them away from Jesus long enough for them to get away. But those guys were probably good sword-fighters back then. Back then they probably practiced a lot. It wouldn't have mattered to him, though. He'd have given his blood, all of it, and gladly to help Jesus.

The kids are all gone now. Old Frank's gone. His wife's still at the beauty parlor. She won't be in for a while. He gets another drink of the whiskey. It's awful good. He hates to stop drinking it, but he hates to keep on. With Jesus watching him and all.

The clock's ticking on the mantel. The hair needs sweeping off the hearth. He knows that cow's still got that white stuff running out from under her tail. But somebody else'll just have to see about it. Maybe the guy who sells the siding can see about it.

Mr. P. figures he ought to make sure it'll work first, so he pulls it out from under the couch and points it at the screen door in back. Right through the kitchen.

He figures maybe they won't be able to understand that. It'll be a big mystery that they'll never figure out. Some'll say Well he was making sure it'd work. Others'll say Aw it might have been there for years. They'll say What was he doing on the couch? And, I guess we'll have to go to town for a haircut now.

They'll even talk about how he borrowed it from Hulet for rats.

Old Frank has already gone through this. He didn't understand it. He trusted Mr. P. and knew he'd never hurt him. Maybe Mr. P. was a father to him. Maybe Mr. P. was God to him. What could he have been thinking of when he shot his best friend?

What in God's name can he be thinking of now?

Mr. Parker, fifty-eight, is reclining on his couch.

Boy and Dog

The dog was already dead.
He was in the road.
A kid watched behind trees.
Tears shone on his face.
He dashed into the road.
Then a car came along.
He retreated to the sidewalk.
He heard his mother calling.
More cars were coming now.
The dog was really dead.
Blood was on the asphalt.
He could see it puddling.
The hubcap was bloody too.

It was also badly dented.

It came off a Mustang.

He ran to the dog.

A car drove up fast.

He caught up the tail.

He pulled on the dog.

It slid in slick blood.

The car got even closer.

He dropped it and ran.

His mother called to him.

She was on the porch.

Johnny what are you doing?

She couldn't see him crying.

His Spam was getting cold.

Bozo was the dog's name.

Bozo was an old dog.

The boy was only eight.

Bozo would be eleven forever.

He ran back to Bozo.

Then he pulled Bozo closer.

But another car came along.

It was the killer Mustang.

It was hunting its hubcap.

The boy had seen it.

He picked up a brick.

The driver was going slow.

He looked out the window.

He really wanted that hubcap.

It was a '65 fastback.

It was worth some money.

It had bad main seals.

Black oil leaked each night.

The dipstick was always low.

It had clobbered the dog.

The wheel hit him hard.

The shiny hubcap said BONG!

The kid held his brick.

He was hiding behind trees.

The driver was slowing down.

It was around here somewhere.

The brick was antique lemon.

It had three round holes.

But it was still heavy.

The car got awful close.

The kid held his brick.

The guy turned his head.

He didn't see the kid.

The kid threw the brick.

It landed on his head.

The driver fell over unconscious.

He jammed the gas down.

The Mustang burned some rubber.

It also burned some oil.

A big tree stopped it.

The tree shook pretty hard.

The windshield shattered in spiderwebs.

The horn started blowing loud.

The guy's head was down.

The horn blew and blew.

The kid got really panicky.

He ran out to help.

He had always loved dogs.

He grabbed the tail again.

The dog was pretty heavy.

The blood made him slide.

The kid kept looking around.

Something popped under the hood.

A little smoke rolled up.

The horn was still blowing.

Wires popped and something crackled.

Then the smoke turned black.

The kid got his dog.

The dog was messed up.

One of his eyes protruded.

Tire tracks were on him.

He was starting to stiffen.

All right then young man.

I'll put these Doritos up.

She didn't hear him yelling.

He couldn't yell very loud.

She went back to lunch.

The smoke wasn't bad yet.

The kid ran back across.

The horn was still blowing.

It was weaker than before.

The battery was getting tired.

Flames leaped under the car.

The guy blew the horn.

He looked sort of dead.

He had this big hole.

It was in his head.

The yellow flames went WHOOSH!

Then the paint started burning.

It was really getting hot.

Nobody would want it now.

The guy's hair was curling.

Fire was coming out everywhere.

The gas tank blew up.

There was this big explosion.

It knocked the kid down.

The car rocked with it.

Two of the tires blew.

The car sat lower then.

The kid said oh shit.

He regretted throwing the brick.

He touched the door handle.

Some of his skin melted.

His fingerprints were instantly gone.

It didn't hurt a bit.

He knew it should have.

It scared him pretty bad.

He could hear music playing.

He rubbed his melted hand.

The guy's hair was gone.

Smoke was thick and black.

It choked him something awful.

He coughed and gagged some.

He ran across the road.

He was needing the telephone.

The emergency number was 911.

He learned it in school.
His class visited the firemen.
They mentioned playing with matches.
They didn't mention throwing bricks.
He ran fast toward home.
But halfway there he stopped.
He didn't have enough time.
He had to go back.
The Mustang had turned black.
The tires were burning off.
Coils of wire fell away.
It wasn't worth much now.
The guy's shirt was burning.
The kid could smell it.
It looked like an Izod.
People were pulled over gawking.
One man came running up.
He was evidently a hero.
A shirt swaddled his hands.
The man grabbed the door.
The hero screamed a little.
The door handle had him.
It wouldn't turn him loose.
The fire rolled around him.
It started curling his hair.
He tried rescuing the driver.
The driver was buckled up.
He was also shoulder-harnessed.
The hero finally got loose.
But he screamed a lot.

His clothes were smoking bad.

He fell and rolled over.

The grass was scorched black.

He was beating himself silly.

His arm had turned black.

The kid watched all this.

The hero flailed the grass.

Somebody needed to get help.

But of course nobody did.

Some people won't get involved.

The car was fully involved.

It wasn't worth twenty bucks.

The motor was probably okay.

The aluminum transmission had melted.

The hero was still screaming.

Suddenly they heard an airhorn.

A big red truck arrived.

Firemen jumped off the truck.

They started hollering Jesus Christ.

One fireman hollered holy shit!

The driver was pretty nervous.

It was his first run.

He didn't set the brake.

The nozzlemen pulled the hose.

They were ready for water.

They were holding it tight.

The driver engaged the pump.

This disengaged the rear wheels.

Nozzlemen were screaming for water.

The hose was pulled away.

The truck was rolling backwards.

The firemen were chasing it.

They were really yelling loud.

It rolled into a ditch.

It was a deep ditch.

It was really a canal.

The canal held deep water.

The truck was pointing up.

The motor had already quit.

They couldn't pump any water.

The hoses wouldn't work now.

The Mustang driver got smaller.

The kid took it in.

He looked for the brick.

It was under the Mustang.

He tried to get it.

He thought about his fingerprints.

But he didn't have any.

So he let it go.

The firemen were screaming loud.

One had sense and radioed.

A crowd of spectators gathered.

A van with newsmen arrived.

There was an anchorman inside.

They started setting up cameras.

The announcer straightened his tie.

The Mustang was solid black.

The fire department came running.

They carried some powdered extinguishers.

They weighed almost twenty pounds.

They started mashing the handles.

White clouds of chemicals rolled.

Fire flashed here and there.

People coughed and almost gagged.

The gas tank kept burning.

They couldn't put it out.

They ran out of powder.

It was only baking soda.

Most people don't know that.

Firemen make money servicing them.

These had steak suppers sometimes.

They played bingo and drank.

Once they had a party.

Some of them got drunk.

Then they had a run.

Their food was barbecued goat.

But the goat burned up.

So did the Mustang driver.

The other truck came then.

A captain of firemen arrived.

He issued orders and radioed.

They stretched lines and attacked.

Only one tire was burning.

Bystanders muttered about their incompetence.

The firemen were pretty embarrassed.

An ambulance pulled up next.

The firemen acted very important.

They bullied the ambulance attendants.

They pried open the door.

One joked about Crispy Critters.

This is a breakfast cereal.

The captain's face turned red.

He began questioning some witnesses.

The kid sidled off unobtrusively.

His Spam was still waiting.

He went to the dog.

The dog was getting stiff.

He picked up one leg.

It stayed up like that.

He looked at the car.

A wrecker was driving up.

He'd never seen a wrecker.

He stuck around to watch.

The anchorman made eyewitness reports.

Several people were interrogated live.

They rushed home to brag.

They were almost real celebrities.

They would phone their neighbors.

They would phone their friends.

Neighbors and friends would watch.

The almost-celebrities would celebrate.

The parties would be gay.

The kid would see them.

He would recognize them all.

It would all be over.

Johnny Carson would come on.

He would be safe forever.

He would request a puppy.

His father would deny him.

He would make different promises.

His daddy would say no.

There were licenses and fees.

Puppies always grew into dogs.

And dogs sometimes chased cars.

And cars sometimes killed dogs.

And bricks sometimes got thrown.

Boys still go to woodsheds.

But fathers must be cautious.

Kids are violent these days.

Especially where pets are concerned.

Julie: A Memory

It was muddy where we parked and I had to be careful not to get on soft ground. That's just a blank space. When I tried to touch her, she slapped my hands away. I heard him slip the safety off. "I don't want you to if you don't want to," she said. Then we went inside. I don't know why I drove all the way through. She didn't say. And then Julie came in. I figured that would make her happy. She had some kind of a fit all of a sudden. "Lock the doors," she said. He had the wrench up in one hand and his fingers were greasy and black and trembling. I didn't want to tell her. We got inside and we sat down. The blood had scabbed on my face. "Don't," she said. I crawled on my hands and knees to the first one just as he picked up the rifle. She wanted popcorn. You see all this stuff on TV now about abortions, and once I saw a doctor holding a fetus in his fingers. She'd left me some sandwich stuff in the refrigerator. I got dressed and turned off all the lights and locked the door. I don't know how many times he hit me. She didn't want to. She said that everything was a mistake, that she didn't love me. He begged hard for his life. And for no reason then, he just slapped her. When I thought of all that, I started feeling good. He looked like he was half asleep. The first boy pulled her panties down around her knees and she whimpered. They say they don't cook their hamburgers ahead of time, but they do. There was a little road that ran back behind, where all the black people were buried. I'd have to hunt under the seat for my socks. "Don't open it," she said. I wiped it with my hand and looked at it. But I wasn't really sure. Then he grabbed her legs, panting, and spread them apart. We lost track of time. I could have reached out and grabbed it. I recognized the second boy. He slapped her so hard her face leaped around sideways. Everybody has to have love. And it seemed like it ruined everything. But that car was there again. It happened quickly. What Julie and I were doing was no different. It was an adventure story. I think I said please to him that night. You can't ask things like that. I didn't even know if we could live together. But I knew she'd be on my side anyway. I worried about it for a long time, that I'd get caught. But I knew we had to try. I didn't want to turn his soul loose if he wasn't ready, so I told him to pray. It's a big step. He had a motor jack set up in front of the grill. One of them said that he didn't have any matches. Houses were all around. I had to keep my shirt on in front of my mother so she wouldn't see the scratches on my back. I stopped outside the city limits and got us a beer from the trunk. She wasn't showing yet. I was trying to get up but I felt like I was drunk. I didn't figure he was ready. "Open that door," he said. I got up on my knees. I'd been planning on staying overnight with some friends at the spillway, but it started raining hard about ten o'clock and we didn't want to sleep in our cars, so we just went home. When we'd first started doing it, we'd always used rubbers. I'd put off telling Mother. And it was driving him nuts. He jammed the rifle against my head. I wanted to go for pizza. Just his feet were sticking out from under the car. She said he was always buying her coffee and eating his lunch with her. I didn't say too much. We were quiet for a while then. I was wet with mud and it was cold on my legs. None of that mattered. And then she got pregnant. Trying to get her hot. So I just kept my mouth shut. I thought they were going to kill us. I listened. But she didn't even say anything about it. I thought we were going to talk. "Somebody with car trouble, I guess," I said. I think my mother wanted to ask me why I wasn't going with Julie anymore, but she didn't. We finally got out there, and the woods were dark and wet. She had her hands up in front of her face. I've even seen her in bars. It was so clear when it was happening. It didn't change anything. "I don't want no part of it," he said. Once we did it right there on the couch with her mother in the next room. I knew I had done the right thing. The first one handed the rifle to the second one and pushed her dress up. I could never go over there without thinking about all those dead people under the stones. Finally it was over. I didn't know if it would work. I put my face between her breasts and closed my eyes and just laid there. If we weren't doing it we were talking about doing it. I finished my beer and then got back in the car. He wanted to know who it was but I didn't say anything. "Thanks," she said. I didn't want to marry her. The road was wet so I drove carefully. It's not something you should do without thinking about it. She said he loved to dance. I cranked it and we sat hugging each other until it warmed up. Before she got out of the car, I made her tell me where he lived. She chain-smoked cigarettes and had brown stains on her fingertips. I wondered if maybe she'd had a child born out of wedlock herself. "Don't," she said. "Please don't." I thought, If you were married to her, you could do this all the time. Mother had offered to buy some for me, but I told her I wanted to take care of things like that by myself. I didn't want to embarrass her. She was talking about baby showers and baby clothes. I could see the rifle lying there, pointing toward the road. Her mother was strange to me. We started dressing. "Hurry up," she'd say. "Hurry up and get it in me." There was something about it on the news. He had his finger on the trigger. His soul was what I thought about, and mine, too. Her mother looked up when I went in, but then she turned away, back to the television. She had mud all over her face and she didn't want me to look at her. There was another boy standing in the rain, watching me. "I love you," she said. They had her tied when I came to. I had to go home finally. He didn't hear me walk up to the car. The porch light was on when we pulled in and neither of us said anything. I figured she'd probably scream. I wiped my forearm across my eyes. He was probably about twenty. Maybe it wasn't even my baby. "When you going to tell your mother?" she said. I didn't know what I was going to tell my mother. You could hear that rain drumming on the roof while you were taking your clothes off and then when you were naked together on the backseat, with the doors locked, it was just the best thing you could want. Down behind the fence there were squirrels and deer. They used to live beside her. I didn't know what to do. Give up my whole life for her and the baby? I walked up on the porch and knocked on the door and heard her mother tell me to come in. I got her in my car and the first thing she did was pull my hand up her dress. She wasn't rude, but I could see that she just didn't want to talk. By then I couldn't do anything. He must have brought the whiskey because she never kept liquor in the house. "You bout two seconds away from gettin a bullet through your head," he said. But I wasn't ready to marry her. Then she squatted down, like she was going to pee on the ground. It was where we always went. She said she didn't want to get married. We held hands. " Ya'll done lost your fuckin minds," he said. "I want to," I said. It was cold outside. I parked my car in the woods and walked back down the road quickly, then went over a barbed-wire fence and down through a pasture. I know he was thinking about that night and what he'd done to us. She had her hand on my dick. I looked at Julie. "Don't," she said. That woman always seemed so hurt. I didn't know what to say. "Hell, she wants it," he said. We'd rest for ten minutes, kissing, and then we'd start again. I wanted to tell my mother and ask her what I should do. We pulled out finally and headed out of town. This night was a night we were going to talk. I thought I was going to wreck the car. You can't do without it. I couldn't see anything. We talked some more. She'd take her nails and scrape me so hard I'd almost tell her to stop. The rifle fell into the mud. "What are you waiting on?" she said. I got to be an expert at getting fully dressed sitting down. I was afraid she'd get up and walk in there and see us on the couch, but it didn't stop us. The first boy had her by the arms and he was dragging her toward a tree. "Tell her to open the door," he said. I'd always thought that having kids was something you should give some thought to. There's nothing blacker than woods at night. You could have her whenever you wanted her. There were a lot of people on the square when I cut through. She unbuckled my belt and unzipped my pants. We ate in the parking lot. We had to hurry because the movie was about to start. And then we said we didn't care what it was as long as it was healthy. When I went to bed, I pulled the covers all the way up over my head and saw it all again, every word and every sound and every raindrop. I didn't want her to have an abortion. I guess it was kind of like when you're little, and you've done something your mother or your father is going to whip you for, but you're hoping that if you beg hard enough they won't. I rolled the window down. He ran off into the woods with a crazy little cry. I got up quickly and went to meet her. "You get out of that car," the boy with the rifle said. He sounded drunk. I took a drink of it. I like adventure. It surprised me when she said she did. I think she felt guilty about the night we got rained out on our fishing trip. She slid up on the console next to me and we left. The second one turned around and looked at me with his dick sticking out of his pants. She laid her head back down. I couldn't understand why they were doing what they were doing. She pushed her dress up and pulled my hand in between her legs. I tried to talk to her for a while, but it was never any use. She got to telling me all about her job, and how this man who worked there was always trying to sweet-talk her on break. I had an old pistol that had belonged to my father. She said leave it alone. I had some beer iced down in my car and I asked her if she wanted one. Or three. "Get out," the one with the rifle said. She did say that Julie would be ready in a few minutes. I sat in the driveway for a long time just looking at the house. The one I hit got up off the ground. People were watching television within sight of us. I was running late when I got home, but she had my clothes ironed and laid out for me. It couldn't have been easy for her. I'd thought he was hurting her because of the way she was moaning. I went inside quietly and washed the blood off my face with a wet towel. They had a nice home there, but he was a long way from the house. I romped on it a little and the back end slid. She said if I wanted to take care of her, take her home. Something cold touched the side of my head. "Please, God," he said. I asked her what she would do about her clothes. When it was dry we'd take a blanket out of the trunk and spread it on the ground. The first thing she did was go over to the boy and spit on him. I knew we'd have a good time. She always made me lock the doors. I couldn't understand why nobody was coming to help us. "Listen," I said, "I don't know what you guys want." I could tell that she was happy. But one night we ran out or I forgot to buy some, or something. It didn't have a jack under it anywhere. The dates were so faded, and the names, too, that you couldn't read them. She didn't know the third one. Sometimes we'd tear each other's clothes getting them off. She told me on the way home. I knew the leaves were wet and cold and I knew how they felt on her skin. She raised up and looked at me. The tires were spinning in the mud. But then I thought that maybe she was just lonely. "You want to do it up here?" I said. "Or you want to get in the back?" But we were running late. She was on her knees and I could see him lunging at her face. I asked her if we were finished and she said yes. We'd have to find a place to live. I didn't want it growing up with just its mother's name, either. She had enough on her already. She was like me. I could have let him live. There were cars passing on the road and I kept thinking that one would surely pull in. I didn't even know where Julie's daddy was. There was a fifth of Wild Turkey on the kitchen table. I used to hunt there. He put his hands up in front of his face and closed his eyes and said, "Jesus, Jesus, oh please Jesus." The night I came in from fishing, I went to bed quietly and tried to go to sleep, but I could hear them moving in her bed, and once in a while, her moaning. But she got up that night and put on a robe and told me it was all right. I was afraid it would hurt her too much. I could do it, too. I just wanted her to be happy. The only thing we could think about was getting it into her as quickly as possible. I loved that rain. She said, "If I could dance, I'd marry that man." I was hungry and wanted to fix myself some breakfast. Some were killed in the Civil War. Blood was in my eyes. You could see the ruts deep in the mud where the tires had gone before us. That night was no different. I took her blouse and bra off and she got on top of me. I told her that I wanted to take care of her. He was gone the next morning and we didn't talk about it. I said I hoped it was a boy. "You just shut your mouth," he said. I thought about it. His eyes didn't close. Give me a good old love story anytime. It was one of those space movies. The foot of the fetus was smaller than his thumb. It was just like shooting a dog. I yelled for him as loud as I could. The first boy went around and tried to open the door. I made a decision right there on that backseat, naked, holding her. Julie drew up and leaned against her side of the car. I didn't say anything. My mother would be a grand-mother. "You can't hide it forever," I said. But sometimes when you do things, you have to pay for them. She had on a red dress and white shoes. She had already gone somewhere, on a date, I guess. Almost all of her friends were married and she wasn't used to dating and she probably worried over what I thought about it. I went into her room and I woke her up. I thought about it. I don't know how long we did it that night. It seemed like that broke the ice. There was blood drip-ping off my face. It made everything seem so nice. "What do you think?" she said. You can't place your order and pull on around and have it ready within thirty seconds without having it cooked ahead of time. She was two months pregnant. So I went out there and got her one. His hands relaxed and one of his feet kicked. They have to. But it was only a matter of time. "We don't want any trouble," I said. On that backseat with her I felt I had all the happiness I'd ever need. They had her tied on the ground with her arms around a tree. In Memphis. All this is fuzzy. I had to keep wiping the blood out of my eyes. Mother stays gone all the time. I couldn't tell her. It had already been in all the papers about the boy they found. Maybe even me. He stomped on my head. The third boy was still standing in the road. I remember he just rolled over and pulled the covers up over him. We'd taken all kinds of crazy chances. She said what was done was done. His face was down in the mud. I'm for life. There weren't any napkins and they didn't give us enough ketchup. "You told her?" I said. She said think about it. She hadn't come right out and said it. Nobody wants to. I eased it up into park and got out with my hands up. It had taken her a long time to get over Daddy leaving her, but she was beginning to make the most of it. It was sharp. They must have known I was there. "You kids have a good time," her mother said. I asked her if she wanted to go to the police or the hospital or what. I don't know how we got over in the woods. Julie wasn't anywhere around. She told it like she was in a trance. There were junked cars all over the pasture. "Just tell me what you want me to do," I said. "If you want this car you can have it." We'd get so hot we just wouldn't think clearly. He'd laid the rifle down. I just unlocked the door and went on into the kitchen. I knew he'd hurt her. "Please," I said, "don't hurt her." He was trying to pull the motor out of a '68 Camaro down in the pasture. I think my mind has tried to cover it up some way. "Please," he said. "Please please please." It wasn't that bad. I didn't think anything about it. "What's wrong?" she said. They had homemade tombstones, carved out of sandrock. I didn't want to hurt her. The first one was doing something to her. The glass was fogged over with our breathing. My car was over there. I didn't want to get up. I couldn't see her getting an abortion. It was pretty good. The first one was puking against a tree. It's a hell of a thing, to see your mother doing that. "Would you just hold me for a little while?" I said. The gun went off. "What?" I said. The one who kicked me put a knife against my throat and I didn't do anything else. "Then we'll tell yours," she said. But I probably wasn't the only kid who'd ever seen something like that. I just had gotten my car paid for, but it needed new tires. It squealed once in the road and was gone. He didn't want to die. I got out to take a leak and the ground was soft. When I grabbed for it, the other one kicked me. The vinyl top was rotted. He screamed when he came. And I wondered what she'd say. They must have heard my car pull up. She wouldn't even look up from the TV when I said something. "Are you sure?" she said. I cared about her. "I'm sure," I said. He rolled out from under it with a wrench in his hand and a pissed-off look on his face, and he knew me then. It was a green '72 Camaro with a black top. He slammed me against the fender. He dropped the wrench. "Don't ask me any questions," I said. "Just hold me." I didn't know if I loved her. "You having trouble?" I said. I thought my nose was running. She was watching "Knot's Landing" and I watched it with her for a while. Randy Hillhouse lived not an eighth of a mile away. I missed Daddy, sure. "Remember me?" I said. I wound up getting about half fucked-up in the kitchen before I got my sausage and eggs fried. "We won't be out late," she said. It was the muzzle of a .22 rifle. I knew she wanted me to marry her. "I wonder what that's doing there," she said. I thought I'd seen the boy some- where before. Julie was quiet. I went down like I'd been shot. "Oh, man, no," he said. It was raining, not hard, just enough to where you had to keep the wipers going to see. The movie wasn't that great. I could have let it go, I guess. We never did it less than twice. I've seen hogs do like that. I stuck it in his face. After it was over, we held each other for a long time. Later on I remembered it like a nightmare. It seems like I cried. Every night. I wanted a cigarette and couldn't smoke in there. She won't even talk to me now, doesn't act like she remembers who I am. "You told her?" I said. I didn't love her. Pow! I think now that I must have been trying to choke him. We'd talked about telling her. But I loved my mother. The first one and the second one were brothers. About the same age as me. I turned and looked at it. "It's okay to cry sometimes," she said. The car was parked at the end of the turnaround. I could see this kid in my mind, running around on a softball field. "You want to tell her?" I said. When I pulled the door shut, I thought about it and unlocked it and stepped inside the living room and turned on the lamp. It's more like a dream now that never really happened. She was screaming for me to help her. She hadn't held me like that in a long time. I waited a week. Her mouth tasted like chewing gum. I think I cried some. It got hard again. I'd already put it up in reverse when the first one knocked on the window. We kissed. I was late when I got over there. I must have passed out. She kissed me, and then she looked at her mother. "For God's sake," I said. I only put one shell in it. I always felt like her mother knew what we were doing. We'd have clothes lying everywhere. I remember one time I walked in on them when they were in bed. I made sure it was him. "You can talk to me anytime you want to," she said. I can't forget how he looked lying there. She said take her home. There was a strange car in the driveway when I pulled up. It was about fifteen miles from town. I stopped and watched for a long time before I went up. They were waiting for us. I thought I was going to vomit, but I didn't. I smashed his head into the fender and caught his hair in both my hands and kneed him in the nose. I'd never done anything to him. We heard their car leave. I kissed her and opened her blouse. I shot him and he fell. "You can get me so damn hot," she said. Then I got myself some Coke out of the icebox and mixed a drink. One was all I needed. She told me how this man had three kids and a wife who didn't like to dance. I didn't move. I could just touch her between her legs and she'd be ready to come. I guess we were both surprised. We were both quiet. "Let's get up and go home, and we'll tell your mother first," I said. I didn't know whether to just go on in or knock on the door. The one on Julie's side said something to the one with the rifle. His pants were down around his knees and she sounded like she was choking. "No," he said, "I don't know you." It seemed that she was what I had been wanting my whole life. I turned around and grabbed his head. They didn't look like people who would raise a son like that. "We've got a flat," he said, but the car looked level. The second one went over to her. I didn't know what they were doing. "Yes, you do," I said. Another, third boy stood in the rain with his hands in his pockets. I was lying on the ground in front of the car. Her body was the temple where I worshipped. They hit me in the head with the gun and then I couldn't see what they were doing with her. I blame that on him. He might have been their cousin. I'd seen his parents before. I eased through town. "Let's get married," I said. The rain was falling in front of the headlights. I had to pull over and stop. It was the best thing I'd ever done. I didn't have an inspection sticker and I was trying to stay away from the law. She'd never mentioned him. But they do. He'd been to the funeral of his brother. I didn't know what to do. "I'll do anything if you don't," she said. I thought she was full of bullshit. Sideways. I didn't like them anyway. I pulled the trigger. I saw then what they'd done. We pulled up into the graveyard and the tires slid in the mud. "He's got a gun," she said. I don't remember driving there. They were both naked and he was between her legs. He was dead, just like that. But the fetus was alive. We hadn't talked about telling anybody. I watched it, but I couldn't concentrate on it for thinking about what we were going to do later. She was still getting ready. He had it out and was holding it in his hand. There were a lot of things I could have said to him, I guess. She said she hoped it was a girl. I know I was scared. I cranked the car and let it warm up. The third one looked like he was puking in the ditch. It made a little red hole between his eyes. She had an abortion. What's bad is that he may be burning for an eternity because of me. She couldn't stop kissing me. I could remember, faintly, seeing them doing it when I was little. When I grabbed the barrel, he turned loose and ran. When it was raining, it was wonderful to park with her. We'd have to get married soon. I know she was thinking about doing it just like me. I kicked the bottoms of his feet. But it's all posted now and you can't hunt on it. I helped her into the car and we looked for the third boy but we didn't see him. There was so much I had to tell her and so much I needed to tell her and in the end I told her nothing. And maybe we wouldn't even be able to make it. I couldn't feel her with one on. I took a shower and shaved, walking around naked in the house. I didn't want to see her hurt. She knew them. "Hey," I said. Jeans and a striped shirt. I didn't know what in the hell to do. I didn't mind killing him so much, after what he'd done. It was my child. I guess he was loosening the transmission bolts. So safe and warm. "Whenever you tell yours," I said. I turned on the defroster when it warmed up. I kept messing around with her. They used to come over and talk to her. The grass was high and there was an old dog pen or hog pen in the pasture with rotten posts and rusted wire. I'd always come right away the first time. We'd been going at each other for the last five months. He was crying and begging me not to do it. I begged him not to hurt her and he kicked me in the face. It hurt.

Samaritans

I was smoking my last cigarette in a bar one day, around the middle of the afternoon. I was drinking heavy, too, for several reasons. It was hot and bright outside, and cool and dark inside the bar, so that's one reason I was in there. But the main reason I was in there was because my wife had left me to go live with somebody else.

A kid came in there unexpectedly, a young, young kid. And of course that's not allowed. You can't have kids coming in bars. People won't put up with that. I was just on the verge of going out to my truck for another pack of smokes when he walked in. I don't remember who all was in there. Some old guys, I guess, and probably, some drunks. I know there was one old man, a golfer, who came in there every afternoon with shaky hands, drank exactly three draft beers, and told these crummy dirty jokes that would make you just close your eyes and shake your head without smiling if you weren't in a real good mood. And back then, I was never in much of a good mood. I knew they'd tell that kid to leave.

But I don't think anybody much wanted to. The kid didn't look good. I thought there was something wrong the minute he stepped in. He had these panicky eyes.

The bartender, Harry, was a big muscled-up guy with a beard. He was washing beer glasses at the time, and he looked up and saw him standing there. The only thing the kid had on was a pair of green gym shorts that were way too big for him. He looked like maybe he'd been walking down the side of a road for a long time, or something similar to that.

Harry, he raised up a little and said, "What you want, kid?" I could see that the kid had some change in his hand. He was standing on the rail and he had his elbows hooked over the bar to hold himself up.

I'm not trying to make this sound any worse than it was, but to me the kid just looked like maybe he hadn't always had enough to eat. He was two or three months overdue for a haircut, too.

"I need a pack a cigrets," he said. I looked at Harry to see what he'd say. He was already shaking his head.

"Can't sell em to you, son," he said. "Minor."

I thought the kid might give Harry some lip. He didn't. He said, "Oh," but he stayed where he was. He looked at me. I knew then that something was going on. But I tried not to think about it. I had troubles enough of my own.

Harry went back to washing his dishes, and I took another drink of my beer. I was trying to cut down, but it was so damn hot outside, and I had a bunch of self-pity loading up on me at that time. The way I had it figured, if I could just stay where I was until the sun went down, and then make my way home without getting thrown in jail, I'd be okay. I had some catfish I was going to thaw out later.

Nobody paid any attention to the kid after that. He wasn't making any noise, wasn't doing anything to cause people to look at him. He turned loose of the bar and stepped down off the rail, and I saw his head going along the far end toward the door.

But then he stuck his face back around the corner, and motioned me toward him with his finger. I didn't say a word, I just looked at him. I couldn't see anything but his eyes sticking up, and that one finger, crooked at me, moving.

I could have looked down at my beer and waited until he went away. I could have turned my back. I knew he couldn't stay in there with us. He wasn't old enough. You don't have to get yourself involved in things like that. But I had to go out for my cigarettes, eventually. Right past him.

I got up and went around there. He'd backed up into the dark pan of the lounge.

"Mister," he said. "Will you loan me a dollar?"

He already had money for cigarettes. I knew somebody outside had sent him inside.

I said, "What do you need a dollar for?"

He kind of looked around and fidgeted his feet in the shadows while he thought of what he was going to say.

"I just need it," he said. "I need to git me somethin."

He looked pretty bad. I pulled out a dollar and gave it to him. He didn't say thanks or anything. He just turned and pushed open the door and went outside. I started not to follow him just then. But after a minute I did.

The way the bar's made, there's a little enclosed porch you come into before you get into the lounge. There's a glass door where you can stand inside and look outside. God, it was hot out there. There wasn't even a dog walking around. The sun was burning down on the parking lot, and the car the kid was crawling into was about what I'd expected. A junky-ass old Rambler, wrecked on the right front end, with the paint almost faded off, and slick tires, and a rag hanging out of the grill. It was parked beside my truck and it was full of people. It looked like about four kids in the backseat. The woman who was driving put her arm over the seat, said something to the kid, and then reached out and whacked the hell out of him.

I STARTED TO go back inside so I wouldn't risk getting involved. But Harry didn't have my brand and there was a pack on the dash. I could see them from where I was, sitting there in the sun, almost close enough for the woman to reach out and touch.

I'd run over a dog with my truck that morning and I wasn't feeling real good about it. The dog had actually been sleeping in the road. I thought he was already dead and was just going to straddle him until I got almost on top of him, when he raised up suddenly and saw me, and tried to run. Of course I didn't have time to stop by then. If he'd just stayed down, he'd have been all right. The muffler wouldn't have even hit him. It was just a small dog. But, boy, I heard it when it hit the bottom of my truck. It went *WHOP!* and the dog—it was a white dog—came rolling out from under my back bumper with all four legs stiff, yelping. White hair was flying everywhere. The air was full of it. I could see it in my rearview mirror. And I don't know why I was thinking about that dog I'd killed while I was watching those people, but I was. It didn't make me feel any better.

They were having some kind of terrible argument out there in that suffocating hot car. There were quilts and pillows piled up in there, like they'd been camping out. There was an old woman on the front seat with the woman driving, the one who'd whacked hell out of her kid for coming back empty-handed.

I thought maybe they'd leave if I waited for a while. I thought maybe they'd try to get their cigarettes somewhere else. And then I thought maybe their car wouldn't crank. Maybe, I thought, they're waiting for somebody to come along with some jumper cables and jump them off. But I didn't have any jumper cables. I pushed open the door and went down the steps.

There was about three feet of space between my truck and their car. They were all watching me. I went up to the window of my truck and got my cigarettes off the dash. The woman driving turned all the way around in the seat. You couldn't tell how old she was. She was one of those women that you can't tell about. But probably somewhere between thirty and fifty. She didn't have liver spots. I noticed that.

I couldn't see all of the old woman from where I was standing. I could just see her old wrinkled knees, and this dirty slip she had sticking out from under the edge of her housecoat. And her daughter— I knew that was who she was—didn't look much better. She had a couple of long black hairs growing out of this mole on her chin that was the size of a butter bean. Her hair kind of looked like a mophead after you've used it for a long time. One of the kids didn't even have any pants on.

She said, "Have they got some cold beer in yonder?" She shaded her eyes with one hand while she looked up at me.

I said, "Well, yeah. They do. But they won't sell cigarettes to a kid that little."

"It just depends on where they know ye or not," she said. "If they don't know ye then most times they won't sell em to you. Is that not right?"

I knew I was already into something. You can get into something like that before you know it. In a minute.

"I guess so," I said.

"Have you got—why you got some, ain't you? Can I git one of them off you?" She was pointing to the cigarettes in my hand. I opened the pack and gave her one. The kid leaned out and wanted to know if he could have one, too.

"Do you let him smoke?"

"Why, he just does like he wants to," she said. "Have you not got a light?"

The kid was looking at me. I had one of those Bics, a red one, and when I held it out to her smoke, she touched my hand for a second and held it steady with hers. She looked up at me and tried to smile. I knew I needed to get back inside right away, before it got any worse. I turned to go and what she came out with stopped me dead in my tracks.

"You wouldn't buy a lady a nice cold beer, would you?" she said. I turned around. There was this sudden silence, and I knew that everybody in the car was straining to hear what I would say. It was serious. Hot, too. I'd already had about five and I was feeling them a little in the heat. I took a step back without meaning to and she opened her door.

"I'll be back in a little bit, Mama," she said.

I looked at those kids. Their hair was ratty and their legs were skinny. It was so damn hot you couldn't stand to stay out in it. I said, "You gonna leave these kids out here in the sun?" "Aw, they'll be all right," she said. But she looked around kind of uncertainly. I was watching those kids. They were as quiet as dead people.

I didn't want to buy her a beer. But I didn't want to make a big deal out of it, either. I didn't want to keep looking at those kids. I just wanted to be done with it.

"Lady," I said, "I'll buy you a beer. But those kids are burning up in that car. Why don't you move it around there in the shade?"

"Well." She hesitated. "I reckon I could," she said. She got back in and it cranked right up. The fan belt was squealing, and some smoke farted out from the back end. But she limped it around to the side and left it under a tree. Then we went inside together.

THE FIRST BUD she got didn't last two minutes. She sucked the can dry. She had on some kind of military pants and a man's long-sleeved work shirt, and house shoes. Blue ones, with a little fuzzy white ball on each. She had the longest toes I'd ever seen.

Finally I asked her if she wanted another beer. I knew she did.

"Lord yes. And I need some cigrets too if you don't care. Marlboro Lights. Not the menthol. Just reglar lights."

I didn't know what to say to her. I thought about telling her I was going to the bathroom, and then slipping out the door. But I really wasn't ready to leave just yet. I bought her another beer and got her some cigarettes.

"I'm plumb give out," she said. "Been drivin all day."

I didn't say anything. I didn't want anybody to think I was going with her.

"We tryin to git to Morgan City Loozeanner. M'husband's sposed to've got a job down there and we's agoin to him. But I don't know," she said. "That old car's about had it."

I looked around in the bar and looked at my face in the mirror behind the rows of bottles. The balls were clicking softly on the pool tables.

"We left from Tuscalooser Alabama," she said. "But them young-guns has been yellin and fightin till they've give me a sick headache. It shore is nice to set down fer a minute. Ain't it good and cool in here?"

I watched her for a moment. She had her legs crossed on the bar stool and about two inches of ash hanging off her cigarette. I got up and went out the door, back to the little enclosed porch. By looking sideways I could see the Rambler parked under the shade. One of the kids was squatted down behind it, using the bathroom. I thought about things for a while and then went back in and sat down beside her.

"Ain't many men'll hep out a woman in trouble," she said. "Specially when she's got a buncha kids."

I ordered myself another beer. The old one was hot. I set it up on the bar and she said, "You not goin to drank that?"

"It's hot," I said.

"I'll drank it," she said, and she pulled it over next to her. I didn't want to look at her anymore. But she had her eyes locked on me and she wouldn't take them off. She put her hand on my wrist. Her fingers were cold.

"It's some people in this world has got thangs and some that ain't," she said. "My deddy used to have money. Owned three service stations and a sale barn. Had four people drove trucks fer him. But you can lose it easy as you git it. You ought to see him now. We cain't even afford to put him in a rest home."

I got up and went over to the jukebox and put two quarters in. I played some John Anderson and some Lynn Anderson and then I punched Narvel Felts. I didn't want to have to listen to what she had to say.

She was lighting a cigarette off the butt of another one when I sat down beside her again. She grabbed my hand as soon as it touched the bar.

"Listen," she said. "That's my mama out yonder in that car. She's seventy-eight year old and she ain't never knowed nothin but hard work. She ain't got a penny in this world. What good's it done her to work all her life?"

"Well," I said, "she's got some grandchildren. She's got them."

"Huh! I got a girl eighteen, was never in a bit a trouble her whole life. Just up and run off last year with a goddamn sand nigger. Now what about that?"

"I don't know," I said.

"I need another beer!" she said, and she popped her can down on the bar pretty hard. Everybody turned and looked at us. I nodded to Harry and he brought a cold one over. But he looked a little pissed.

"Let me tell you somethin," she said. "People don't give a shit if you ain't got a place to sleep ner nothin to eat. They don't care. That son of a bitch," she said. "He won't be there when we git there. If we ever git there." And she slammed her face down on the bar, and started crying, loud, holding onto both beers.

Everybody stopped what they were doing. The people shooting pool stopped. The guys on the shuffleboard machine just stopped and turned around.

"Get her out of here," Harry said. "Frank, you brought her in here, you get her out."

I got down off my stool and went around to the other side of her, and I took her arm.

"Come on," I said. "Let's go back outside."

I tugged on her arm. She raised her head and looked straight at Harry.

"*Fuck* you," she said. "You don't know nothin about me. You ain't fit to judge."

"Out," he said, and he pointed toward the door. "Frank," he said.

"Come on," I told her. "Let's go."

IT HADN'T COOLED off any, but the sun was a little lower in the sky. Three of the kids were asleep in the backseat, their hair plastered to their heads with sweat. The old woman was sitting in the car with her feet in the parking lot, spitting brown juice out the open door. She didn't even turn her head when we walked back to the car. The woman had the rest of the beer in one hand, the pack of Marlboro Lights in the other. She leaned against the fender when we stopped.

"You think your car will make it?" I said. I was looking at the tires and thinking of the miles they had to go. She shook her head slowly and stared at me.

"I done changed my mind," she said. "I'm gonna stay here with you. I love you."

Her eyes were all teary and bitter, drunk-looking already, and I knew that she had been stomped on all her life, and had probably been forced to do no telling what. And I just shook my head.

"You can't do that," I said.

She looked at the motel across the street.

"Let's go over there and git us a room," she said. "I want to."

The kid who had come into the bar walked up out of the hot weeds and stood there looking at us for a minute. Then he got in the car. His grandmother had to pull up the front seat to let him in. She turned around and shut the door.

"I may just go to Texas," the woman said. "I got a sister lives out there. I may just drop these kids off with her for a while and go on out to California. To Los Vegas."

I started to tell her that Las Vegas was not in California, but it didn't matter. She turned the beer up and took a long drink of it, and I could see the muscles and cords in her throat pumping and working. She killed it. She dropped the can at her feet, and it hit with a tiny tinny sound and rolled under the car. She wiped her mouth with the back of her hand, tugging hard at her lips, and then she wiped her eyes.

"Don't nobody know what I been through," she said. She was looking at the ground. "Havin to live on food stamps and feed four younguns." She shook her head. "You cain't do it," she said. "You cain't hardly blame nobody for wantin to run off from it. If they was any way I could run off myself I would."

"That's bad," I said.

"That's terrible," I said.

She looked up and her eyes were hot.

"What do you care? All you goin to do is go right back in there and git drunk. You just like everybody else. You ain't never had to go in a grocery store and buy stuff with food stamps and have everbody look at you. You ain't never had to go hungry. Have you?"

I didn't answer.

"Have you?"

"No."

"All right, then," she said. She jerked her head toward the building. "Go on back in there and drank ye goddamn beer. We made it this far without you."

She turned her face to one side. I reached back for my wallet because I couldn't think of anything else to do. I couldn't stand to look at them anymore.

I pulled out thirty dollars and gave it to her. I knew that their troubles were more than she'd outlined, that they had awful things wrong with their lives that thirty dollars would never cure. But I don't know. You know how I felt? I felt like I feel when I see those commercials on TV, of all those people, women and kids, starving to death in Ethiopia and places, and I don't send money. I know that Jesus wants you to help feed the poor.

She looked at what was in her hand, and counted it, jerking the bills from one hand to the other, two tens and two fives. She folded it up and put it in her pocket, and leaned down and spoke to the old woman.

"Come on, Mama," she said. The old woman got out of the car in her housecoat and I saw then that they were both wearing exactly the same kind of house shoes. She shuffled around to the front of the car, and her daughter took her arm.

They went slowly across the parking lot, the old woman limping a little in the heat, and I watched them until they went up the steps that led to the lounge and disappeared inside. The kid leaned out the window and shook his head sadly. I pulled out a cigarette and he looked up at me.

"Boy you a dumb sumbitch," he said.

And in a way I had to agree with him.

Night Life

I decided a long time ago that it isn't easy meeting them, not for me. Some guys can just walk up to a woman and start talking to her, start saying anything. I can't. I have to wait and work up my nerve, have a few beers. I have to sit at a table for a while, or the bar, and look them over and find the one who looks like she won't turn a man down. This sometimes means picking one who is sitting by herself, who is maybe a little older than most, maybe even one who doesn't look very good. Sometimes I wait until she dances with another man, then go over and make my move after she sits back down. Sometimes, if I see one whose looks I like, I send a drink over to her table. But it isn't easy meeting them.

I'm in a bar just outside the city limits Friday night when three women come in and take a table next to the dance floor, the last table not taken.

I order another beer and look out over the crowd, the band playing, the couples who have found each other drifting over the floor like smoke. Some of the tables have three and four women, some have couples, some have men, and one table has a girl by herself. I check her out.

She has on a black dress and white stockings, is dressed, I think, a little like a witch. She has a bottle in a brown paper sack sitting on the table and she holds onto her solitary drink with both hands. She seems to have eyes for only this. I sip on my beer for a while and eye the creeping clock above the taps and finally I go over. She looks up and sees me coming her way and looks away.

"Hi," I say, when I stop beside her chair. I wish the band wouldn't play rock and roll; you can't even talk over the noise. She smiles but she doesn't say anything. I'm going to be shot down.

I lean over and shout above the music: "How you doing?" She says something that I think is "okay" and I feel completely stupid, leaning over her like this. She looks like she just wants me to go away quickly and leave her alone. I won't score. She won't dance. Friday night is flying away.

"Want to dance?" I shout in her ear. The black horn player is crouched on the stage in front of the mike, the spotlight on him, his cheeks ballooned out as he blows and sweats, his jeweled fingers flying over the valves. She shakes her head and gives me a sad look. Smoke two feet thick hangs from the ceiling.

"Hell, come on," I say, putting on my friendliest smile, feeling my confidence—what little I had to start with—ebbing away. They're all like this. They won't talk to you, they won't dance. Why do they come out to a place like this if they don't want to meet men? "I'm not going to bite you," I say.

She takes one hand off her drink and leans slightly toward me. "Thanks anyway," she says. The flesh around her eyes looks dark, it's bruised, she's hurt. Maybe somebody slapped her. Maybe she said the wrong thing to the wrong man and he popped her. I know it can happen between a man and a woman. It can happen in a second.

"You live around here?" I say. I don't know what to say; I'm just saying anything to try and keep her talking.

She shakes her head, closes her eyes briefly. Patience. She's weary of this, maybe, these strange men asking, always asking, never stopping. "No. I live at Hattiesburg. I'm just up here for the weekend."

"You waiting on somebody?"

She draws back and blinks. Now she'll tell me it's none of my business. "Not really," she says. "I'm just waiting."

"Well come on and dance, then," I say.

She opens a small brown purse that looks like a dead mole and pulls out a white cigarette. I fish up my lighter and give her some fire. She inhales and coughs, her tiny fist balled at her mouth. Maybe she's had a bigger fist at her mouth. Maybe she likes it.

"Thanks," she says.

"You going to school at Hattiesburg?" I say.

She nods, looks around. "Yeah."

"Just up here living it up on the weekend."

"Not really. I just came up to Jackson to sort of be by myself for a while."

Something's bothering her, I can tell. She only wants to be left alone. She doesn't want to dance. She has her own bottle and her own table, her own troubles of which I know nothing. So I draw back a chair and put one foot up in it, rest my elbow on my knee. "How come?" I say.

She cups her face in her other hand and dabs at the ashtray with the cigarette.

"Oh. You know. Just getting away from everything."

"Yeah," I say. I know the feeling. I begin wishing I'd never walked over here. "What's your name?"

"Lorraine," this Lorraine says. She doesn't ask me my name.

"You look sad, Lorraine. What's wrong?"

"Nothing," she says, apparently only mildly pissed. "Nothing's wrong. I just want to be by myself for a while. I've just got some things I have to deal with."

I know. I know all people have things they must deal with. I have things I must deal with. I must deal with lonesome Friday nights, and these little semihostile confrontations sometimes occur as a result. But I don't know when to stop.

"Don't you like to dance?" I say. I feel like a fool. Am a fool.

"Sure. Sure I like to dance. I just don't feel like it tonight."

"Well," I say. I hate to get shot down, blown out of the saddle. But most of the time, I get shot down. I hate to have to turn away and go back to the bar without even a dance. I hate for them to beat me like this. But she probably does have some problem. There's probably a man involved somewhere, somehow. Possibly even a woman.

"Don't take it personally," she says. "Maybe some other night."

"Sure," I say, and I turn away. I walk a few steps and stop. I look back at her. She's taking the top off the bottle. I don't know what's the matter with me. I go back to her table.

"You sure you don't want to dance?" I say.

"No," she says, not even looking up. "Not now. Please leave me alone."

She's just lucky is all. She doesn't know just how damn lucky she is. The last of the Budweiser is almost warm, so I raise it aloft and signal to the sullen barmaid. I know her. She knows me. Her wet swollen hands reach into a dark cooler. I give her money but she doesn't speak. She doesn't want to look at me. Her heavy breasts sway as she rubs the bar hard, her eyes down. I watch them move. I watch her move away. She finds something to do at the other end of the bar. I take a drink.

A large number of people are wanting in the bathroom. I wait for three or four minutes before I can get inside the door, and then it's old piss, wet linoleum, knifecarvings above stained urinals that shredded butts have clogged. Water is weeping out from the partitioned commode stall where there is never any toilet paper. Others in line behind me are now waiting their turn. Their faces are scarred and murderous; it won't do to bump into them. To these no apology is acceptable. They'll cut their knuckles again and again on my broken teeth after I'm on the floor.

I go back out, into the noise and the smoke and the dark. A woman touches my wrist when I go by her table, one of the three I saw earlier.

"Hey," she says. "How come you ain't asked me to dance yet?"

And there she is. Dark hair. Pale face. Sweater.

"I was fixing to," I say. "You want to wait till the band starts back up?"

"Set down," she says. She pulls out a chair and I sit.

"Where's your friends?" I say. I hope they won't come back. I don't know why she's picked me, but I'm glad somebody has. Even if the night turns out wasted there is hope at this moment.

"They over yonder," she points. "I've seen you before."

"In here?" I need my beer. "Let me go over here and get my beer and I'll be right back." She nods and smiles and I can't tell much about her except she's got knockers. I get my beer and come back.

"I saw you in here other night," she says. "Last weekend."

That's not right; I worked all weekend last weekend, trying to make more money. But I say, "Yeah. I come in here about every weekend."

Dark hair. Pale face. Sweater. Knockers. Jeans. I look down. Tennis shoes. With black socks.

"I used to come in here with my husband all the time," she says. "You want a drink?"

I lift my beer. We sit for a while without saying anything. The band is coming back, moving around on the stage and talking behind the dead mikes.

"That's a pretty good band," I say.

"Yeah. If you like nigger music. I wish they'd get a good country band. You like country music?"

"Yeah," I say. "Sure." But I wish I knew George Thorogood personally.

"Who you like?"

I have to think. "Aw. I like old Ricky Skaggs pretty good. Vern Gosden, I like him a lot. John Anderson."

"I used to be a singer," she says.

"Oh really?" I'm surprised. "Where?"

She looks around. She shrugs. I watch her breasts rise and fall. "Just around."

"I mean, professionally?" I sip my beer.

"Well. I sung at the Tupelo Mid-South Fair and Dairy Show in nineteen seventy-six. Had a three-piece band. That's where I met my husband."

"You're divorced," I say.

"Huh. Wish I was."

Here's the one thing I don't need: to get hooked up with somebody who has more problems than I do. I'm already on probation. I don't need to get hooked up with somebody who will sit here all night telling me how her husband fucked her over. But she has some really nice, truly wonderful breasts. It won't hurt to sit here and talk to her for a while. Maybe she's as lonely as I am.

"What? Are you separated?" I say.

"Yeah."

"How long?"

"About two weeks. Listen. I don't give a shit what he does. He's a sorry son of a bitch. I don't care if I don't never see him again."

"You're just out to have a good time."

"Damn right."

I tell her I think we can have one.

BY TEN WE'RE out on the parking lot in her new Lincoln (surprise) and she's braced up against the driver's door. I have her sweater and bra all pushed up above her breasts and I'm moaning and kissing and trying to get her pants down. We're half hidden in the shadow of the building, but the neon lights are shining on the hood and part of the front seat. People in certain areas of the parking lot can see what we're doing. I don't care; I'm hot. Her nipples have been in and out of my mouth and she's halfway or halfheartedly trying to fight me off. She smells of talcum powder and light sweat. We've been kissing for ten minutes, but she doesn't seem to be excited. I know already, deep down, that something is wrong. She keeps looking out over the parking lot.

"Oh baby," I moan. I kiss the side of her neck and taste makeup on my tongue, slightly bitter. Patooey. "Let's do it," I say.

"Not here," she says. She pushes out from under me and takes both hands and tugs her bra and sweater back into place. I look at her for a moment and turn away. Not here. That might mean maybe somewhere else.

"Oh we'll *do* it," she says. Sure. "We just can't right now."

She rubs the side of my face. "My husband might be around here."

"Your husband?" I say. What's this? "I thought you said you weren't worried about him." It's always like this. They all have some problem they have to lay on you before they'll give it to you, and even then sometimes they won't give it to you. "What? You think he might come around here?"

She brushes the hair up away from her eyes and pulls at her pants. She pulls down one of the visor mirrors and checks her face.

"He might. I told you we used to come over here."

"You said you didn't give a shit what he did."

"I don't."

"Then what are you worried about?"

"I'm not worried. I just don't want him to catch me doing anything."

"Aw," I say. "Okay." I understand now. She's another one of the crazy ones. I don't know why I'm the one who always finds them, goes straight to them like a pointer after birds. They're not worth the trouble. They drive me nuts with their kids and their divorces and their diet pills and their friends in trouble and their ex-husbands for whom they still carry the torch. They promise and promise and promise. I know she's crazy now, I know the thing to do now is just forget about it, go back inside, leave her out here. "Well, I'm going back in here and get me a beer," I say. "I don't want to get mixed up with you and your husband. I'll see you later."

I slide over to the door—I don't have to slide far—and open it. I step out onto the parking lot and look back in at her. She doesn't look up. She has some secret hurt in her heart that matters to her and doesn't matter to me. I think about this for a moment. I weigh various possibilities and things in my head. For a moment I'm tempted to get back in and talk to her. But then I shut the door and walk away.

THEY CALL ME in from the car bay the next day and tell me I've got a phone call. I figure it's probably my mother wanting me to bring home something from the store, eggs or milk. I have grease all over my hands, under my fingernails, too, where it's always hard to get out, so I tear off a paper towel and pick up the extension with that.

"Hello," I say.

"Hey!"

I answer slowly. "Oh. Yeah." I recognize the voice.

"This is Connie. What you doing?"

"Well," I say, "right now I'm trying to fix a Buick. What can I do for you?" I look around and eye the shop foreman watching me. They don't pay me to talk on the phone unless I'm ordering parts.

"I just wanted to see what you's doing tonight. I wanted to talk to you about last night. Can you talk?"

I slip the receiver down between my head and my shoulder and wipe my hands with the paper towel. "Yeah," I say. "I guess I can for a minute. What's on your mind?"

"Well, I just wanted to tell you I was sorry about last night. About the way I acted. I'd been drinking before I ever got over there and we—Sheila and Bonita and me—we'd been talking about Roland and me before we ever come over there."

"Roland," I say. "Your husband."

"Right," she says, seems happy to say it. "We been married eight years. We got two kids. You know the kids is the ones always suffers in something like this."

"Yeah," I say. Well, sure. Sure they do. "I guess so," I say.

"I'm at home and I was thinking about last night. I mean, when we was out in the car and all. I was just upset. I didn't mean to act like that."

She's talking like she did something wrong. But all she did was refuse to take her pants off. In a public parking lot. Where anybody could have walked up to the car and looked in, seen her in all her naked glory for free. I'm uneasy remembering this, my half-drunk horny stupidity. I could have gone too far. I'm not supposed to be in bars anyway.

"Well," I say. "Hell. You don't owe me any apology or anything. I mean. We just met. You know. Out in the car and all. . . . you don't have to explain anything to me."

"I feel like I ought to, though," she says. "I was just wondering what you were gonna do tonight. I thought I'd see if you wanted to get a drink somewhere. If you're not busy." She lowers her voice. "I mean I liked it. In the car."

I know now that I shouldn't have tried that anyway. She just had me so turned on. . . .

I say, "You did, huh?" I'm seeing it again now, how the light played over her breasts, how they looked when I pushed her bra up.

"Well," I say, "I don't have anything planned."

"Okay," she says. She sounds glad she called. "You want to meet me somewhere?"

"Sure," I say. "I guess so. Hell, we can drink a beer or something."

"I'd really like to tell you why I acted the way I did last night, Jerry."

"It's Gary."

"Right. Gary. I knew it was Gary. You want to go back out there? Where we were last night?"

I start to say no, let's go someplace else, but she says, quickly, "It's close to my house and all. I'll have to get somebody to keep my kids and they know the number there if anything happens."

"Okay," I say. "Listen. I've got a lot of work to do, so it may be late when I get off. Maybe around six or seven. I get all the overtime I can. Why don't we try to get out there about nine? That'll give me time to get home and get cleaned up and all. I've got to catch a ride."

"That's fine," she says. "I'll get us a table."

"Okay," I say. I think for a moment. I might as well go ahead and ask her. "Listen. You want me to get us a room?"

She waits three seconds before she answers. "Well. You can get one if you want to, Gary. I'm not promising anything. But you can get us a room if you want to."

SHE'S ALREADY HAPPY and high when I slide into a chair beside her. It looks like the only seat left in the place is the one she's been saving for me.

"Hey," I say, and I set a fifth on the table. She leans over and kisses me. Her eyes are bright even in the darkness; they seem to belong to a woman different somehow from the one I wrestled with in the car the night before. The table is no bigger than a car tire. "How long you been here?" I say.

On the floor to the music she moves with drunken feet, pressing herself against me, her washed hair in my face sweet and soft. We dance a few times and then she tells me she wants to talk.

"What it is, see, he's wanting to catch me. Messing around."

"I don't get it," I say. "How come?"

"He wants me to give him a divorce. But I ain't gonna do it. I ain't gonna do one thing that'll make him happy."

I don't care about any of this. I don't want to know her problems. She acts like she's the only one who has any.

"Let's talk about something besides you and your husband," I say. "Why don't you quit thinking about him? You'd probably have a better time. You know it?"

She seems to realize with sadness that what I'm saying is true. "I know it," she says. "I'll hush about him."

But she doesn't. She keeps bringing his name up and looking all around in the bar, trying to spot him at large. I know there is nothing to do but be patient. I have a motel key in my pocket.

WE PULL INTO a parking space next to the wall of a Day's Inn and she turns off the lights and ignition. The aluminum numerals on the red metal door read 214.

"Let's go in," I say. I open my door.

She turns her face away from me and stares at something across the parking lot. She's very quiet. Unhappy. Almost angry.

"What are you looking at?" I say. I see the back of her dark head move.

"Nothing." She pulls the keys out and opens the door. "Let's go on in. Now that you've got me out here we might as well."

I haven't twisted her arm to get her out here. She's driven us over here willingly. Now I don't know what's wrong with her. She gets out and comes around to the front of the car looking down, not looking at me. I slip the key in and unlock the door. I turn on the light. A motel room like any other. I set what's left of the fifth on the plastic woodgrain table and go back and lean against the door. She is standing below the sidewalk, hugging herself with her arms, facing away. She seems to be looking at a blue Chevy pickup parked across the lot.

"You coming in?" I say.

Without answering she turns and comes by me and goes to sit on the bed. I shut the door and bolt it. I'm a little drunk. She'd better be careful. I take the bottle out of the sack and open it, tilt a burning drink down my throat. I hold it out to her.

"You want a drink?"

She shakes her head violently and stares at the floor.

"Well," I say. I look around and see the TV. "You want to watch some TV?"

"It doesn't matter," she says. "Nothing matters."

"Boy ain't we having just loads of fun," I say.

I turn on the TV and kick off my shoes and stretch out on the bed beside her, turning one of the pillows around so I can prop my head against it. I find an ashtray and move it over beside me. I sip from the bottle and wish I had some Coke. CNN news is on. After a while she turns around and lies down beside me. She doesn't say anything.

"You didn't have to come over here, you know," I say.

"I know," she says.

I don't know why I always have to pick some crazy woman. I used to be under the impression that after a man has put up with one of them, that that will do it for the rest of his life, that the others will all be halfway normal.

"You want to go back?" I ask her.

I turn just my head and watch her. She's lying on her side with her legs drawn up. She's wearing light blue slacks and a black top with red flowers.

"No," she says. "I want to stay here with you."

"Oh yeah?" I say. "Damn if you act like it."

For answer she reaches out and takes my hand and puts it on her breast. She rubs the hand over it for a moment and then slips it inside her blouse. I lean over and kiss her and push my fingers down into the cup of her bra. She slides a hand up my leg and I break away long enough to set the whiskey on the table, then roll on top of her.

"Cut the light out," she says.

"What?"

"Cut the light out."

I get up and pull off my shirt and flick off the light and we are left in the blue glow from the TV. Some massacre in a foreign country is being documented on the television screen: swollen bodies, murdered live-stock in the streets. Black bloodstains on shattered brick walls. I push her shirt up and reach behind her and unsnap her bra, the heavy round meat easing into my hands. I kiss at her with an urgency she doesn't seem to share. I rub at the waistband of her pants and run my hands all over her. But there is no feeling in her kisses. She's tense. I twist her thick nipples between my fingers and after five minutes I quit. She has worked her way upright in the bed and she sits now with her nice knockers poking out from underneath the twisted entanglements of her shirt and bra, looking not at me or the TV or her clothes but the wall.

I sit up and swing my legs to the floor and find my cigarettes. I light one and get my shirt off the floor.

"You ready to run me back to the club?" I say. "There's no need in us staying over here." Something is wrong with her. She doesn't even get excited. It's no wonder her husband has left her. She's cold as a fish.

"That's his pickup," she says.

"What?"

"That's Roland's pickup outside. He's got some woman over here. In one of these rooms." She looks at me. "Maybe right next to us."

I hate myself for being this way. For being so desperate. I already knew how it was going to turn out. I knew it would be exactly like this.

"Well, so what?" I say. "If he's screwing around on you, what are you so worried about?"

"I'm not worried," she says.

"The hell you ain't." I stand up and pull on my shirt. I know I need to get myself out of this room and away from her. It's not too late to go back to the bar and try to meet somebody else. Anybody will be better than her. Even the fat ones will be better than her. At least I can have a good time with them. They don't have problems. They don't waste the nights. "You're afraid he'll see you with me," I say.

"Would you just listen for one minute?" she says. "I been married to him since I was sixteen. We got some rental property we own together. He's a contractor. He didn't leave me. I left him! You don't understand."

"Yeah," I say. "I understand. I understand all of it. You're wanting somebody to listen to all your problems and I ain't no fucking head doctor. Just take me back to the club or let me out somewhere and I'll catch a ride home. Hell, it's Saturday night. I got to go back to work Monday. You know what I'm saying?" She fastens her bra back together and pulls her shirt down. By the time I get out the door to the running car, I'm surprised she hasn't left me. The truck we saw earlier is gone, but she doesn't mention it. I get in with her and sit close to the door all the way back. I look at her breasts. They are magnificent. I want to suggest another scenario, but I don't.

I'M LIVING WITH my mother again and Sunday is a chicken dinner, just the two of us. Mashed potatoes and English peas, gravy. I sleep late on Sunday, then go down to the road and pick up the papers, the *Commercial Appeal* from Memphis and the *Clarion-Ledger* from Jackson. The rest of my morning is taken up with reading these papers, especially the movie and book pages, and drinking coffee and smoking cigarettes until my mother comes in from church and calls me to dinner. I don't have a car now; a lawyer has the money it brought, so now I read the pages with the car ads, too. I want to buy a new one, have been toying with the idea, and try to save my money for that.

Sunday afternoon, I'm asleep in the bed that held me as a child when the phone rings. I wake and turn and hear my mother moving toward me in the empty house, her feet and weight ponderous on the old boards, hesitant. She's coming to see if I'm asleep and she probably hopes I am. She opens the door and sees me. She says there is some woman who wants to talk to me. I know somehow, freshly awake from dreams of erotica and hanging breasts, deliciously rested, ready for the last night of the weekend. I get up and go to the kitchen and shut the door. It's her.

"Gary?" she says.

"Yeah."

"It's Connie."

"Yeah. I know." What does she want and why has she picked me? Why can't she see that I'm bad for her? That I can't take much more?

"Did I wake you up?"

"Yeah, matter of fact you did."

"Aw, I'm sorry. I didn't mean to wake you up. I guess I shoulda called later. I didn't mean to wake you up."

"Listen," I say. "What do you want?" There's no need to be nice to her anymore. I'm through with her, I don't want her to start calling over here and bothering my mother when I'm not home. I don't even want her calling over here. My mother asks too many questions as it is. Any man twenty-eight years old ought to be able to come and go without his mother asking him where he's going every time.

"I just wanted to talk," she says, and she says that in a pleading voice. "Can you talk?" Suddenly she sounds cheerful and sober.

"I don't know," I say. "I mean, I don't see much point in it. I don't even know what you want. I don't think you know what you want." I can't see my cigarettes. "Hold on," I say. "I've got to find a cigarette."

I don't wait for her to answer. I go into the living room and get my pack and my lighter. I light one and look out the window at the passing cars, the uncut grass. My mother watches from behind her eyeglasses where she sits with the Bible of God cupped in her lap. She says nothing, but I see the fear she has. After a while I go back and pick up the telephone again. "All right," I say, making the weariness in my voice plain.

It's kind of hard, not having a car. I have to be careful to get with somebody who has wheels. I have to make sure of that early on. I don't mind paying for a room if the woman doesn't mind us going in her car. It complicates things, makes them more difficult. But I can't take them home, not while I'm living with my mother. She wouldn't allow it. I know what would happen if I tried it. I've imagined it before, and it isn't nice. It's awful. Doors jerked open and covers grabbed.

"Listen," she says. "I know I acted terrible last night. It was just his truck over there that did it. You got to understand, Gary, we been married ten years. You just don't throw ten years away without thinking about it."

"Right," I say. First eight years, now ten years. I must deal with her, get rid of her. "But it ain't none of my business. Let me explain something to you. When I go out on the weekend, all I'm looking for is to have a good time. All right? I mean I don't think I have to go to bed with every girl I meet. I've been married. Not as long as you, but I've been married. I know what it's like." I'm not saying what I mean to say. "You just act too damn strange for me, okay? You get depressed, and I don't need to be around somebody that's depressed all the time. It gets me depressed, too. Now that's all it is. If you still love your husband, fine. You need to try to work everything out with him. That's between you and him. I don't have anything to do with it. I just don't want you to call me anymore."

That should do it. That should make her mad enough to where she'll say something, then hang up on me. She doesn't. "Oh, Gary. Don't be mad. I've been thinking over everything today. Listen. I called my husband and you know what I told him?"

"What?" I don't want to hear this shit.

"I told him I wanted a divorce. I told him I was going to try to get eight hundred dollars a month out of him. He started talking sweet then. He wants us to get back together now. What you think about that?"

"I don't know," I say. "I don't care," I say. I open the icebox and find a beer. Then I look a little longer and find the schnapps.

"I told him I saw him last night. At that motel. But anyway, that ain't what I called you about. I called you about something else."

"What?"

"I got us a room tonight. Just you and me. At the Holiday Inn. I already got it. I got the key right here."

I don't really believe that. "I don't really believe that," I say.

"Listen, Gary. I know I ain't acted right. I don't blame you for being disgusted with me. But it was just all that stuff with my ex. He's been going out on me for the longest. Friday night was the first time I'd ever been out without him. In ten years. Honest."

"Is that right?" I say. She's probably lying. She's probably just telling me all this so she can get me off again and drive me some more nuts telling me some more about it.

"I swear. Gary, I swear to God. May God strike me dead if I ain't telling the truth."

"Well," I say. I take a drink of my beer. Maybe she is telling the truth. Maybe they've had what she thought was a good marriage. It's happened before. You can go along fine for years and it can fall apart in a second. You can do things to each other that can never be forgiven. One word can lead to another word. You can lose control and a whole lot more. They can make you pay for one second of anger. They can make you pay with your house, and your car, and your money and self-respect. She doesn't have to tell me about marriage. I know already. Marriage is having to live with a woman. That's what marriage is.

But I won't have to see her after tonight. I won't put up with any more shit from her. I don't have to. I'm not married anymore. I won't be again.

"How's that sound?" she says.

"I guess it sounds all right," I say.

"Listen, baby, I'm gonna make up for everything tonight. I mean, everything."

"Well, okay," I say. She's convinced me. There's only one thing. I don't want her to pick me up here, at my mother's. "Where do you live?"

"I can come get you," she says.

"No. I'd rather you wouldn't," I say. "Listen. I've got a friend who'll give me a ride out to your house. You staying in the house?"

"Hell yes," she says. "I'm not gonna give it to my ex."

"I'll just get somebody to carry me out there, then. Where do you live?"

She tells me. I say I'll be there by seven. I feel a lot better about everything when I hang up the phone.

"You sure this is it?" I say to my friend.

The boy I'm riding with looks at the mailbox.

"That's the number. One hundred Willow Lane. Hell, Gary, there ain't nothing but rich people live up in here."

"Well damn," I say. "This is the address she gave me."

"Well, this is it then," my friend says. "You want me to wait on you?"

"I don't know. You might ought to."

"We'll just pull up in here and see if this is it."

We drive up a blacktopped lane to a house designed like a Swiss chalet. I guess that it's over four thousand square feet under this roof. It has big dormers and split shingles and massive columns of rough wood on the porch. There is a pool full of blue water in the backyard. The Lincoln I've been riding in and nuzzling her knockers in is parked in the drive.

"Hell. That's her car," I say. "I guess this is it."

She comes to the kitchen window and pushes the curtains aside.

"This is it," I say, when I see her. "I just didn't know it was this fancy."

"You better hang onto her," my friend says.

"Yeah. Maybe so. Well, thanks for the ride, Bobby. Let me give you some on the gas."

"Get outa here," he says.

I start pulling five dollars out of my billfold, but my friend leans across me and opens the door. "Get your butt outa here," he says. "Put that money back up."

"Hell, Bobby," I say. "It's a long way out here."

"I may need a ride from you sometime."

"You better take it."

"Go on. I'll see you later."

I get out, sticking the money back in my billfold, waving to my friend backing out of the driveway. The headlights retreat, swords of light through the motes of dust that hang and fall until he swings out and grabs low and peels away with a faint stench and high squeal of rubber. I listen to him hit the gears, to the little barks of rubber until he is gone. For a moment I wonder what I'm doing here. On another man's concrete. Another man's ride. Everything about this house is elegant. It's hard to believe this woman comes out of this place. But there she is, opening the door. I go up to her. She kisses me.

"Come on in," she says.

It's a dream room. High, vaulted ceilings, enclosed beams. Rams, bucks, bear heads mounted over the fireplace, and it of massive river stones. Carpet that covers my toes. I don't know what to say. I know

now she wasn't lying about the contractor and the real estate. Or the kids. Two beautiful little girls are seated on the thick carpet in their nightgowns, one about two, the other about four. Dark hair like her, shy smiles.

"Hi," I say. They look up at me, smile, look down. They have toys, trucks, Sylvester the Cat on the floor. The remnants of their suppers are on paper plates beside them. Potato chips. Gnawed hamburger buns. They whisper things to each other and cast quick glances at me while they pretend not to watch.

"I'll be ready in just a minute, Gary," she says.

I look around. "Yeah. Okay," I say. I'm watching the little girls. They've taken my interest. They're so precious. I know they cannot comprehend what has happened to their daddy. I feel myself to be an intruder in this house, a homewrecker. The husband, the father, could come home and kill me this minute with a shotgun. Nothing would be said. No jury would convict the man. I don't belong here.

She has gone somewhere. I sit on the couch. The girls play with their trucks and croon softly to each other little songs without words, melodies made up in their own fantastic little minds. They move smooth as eels, boneless, their little arms and legs dimpled with fat.

"I'm ready," she says. I look around. She has her purse. She seems brisk, efficient. She has her keys. It's like she's suddenly decided to stop slumming. She has on trim black slacks, gold toeless shoes with low heels, a short mink jacket. Diamonds glitter in the lobes of her ears. Her breasts hang heavy and full in the lowcut shirt, and I know that tonight she will deny me nothing. She's smiling. She takes my arm as I stand up and she kisses me again. The children watch this puzzle in soundless wonder, this strange man kissing Mommy.

"Okay, girls, we'll be back after while," she says. They don't look up, don't appear to hear. "Sherry?" she says. "We're gone." She must be talking to somebody else in the house, somebody I can't see, the babysitter, I guess. "Sherry?" she says. "Did you hear me?"

"Let's go," she says to me, and she starts toward the door. She's searching for a key on her key ring.

"Bye, girls," I say. The oldest one gives me a solemn look, a dignified nod.

"Stay in here, now," she says. "Don't mess with the stove." We're halfway out the door when it hits me.

"Wait a minute," I say. She's locking the door, locking the children into the house. I hear the lock click. "Where's your babysitter?"

"They're all right," she says. "We won't be gone long anyway. Not over a few hours."

"*Wait* a minute," I say. "You gonna leave them alone? Here?"

I've got my hand on her arm, I'm turning her to look at me in the lighted carport. She looks down at my hand and then up at me, surprised. She steps away.

"Well, it's not gonna hurt anything. They'll be all right."

"All right?" I say. "They're just little kids. I thought you said you had a babysitter."

"I couldn't get one," she says. "Now come on. Let's go. They've stayed by themselves before." She's going toward the car. I stand watching her dumbly, like a dumbass, like the dumbass I am.

"What if something happens, though?" I say. "What if the fucking house was to catch on fire?"

She stops and looks back. She holds her face up slightly, puts one hand on her hip. "Do you want to go or not?" she says.

"You told me last night the babysitter had your number so she could get ahold of you," I say. Then I realize. She's never had a babysitter. They've been locked up in this house the whole weekend, these children.

"Do you want to go or not?" she says.

I look through the curtains on the door. The girls have been watching it, but now they look back down at their toys. The youngest one gets up and walks away, out of sight. The oldest rolls her truck. I look at the woman standing by the door of a new Lincoln, waiting to carry me to a Holiday Inn. She's ready now, finally. And so am I.

"Come here," I say.

"What?"

"I said come here."

"Why? Get in, let's go."

I go around the hood after her, slowly. Her face changes.

"What is it?" she says. "What's wrong with you?"

"Come here," I say, and I know my face has changed, too.

"Hey," she says. "I don't know what you think you're doing."

I know what I'm doing. I have my hands on her now, and she can't pull away. She probably thinks I'm going to kill her, but I'm not. I'm going to keep my hands open this time, and not use my fists. I don't want to scare the little girls with blood. They would be frightened, and might remember it for the rest of their lives.

Leaving Town

Her name was Myra and I could smell whiskey on her breath. She was nervous, but these days, you don't know who to let in your house. She'd seen my ad in the paper, she said, and wanted some new doors hung. We talked on the porch for a while and then she let me in.

It looked like she didn't have anything to do but keep her house clean. She gnawed her fingernails the whole time I was figuring the estimate. She kept opening and closing the top of her robe, like a nervous habit. Both the doors had been kicked out of their locks. The wood was splintered. She needed two new doors, some trim. Maybe two new locks. She wanted new linoleum in her dining room. I gave her a price for the labor and went on home, but I didn't think I'd get the job.

HE WAS A polite young man. His name was Richard. He seemed to be very understanding when I explained that Harold had kicked the doors in. Of course I didn't tell him everything. All I wanted was to forget about Harold, and every time I looked at the doors I thought about him. I tried to talk to him a little. I told him that I was divorced now and that it was a lot different when you're used to two salaries and then have to live on just one. I told him I didn't want to pay a whole lot for the work. He said the doors would run about forty dollars apiece. I had no idea they would be that high.

He had very nice-looking hands. They looked like strong hands, but gentle. I doubted if they'd ever been used to slap somebody, or to break down a door.

He didn't talk much. He was one of those quiet people who intrigue you because they keep so much inside. Maybe he was just shy. I thought the price he gave me was twenty or thirty dollars too high. I told him I'd think about it. But I needed the work done.

After he left, I fixed myself another drink and looked at the doors. They were those hollow-core things, they wouldn't keep out anybody who wanted in bad enough. I kept thinking about Richard. I wondered what it would be like to kiss him. I could imagine how it would be. How warm his hands would be. My life is halfway or more than halfway over. There's not much time left for things like that. I don't know why I even thought about it. He had the bluest eyes and they looked so sad. Maybe that was the reason. Whatever it was, I decided to call him back and let him do the work. I couldn't stand to look at those doors any longer.

I WAS FEEDING Tracey when she called. Betty was reading one of her police detective magazines. The phone rang three or four times. Betty acted like she didn't hear it. I got up with Tracey and went and answered it.

I was surprised that she called back. She'd already talked like I was too high. But people don't know what carpentry work is worth. You have to have a thousand dollars' worth of tools to even start.

She sounded like she was a little drunk. I guess she was lonely. When I was over there, she'd look at the doors and just shake her head. But I'd given her a reasonable price. It was cheaper than anybody else would have done it for. I didn't tell her that. She wouldn't have believed it.

I told her I could start the next night. She hadn't understood that I was going to do it at night. I had told her, though. She just hadn't been listening. She said she thought I was in business for myself. I told her I was, at night. I told her I had to work my other job in the daytime. Then she wanted to know all about that. She just wanted somebody to talk to. Tracey was going to sleep in my lap. I asked Betty if she'd take her but she wouldn't even look up. She was still reading her magazine.

She wanted to know didn't I get tired of working all the time, at night and on weekends. Hell, who wouldn't? I told her, sure, I got tired of it, but I needed the money. That was all I told her then. I didn't want to tell her about Tracey. I didn't want to tell her all my personal business.

She sat there for a while and didn't say anything. Then she wanted to know if there was any way I could come down on the price. That pissed me off. She wanted to know if that was the very least I could do it for. At first I told her I didn't see any way I could, but I needed the money. Hell, I have to put gas in my truck and all. . . .

I told her I'd cut it twenty more dollars but that was it. I told her if she couldn't live with that, she'd just have to find somebody else to do it. And I told her that if she found somebody cheaper, she wouldn't be satisfied with it.

I had to tell her a couple of times that I'd be there the next night. I told her I had to go by the building supply and get the doors.

She wanted to talk some more, but I told her I had to put my baby to bed. Finally I got away from her. I wasn't really looking forward to going back.

I got up with Tracey and Betty wanted to know who that was on the phone. I told her a lady I was going to do some work for. Then she wanted to know what kind of work and how old a lady and was she married or divorced and what did she look like. I told her, Hell, normal, I guess, to let me put Tracey to bed.

She started crying when I laid her down and I had to stay in there with her and pet her a while. I guess her legs hurt. She finally went to sleep. Betty won't even get up with her at night. I have to. It doesn't matter if I've worked twelve hours or fourteen hours. She can't even hear an alarm clock. You can let one go off and hold it right in her ear. She won't even move.

She was smoking the last cigarette I had when I went back in the living room. She said that kid hated her and I told her she just didn't have any patience with her. I picked up the empty pack and asked her if she had any more. She said she was out. I just looked at her. She'll sit in the house all day long and won't walk a half block to the store and get some, then smoke mine until she makes me run out. Then I have to go.

I got my jacket and told her I guessed I'd have to go get some. She told me to bring her some beer back. I told her I didn't have enough money to buy any beer. I wanted some too but I was almost broke. She told me to just write a check. She says that shit all the time. I told her we had enough to pay that doctor bill and that was it. Then she said something about the saw I bought. It was eighty-nine dollars. But good saws cost good money. And if I don't have a saw, I don't have a job.

She wanted to know when I was going to marry her. I told her I didn't know.

I went by the building supply the next day, after I got off from work. I priced the locks, but they were almost twenty dollars apiece. I decided to see if I could use the old locks on her doors and save her that much anyway. I signed for the doors and the trim, the linoleum.

I didn't want to go straight over there. I wanted to go home for a few minutes and see Tracey and get Betty to fix me something to eat. I'd asked Leon to let me borrow ten dollars until Friday, so I stopped at the store and got a six-pack of beer. You can't just go through life doing without everything.

I loaded up my sawhorses and left the linoleum in the carport. Tracey was sitting on the floor, wanting me to pick her up. I set the sack on the table and told Betty I'd brought her some beer. She was reading another magazine so I played with Tracey for a while. Then I got her building blocks and set her down with them and got one of the beers out of the sack. Dirty clothes were piled up everywhere. She won't wash until we don't have anything to wear. I lit a cigarette and just watched her. She didn't know I was in the room. I drank about half my beer. I had a lot of shit going through my head.

Finally I asked her if she could fix me something to eat before I went over there. I told her it would probably be late when I got back. I told her I was hungry.

She asked me what I wanted. I told her I didn't care, a sandwich, anything. She said she didn't know of anything we had to eat. She said I could go in there and look.

I told her I wanted some supper. She didn't look back up, and I thought, Work your ass off all day and come home and have to put up with some shit like this.

I sat there a while and then I got up and made out like I was going to the kitchen. She wasn't watching me anyway. She had her magazine up in front of her face, picking at the buttons on her blouse. I bent down behind the couch. I peeked over her shoulder to see what she was reading. THE LAUNDROMAT AXE MURDERER WOULDN'T COME CLEAN. I don't know how she can stand to read that shit. She gets so deep into it, she'll get her nails in her mouth. I got up on my knees right behind her. She was nibbling her bottom lip. I was just trying to have a little fun.

She jumped about two feet high when I went boo in her ear. Turned around and slammed her magazine down. She was pissed. Bad pissed.

I told her I was just playing with her. She told me to just go on and leave. Said I was always hollering about saving money. Why didn't I go out and make some? Instead of worrying the hell out of her?

I got up in her face, said let me tell you one goddamn thing. You lay around here on your ass all day long and don't do nothing. Won't clean the house up. Won't even wash Tracey's face. I told her if I could go out and work at night, she could fix me something to eat.

She said there wasn't anything to eat.

I said by God she could buy something.

She said give her some money and she might.

I told her I gave her money, and she spent it on those stupid fucking magazines.

She whispered to me. Hateful. If I was so damn unhappy then why didn't I just leave? Just pack up and go right now?

I didn't answer. I picked up Tracey and she put her arms around my neck. We went into the kitchen. I looked in the refrigerator. There was some old bacon, and a half cup of chili in a Tupperware bowl, and a quart of milk, and a little brown hamburger meat, and one hot dog. I found some Rice Krispies under the counter. I fixed two bowls and ate with Tracey. I washed her hands and her face.

I didn't want to leave. I'd said some of the words I'd been wanting to say but I hadn't said all of them. My words wouldn't hurt her as bad as hers hurt me. I held onto Tracey and looked at my watch. There wasn't much time. Your life goes by and if you spend it unhappy, what's the point? If staying won't make you happy, and leaving ruins somebody else's life, what's the answer?

I didn't know. I still don't. But I'd told her I'd be there by six. And finally I couldn't wait in the kitchen any longer.

I WAS SO nervous I changed clothes three times before he got there. I ended up wearing a dress that was too short. I cleaned the house twice, even though I knew there would be sawdust and tools on the floor. I'd been thinking about him all day, I couldn't help it. He was so quiet and mysterious and he had such lovely hands. I'd had a few drinks, and I was going to offer him a drink when he got there. Just thinking about him being all alone in the house with me excited me. Maybe if he had a few drinks, he'd loosen up and talk to me. I wanted to talk to somebody so badly. It's not easy being alone after being married for thirty years. It's not easy to come home to a house so quiet you can hear a clock ticking.

I kept waiting and looking at my watch, and I kept drinking. I thought it would calm me down. I was so nervous my hands were just trembling.

Finally he pulled up and I looked out through the curtain in the living room. He had two doors and two sawhorses in the back of his pickup. I watched him get out and put on a tool belt and lift the doors from the truck.

I opened the door for him and smiled and told him he was right on time. He said hi or something, and then started bringing everything in. He didn't have much to say. I just watched him and smiled. He brought in some kind of a crowbar and a power saw and a long orange extension cord. I couldn't get that idiotic grin off my face. I had a drink in one hand and a cigarette in the other. Harold used to tell me that if I didn't drink myself to death, I'd smoke myself to death. But he was always so cruel. Always so cruel.

I asked him if he would like a drink. He said he didn't like whiskey, and took the crowbar and tore the facing off the wall like he was mad at it. It made this awful screeching sound when the nails pulled loose. He just . . . attacked it. Within five minutes he had the frame and the door lying in the carport and was pulling finishing nails from the studs. The nails screamed when he pulled them. I said something about how he didn't waste any time. I was smiling. He said he wasn't making much money on this and had to get through as quick as he could.

I thought he was probably mad at me for talking him into coming down twenty dollars. But I'm single, I don't have Harold's money, I have to get by, too.

I told him I had some beer if he wanted one. He said let him get this door up and he might take one. He pulled a screwdriver out of his tool belt and stepped outside to the carport and closed the door behind him. Almost like he didn't have time to talk to me. Or was angry with me. I hadn't done anything to him. The paneling was rough and splintered where he'd taken the door off. You could see the wires inside the studs. You could see the nails. It all looked so raw.

I made myself another drink, and checked my makeup in the hall mirror. You would have thought I was having a cocktail party the way I was acting. He was out in the carport and I watched him through the window. He was kneeling beside the door, doing something, I couldn't tell what. His shirt had come up and I could see the bumps of bone in his back. His back looked so smooth. I wanted to feel it with my hands, run my hands over it, up his ribs, down over his hips, I wanted him to put his mouth on my throat and slide it down to my breasts and take one of my nipples in his lips and say Myra, Myra. . . .

MY GODDAMN BACK was killing me. If I bend over for more than five minutes at a time I can't straighten up. Sometimes in the mornings it hurts so bad I can just barely get out of bed. I have to get up and walk around and bend and stretch to get to where I can go to work. It usually stops hurting midway through the morning and starts hurting twice as bad around three. I'd been laboring for a bricklayer all that day, mixing his mortar and handing him his blocks. They just scab us out to whoever needs help on a big job. If you're not in the union you don't have any say. I can't stand the dues so I pay my own. But I'm afraid I'll get disabled. I'm afraid I won't be able to work anymore. I worry about that every day.

I fell three months ago. We were bricking a bank. A scaffold leg collapsed, one of those cheap ones they rent from the building supply. I was fourteen feet up, not that high, but I landed on a sheet of plywood that was propped up against a water cooler. I thought I'd broken my back. Everybody who saw me fall thought I'd broken my back. When the ambulance came for me, they treated me like a patient with a broken back. They pulled traction on me and immobilized me. I was screaming. I bit my tongue.

My foreman came to see me in the hospital. He told me the company took care of its employees. He only stayed a few minutes. I could tell he couldn't wait to get out of there.

I had to go on workmen's comp after I got out of the hospital. What I drew was about half my pay. You can't live on half money. You've got to have whole money. I went over to the job a few times, to talk to the guys I worked with, but I was just in the way. They couldn't work and talk to me, too. I stopped going after a while. I stayed home and drank beer with Betty and read those Little Golden Books to Tracey.

I'd never felt so useless in my whole life. There wasn't anything to occupy me. Betty didn't want to do it. I had to do the grocery shopping to make our money stretch. We fought over the money, over the TV, over anything and everything. I had to put up with these assholes every week in the office where I got my check. Some days I wanted to just go away somewhere and never come back again. I was supposed to stay off for four months, but I went back after two by forging my doctor's signature on an insurance release. They set me to mixing mortar and carrying twenty-pound blocks.

I got the knobs and the lock out of the old door and took them back into the house. She was sitting on an ottoman. She had on dark stockings. I told her I'd probably bring another boy with me the next night, to lay the linoleum. She just nodded. It was like she was listening to something in her head. I didn't know what I'd do if my back got to hurting so bad I couldn't work. I didn't know how bad it would have to hurt before it stopped me. I didn't know how I'd pay Tracey's doctor bills if that happened.

I told her I'd take that beer now if she didn't care. She nodded and smiled and went to get it. I watched her, and I thought about the twenty dollars she had talked me out of. I should have just told her to forget it. I should have just told her to get somebody else and keep her lousy twenty dollars.

HE WAS CERTAINLY a fast worker. I didn't know if he wanted a glass or not. I figured carpenters usually drank theirs straight out of the can. He wasn't making it easy for me to talk to him. He acted like he had things on his mind. We couldn't talk at all with all that ripping and hammering going on.

I carried the beer out to him and he drank about half of it in one swallow. I sat down again to watch him work and asked him if he wanted a cigarette. He had some of his own. He picked up the lock and the knobs and started putting them into the door.

I ASKED HER if she was going to be at home the next night. I had to ask her twice. She looked up and I told her that I'd probably get through with the doors that night. I told her that if she didn't care, I'd go ahead and tear out the old linoleum and lay the new the next night. If she didn't care.

She'd pulled her dress up over her legs. Her legs were kind of skinny but they weren't that bad. I didn't know if she meant to do it on purpose or not. Maybe she was so drunk she didn't notice it.

She didn't know if she was going to be home the next night or not. She asked me if I wanted to come back the next night. I told her I'd just like to get through. The quicker I got through, the quicker I got paid. She said she'd have to decide.

I KNEW HE wasn't going to be interested in me. The only thing he was interested in was the money. He couldn't wait to get out of my house. And I'd been sitting there thinking such foolish things. I was ashamed of myself. I don't know anything about dating, I've been married so long. Going out to bars alone, hoping for some man to pick me up: I don't want that kind of life. My drink was almost empty.

I told him I needed a fresh one and got up to make it. I didn't know I was in such bad shape. My head started swimming when I got in the kitchen. I dropped my glass.

I HEARD A glass break and I stopped what I was doing. I got up and looked around. I didn't see her anywhere. Then I heard her. I thought maybe she'd fallen and hurt herself. She sounded like she was crying. I went down the hall and found her in the kitchen. She was down on her knees, on a towel she had folded underneath her. She was crying and picking up the broken pieces of glass. I didn't know what the hell to do.

I KNOW YOU'RE not supposed to feel sorry for yourself. But I had always had somebody to take care of me and tell me what to do. It's so frightening to be alone. I was only trying to reach out to somebody. All I wanted was a little conversation. I was just trying to be nice to him.

I was so ashamed for him to see me crying. I'd just had too much to drink and I'd gotten depressed. He was standing behind me. He asked me if I was okay and I said I was. It was so quiet. The glass had gone everywhere. I wanted to make sure I got it all up so I wouldn't step on a tiny piece while I was barefoot one morning. I told him that it was okay, that he could go back to work, that I'd get him another beer in a minute. Then he knelt down beside me and started helping me pick up the glass.

SHE SEEMED SO helpless and so weak. She wasn't anything like Betty. She wasn't hard like Betty. I know it embarrassed her for me to see her like that. And I was afraid she might cut herself, so I got down on the floor to help her. She was trying to stop crying. I didn't know what was wrong or what to say. I felt bad for her, and I wanted to help her if I could. All her mascara had run down from her eyes in black streaks. She'd smeared some of it wiping at her eyes. She said it was nice of me to help her. Then she said Richard. That was the first time she'd said my name.

I LOOKED AT HIM. He was just as embarrassed as I was. I thought about how I must have looked to him, half drunk, with my eyes red from crying. I had cried so much because of Harold. Nobody knows what I went through. He wasted so much of my life. All those years that were just thrown away. I wanted to tell him so bad about what had happened to me. I had so much on me that I wanted to unload. I turned to him and I put my hand on his shoulder. I wanted

him to kiss me, or to put his hand on my breast. Or to at least hold
me. I wanted to tell him what was wrong with me.

I DIDN'T KNOW what to say when she touched me. I stopped
what I was doing and I looked at her. She was trying to smile. Her eyes
were wet. I didn't know what she wanted. Maybe just somebody to listen
to her. Maybe something else. But she was old enough to be my mother.

She said what if somebody asked you to do something. And it
wouldn't hurt you, if it was just a favor that somebody wanted you to
do, would you do it? If it didn't cost you anything and it would help
the other person. She said if I just knew. She said he had other women.
That he'd beaten her. That nobody knew what she'd been through.

She started crying again. She put her head on my shoulder and she
took my hand and slipped it around her waist. I didn't know what else
to do but hold her. She started sort of moaning. I didn't have time to
do anything. She said I want you. She put her mouth on mine. She
was holding my ears in both her hands. I tried to pull back. I tried to
tell her that she was drunk and she didn't know what she was doing.
But she unbuckled my pants. It happened in a second. She pulled it
out and started rubbing it with her hands, moaning. She leaned back
and pulled up her dress and I ran my hands up underneath her. I
couldn't help it. I didn't know what to do. I knew she was drunk and I
was afraid she'd holler rape when she sobered up. We got up somehow
and went back against the counter. She opened her dress and pulled
my head down to her. I couldn't get away and didn't want to.

I JUST WENT crazy for a minute. Once I touched him I
couldn't stop myself. He started running his hands all over me. I knew
I should stop but I couldn't. I didn't even know him. I knew he was
going to think I was a whore.

I just lost control of myself. I didn't even care what he thought. I just wanted someone to put his arms around me and hold me tight. I didn't want to stop. I knew if we kept on it was going to happen. I wasn't even thinking about how I'd feel the next morning, or how I'd feel after it was over. I was just thinking about how I didn't ever want him to stop. But finally he did. He stopped and backed away from me. He looked like he was scared to death. I don't know what I looked like. Half my clothes were off. I think I asked him what was wrong.

I FINALLY GOT ahold of myself. I think I said shit or something. We were both breathing hard. I fastened my pants back up. She was staring at me like a wild woman. There was a chair pulled out beside the table and I went over to it and sat down. She didn't say anything for a minute. I think she was buttoning her dress. I waited until I thought she was done and then I turned around and looked at her. She was wiping her eyes with her fingers. She fixed herself another drink. Then she went to the refrigerator and got me another beer. I started to just get up and leave. But she brought the beer and her drink over and set them down and dropped into the chair beside me. She looked dazed. We almost did it, she said. Yeah, I said. We almost did.

HE STARTED TALKING about the little girl. At first I wasn't listening. I was almost in shock. It took a long time for me to calm down. My heart was beating too fast, and I was wet. I wanted to kiss him again but I was scared to try. He said she wasn't his. It was something about her telling him she was divorced and then later after he'd been living with her for a while, admitting that she had never been married. I think I was just staring at my drink when he started talking. But then what he was saying started sinking in and I started listening to him. I couldn't believe what we were doing, just sitting there in my kitchen talking and drinking after what we'd done. He said it didn't matter to him for a while about the lie she had told him because he loved the little girl and felt like she was his. He was the only daddy she'd known. But he didn't love the woman. I could tell that just from hearing him talk. He said he carried the little girl everywhere he went, even if he was just going to the store for something.

There was something wrong with her legs. She couldn't walk right. They had all these tests done on her and had her fitted with braces and then his insurance company wouldn't pay the bills because he wasn't married to her mother. I wondered what she looked like. I had this picture of black hair and a frowning face for some reason. He said he was afraid to leave her. He said he didn't love her, but he couldn't leave the little girl. He said he didn't know what would happen to her. I felt better about everything, about losing my head, after we talked for a while. But he was working all these jobs at night to try and pay the doctor bills. I felt like . . . I just don't know what I felt like. Cheap. Stingy. For getting him to lower his price. And I felt awful for drinking too much and having those daydreams about him, and then kissing him and all. He kept talking. The more he talked, the worse I felt over feeling so sorry for myself about Harold.

I asked him what he was going to do. He said he didn't know. He said if he left her there was no telling what would happen to them. He said the woman had never worked a day in her life and didn't finish high school and had been brought up on welfare. He said she didn't know what it was like to have to work for a living.

I SHOULDN'T HAVE talked so much. I didn't mean to tell her all my problems. I know everybody's got problems, and everybody thinks theirs are worse than everybody else's. I know she had it bad. Married to a son of a bitch that slapped her around. She felt like her whole life had been wasted. She talked some, too. She said she knew what it felt like to have to stay with somebody without love. She knew what I felt like. She was as miserable as I was.

I probably could have taken right back up where we left off. I was tempted to. I don't think I've touched a woman who was that hot ever. I thought when women got older they didn't care anything about sex. Or maybe she was just trying to reach out to somebody. She didn't come right out and say it, but just from the things she said, I could tell she hadn't slept with her ex-husband for years. I felt so goddamn sorry for her. But I didn't want her to feel sorry for me. I didn't want to work anymore, though. I just wanted to load my shit up and go somewhere. I thought about asking her if she wanted to go drink a few beers with me, but really I wanted to be by myself. I had to decide what I was going to do. I knew I couldn't keep going the way I was going.

I ASKED HIM what he was going to do and he said he didn't know. He said he'd keep on working. He was hoping she'd grow out of it. He said he didn't mean to dump all his problems on me. But he said the little girl would sit on the floor and hold her arms up to him when he came in from work and beg him to take her. He said he thought she sat on the floor all day because her mother wouldn't help her try to walk or even pick her up. He said all she did was read magazines and watch TV. I don't know how he could have gotten mixed up with somebody like that. I don't know why he couldn't have gotten somebody who deserved him.

I TOLD HER that if she didn't care I'd just leave the doors and finish up the next night, or the next. I had to get away. I hated to just leave her wall like that, but there wasn't any way I could finish hanging the door that night. She said it would be okay, that I could come back and finish it whenever I wanted to. She said she never had any company and nobody would see it anyway.

I WATCHED HIM roll up his cord and put away his tools and get ready to leave. I wanted him to stay, but I didn't ask him to. I could tell he had a lot on his mind. His hands had felt so good to me. I knew I was going to cry after he left. I knew I was going to cry and I knew I was going to drink some more. I wanted him right then more than I've ever wanted anything in my life. I would have given him anything. But all he wanted was to leave. I wasn't going to try to hold him. I wasn't going to make a fool of myself again. But right up until the time he left, I would have made a fool of myself. Gladly. When he went out the door I knew I'd never see him again.

I RODE AROUND for a while. I didn't want to go back home just yet. I wanted to run but I didn't have any place to run to. Some people can just walk away, turn their backs and go on and forget about it. I couldn't. But it didn't stop me from thinking about it.

I went to a bar on Jackson Avenue and counted my money before I went inside. There was just enough left from what I'd borrowed from Leon to get a couple of pitchers of draft. There wasn't anybody in there I knew. I sat at a table by myself, in a booth in a dark corner. I thought that if I sat quietly by myself in the dark and drank, I'd be able to figure out what to do with the rest of my life.

Florida was the best place to go. There was no cold weather to stop you from laying brick. There was plenty of building going on. Jobs were supposed to be easy to get.

But I couldn't stop thinking about Myra down on the floor, crying. Or about how she felt when I was kissing her. I'd never had anybody want me that bad. I'd never had anybody so desperate reach out to me like that. And I'd turned her down. I regretted it.

I kept drinking. Betty didn't know what it was like to have to work, to be strapped into a job like a mule in a harness. The company I worked for didn't give a fuck if I broke my back. They'd just hire somebody else. There were people standing in lines all over the country wanting jobs. She didn't understand that. She didn't know what it was like to have to work when you were hurt. You either kept up or you didn't. If you didn't keep up they'd let you go.

She looked so awful down on the floor. I was still thinking about her by the time I finished the first pitcher. I had to scrape all my change together to make the price of the last one. I knew I'd be drunk by the time I finished it, but I didn't care. I wanted to get drunk. I felt like getting drunk would help me more than just about anything right then. So I got the other pitcher and sat back down in the corner with it. I knew by then that it had been wrong for me to turn her down. And I needed to talk to her some more anyway. She had listened to me and she had seemed to understand. She was so much kinder than Betty, so much gentler. Her body had been so soft. I wanted to take all her clothes off gently and touch her whole body and make her happy. I wanted to heal her. I kept drinking. The more I thought about it, the more it seemed like a good idea.

I know I was too drunk to remember what happened exactly. I came to in the parking lot. Somebody had hit me because there was blood in my mouth. I tried to stand. I made it up to my knees and then I passed out.

I woke up again. I was lying beside my truck. I got ahold of the door handle and pulled myself up with that. I leaned my arms on the bed and tried to remember what had happened. Somebody had been yelling at me. I remembered swinging one time. Then nothing until I came to in the parking lot.

I knew what I had to do. I knew where I had to go. I got in my truck and cranked it up. I had to close one eye to see how to drive. Some of my lower teeth were loose. There was a cut inside my mouth. But I knew somebody who would take care of me. I knew somebody who would be glad to see me.

ALL MY CRYING was over with. You can only cry so much. You can't just keep on feeling sorry for yourself. I was lying in bed watching "The Love Boat" and hoping somehow that he'd come back. But I knew he wouldn't. I didn't know if he'd even come back and finish the work. I thought he would probably be too embarrassed to.

I was watching the show but I didn't believe in it. It wasn't like real life. There were too many happy endings on it. Everybody always found just exactly what they were looking for. And nobody on there was mean. Nobody on there was going to break down a door and slap somebody off the commode.

I wanted to talk to him again. He seemed to be such an understanding person, a person who would take the time to listen to another person's troubles. I was wishing I could see what his woman and his baby looked like. I was still having some drinks.

I knew there were nice men in the world, men who would love me for myself and not mistreat me. But how did you find them? How did you know they wouldn't change years later? There weren't any promises that would keep forever. Things altered in your lives and people changed. Sometimes they even started hating each other. I hated Harold so bad when I divorced him that I couldn't stand to look at him. But I can still remember how tender his hands used to be. I can still remember the first time he undressed me and how he looked at me when I was naked.

But who would want me now? I shouldn't have been surprised when Richard pulled away. I have varicose veins and my breasts are sagging. I've got those ugly rolls of fat around my middle. I've gone through the change. No, a young man doesn't want an old woman. It's the old woman who wants the young man.

I hoped he wouldn't tell anybody. I hoped he wouldn't tell his woman about it. I knew he wouldn't. Not a nice boy like him. I wanted to blame something, so I blamed the drinking. But I couldn't blame all of it on the drinking. I had to blame part of it on me.

I even thought about calling him. But I couldn't call him. What if his woman answered? What would I say then? He might have already told her and she might want to know if this was the old drunk bag who tried to get Richard in the bed with her. She might say, Listen, you old dried up bag of shit. . . .

But what if he answered? It wasn't late. It wasn't even ten o'clock. But what if the baby was asleep and it woke her up? It was stupid to even think about it. But I wanted him to come back so bad. Nobody thinks the things I think. The crazy things, the awful things, the insane things. That's what I was thinking when I heard him pull up.

I DON'T EVEN know what I said to her. I was almost too drunk to walk. She turned the porch light on and came to the door. I talked to her. I guess I scared her with all the blood I had on me. I know I looked awful. I can't even remember what I said to her. There's no telling what I said to her. It's a wonder she didn't call the police.

I COULDN'T BELIEVE he came back. All that time of lying there thinking about him and wishing he'd come back and then he did. I just had on my housecoat and my underwear. I still had my makeup on. I couldn't wait to let him in.

I turned on the porch light and watched him try to get out of his truck. I didn't know what was wrong with him at first. He was staggering. And his face was all bloody. He'd been in a fight.

I got scared then. It took him about three tries to get up on the porch, and then he had to hold onto a post. He was the drunkest human I'd ever seen. I almost didn't recognize him.

He knocked on the door. I didn't know whether to open it or not. I hadn't been expecting him to be the way he was. I didn't know what to do. He kept knocking and finally I slipped the chain on and opened the door just a crack. I was scared to let him in.

He was weaving. He had blood all over his chin. He could just barely talk. It was hard to understand what he was saying, but he said something about it being so late. I said Yes, it was, and I asked him what he wanted. He said he just wanted to talk to me. I don't know what I could have been thinking of. He looked dangerous.

I told him he was drunk and I asked him again what he wanted. He kept saying that he'd sober up in a little bit. Then he asked me if he could come in. I told him it was awfully late. I didn't even really know him. I didn't know what he might do while he was drunk. He'd already been fighting, what else would he do? I knew that if I let him in he'd never leave, or he'd pass out and I wouldn't know what to do with him. Or what if he tried to rape me? I couldn't let him in.

I tried to be as gentle with him as I could. I told him it would be better if he went on home. I told him it was after ten. He asked me if I had any coffee. He said if he had some coffee he'd sober up. But he could barely stand. And he was driving. I thought, What if he left in his truck and killed somebody, or himself, before he got home? Maybe I should have let him stay. But I was scared to let him stay. He looked so wild. His eyes were as red as blood.

He said something about a favor. He said something about if it wouldn't hurt you and would help the other person. I didn't know what he was talking about. I told him to please go home.

He said he needed to talk to me, that nobody understood. I told him I didn't want to do anything that would hurt him, but that he needed to go home right away.

I knew I had to be firm. I told him I was going to close the door. He hung his head. Then he looked up and looked into my eyes. Looked right into me. Everything changed in that moment. I saw how the rest of my life was going to be. I knew that I would always be lonely, and that I would always be scared. I told him to go home again and then I shut the door.

I DON'T REMEMBER driving home. I just woke up the next morning in bed with Betty. Tracey was crying. It was dark. I put my hand on Betty and I moved against her and I put my chin in her neck. She squeezed my hand in her sleep. She moved it down between her legs and moaned. Maybe she was having a bad dream. It all came back to me suddenly, what I'd done the night before. I just closed my eyes. I didn't want to think about it. I had to get up in thirty more minutes. I had to get up and fix myself some breakfast.

SOME MEN SHOWED up a few days later. One of them was short, with a red beard. His shirt was spattered with paint. He did all the talking. The other one just stood on the porch and looked around.

I let them in after they explained why they were there. They brought their tools in, and the linoleum in. I stayed in the bedroom while they hammered and sawed and nailed. I thought they never would get through.

Finally he knocked on the door and asked me if I wanted to come out and look at it. I went out and looked. The doors were hung and the new linoleum was down. They'd done a neat job, a good job. But I wanted them out of my house. I wrote him a check quickly, for the same price that Richard had named. They took his sawhorses. They said they could do other things: remodeling, build decks, paint my house. I thanked them and told them I didn't need anything else right now. I didn't ask them anything about Richard.

It was almost a month later when I saw them in the supermarket. I like to do my shopping at night, when the stores aren't full of people, when the aisles are clear and you can take your time. A young woman turned into the aisle ahead of me, a girl with a sweatshirt and blue jeans and fuzzy blue house shoes. I wouldn't be caught dead out like that. There was a little girl with yellow hair sitting in the cart, and she was reaching out for everything they passed. The woman slapped at the child's hands like an automatic reaction, without even looking. I watched them for a while. And then I went on past them. I wanted to finish and get out of the store quickly, as soon as possible, before it was too late. Their lives were things that didn't concern me and the world is full of suffering anyway. How can one person be expected to do anything about it?

I turned the corner and he was standing at the meat counter with a pack of bacon in his hand. His back was turned and I thought I might slip by. But he turned his head, just a little, and he saw me. He didn't seem surprised, or even embarrassed. His head bent just a little, and he said something. Hey, something. I thought for a moment he was going to start talking to me. But he didn't. He turned away. I thought that was nice of him, to make it so easy for me to go on by. I didn't let myself hurry. I stopped a little ways past him and looked at some dill pickles in a display set up in the middle of the floor. There were hundreds of bottles. I didn't want to buy any, but I picked up one and read the price. It was fifty-nine cents. I looked over my shoulder and he was looking at me. Richard. My hand must have been trembling. I wanted him even then. I set the jar back without looking and the whole display crashed down. I jumped back. It was unbelievable the way it looked. Broken glass everywhere, and thousands of tiny green chips. Green juice that started puddling around my cart. It ran across the floor and people stepped out of the aisles to look at me. I was trying to think of something to say. I didn't look over my shoulder to see if Richard was watching. I was scared of what I might see.

I PUT THE groceries away and took a shower and put on clean clothes. Tracey was asleep in her bed and Betty was asleep in hers. I waited until she started snoring and then I started gathering things up. I had a week's pay in my pocket and the truck was paid for. I had the title in the glove box. I could trade it off, buy another one, whatever.

Tracey doesn't sleep well most nights, but that night she did. She slept through Grenada, through Jackson, on through Hattiesburg. The miles piled up behind us. I knew Betty wouldn't send anybody after us. I knew Betty would probably be relieved.

I had Myra's number in my pocket and I thought I might call her when we got to where we were going. I thought I might wish her some luck.

The End of Romance

Miss Sheila and I were riding around, as we often did in those days. But I was pretty sure it was going to be the last afternoon of our relationship. Things hadn't been good lately.

It was hot. We'd been drinking all day, and we'd drunk almost enough. We lacked just a little getting to a certain point. I'd already come to a point. I'd come down to the point where I could still get an erection over her, but my heart wouldn't be going crazy and jumping up in my throat like a snake-bit frog. I wouldn't be fearing for my life when I mounted her. I knew it was time for me to book for a fat man's ass. She bitched about how much time I spent locked in my room, how my mother was bossy, when would I ever learn some couth? And you get them started nagging at you, you might as well be married. Well. I'd been out of women when I found her and I'd be out

of women again until I found another one. But there were hundreds
of other women, thousands, millions. They'd been making new ones
every day for years.

"I ain't drunk," she said.

"Well, I'm not drunk, either."

"You look like you are."

"So do you."

"You got enough money to get some more? You can take all that
Nobel Prize money and get us a coupla sixers, can't you?"

She was bad about chagrinning me like that.

"I magine I can manage it," I said.

So she whipped it into one of those little quick-joints that are so
popular around here, one of those chicken-scarfing places, whipped it
up in front of the door and stopped. She stared straight ahead through
the windshield. Nothing worse than a drunken woman. Empty beer
cans were all piled up around our feet. The end of romance is never easy.

"What matter?" I said.

"Nuttin matter. Everything just hunkin funkin dunky."

"You mean hunky dory?"

She had some bloodshot eyes and a ninety-yard stare. I'd known
it would come down to this. The beginning of romance is wonderful.
I don't know why I do it over and over. Starting with a new one, I
can just about eat her damn legs off. Then, later, some shit like this.
Women. Spend your whole life after the right one and what do they
do? Shit on you. I always heard the theory of slapping them around
to make them respect you, that that's what they want. But I couldn't.
I couldn't stand to hit that opposite flesh. That slap would ring in
my head for the rest of my life. This is what I do: take what they give
and give what I can and when it's over find another one. Another
one. That's what's so wonderful about the beginning of romance. She's

different. She's new. Unique. Everything's fresh. Crappola. You go in
there to shave after the first night and what does she do while you've
got lather all over your face? Comes in and hikes her nightgown and
then the honeymoon's over.

I'm not trying to get away from the story. I mean, just a few minutes later, some stuff actually happened. But sitting in that car at that
moment, I was a little bitter. I had all sorts of thoughts going through
my head, like: *Slapper. Slapper ass off.* I held that down.

She looked at me with those bloodshot eyes. "You really somethin,
you know that? You really really really."

I knew it was coming. We'd had a bad afternoon out at the lake.
Her old boyfriend had been out there, and he'd tried to put the make
on her. I and seven of my friends had ripped his swim trunks off of
him, lashed him to the front of her car, and driven him around blindfolded but with his name written on a large piece of beer carton taped
to his chest for thirty-seven minutes, in front of domestic couples,
moms and dads, family reunions, and church groups. She hadn't
thought it was funny. We, we laughed our asses off.

I got out of the car. She didn't want to have any fun, that was fine
with me. I bent over and gathered up an armload of beer cans and
carried them to the trash can. They clattered all over the place when I
dropped them in. I was a little woozy but I didn't think anybody could
see it. Through the window of the store this old dyed woman with
great big breasts and pink sunglasses looked out at me with a disap-
proving frown. I waved. Then I went back for more cans.

"Don't worry about the damn cans, all right?"

"I can't move my feet for them," I said.

"I'll worry about the damn cans," she said.

It sort of crumpled me. We were in her convertible, and once it
was fun to just throw them straight up while we were going down the

road. The wind, or I guess just running out from under them was fun. It was a game. Now it didn't seem to matter. I think we both had the creep of something bad coming up on us. She could have beat the shit out of me, I could have beat the shit out of her. It's no way to live. You don't want to go to sleep nervous, fearing the butcher knife, the revolver, the garrote.

"Just go in and get some beer," she said. "We got to talk."

Then she started crying. She wasn't pretty when she was crying. Her whole face turned red and wrinkled up. I knew it was me. It's always me.

"You're just so damn great, ain't you?" she said. "Don't even want nobody overt the house, cept a bunch of old drunks and freaks and whores."

My friends. Poets, artists, actors, English professors out at Ole Miss. She called them drunks and freaks. *Slapper. Slap shit out of her.*

"Just go on git the damn beer," she said. "I got something to tell you."

It's awful to find pussy so good that treats you so bad. It's like you've got to *pay* for it being good. But you've got to be either a man or a pussy. You can't just lay around and pine. I thought at that point that maybe I'd gotten out of that particular car for the last time.

I went on in. I was even starting to feel better. If she left, I could go home, open all the doors, crank up the stereo, get free. I could start sleeping in the daytime and writing at night again, nonstop if I wanted to, for eight or ten hours. I could have a party without somebody sullen in one corner. Everything would be different and the same again.

Well, hell, I wasn't perfect though, was I? I'd probably been a shit-ass a few times. Who's not? Even your best friend will turn asshole on you from time to time. He's only human.

I knew somebody else would come along. I just didn't know how long it would be. So I did a little quick rationalizing inside the store.

Whatever I was going back outside to wasn't going to be good. She was bracing herself up to be nasty to me, I could see that. And there wasn't any need in a bit of it. I could do without all the nastiness. I could take an amicable breakup. All I had to do was hang around inside the store for a while, and she'd probably get tired of waiting for me, and run off and leave me. So I went back toward the rear. The old bag was watching me. She probably thought I was a criminal. All I was doing was sitting back there gnawing my fingernails. But it was no good. I couldn't stand to know she was out there waiting on me.

So I got back up and went up the beer aisle. I figured I might as well go on and face it. Maybe we'd have a goodbye roll. I got her a six-pack of Schlitz malt liquor and got myself a sixer of Stroh's in bottles. The old bag was eyeing me with distaste. I still had my trunks on, and flip-flops, and my FireBusters T-shirt. I was red from passing out under the sun.

I could see Miss Sheila out there. I set the beer on the counter just as a black guy pulled up beside her car and got out. I started pulling my money out and another car pulled up beside the first one. It had a black guy in it, too, only this one had a shotgun. The first black guy was up against the door, just coming in, and the second black guy suddenly blew the top of the first black guy's head off. The first black guy flopped inside.

"AAAAAAAAAAAHHHHHHHHHHH!" he said. "HHHHHH WWWWWWWAAAAAAAAAAAAAAAHHH!" Blood and meat and black hair had flown inside everywhere with him, glass. It stuck to the walls, to the cigarettes in the rack over the counter, to the warming oven where they had the fried chicken. I'd eaten a lot of that fried chicken. The guy flopped down the detergent aisle. "WAAAAA AAAAAAAAAH!" he said.

I just stood there holding my money. I'd been wrong. The top of his head hadn't been blown off after all. He just didn't have any hair up there.

"HAAAAAAAAAAAAAAAAAAH!" he said. He was flopping around like a fish. He flopped down to the end of the aisle, then flopped over a couple of tables where people ate their barbecue at lunchtime, (where I'd been sitting just a few minutes before) and then he flopped over in the floor. I looked outside. The second black guy had gotten back into his car with his shotgun and was backing out of the parking lot. I couldn't see Miss Sheila.

"Let me pay for my beer and get out of here," I said, to the woman who had ducked down behind the counter. "The cops'll be here in a minute."

The black guy got off the floor back there and flopped over the meat market. "AAAAAAAAAAAAAAH!" he said. He flopped up against the coolers, leaving big bloody handprints all over the glass. He started flopping up the beer aisle, coming back toward us.

"Come on, lady," I said. "Shitfire."

He flopped over a bunch of Vienna sausage and Moon Pies, and then he flopped over the crackers and cookies. Blood was pouring out of his head. I looked down at one of the coolers and saw a big piece of black wool sliding down the glass in some blood. He was tracking it all over the store, getting it everywhere.

I knew what the beer cost. It was about six dollars. I didn't wait for a sack. But I watched him for a moment longer. I couldn't take my eyes off him. He flopped over the candy and the little bags of potato chips, and across the front, and flopped across the chicken warmer and the ice cream box and the magazine racks. "HAAAAAAAAAAAH!" he said. I put some money up on the counter. Then I went outside.

The guy had shot the whole place up. All the glass in the windows was shattered, and he'd even shot the bricks. He'd even shot the newspaper machines. He'd murdered the hell out of *The Oxford Eagle*.

When I looked back inside, the guy had flopped up against the counter where the woman was hiding, flopping all over the cash register. Sheila wasn't dead or murdered either one.

I asked her, "You all right?" She was down in the floorboard. She looked up at me. She didn't look good.

"I thought you's dead," she screamed. "OH, GOD, HOW COULD I HAVE BEEN SO FOOOSH?"

I set the beer on the back seat and got in. "You better git this sumbitch outa here," I said. I reached over and got me a beer. I could hear the sirens coming. They were wailing way off in the distance. She latched onto me. "WOULDN'T LEAVE YOU NOW FOR NOTHING," she screamed. "COULDN'T RUN ME OFF," she hollered.

"I'm telling you we better get our ass out of here," I said.

"Look out," she screamed. I looked. The wounded black guy was flopping through the door where there wasn't any door anymore. He flopped up beside the car. "WAAAAAAAAAAH!" he said. He was slinging blood all over us. But other than that he seemed harmless.

"What I wanted to say was maybe we should watch more TV together," she said. "If you just didn't write so much. . . ."

The cops screamed into the parking lot. They had their shotguns poking out the windows before they even stopped. Five or six cruisers. Blue uniforms and neat ties and shiny brass. They'd taken their hats off. They had shiny sunglasses. You could tell that they were itching to shoot somebody, now that they'd locked and loaded. The black guy was leaning against the car, heaving. I knew I wouldn't get to finish my beer. I heard them shuck their pumps. I raised my hands and my beer. I pointed to Miss Sheila.

"She did it," I said.

The Crying

It was old timber, good, heavy timber, some of the best left in the land. There was enough of a canopy in the tops to keep the sunlight blocked and prevent the undergrowth from taking over, and I'll tell you that's something rare in this day and time. The floor was so clean you had shooting lanes anywhere you wanted to look, and it was easy to see any movement in all that open space of dead leaves. I was lucky to be able to hunt on it. I knew it might not last much longer. Not that you can blame people for wanting to sell land and make money, or for getting old and in bad health and unable to pay the taxes on it. You just hate to see it leave, because you know that particular forest will never be back. It takes a hundred years to grow a forest like the one we had. And Weyerhauser and U.S. Plywood and Georgia-Pacific don't want hardwoods anyway. They want pine trees about

twenty years old, for more lumber for more houses for more people
to spend their lives paying for. They can grow five of those forests in a
hundred years. But when the logging crews come into untouched area
like that, with their long-bar saws and dozers and skidders and trucks,
it's an awful thing to see.

We had a five-year lease. All written down on paper and typed up
in a lawyer's office, all duly signed by all involved parties, the money
paid. It was safe, at least for a while. We didn't know what we'd do if
Mr. Barlow upped the ante the next time around. We were all getting to the age where we had to start thinking about things besides
deer hunting, things like college educations and car insurance for the
teenaged boys, additions on our homes. Our sons were growing up,
you see. That was the kicker. We hadn't leased all that land just for
ourselves. We'd leased it for our boys, too.

None of them were along that morning, though. Randy had played
in a football game a hundred miles away the night before, and Jim said
that when he came in a little past midnight, he was beat up and worn
out and too bruised to go. They'd lost a heartbreaker, too, 20–21, for
their division title. Bobby's boy, Ted, had a broken leg that was still in
the cast, and I hadn't been able to pull Alvin out of the bed at 4 a.m.
So the three of us went by ourselves.

It was one of those mornings when I thought the sun would never
rise. The woods were as quiet and cold as I'd ever seen them. Even
before it got daylight you could see the thick white rime of frost laying
on everything so hard it looked like snow. And within an hour I was
in agony. It wouldn't have mattered if a real trophy buck had walked
up; I was shaking too hard to draw a bead on anything. I'm always in a
hurry, always forgetting my thermos of coffee or my gloves, or another
pair of socks. I'm always in a hurry to get into my stand. Later that day
I heard that it had gone down to three degrees.

I'd always wondered how the animals could stand cold like that. I don't mean things like squirrels and coons that have dens lined with warm leaves they can burrow down into, animals that can cover their faces with their tails. I mean the ones that live on open ground, like the deer. A brushpile or a thicket is all they can get into, and on mornings when the ground is frozen, lying on it must be bad for them. Maybe they don't feel it like we do. Maybe they don't have any choice.

I was shaking too hard to even light a cigarette. I tried, and I dropped my lighter. I told myself that I didn't need to be smoking in my stand anyway, but I've always been a poor disciplinarian. I rooted around in my field jacket until I found some matches. I thought maybe smoking would help me throw off the shivering. It didn't. If anything, it got worse.

My hands were like claws by then, just wooden lumps that could hardly feel or hold onto my rifle. I crossed my legs on the old, weathered boards and lowered my head. I put my hands in my armpits, trying to shake myself out of the shaking. My teeth were clattering like those windup chompers you see. The only comfort I had was in knowing I had raised a son with enough good sense to know when to keep his head under the covers and stay in the bed. I thought of how warm Mary Annie's thighs and back and belly were under her flannel gown, of how I could have been lying against that warmth at that moment. My feet didn't seem to be connected to my ankles any more. They were just vague aches.

When the clouds came over, and the wind sprang up, my heart sank. I almost got down and built a fire. The sun wasn't going to come out and warm me after all. The temperature wasn't going to rise much about close to freezing, and the wind was already bringing some tiny sleet that stung my face. I always try to rationalize everything, but there were only two choices: stay in the tree the rest of the morning and maybe not even see a deer anyway, and freeze, or get down and build a fire and give up any chance of seeing a deer once I made all that noise and created all that smoke. I stayed in the tree by rationalizing this: Jim and Bobby were probably no colder than I was, and neither of them was going to climb down and build a fire.

When I first heard it, it didn't register. It was just a noise that came along with the wind. Trees make their own voices in the woods sometimes, when two grow together and rub their bark away in the breeze. They moan, creak, cry out. Eventually I began to think that I was hallucinating from the cold, and that scared me. Of course I thought of hypothermia then, and again I considered getting down and rounding up some firewood. There were plenty of pine knots lying around. The woods were full of dead branches. But I kept thinking that soon it would warm up, that soon I'd stop shaking. And I was so deep in my own misery that I didn't even listen to it closely for at least ten or fifteen minutes. Then the wind laid a bit, and I heard it plainly: *oooooooooh help me.*

My head snapped up. It wasn't coming from the ground. The voice was in the air. But when the wind gusted, it lessened.

It's Jim, I thought. It's him or Bobby, one or the other. One of them has fallen out of his stand, and broken his leg, or landed on his knife. I started up, then stopped. It was coming from right in front of me. Bobby was a few hundred yards to the right of me, and Jim was far away to the left. This voice was close. It stopped then, and there was nothing to hear but the limbs moving, and the dead leaves rattling over the ground. I sat as still as I could and held my breath for a short time. I stopped noticing that I was cold. There was nothing, no sound but the wind. There was not an animal stirring anywhere, not even a squirrel. No birds. And it was only then that I noticed what had been missing all morning: the sound of any kind of life. In a place that is always teeming with life, it all appeared as dead as dead can be.

I told myself that it was too cold for anything to be stirring, that the animals knew when to stay hidden and warm better than men did. I told myself that I had been mistaken about the voice. If Jim or Bobby had been hurt, they would have fired three times. We had a prearranged signal for trouble. We all carried extra cartridges just for that purpose. Nobody else was supposed to be there.

I heard it again. Softer now. *heeeeeeeeelp oooooooooh help*

It was a weak voice, the voice of someone who had been crying out for help for a long time, so long a time that his voice was almost gone, either that or his life. And it didn't matter if somebody was on our land who wasn't supposed to be there, or if I spooked all the deer by getting down and trying to find him. The thing was, I had to find him. Soon.

I unloaded my 30.30 and slung it over my back. I slipped once, going off the platform, and I had that wild sudden leap of fear in my throat before I caught myself and held on. I was twenty feet off the ground. I couldn't afford a mistake like that. I hung on until my breathing slowed back down, and my heart, and I went down the tree a step at a time, the cotton picker spindles I'd driven in hard and cold beneath my hands. My breath fogged in front of my face. The sleet started turning to rain.

I didn't draw an easy breath until I got both feet on the ground. Then I hobbled around like an old man, trying to walk some feeling back into them. They were just dead nubs on the ends of my legs. I wondered if I had frostbite.

I tried to reload my rifle, but I couldn't make the cartridges go back into the magazine. One by one they fell out of my fingers. Finally I said: to hell with it, you couldn't pull the trigger anyway.

There was a ridge directly in front of me that towered over the ridge my stand was on; I'd watched lots of does come down it before, pawing in the leaves and scraping them away to find the acorns, looking up suddenly when the squirrels darted between their legs. There were not deer on it now. The crying was coming from the other side of it. It was the most pitiful thing I'd ever heard. It made me colder than I already was.

It took some effort, but I knelt in the leaves and scraped my hands together and gathered up the shells I'd dropped. It was impossible to keep from picking up scraps of leaves and bits of trash and tiny sticks with them. I just shoved all of it in my pocket. I knew there wasn't much time. And there were other things going through my mind. After I found whoever it was, I would still have to go for help. I would have to get Bob and Jim to help me. I might have to run for help on my dead and frostbitten feet. I cursed myself for a fool and for being where I was. I cursed this fool for being on land that was plainly posted and causing me to have to go through this.

There was no one on the other side of the ridge.

It was a shock to me, because I was out of breath and my legs were trembling, and I had braced myself for whatever I was going to find. I'd already thought the worst, that someone had been shot accidentally the day before and had suffered all night, half-frozen, probably wishing for the mercy of death. To find nothing there was unbelievable. I shifted to the east, toward Bobby's stand. I stood on top of the ridge, panting, bent over, my hands on my knees. I wasn't cold anymore, but there were thirty or forty pins sticking in the bottoms of my feet. It's good for you, I said under my breath, it's good for you. You're so bad out of shape. You ought to be running five or six miles a week.

The first thing I did was take off my field jacket and my insulated coveralls. I wadded them up tightly beneath an oak and loaded the rifle. I could flex my fingers fairly well by then, but I didn't know whether to fire the trouble shots or not. The voice kept calling, so weak, so softly: *ooooooooooooooooo-help*

It made me mad. If he was hurt, why in the hell didn't he stay in one place so somebody could help him? It was probably some idiot drunk out of his mind on whiskey, wandering around with a sprained ankle or something, lost.

There was nothing moving down there. Just the great brown trunks and grapevines and the dead brown leaves. I went down the side of the hollow slowly, trying to slip with the loaded rifle. A fine steady rain had begun, and my head was soon wet. That was all I needed, pneumonia on top of hypothermia and frostbite. I decided that if I found the guy and he was drunk, I might just let him find his own way out. Or by God even prosecute him. We had posted signs every fifty feet along the road. Even an illiterate knows what a posted sign looks like.

When I got down to the creek, the voice had moved away again. Somehow, in some way that I couldn't understand, he knew where I was and wasn't letting me get any closer. I stopped then. I sat down, winded, and held my rifle between my knees. I was sweating underneath my long underwear. That was going to bring a chill later. I wasn't going to chase some nutty asshole over half of Lafayette County.

"Hey!" I yelled. *heyeyeyeyeyeyeyey*, the echo said.

"Where you at?" *at tat tat tat*

The sounds rolled back into silence. Everything quiet. Except: *oooooooooooooooooh plleeeeeeeeeeeeeeee haaaaaaaaaaaaayyyyyyyyyyylllppp*

Shit, I thought. What in the . . . I began to not like it very much at all. I could have been anybody. You read the papers every morning, what do you find? Absolutely insane people, maniacs, wandering loose, murdering other people. Dead nude women who've had car trouble, missing people who are never found. Someone disappears and the police look for them for a while, but after a few days it's not news anymore. You stop hearing about it. But the missing people are still missing. It matters deeply to a family somewhere. Their loved one is somewhere, make no mistake. You read the small articles and you say to yourself: Dead. Murdered. They'll find her in five or six years. Or never. Anything or anybody could be out in the woods. Lunatics escaped from maximum security, luring people deeper back into the woods. . . . I stuck cartridges into the Marlin until her belly was full. I wasn't taking any chances.

I had made up my mind to fire three shots when I saw Bobby. He was coming slowly down the hollow ahead of me, stopping and listening. He and I were both listening to the same thing. It was weaker, softer, it didn't want him going the wrong way. I knew that then.

I met him halfway up the hollow. He had the strangest look on his face. We didn't say anything at first. We stopped about ten feet away from each other and squatted on the ground. I lit a cigarette and laid the barrel of the rifle alongside my face, leaning on it, staring at the woods. He hunkered down like a country man, his Browning across his knees. We just listened for a while. Every so often I'd see him raise his head and turn one ear toward the sound, tracking it. Then he'd shake his head.

"What do you think?" he said, finally.

"I be damn if I know, Bobby. I can't figure it. How long you been hearing it?"

He looked down and raked at the leaves with a stick.

"Ever since I got up in my stand," he said. "I heard it before daylight."

"What about Jim? You think he . . .?"

"Yonder he is. Let's ask him."

I looked up. I could see Jim's blue cap coming down toward us. He'd already seen us and had stuck his rifle under his arm, walking quickly, not trying to be quiet. He stopped about fifty feet away and grinned. I damn sure didn't feel like grinning.

"What is that?" he said.

"Don't know," Bobby said. "Gimme a dip, Jim."

He came on over to us and sat down. He pulled his Skoal out of his pocket and passed it to Bobby. Then he took off his cap.

"I thought it was somebody lost at first," he said. "First I heard it, it was coming from the west."

"West?" I said.

"Yeah. At first. It sounded like it was close to my stand. I got down after about ten minutes. Sounded like somebody hurt bad. And I started walkin' and lookin'. Every time I thought I's getting close to it it'd move." He looked at me and Bobby. "Then I noticed. Ever time I stopped, it stopped." He gave me the same funny look that Bobby had given me. Something strange. Unreadable. It was like all of us knew something that none of us wanted to speak aloud.

We just sat there for a while, listening to it. It seemed to me that once it had us all three in the same place, it got louder. Maybe I was just concentrating harder. I don't know. But it seemed to get closer, and louder. Finally, Bobby stood up and said, "Well, shit, let's go see what it is."

The long and short of it is that we walked for over two hours. We didn't find anything. It was a little before noon when we decided to call it off. There was nobody in those woods but us. We knew that. Nobody we could see, anyway. We could still hear the voice, but it seemed to get fainter when we turned toward the road. When we got within sight of my truck, we couldn't hear it at all.

We racked the guns and stood around in the road. I had three hot beers in the back end and we started drinking those. Jim said he thought we ought to call the Civil Defense in and let them worry about it. I didn't say anything. Bobby was like me, he thought like I did. We didn't want to look like fools, but I'd seen something like

this once before, in Alabama, when I was five years old. My mother
knew of it, and my older brother. No one else. Not even Mary Annie.
I thought about that when Bobby said that maybe it wasn't something
that anybody would be able to find.

Jim's face gave a little funny jerk when he said that. He sells insurance for a living and deals with the reality of life and death, the cash
value of a person's demise. He laughed.

"You crazy, Bobby," he said. "You know that? You crazy."

I wouldn't have wanted to have told Bobby that. I saw him put
a guy through a plate glass window in a bar uptown years ago. He
almost went to the pen over it. No, I wouldn't have said that.

"It ain't no need in calling out the Civil Defense," Bobby repeated.
"They wouldn't find nothin'."

Jim's face twitched like he wanted to say something else. He didn't.
We left it at that.

THE PHONE RINGING lifted me out of my thoughts one
night. It was between seasons, a Friday night. Alvin was off with some
girl who had just gotten her driver's license and Karla was up in her
room with her mother, talking out something she'd already been told
about and had been expecting, and that had finally happened. Mary
Annie was just glad it had happened at home, instead of at school, or
when she was off with some of her friends at the pool. I took it as a
sign to go down into the den and mix myself a good drink and not
even pay attention to the television, just marvel at the way a baby girl
grows into a woman in twelve short years. I left them alone. I wasn't
empty so much as lonely, and feeling old. I was glad to hear Bobby
on the line.

"Boy, what you doing?" he said.

"Just laying around. What you up to?"

"Nothin'. Sherrel's taken the kids to see Santa Claus and a movie. I'm over here by myself. Can you get off?"

I glanced up at the stairs. Better if I was gone anyway, probably. "Yeah," I said. "You want me to come pick you up?"

"Just get ready," he said. "Got something I want to talk to you about."

I pulled my boots on and grabbed a sweater. I took my drink into the kitchen and sat on one of the barstools until I finished it. I yelled up the stairs at Mary Annie where I was going. And before long Bobby pulled up.

We rode the night woods. That took me back about ten years, when I did that most every night. The hardest memory was of a fist-fight with a state trooper and the cuffs on my wrists, my little babies out in the car the next morning when she came to the jail to get me after borrowing the money from her mother. Yeah. Those days, bad times on the land, bad times all around. I could have been nothing so easily. Sometimes I still wanted to be. I pretended to be something, like everybody else. It was good to be off like that again.

Bobby had a fifth of Crown and a two-liter Coke and cups and ice. "Jim's fulla shit, ain't he?" he said, and I didn't say if he was or wasn't. "I didn't know what to tell him that day. Here. Mix yourself a drink." He turned the interior light on and I mixed up two strong ones. We rode for a while, made small talk. He'd had his old truck for about twenty years. He just kept putting motors and transmissions in it, said he wouldn't ever buy a new one. He talked that around for a while, before he got down to it.

"Long time ago," he said, "when Daddy was just a young man. During the war. His mama died when he was four years old. Just died suddenly one night. They don't even know what she died from. Things was different back then, though. I think she'd been sick for a while. He talks like he remembers her. He says he does. But I think he wanted to remember her so bad he made up a lot of stuff when he was a kid, you know?"

"He probably did," I said. I was going with the flow. I knew that Bobby was about to tell me something that was close and deep within him, something that maybe nobody else had ever heard. I was ready to hear it. I wanted an answer for that day, even though I was pretty sure I already knew it.

"He said Papaw would sit out on the porch with him and tell him stuff about her. About what they did when they were young and all. Back when they were goin' together they courted in buggies. Can you imagine that? Hitching up a horse and going on a date?"

"Yeah," I said, and that was all I said.

"Daddy was in the marines," he said. He was goin' across the ocean on a ship in 1945, a whole ship full of men. He said you had a little place about four feet wide and six feet long that was yours. All your clothes, all your gear. He said you had to sleep so close to another man you'd touch him. Couldn't even turn over in your bunk. He said it was bad."

I'd heard Daddy talk about it, of course. But he was shipped over early, I guess around '42 or '43. He was in the army and went to Europe anyway.

"It was early one mornin'," he said. "Just off the coast of Iwo Jima. They was waitin' orders to land, I guess it was so many ships they had to wait their turn. They'd done been told to saddle up, that they were goin' in. The navy had been shelling Mount Surabachi for something like two weeks, trying to soften it up. They knew they was goin' in over open beach, no cover. And every Japanese had sworn not to be taken alive. But they'd been waiting something like three hours with full packs on and all. He said it just come down the hall in front of everybody. Like a silhouette, he said. All black, like lace, but not exactly like that either. More like a shadow was what he said. And he said it got just as quiet as anything when the first ones seen it. Said he guessed most of 'em thought they's fixin' to meet death anyway and it had come on the ship to meet 'em. There was some black guys in this platoon, you know how they are over something like that. But they didn't say nothin'. Said their eyes got big and white, but they just leaned back and let it pass. And it came on down the aisle, every man there watchin' it. Said two or three tried to touch it but it wasn't nothin' there to touch."

We had stopped by then, and I don't know how long we'd been stopped. It might have been a long time. I know we were in woods. Black woods. So black your cigarette was a red rocket coming up to your mouth. There's something to be said for Crown Royal in the proper doses.

"Did he know what it was?" I said.

He fell silent for a moment. God, I was glad he'd come after me. "Oh yeah. He knew. He said he believed everybody in there knew. Said that was why some tried to touch her. But she come on down to him. Stopped right in front of him. He was nineteen years old. He thought it was the sign of his death, see. But it wasn't."

Bobby sounded almost ready to cry, and I knew to be silent. I found the bottle on the seat, and drank straight from it.

"She touched him," Bobby said, and he reached his fingers out lightly, and touched my left temple, twice. I hadn't known that his touch could be so light. "Like that," he said.

We were somewhere around Tula, Edie Hill or London Hill or Round Station, I don't know. You couldn't see anything where we were sitting but blackness.

"She touched him," Bobby said. "And he said he even saw her face for a moment. He knew her. It was his mother. My grandmother. Said it was like just a glance at her face, but he knew her from the pictures. He knew it wasn't his death then, when he saw her face. He knew he was going to be protected, be able to survive Iwo Jima and the whole war and get out of the marines and come home and marry and have a family. But he said he knew there was death all around him, in all those boys he was sitting with, that they were all going to die, most of 'em before the end of that day. But she left. They didn't even see where it went. They dropped anchor a minute later, and they called 'em up out of the hold and over the sides, down the nets to the landing craft. Then they left for the beach. He said it was a beautiful mornin', the water was so blue. They were slaughtered, Daddy said. Three thousand marines killed the first day at Iwo Jima. And he said he should have been killed fifty times. The bullets wouldn't hit him. He never got a scratch. Seven hundred and sixty-two out of the eight hundred on his ship killed before dark."

I didn't see so much as I felt him look at me in the night.

"Now what do you think it was hollerin' at us over there that day?"

I told him.

THIRD SEASON COMES and the fire is off you. Jim had clients to see, policies to sell. He told me two or three times over the phone about all the clients he had to sell to. I got pissed off finally and asked him did he want to just give up the land deal or what? He never would say.

And Bobby wouldn't go, he was stuck in California, between there and Oregon, hauling strawberries or cows or mattresses or something. It fell to me to go back, as I'd always known it would.

It wasn't cold that day. January in Mississippi sometimes has all these sunshiny weeks, that false spring when you think it's all over. You can catch catfish in the river, or crappie in the spillway. I guess anything wears off after a while.

The cold I'd gone through that morning was only a memory, and when I got out of the truck and stepped into the woods I knew I was going to hear it, just like Bobby's daddy had known that the machine guns wouldn't kill him on the beach at Iwo Jima.

I don't remember walking up there. Suddenly I was leaning on a tree close to my stand. I stood my rifle against the tree and stepped upon the picker spindles high enough to look at it and see what kind of shape it was in. It was covered with leaves, and the squirrels had sat there and cut their hickory nuts and acorns, leaving their tattered scraps behind for me.

ooooooooh pleeeeeeese hellllllllllp meeeeeeeeeeee

The wind soughed through the naked branches and I saw that winter wasn't gone, that the nights were still cold. I turned my wooden feet toward the sound, and I followed it. Down through the hollow, over two ridges, and down again, into a little seepy place that I'd never seen before. I stood there for a long time, just at the edge of it, before I went in. I knew there was nothing in there that was going to hurt me. I leaned the rifle against a bush.

The ground was soft, spongy. The spring came out of the side of the hill and the water lay over the ground in a thin coat. A thin sheet of ice in the winter, on those mornings of three degrees. A place that would crack and break, give way beneath old, trusting feet, beneath eyes and judgment that weren't as good as they used to be.

When a turtle dies, his shell lies close to the ground. Over the years the scales come off one by one, the tortoiseshell panes falling, the leaves of the years covering them, until only the naked white dome of bone remains to be seen. People pick them up for ashtrays, but first they turn them over with their feet, as I did this one.

I was careful not to touch anything with my hands. I raked leaves away with my boot, and there were the remnants of his own boots. The cancerous barrel of the rifle lay close beside him, the shells rusted solidly into the magazine. A young tree had grown up through him, between his spine and his ribs. And his billfold was there, and his belt with the tarnished green buckle, as was an old Case pocketknife that a careful deputy patiently searching finally uncovered beneath the leaves. There wasn't much left of the deer horns beside his hand. The squirrels had been at them for the calcium.

The red lights and the blue lights winked for a long time on the road that night. I thought they would never get it over with. The next day I found out who he was.

Lucius Thaddeus Tarver. Black male, aged sixty-two in the year 1971. He had gone hunting one November day and his family had never heard from him again. They had found his truck a few days later, of course, and his family still had it. They had kept hoping through some of those years anyway. What I wondered was how long he'd been crying out, and how many men, like us, had heard and refused to listen. I came close to it. I don't like to think about him lying there in winter and summer, with his bones exposed, wanting only the peace that six feet of dirt would finally bring.

But that timber's gone now. There are millions and millions of young pines on it. That's all you can see. Jim lost his marriage and Bobby's not around much any more. I couldn't keep the land by myself. Alvin is in New York anyway. I see him rarely. But I'm still hunting.

I found a little place of fifty-two acres not far from my house. I can drive up in there and be in my stand in five minutes. But I'm careful now. I carry hot coffee to my stand, and if it's too cold outside, I simply don't go. I've taken Mary Annie with me into the woods and showed her my stand. She knows the place where I will be. Each morning I go out, I tell her how long I will be gone. All the phone numbers she might need are written on the calendar. But she doesn't really need them. You can almost set your watch by when I pull back into the driveway. I am always exactly on time.

And Another Thing

You hear things under people's houses. You can hear them walking on the floor, hear them talking to each other, but strange, like they're underwater.

These people I went over to see about, I didn't see the woman. I just saw the man. Frankie took the call. Frankie's just a kid, a large one. He wears these boots you wouldn't believe the size of, with cleats on the bottom like he's going to climb a mountain any minute. He answers the phone and calls me on the radio and tells me where to go next.

Me, I'm a plumber.

It was already quitting time that evening and I was thinking about a few cold beers and a few racks of eight ball at Ireland's. But here was this problem waiting for me back at the shop.

"One eighty-four Vance," Frankie said. "Man called and said his toilet was stopped up."

I checked my watch. It was after five.

"What'd he say?" I said.

"I don't know, he just said his toilet was backed up and water was running all over the floor," Frankie said. "I think his wife was yelling at him. I could hear somebody yelling in the background."

So I told him okay, I'd go take care of it. I told Frankie to go on home before I left. He gets time-and-a-half after five.

This man met me before I even knocked on the door. I had my hand lifted and he just opened it. He was a big man with gray-black hair and a loose shirt cut evenly around the bottom hanging out of his pants. He had on some of those deerskin moccasins. I couldn't hear his wife yelling.

He said his toilet was stopped up, so I got the sewer snake and an adjustable wrench and crawled under the house. That was when I heard them talking. But they weren't talking. They were yelling.

"And another thing!" this woman's voice said. It was odd hearing it like that, under the house. I decided I'd just take my time and see what all they were yelling about. I turned on my flashlight and found the cleanout. It was plastic with a one-inch nut. The house was pretty high off the ground, so I crossed my legs and lit a cigarette. I didn't take the nut off, though, not while I had that Marlboro going. I didn't want to blow myself to Kingdom Come. You know, with sewer gas.

"I'm tired of you talking about how fat I am!" So evidently she was fat. But maybe not. Maybe he just thought she weighed too much and stayed on her ass about it all the time. I had a half pint schnapps in my overall pocket and I got me a little drink. I mean, after all, it was after five o'clock.

It was nice and dry under there, not like some houses you go under where pipes are leaking everywhere and there's mud you have to crawl through. It was insulated, too. That house had been taken care of.

"Yeah, well I'm tired of this goddamn life we're living!"

This was him screaming.

They lowered their voices, but I heard them. I was listening.

"You think he can hear us?" she said. Talking about me.

"Fuck him! I don't give a shit if he hears us or not!"

Well, when he said that, I didn't give a shit if he got his toilet unstopped or not. But since I was making $47.50 an hour, I decided to stay under there.

"Listen. I've worked my ass off for you for thirty years and you don't appreciate it. You can't even mow the yard!"

"I don't know how to mow a yard! That's your job!"

"Hire somebody!"

"With what?"

"With some of that money you're always spending on clothes and shoes!"

So, she was fat, and she spent too much money, and she wouldn't mow the yard and she didn't appreciate him working so hard. I wished I could see for myself what she looked like, whether she was really as fat as he said she was.

I put my cigarette out and put the wrench on the nut. First thing that happened was, it broke. I don't know why they put that plastic crap on there. It was backed up, too. You wouldn't believe the stuff that ran out of there. You wouldn't believe the things they were saying to each other in that house.

"I gave you the best years of my *life!*" she shouted. Then it sounded like she threw herself down on the couch or something. I could hear all sorts of crying going on. I could tell things were coming to a head after thirty years. I knocked all that plastic out of the way with the end of my wrench and started uncoiling the sewer snake. I had a good brass nut in my pocket I could sell him for fifteen bucks. Or maybe twenty-five, depending on how he treated her and whether she deserved it or not.

"Yeah, cry! That's all you can do is cry! I've had it up to here with that crying! You think I wouldn't like to cry sometimes? You think you're the only one that knows how to cry? I could cry over wasting my life with you!"

There were a bunch of terrible words being said and I was feeding the snake down the pipe an inch at a time. I stopped and wiped off my hands and got another drink of the schnapps. I was wondering what she was going to come back with. I hated to hear all that. Nobody should have to hear things like that between a woman and her husband.

Something broke up there. There was a big crash.

He said: "Why goddamn you!" And he must have hit her. She fell on the floor with a thud that shook the joists.

"You ran them off!" she yelled. "You ran every one of your own children off!"

"Don't you say that! I didn't run them off! You smothered them, every one of them! You wanted them to be perfect!"

I could see it. Her on the floor, maybe with blood running out of her mouth, and him standing over her, yelling. A very dramatic scene. Boy, what a mess. There were gobs of toilet paper and crap and something that looked like a used cereal box coming out on the snake. Things were heating up. I was beginning to wish I'd just gone on to Ireland's. I could have been beating Tommy at eight ball right then.

"He's dead!" she screamed.

"Yeah! Dead because of you! You drove him to it! Twenty-one years old and in his grave because of you!"

I had to stop. What could she possibly come back with against *that*? I tell you, you can find out about the intimate lives of people just by staying under their houses.

"What about you? You never sympathized with him. Oh no, not you. He had to be a pro linebacker, didn't he? Calling him Nancy in front of his friends. Don't you know what that did to him? Don't you know how that made him feel?"

I can tell you that I wanted out from under that house right then and there. I didn't care about the $47.50. No sir.

"How do you think *I* felt? Everybody knew it!"

"So what? He was your son!"

"He was your son too! Don't you lay it all off on me! If your mother hadn't been so crazy . . ."

"Don't you bring my mother into this! Don't you blame my mother for your mistakes! You sonofabitch!"

That was the end of it. It couldn't go any deeper. It was a good thing, too. I only had about a foot left. Any more and I'd have had to go back to the shop for the Roto-Rooter.

"Don't you call me that! Don't you ever call me a sonofabitch!"

"Sonofabitch, sonofabitch, sonofabitch!"

I heard that lick. All the way under the house, through the insulation and the boards and the subflooring and the linoleum and the carpet or whatever, I heard it. Larry Holmes has never been hit with a lick like that. I don't know how it kept from killing her. It hurt me just hearing it. A man should never get to the place where he has to hit his wife like that. She fell on the floor again and the whole floor shook. That made me think he was right about her being too fat. But it wasn't any of my business. I didn't want to think about it. All I wanted to do was get the pipe unclogged and leave. I didn't even want to have to go to the door and give him the bill. I didn't want to have to look at his face.

Everything went quiet up there. I worked the snake back and forth, pushing everything around in there. I thought maybe he *had* killed her. And if he had, I was kind of like a witness. I mean, I'd heard it. And if he had killed her, and I was the only witness, he might want to kill me, too. So I decided that when I got out from under the house, if he made any funny moves, I was going to bust him right upside his head with my wrench. I'll tell you, I was not looking forward to crawling out from under that house.

But after a while I heard her moaning. That was the only thing I could hear. That, and him crying. The line made a sucking noise when the clog broke through, and that was that. I pulled the snake back out and coiled it up and put the clips on it. I got the brass nut out of my pocket and screwed it in tight.

They were saying things to each other in soft voices, in comforting voices. I thought maybe they were sitting on the floor together, holding each other, telling each other how sorry they were for the hurts, promising to not ever do anything like that again, ever, never, ever never ever. Making promises they'd never keep.

"Hey!" I screamed. "Can you flush the commode up there? Hey!" I was screaming as loud as I could scream. I had my face turned up to the floor. "Can somebody up there flush the commode?" I had my eyes closed. I was screaming with my mouth wide open. "One of you guys want to flush the commode?"

Tiny Love

Tiny was tiny, but he had a wife and he loved her. The love he had for her was a lot bigger than he was. He did it all for her, ate the bologna sandwiches, changed the flats on the side of the road in the cold winter evenings when the rain was coming down, worked in the danger of the factory. Especially the factory, where gigantic presses could smash his hands and crush them, make nubs of his fingers. The machines crashed and pounded, and the huge wheels at the tops of the presses turned, and Tiny slid his little piece of metal under the die and hooked both hands on the buttons, and the presses turned over and came down with unbelievable force and stamped out one part at a time. He hooked the part with a little rubber suction cup on a rod, drew it safely out of the way, and inserted another piece, inhaling the exhaust of the Towmotors while standing on a skid to raise himself up to the level where other men stood.

He smoked constantly, not looking around, always watching his hands and where they were, because he knew Sonny Jones and Duwayne Davis who worked in the stockroom with their nubbed and shortened hands, victims of the same machines he stood before. The young boys drove the forklifts with cigarettes dangling from their lips and threaded the forks of the lifts into the pallets with insolent skill, blue fumes roaring from the grilled exhausts in the back.

Every afternoon Tiny spent his two dollars. Every day he drove by the liquor store, the last one on the way out of town, and picked up a half-pint of Four Roses or Heaven Hill or Old Grand-Dad or any of the other cheap and hangover-producing brands of whiskey, whichever one she had summoned from her bed that morning as he stood with his lunch sack in his hand at the bedroom door. All day he kept the name of that label in his head and that afternoon he fired up his rusty '71 Ford Fairlane with the busted muffler and drove out of town with a smoke hanging from his lip, winter and summer, good times and bad, and stopped by the little store on the outskirts of town where he was a regular but unknown customer, a place run by college boys whose faces always changed, and there he would shuffle in and pick what she wanted from the shelf and produce his two dollars and change and take his bottle once they'd sacked it and move once again through the coming darkness toward his small house in the country, where he had a little vegetable garden, a car shed, some rusted and warped pianos sitting in the yard in a muddy collection like a neglected group of behemoths.

He would stop the car in the driveway and get out and grab his jacket and go in, pulling on the screen door, and there she would sit on the couch in front of the gray television screen, in her robe and her nightgown, her nicotine-stained fingers trembling, her mouth moving in the first tremblings of a smile, and Tiny would think, Lord, I love her. She would reach for him and the bottle at the same time, and Tiny knew that the hug she had for him was at once a hug for him and a hug for him for bringing the bottle, and he would bend and kiss her quickly and go to the kitchen and fix her a glass of Coke with ice so she could mix her first drink, and then he would sit down and she would begin to tell him about her day.

Men lost their hands in the presses. The presses were thirty feet high and they had wheels that were twelve feet in diameter, and they were made of iron and they weighed hundreds of tons, and a man's hands were a small thing in the face of the quarter-inch thickness of metal parts the presses stamped out without stalling. A man had no power in the face of power like that. The press-department bosses looked sharply in the press department and watched where men put their hands and talked to them and measured small pieces of metal with micrometers and checked blueprints and eyed everything and ordered runs for the presses, and Tiny hooked both his hands on the buttons and watched the die come down and make another part. He hooked it with his little rubber-suction-cup rod and drew it out safely and inserted another piece. He leaned on his machine and thought, Lord, I love her, and the press came down and Tiny, locked in his life-time's work, watched his hands and where they were and rehearsed the name of that afternoon's bottle in his mind.

He ate bologna sandwiches every day. It never changed. It was always bologna, and he bought a pound a week, seven slices, where Mr. Carlton Turner sliced it on his machine and where the people who lived in the community with Tiny and his wife knew him and knew that she drank. Tiny would always hang around the store for a while, looking lost, talking about the weather or whatever had just happened, and he would twist the neck of the paper sack that held the bologna tight around the small, cold mound of meat inside there, and he would tell everybody to just come on and go home with him. But nobody ever did. It was just something to say, like people in the country often say.

He fixed the bologna sandwiches in the kitchen each morning while she was sleeping, quiet in the kitchen with only the radio playing, two pieces of bread and mayonnaise, wrap it in waxed paper, put it in the sack. She hardly ever went anywhere. Her day began when his ended. She was articulate to the point of wittiness once she'd had her first drink, but he couldn't sit up with her all night watching network television.

He ate the sandwich in the break room with one of those mixed soft drinks that came from machines that drop first the cup and then some ice and then several squirts of different liquids and finally fizz up the drink and click to signal when they are ready. He watched checkers games sometimes or just talked with other people about work or how the fish were biting or who had died, and he kept his eye on the phone booth and waited until almost everybody had headed back to punch in and then dashed to the booth to call her and speak to her for just a few moments. Sometimes she was up. Sometimes she wasn't. He needed to hear her voice always. Sometimes he did. But sometimes he didn't.

HE'D TRY TO get her out to go places with him, but she hardly ever would. She'd say she didn't look right, or her hair wasn't ready, or she hadn't had a bath. He was sometimes only asking for her to go buy groceries with him. They couldn't go dancing because she was semicrippled, from a car accident a long time ago. It wasn't that she couldn't actually walk. She actually could. She just preferred not to. Tiny had to help her bathe. He would roll her in her wheelchair with her thin legs crossed under a robe and lovingly draw a tub of warm water, testing it frequently with his hand, talking softly to her, making sure the water wasn't too cold or too hot, and then together they would work her out of her robe and he would help her pull her arms out of the entrapments of the sleeves until she sat naked and pale and defenseless and semicrippled and slightly drunk in the chair, and he would slide his hands under her legs, feeling the movement of her loose skin under the slack muscles of her thighs, and lift her, gently, careful not to bump her, and pick her up, stand balanced with the precious weight of her in his arms, his hands cradling the soft, withered flesh of her back and legs, and lower her, gradually, slowly and carefully, almost herniating himself sometimes, into the warm water, and bring her an ashtray and replenish her drink, and he would sit there and bathe her back, her little sad and drooping breasts, and she would talk about David Letterman and what he'd said, and he would rinse her back slowly, lovingly, and try to fix her eyes with his eyes, and she would prattle on, the water cooling, her toes red and distorted and pruney.

It seemed to go on forever sometimes, the two of them sitting in the bathroom, because she could lean forward and turn on the faucet with her toes and let more hot water in, and Tiny would keep replenishing her drink, because it was a prelude to love. Once the bath was done and she was done and she said that she was ready, he would let the water out and dry her partially where she sat in the tub, because he didn't want to pick her up while she was wet and risk dropping her, and she would lift her legs and let him dry her under each one, and he would carefully run the towel under and over everything involved, so that she would be dry, and safe to hold, and he would, once he was sure of this, bend once again and put his hands under her legs and behind her back and lift her up, and reposition her in the wheelchair, toss her little robe over her, and wheel her back to the bedroom.

He would kiss her and tell her how much he loved her before he took her out of the chair. There would be only a small lamp burning. She would nod and smile, holding out her empty glass, and he would hurry to make her another drink. He would bring it to her and sit beside her on the bed until she was ready, and then he would lift her out of the chair and put her on the bed and pull the covers up over her, so that she was not exposed, and undress quickly in one small dark corner of the room, and go to her, naked and fully engorged, and spread her thin withered thighs and get in between them and try to give her all the love he could feel.

IT WAS DIRTY, dangerous work, and there was no way to get out of it, because once it started you were locked into a clock you had to punch into for forty hours a week, and that left no room for looking for other jobs, and Tiny never expected that his life would merit more than this anyway. He believed in Social Security and he believed that he would live a long and healthy life and he believed that his job was a form of security as solid as anything anybody could ever hope for. Sometimes he longed to drive the forklifts. Sometimes he longed to be the foreman over the assembly line where fifty people put stoves together and drilled holes with drills and inserted screws with air-driven screwdrivers and sent them on down the line, because the press department was too loud for talk and almost too loud for thought, but Tiny had only two thoughts anyway and they were, Lord, I love her, Kentucky Tavern.

He tried not to think about her too much when he was at work. He tried to think about his hands and where to keep them as the huge wheels turned and the die came down and shook the concrete floor where he stood on the skid with his cotton gloves and his rubber-suction-cup rod. There was two weeks' vacation a year, time he usually spent in his garden, early in the spring when everything needed to be tended to, when the pole beans needed poles and the tomatoes needed staking and tying off, when the grass was coming strong in the watermelons and they needed a good hoeing out. If she was okay, or sleeping, sometimes he would fish, settled against a tree on the riverbank, a small can of worms beside him, the line lying slack in the slow, muddy river current, flotsam piled in the eddies, empty milk jugs and beer cans and tiny sticks and trash. But he thought of her even then, wondering if she was all right, if he should stop fishing and go see if she needed anything. The two weeks always overwhelmed him. Here were two whole weeks where almost anything might be accomplished, where a man might search out and find a better job, one that paid more money, that was not so dangerous and depressing, one that might allow him to buy a better car, new furniture, a motorized wheelchair, any number of things that might improve their lives. She had never been able to have any children and Tiny had accepted it early, but he still grieved in his heart for the loss of what might have been, children to come home to, to help with their homework, to take fishing. And there never seemed to be enough time in the two weeks to do all the things that needed doing. Each year he told himself that he was going to get ahold of a truck and some men to help him move the pianos out of the yard, but there were always other things to tend to, a coat of paint on the house, the reworking of her little flower gardens, and every afternoon the trip to town for the little half-pint bottle. She would not allow him to buy a fifth. She would say that she was not alcoholic and did not need a fifth. She would say that all she needed was a little half-pint. And Tiny never even thought, for a long while, of arguing with her. He loved her too much.

Sometimes Tiny fried the fish he caught, when he caught some, rolling the headless lengths of pink catfish flesh in yellow cornmeal and dropping them into hot grease and turning them with a fork until they were a nice, even brown. She would help him, sitting by the stove in her wheelchair, offering advice as to the doneness of each piece, chainsmoking and drinking her little drinks. Tiny knew that she didn't have anything else to do, that she was lonely, that the drinks helped her cope with her life and her reluctance to walk. He dreaded the end of his vacation and the return to the brutalizing noise of the factory, the danger of losing his hands, the same cold, tired bologna sandwiches. He never complained, never regretted being saddled with her and his life, never asked the big Why? He enjoyed his two weeks off as best he could and when it was over went back to the thing that brought in his three dollars and sixty cents an hour.

Her liver was not in good shape and there were frequent trips to the doctor. There was no one else to take her and so Tiny would have to be excused from work for a few hours. The press-department foreman didn't like it because then he had to pull somebody out of spot welding and put him on Tiny's machine. Sometimes she would call the factory and ask for Tiny and somebody would have to come and get him, usually the press-department foreman, and he would never fail to tell Tiny that they weren't paying him to talk on the phone. Tiny would nod his head and agree and thank the foreman and go into the foreman's tiny office where the phone was lying on its side and he would listen to whatever his wife was telling him, nodding his head rapidly, trying to get off the phone as soon as possible, and it was always bad for him to have to go back out and tell the foreman that he needed a few hours off so he could take his wife to the doctor.

The foreman would more often than not get mad at him, and cuss, and then tell him to go on, but hurry up, goddamnit, and Tiny would rush to the time clock, punch out, rush home, load his wife up, rush to the doctor's office, see the doctor, then rush back home and unload her, and rush back to the factory, where the foreman would be so mad he wouldn't speak to him for the rest of the day. And anyway, after a trip to the doctor, there was never much left of the rest of the day. And after a trip to the doctor, Tiny could never stop thinking about what the doctor had said, because he always said the same things. He always told Tiny that her liver was in bad shape, that her drinking was going to kill her, and that Tiny had to stop buying it for her. After Tiny had pushed his wife back out to the waiting room, he and the doctor would have these small private conferences in the doctor's office, behind a closed door. The doctor would say that he understood she had a need, but her liver was getting worse, and if she didn't stop drinking, one day it was going to kill her. The doctor would say for Tiny to just stop buying it, but Tiny would shake his head and tell the doctor that he could hardly stand to do that, that she needed it, that she was lonely, that she would cry if he didn't buy it for her, and that there were a lot of things he could stand but seeing her cry wasn't one of them. Then the doctor would shake his own head and write a prescription and tear it off the little tablet and tell him a definite and somewhat huffy good-bye.

HER HEALTH HAD never been good and it continued to get worse. She seemed to get weaker each year. And neither one of them was a spring chicken. She coughed badly from the cigarettes, and at night Tiny would sit on the bed with her and pat her back while she coughed herself into strangling fits and wheezing spells that he tried to cure by slapping her gently on the back. He'd hold her close and think, Lord, I love her, and then she'd ask for another drink and Tiny would get up and fix it. One time he told her that he wasn't going to fix it, and she cried and immediately Tiny relented and fixed it. He sat there watching her drink it and wondered if he could bring himself to be strong enough to do what was best for her. He knew it wouldn't be easy. He knew she'd cry. He didn't know if he could take that or not. But the doctor knew what he was talking about. He was a doctor. He'd been to college and had learned all those things. And if he said it was killing her, then, by God, it *was* killing her, and he, Tiny, was the one who was doing it by buying it for her, so in a way, *he* was killing her, and if he kept buying it, and it *did* kill her, then what would he do? What would he do for love?

TINY TRIED TO save a little money from time to time. It wasn't easy, because he didn't make much, and he spent a lot, but he managed to stick back a little here and there. One Saturday afternoon when things were pretty smooth, when she was happy in front of the television with a Tarzan movie on, Johnny Weissmuller in *Tarzan Finds a Son!*, and a drink in her hand, Tiny told her he was going to go look at another car. He asked her if she wanted to go. She didn't. She just happily waved him on out the door. Tiny thought, Lord, I love her, and drove eight miles to the driveway of a man with a '78 Buick for sale, high mileage but clean, good floor mats, the paint faded just a little. Tiny got in and cranked it up and revved it up. It was a smooth-running little engine. The man swore it wouldn't use a drop of oil. He said there wasn't any way you could get it to use a drop of oil. He said you could run the dog*shit* out of it and it would, it wouldn't *ever* register the *least* bit *low* on the *stick*. He said it was the best car he'd ever had. He said the only reason he was getting rid of it was because he'd bought a new one, and there it sat in the carport, all shiny and new.

Tiny cut it off and got out and kicked the tires. They didn't have a whole lot of tread left. But the man was only asking four hundred dollars for the whole thing.

Tiny asked the man if he could drive it. The man said he could. Tiny drove it and liked it. It handled well. It cruised like a Buick ought to. Tiny came back and parked the car and told the man he believed he'd take it. He pulled the money from his pocket, the carefully saved twenties and tens, a whole wad of them, and counted it into the man's hand. Then he asked the man if he'd mind following him home in the car, since he only lived eight miles away, and then Tiny could bring him back home, and the man said he'd be glad to. So that's what they did.

Tiny told his wife, "Come on, let's go riding around." He bundled her up in a robe and fixed her a big drink in a jelly glass, stirred it with a spoon, and they got in the car and took off. It was a warm summer evening that evening, and people were riding around, and they rode down some roads, and she drank, and Tiny smoked, and they talked. The air smelled good, and once in a while they'd meet somebody they knew, and Tiny would wave. He felt good, having her with him, in this new (to them) car. She told him how much she liked the Tarzan movie. They talked about what a good swimmer Johnny Weissmuller was and about what a good Tarzan yell he had. Tiny felt so good he let out a Tarzan yell himself, but it wasn't nearly as good as Johnny Weissmuller's. It didn't matter. The cotton fields were growing and it had rained earlier and the air smelled clean, wonderful, and Tiny had hopes that things would get better.

They stopped by a small store and bought some ice and some more Cokes. She had secreted the better half of a half pint in her purse so there was no need, really, for them to stop riding and enjoying the scenery. But they happened upon a bad wreck. Law officers were directing traffic in the middle of the road. A bridge railing had been crashed through, and as they crept past they could see a car upturned in a creek, the muffler exposed, all the underparts showing. People were standing in the road, watching. They crept past. Cars were parked everywhere. An ambulance was waiting. People with white coats were standing down on the bank of the creek. There was a stretcher on wheels they were standing beside. Somebody was being pulled out of the car, and he looked dead, an old man, with gray hair, a bloody wound in his chest. A man standing in the road wearing overalls told Tiny they thought he was drunk. The lawmen waved to Tiny to move on through. Tiny and his wife craned their necks to see as they crept past. But other people were waiting behind them, and they didn't get to see the dead man brought all the way out and placed on the stretcher with a sheet over him for his ride to the morgue.

IN THE WINTER it got dark early. Sometimes it would be almost dark when Tiny got home. He cooked hamburgers sometimes, smoking in the kitchen, drinking coffee, never touching a drop of what she loved so much. Usually on Friday evenings he bought groceries with part of his paycheck and in the winter it was always dark when he got home with the groceries. That made him late with her bottle, and she was always a little ill on Friday afternoons and would want her bottle brought in before the groceries were brought in. Tiny was used to that and did it and didn't mind it, although the doctor's words kept nagging in his head. He could see the doctor's head, and how he'd shake it, with the air of resignation he had, and sometimes Tiny would actually think about trying to do what the doctor had told him he should. And one Friday afternoon, he tried it.

He didn't stop by the liquor store and get her bottle. He went straight to the grocery store, pushing his cart up and down the aisles, trying not to think about what she was going to say when he came in empty-handed. There was going to be some crying, and some arguing, he was sure, but he felt like he was doing the right thing. He knew she was sitting at home at that moment, anticipating her bottle, and he knew she was going to be disappointed. He knew she might pitch a fit. But he thought he could handle it. When he got home, it turned out he couldn't.

He took the groceries in—it was winter, dark—and set them on the table in the kitchen, two sacks, two armloads. There were all kinds of good things in the sacks, stuff like fresh catfish, some fatback, some cracklings for crackling bread, buttermilk, Jimmy Dean smoked sausage, some nice chicken legs, and candy. Tiny thought he might be able to get her off whiskey and on candy. He was hoping he could, anyway. But she seemed a little furious when she came rolling into the kitchen in her wheelchair.

He turned around to her while he was setting the groceries on the table and she demanded to know where her bottle was. She looked a little wild, and she looked a little shaky. She looked, Tiny thought, like she had revved herself up to do some real nasty talking. He tried to be calm. He tried to be as benevolent as he could. But it didn't work. She knew, right away, that he hadn't brought the bottle. She knew, right away, that he was stiffing her, trying to put her off, and she looked in the sacks and found the sacks wanting. And she went into a rage. She had a cigarette hung in the corner of her mouth and she threw the pack of cracklings against the wall where they slid down behind the stove. Tiny tried to reason with her, but it didn't do any good. She wanted her bottle, and she wanted her bottle right away.

Tiny tried to explain to her that it was killing her, tried to get her to remember all the things the doctor had said, but she wouldn't listen to any of that. She knocked the buttermilk off the table and it broke and ran all over the floor, and she took the Jimmy Dean smoked sausage and tried to hit Tiny with it, and then she backed him up into the corner where the heater was and beat him with the catfish until he finally agreed to drive her back to town and get her a bottle. She just wouldn't listen to reason. It was Friday night and the Grammy Awards were coming on.

BUT THAT NIGHT was a wonderful night. She always seemed to keep a little piece of a drink secreted somewhere, maybe for emergencies, and she had one when they went to town. She sipped on it and moved over in the seat close to Tiny and sort of rubbed on him while they were going to town. She whispered all kinds of wonderful things she was going to do to him once they got back home. Tiny stepped on the gas in the Buick and they went to the liquor store and he got the bottle and they went back home after stopping by Kentucky Fried Chicken for two dinner boxes with coupons they'd saved from the mail. They didn't watch the Grammy Awards, and the chicken got cold in the kitchen. Tiny's wife got him down on the bed and yanked his pants off and did things to him with her mouth that he'd never seen or even imagined before, and he didn't even question where she'd learned it or heard of it or seen it or imagined it, just enjoyed it and thought, Lord, I love her, and woke up the next morning with different thoughts in his head.

NOW THINGS SEEMED to take another turn. Now when Tiny was at the presses he had more things on his mind than Lord, I love her, and Old Crow, and where to put his hands. He began to be trained to know that as long as he brought the bottle, she would do those wonderful things with her mouth. It was hard for him to think about where to put his hands when he thought about where she put her mouth. The presses were still just as big, still just as dangerous, but Tiny had more to live for now. He couldn't wait for the days to get over. He couldn't wait to get back home with that bottle and take it in to her where now she waited on him in the bedroom in her robe, smiling, her lips ready. For Tiny it was deep love, the deepest love, and he'd think, Lord, I love her, and Shit, and Damn, and that was about all the superlatives he knew. After he'd exhausted them, he just had to moan and groan.

THAT WENT ON for a while. A long while. A long, slow, pleasurable, mesmerizing while. It went on through the whole two-week vacation the next year. The pianos didn't get moved, just kept moldering in the yard, but once in a while Tiny would go out there and tinkle the rain-swollen keys, rub his hands over the cracked and splintered veneers. He thought of hiring a bulldozer and having them just bulldozed over into the hollow behind his house. Tiny had to move around those pianos.

SHE SEEMED TO get weaker all the time. Tiny knew the cigarettes and the booze were killing her. She never ate anything, and her phone calls to the factory became more frequent, sometimes at lunch when he was trying to eat his bologna sandwiches. At night he cooked chili, fried chicken, tossed salads, baked potatoes, did roast beefs, but nothing seemed to interest her. All she wanted was her drink and smokes. He knew he was going to have to try it again. He didn't want to. He knew it would be tough. He knew she'd . . . But he hoped there wouldn't be any violence this time.

ONE DAY HE made up his mind. He stood all day long at the press and thought about it. He decided to get tough. He knew it wouldn't be easy.

He didn't buy a bottle that evening. He just went home. He didn't even go in the house at first. He just went out in the backyard and started pulling up some weeds. But before long, she started calling to him. He could hear her in there. She was wanting her bottle. That was plain. He kept pulling up the weeds. He was trying to take his mind off it. He was trying to think about something else.

Before long he heard her crying. She was screaming and ranting and cussing and crying all at the same time, and he heard her say

some things about why God let good men die and bad men live, and
he didn't know what she was talking about, and didn't want to know,
only wanted for her to hush and not keep on about all that. But she
made it back to the kitchen in her wheelchair. She raised the window.
She screamed at him out of that. She screamed some things that were
pretty bad.

She screamed, *"You motherfucker! You little sawed-off midget asswipe!*
You cheap prick!" It hurt Tiny pretty bad to hear all that. But he just
kept pulling up his weeds. He thought he could weather the storm.
He thought maybe she'd cool off if he just stayed out in the yard and
minded his own business.

But she got to knocking over stuff in the house. There were all sorts
of big crashy noises. She was screaming the whole time. It was a good
thing Tiny didn't have any close neighbors because no telling what
they'd have thought. Probably something like, Aw, hell, that's Tiny's
drunk-ass wife again.

Then she got to yelling that she was going to set the house on fire.
She screamed out the window that she'd *burn this goddamn house to the*
ground! Tiny didn't think she meant it. But it turned out that she did.

Before long there was a big orange glow in the living room. Smoke
started coming out of one of the windows she'd been screaming out
of just a few minutes before. Tiny didn't think, Lord, I love her. He
thought, *Oh shit!* and rushed inside. A whole wall of the living room
was on fire. Burning embers were on the floor. Smoke was mush-
roomed near the ceiling like a small atomic bomb. And there was
Tiny's wife, hacking and strangling, trying to get out on the front
porch, her wheelchair hung in the doorway.

Tiny didn't know what to do first, rescue his wife or try to put out
the fire. He ran over to his wife, grabbed her, pulled her wheelchair
back. The smoke was terrible and it was burning his eyes. He could

barely see. He couldn't breath for it. They were both coughing and strangling. Tiny could feel his hair getting singed. He could see his wife's hair getting singed. He lifted her out of the wheelchair, kicked the chair out of the way, and carried her outside and put her on the porch swing. Then he jumped down in the yard and grabbed the garden hose and turned on the faucet The fire was getting bigger in the living room. The heat was awful. Tiny had to go inside and face that with a garden hose.

The fire was licking at the ceiling. Tiny squeezed the nozzle and put his hand over his mouth. The water knocked the fire down quickly, but the smoke turned black and got about four feet thick near the ceiling. Tiny's eyes watered and he thought he might puke. He got down on his knees. Black water and charred debris covered the floor. He could hear his wife coughing out on the porch swing. He kept spraying the water and the fire finally went out. He saw that the house wasn't going to burn down after all. Bur it sure had made one hell of a mess.

Tiny could have done a lot of things. He could have cussed his wife out, slapped her around some, whipped her ass good for setting the house on fire. All he did was drop the hose on the floor and walk out on the front porch to look at her and think, Lord, she sure is a lot of trouble.

ALL OF A SUDDEN, Tiny didn't know what to do with his wife anymore. It looked like she was capable of nearly anything to keep on getting her drinks. He started worrying about her more at work and almost stepped into the path of a moving Towmotor a time or two. People had to yell at Tiny for him to get out of the way. If they hadn't, he might've just stepped on out into the aisle and gotten mashed.

And Tiny had to lie to his insurance company about the fire. They sent a man out to investigate and Tiny told him the heater caught the wall on fire. The man wanted to know why they were running the heater in such hot weather. Tiny told the man that his wife had gotten a chill, and then had pulled a chair over in front of the heater, and had gotten up to go to the kitchen for something, and the chair had caught on fire, and then caught the wall on fire, and the man said he thought Tiny's wife was in a wheelchair, and then looked over at her sitting there in her wheelchair. Tiny had to hem and haw, and finally admit that he didn't really know what had happened. He said it might have been an electrical short.

The man said *Ha!*, and then stood around for a while and acted like he was getting mad. He wanted to talk to Tiny's wife but Tiny didn't want him to talk to his wife. The investigator finally left, with nothing settled. About a week later Tiny got a notice in the mail saying that his house insurance had been canceled. Somebody, maybe the investigator who had come out, wrote a shitty little note in there that said. "You've lucky we didn't sue your lying little ass."

Tiny had to dig deep to find the money to fix his living room back up. Some Sheetrock had to be torn out, and new Sheetrock put in, and sanded, and painted, and new trim had to be put on, as well as new linoleum where those burning embers had melted holes in the floor. The ceiling was all screwed up and that had to be fixed, repatched, and painted. It cost Tiny a wad of money he couldn't really afford to spend. They had to buy new curtains and new venetian blinds, a new window shade. Tiny had to shake his head every time he thought about the whole thing being caused by a little two-dollar bottle of whiskey. He asked himself why he didn't just go on and buy the whiskey. He'd stand there at his press and not think too much about where to put his hands as the wheels turned over and came down and slammed out another part. Tiny got to be kind of like a machine, kind of like the machine he was running, something that moved when it had to, an automation, kind of. He worked like a robot, doing the same things over and over and over and over and over and over and over.

He kept buying the whiskey for her. He didn't know what else to do. And sometimes, late in the evenings when he was headed home, all by himself, just cruising along in the Buick, with the little sack on the seat beside him, things would pile up on him and get to him, and he'd drop his head, a cigarette dangling from his lips, and he'd cry. It wouldn't be loud crying. He'd just shake his head and a little snot would run out of his nose. He'd wipe it off with the back of his hand. And after a while it would end. He'd be all dried up by the time he got home, and saw his wife sitting in the living room, smiling, holding out her arms, making little smooch noises with her mouth, all ready for that Tiny love. But Tiny was about sick of love. He'd just hand her her bottle and head into the kitchen to see what was in the refrigerator to fix for supper. He still, after all, had to eat.

HE WORKED ALL day five days a week and he didn't see anything but the press in front of him. He put the piece of metal under the die and leaned against the press and mashed a button with one hand and smoked a cigarette with the other hand and the press came down and stamped out the part and Tiny hooked it with his little rubber-suction-cup rod or just his hand sometimes and drew it safely out of the way and stuck in another piece of metal and leaned on the machine and pushed the button.

Sometimes somebody had to punch him when it was time to go to lunch because sometimes Tiny wouldn't even hear the whistle. If nobody punched him, sometimes he'd just stand there and work all the way through his lunch break. And when he did take lunch, he just sat there and chewed and stared at the table. People started looking at him and talking about how funny he was acting, but Tiny didn't pay any attention. He had too much other stuff on his mind.

Some evenings he'd go home and hand his wife her bottle and go out on the front porch and sit in the swing, swinging, swinging, staring out at the road. People would drive by and wave and blow the horn, but Tiny wouldn't wave back. He couldn't figure out what to do about her. She'd holler out for him to come inside and see what was on the television, but Tiny wouldn't do it. He'd sit there until it got dark and sometimes he'd sit there until after dark and beyond. But his wife never complained that supper wasn't ready. Sometimes it would be only the screaming hunger gnawing inside his stomach that would drive him back inside. And sometimes the cure for that would only be another bologna sandwich. Tiny just about lost his appetite over his wife. He'd go to bed by himself, lie in the dark bedroom while the television played in the living room, while his wife chuckled over Johnny Carson and Ed McMahon and coughed once in a while. Tiny didn't know what he was going to do. He didn't think he could keep on going the way he was. And it turned out that Tiny wasn't wrong.

THERE WAS A little fat woman who worked down on the assembly line, and she started coming into the break room and sitting down at the table with Tiny, across from Tiny, and looking at him. She had a hot-dog sandwich every day. It never changed, just like Tiny's bologna. She looked at Tiny and smiled at him, and every once in a while Tiny would look up and see her smiling at him, and he'd smile back. Nothing special, just a little grin once in a while. But it escalated.

Tiny would go to the bathroom, which was down by the assembly line, and he'd climb the stairs and the little fat woman would be looking up at him and smiling. And one evening, she asked Tiny if he'd give her a ride home from work. Tiny said, "Sure." He wasn't doing anything but going to the liquor store for a bottle for his wife. He told her he needed to do that first. She said that was fine, that she might just get a little bottle herself.

They went into the liquor store kind of like a couple, kind of like a date. It felt a little funny to Tiny, but it also felt a little good to Tiny, whose wife had never gone anywhere with him in ages.

Tiny didn't mean for it to happen, but one thing sort of led to another. They got back in the car, and the little fat woman started telling dirty jokes and telling him how cute he was, and Tiny laughed and lit a cigarette, and the little fat woman opened her bottle and took a drink. She offered him a drink and Tiny took it. It was the first one he'd had in a long time, seeing as how he'd seen what it had done to his wife.

It turned out the little fat woman lived about twenty miles away and she apologized for that, but Tiny told her that was all right, he didn't mind, that it had been a good while since he'd spent any time with anybody but his wife. The sun was going down and the evening was pretty, and the little fat woman had a few more drinks and got to flirting with him, and crossed her legs under her skirt. Her legs were a little hairy but Tiny didn't care. He thought they were pretty nicely shaped. He opened his wife's bottle and started drinking out of that. It was Ancient Age that evening.

The little fat woman had some nice fat little breasts and the thing she had on was sort of low cut, and whenever she leaned over in the seat toward Tiny, which she did a good bit, Tiny could sort of see right down that little valley. He didn't mean for it to happen, but his love muscle got inflated, and the little fat woman noticed it and giggled and pointed to it, and then told him maybe they ought to pull over and see if they couldn't let a little of the air out of it. Tiny had polished off about half his wife's whiskey, and it sounded like a good idea to him, so they did. It had gotten dark by then and they pulled up into an old cemetery and all of a sudden the little fat woman was all over Tiny, spilling her whiskey on him, smooching on him with her mouth, and she knew things to do with *her* mouth that Tiny's wife had never thought of or seen or even imagined, and they stayed there for about three hours, plenty long enough for Tiny's wife to be totally enraged when he staggered in drunk, whooping and laughing, and then falling like a tree down on the couch, hiccupping and grinning before he passed out.

THE NEXT MORNING, Tiny woke up on the couch and realized that things didn't have to be the way they were. He didn't have to put up with that bullshit from his wife. The little fat woman was a whole lot more fun than his wife had ever thought about being. Tiny had loved his wife a lot at one time, but now he didn't love her so much. As a matter of fact he'd sort of started hating her. All she did was complain and cough and drink and cost him money. There was no telling how much money she had cost him over the years. She didn't have any sense of humor at all, and the sex they had together was kind of like something she paid him just to bring the whiskey. Tiny stayed there on the couch awhile and thought about the little fat woman's fat little naked body and how nice and fat it had been. She really had some meat on her bones. He got all excited again thinking about it. He wondered if maybe she'd want him to give her another ride home sometime. He hoped she would. Tiny thought that maybe he might ought to put a quilt in the trunk and start carrying it around with him, just in case. Just keep it for emergencies, kind of like how his wife kept her little parts of bottles of whiskey hidden.

Tiny got up and walked into the bedroom and peeked in on his wife. She was in bed with the covers up over her head. He couldn't see her face. She wasn't moving at all. She looked dead but he knew she wasn't.

Tiny eased into the kitchen and fixed his bologna sandwich. He eased out the door and got in the Buick and cranked it.

He did some hard thinking on the way to work. He hadn't had anything but misery for a long time with his wife. He'd tried to do everything he could for her, had pampered her, had done what she asked all the time, and it looked like all she did was use him. Tiny wondered what he'd done to deserve all that. He'd always provided for her, and what had she given him in return? Nothing but trouble, that's what. All she wanted to do was watch television and drink. He was tired of it. He didn't know why he couldn't have a little fun in life. A man wasn't supposed to just work like a dog all the time, was he? Just be like a damn machine standing at a damn machine and drawing a damn paycheck that was always spent before the next paycheck came? Tiny started wishing he'd never married his wife. He started wishing he'd never even seen his wife. He started wishing he'd never started working in the factory. He'd done some carpenter work when he was young and he started wishing he'd just stayed with that. He might have been a contractor by now, making plenty of money, having a big crew working for him, being the boss, ordering everybody around. The more he thought about his life and how it was, the sicker he got. He was so sick of the factory that he didn't know if he could walk back in the door. He knew his wife was probably going to call the factory sometime during the day and say she was sick and needed to go to the doctor. Then the press-department foreman would get mad at him again. He felt trapped. He didn't know whether to shit or go blind. He didn't know how he was going to go on with his life. His life seemed so bad he could hardly stand to think about it.

He thought about not going in to work. He thought about just stopping by a pay phone and calling in sick. He didn't feel real good anyway. He had a bad hangover. He wished there was some way he could get the little fat woman off with him and just spend the day with her. But she was probably on her way to work just like he was.

Tiny didn't know what to do. He sure didn't want to go back home. His wife would raise hell with him all day if he did that. Tiny realized that people could get more problems on them than they could handle, and that they could talk themselves into doing away with themselves. He wasn't thinking about doing that, he was just seeing how it could happen.

He guessed he could divorce his wife. That was a possibility, but it sure would look bad on him. Her lawyer would be sure to get her in the courtroom in her wheelchair and create a lot of sympathy for her. She'd probably take his ass to the cleaners, and he knew his ass couldn't stand a trip to the cleaners. He was just barely making a living as it was. But one thing about it was he wouldn't have to buy her a damn bottle of whiskey every afternoon if he divorced her. He wouldn't have to go everywhere by himself. If he divorced her he could probably start going with the little fat woman, maybe steady. Or maybe they could even get married if they fell in love. Maybe that was what he needed to do, just trade in his old wife for a new one. The little fat woman might even want to go dancing on Friday and Saturday nights or something. Then they could go on picnics on Sunday afternoons, or go fishing. Tiny thought about the two of them sitting side by side on the riverbank, fishing. They'd have the quilt with them and the sun would be shining and if the fish weren't biting she could do those wonderful things with her mouth right there while the river flowed past. The more Tiny thought about it, the more it seemed like a good idea. What was the point of staying with his wife if he was unhappy? There wasn't any future in it.

But what would happen to her? Who would buy her whiskey for her? Where would she live? Who'd take her to the doctor? Who'd cook her meals? Who'd help her take a bath?

By the time Tiny got to work he was so confused and sick and sick at heart he hardly knew where he was. He punched in at one minute before seven and grabbed a fresh pair of cotton gloves and headed back to the press department. He wanted to walk down by the assembly line and see if he could see the little fat woman but he didn't have time. He went over and turned on his machine and the whistle blew. He decided he'd ask the little fat woman if she wanted to eat lunch in his car with him and maybe they could talk about some of his problems. Maybe he could talk to her and ask her advice. And maybe he could give her another ride home that evening. Maybe his life could work out all right after all. He hoped it could. Things had been bad for a long time, and he was ready for them to get better. Maybe this new relationship with this little fat woman was the light at the end of the tunnel, where happiness was possible, and life didn't have to be something you merely had to endure until the day you died.

Thinking about these things, Tiny put a piece of metal in, leaned on his button, and then noticed that he had not been careful where he placed his hand.

A Birthday Party

I'd turned forty and it was weighing pretty heavy on me. I was in a bar again, as usual, and I was thinking about my daddy again, as usual, and what all he had gone through, and wishing he was sitting on the bar stool next to me, when in reality he was dead and gone and asleep with the worms since April 19, 1968, and I had just ordered a Crown and Coke that had just arrived and I was looking at the large breasts of a red-haired girl who was sitting next to me and I realized that I was slightly drunk and didn't really gave a damn what happened next. The world had turned around on me and I had been published and all the years I had struggled through were a forgotten memory that sometimes rose up in my head and reminded me.

The price had been high and now I was being constantly assaulted by young writers who offered things if I would read their stories. They offered money, homes in Florida, plane tickets for Denver, hotel rooms in New Orleans, and blowjobs. I didn't want to have anything to do with them. I knew that their stories would break my heart not because they were so good but because they were so bad and I would have to be the one to tell them they ought to probably cut their throats instead of trying to be fiction writers but I knew they wouldn't listen to me.

I saw a well-dressed man start trying to make love to a girl with really snaggly teeth, I mean her teeth were rotted and crooked, she had some kind of bad gum disease, she was loose, a loose woman, a woman who wore loose, dirty T-shirts and was fat in that way that you knew when you looked at her that she could never be any way other than the way she was, no matter how much dieting she did, no matter how much she exercised, that she would always hang out in bars drunk, the last one to be pulled off the dance floor and fucked in the bushes by people who wouldn't give her two glances when they were sober, and this man, this well-dressed man, he made it a point to come up to her and remark that he'd been meaning to talk to her, that he'd meant to talk to her the other night, and that if she had a few minutes he'd like to talk to her right away. She grinned, that awful black-toothed grin, and said she had plenty of time, and they went off into a corner after he bought her a drink.

She'd been running with a little road-lizard who couldn't pay his bar tab and had been cut off for it. Her teeth were awful, something you'd see in a nightmare, something you'd never want to kiss. I thought it was plain to everybody in the bar that the man was wanting to have sexual intercourse with her. It was plain to me. I wouldn't have even bought her a beer. I'd have moved if she sat next to me. I wouldn't have danced with her at all. She seemed to be expecting to hear the good things the man was saying to her. I didn't watch where they went. I knew that the bushes were dark at night and that there were secret things that went on that nobody but the participants saw.

There were a lot of drunk people in there. It felt pretty homey, what with all the friendly smiles and the people who knew each other talking to each other and some people were dancing out on the dance floor although I wasn't. My dog had died, had been killed, actually, by another dog, and it had taken all my self-control to keep from slipping a round into the magazine of my 30.30 and slowly, lovingly, squeezing off one sweet bullet into the head of that dog that had killed him. He'd come up and pissed on one of my fenceposts the day before, and I'd gone as far as to load up the rifle and lay it on the hood of my pickup and watch him, daring him to come on up and piss on my rosebush in the yard. I even sighted on him. I even fixed the crosshairs on his burry head and said to myself, You're a lucky son of a bitch that I'm such a nice guy even though you're not.

I hung around on my stool for a while. I'd paid my income tax and I had hardly any money to drink on at all. I wanted some love myself and knew I was too shoddy-looking to get any. I tried to dance with a few women but nobody wanted to dance with me and I couldn't blame them. I was looking pretty disreputable. I'd had to tape up the toe of one of my boots and my fingernails had a lot of black greasy dirt under them from changing out a water pump on my truck. Doing that had made me thirsty, and since it was my birthday, I had come back to this dark hole-in-the-wall looking for love.

I could see the man and girl at the booth in the corner, talking. I didn't really understand the whole thing. The only thing I had figured out was that men came into bars hoping to pick up women, and drank, and then the women came in a little later, all dressed up and smelling good and wearing tight pants and low-cut blouses that exposed the tops of their breasts, and it drove the men crazy who were wanting them, and the lucky ones, the ones with money and nice haircuts and good shoeshines got the women, and the rest of them had to fight because they couldn't fuck. I had figured out that that was it: if they couldn't fuck they had to fight, and fight they did. A small marathon of face-punching erupted suddenly two bar stools down from me, two guys knocking each other's heads back and forth with frothy, bloody lips and teeth flying. The bartender clouted one of them on the head and the guy left like a good boy, no questions asked. I ordered another drink and counted my money. I knew there wasn't enough to last until closing time and it saddened me immeasurably.

I had been introduced to some women a little earlier by a friend of mine who had tried to buy them a drink, but it quickly became evident that they were much more interested in each other. I'm not saying that they were tongue-kissing or anything, but it was pretty obvious to me that before the night was over all of them were going to have a mouthful of pubic hair. It was all they could do to keep their hands off each other, and I had a sinking spell when I found out that they were all very glad to meet me. I didn't want to have anything to do with them and when one of them asked me to buy her a drink, I didn't. I could tell by looking at her that she'd been in a mental institution and she seemed to be still a little nutty. I'd talked to a dentist who'd worked in a mental institution for a while and he'd told me some horror stories about patients who'd heard voices inside their mouths and had taken Black & Decker drills to their molars. I didn't want to get acquainted with a bunch of people like that. I had troubles enough of my own. I had turned forty. All I wanted to do was sit there and drink my whiskey and then drink another one. I wasn't asking a whole lot out of life that particular night, just to see forty-one.

The well-dressed guy came back to the bar and ordered two more drinks and I looked over his shoulder at the awful woman who was looking in his direction as if she knew something that nobody else did.

Her teeth were beyond funky. If she'd been my dog I'd have shot her. I couldn't help wondering if she'd let her mouth get in that kind of shape what kind of shape she'd let her vagina get in. And here this guy was wanting to ream the depths of it. He tipped the bartender big, two dollars down the empty wine carafe that held his stash. He went back with the drinks and the horrible woman laughed at something he said. My drink came and I counted out my change and paid. The bartender looked at me as if I was a small, partially dissolved turd.

The television was playing but it was silent. I looked at Senta Berger's magnificent breasts in *Major Dundee* while she and Charlton Heston were wallowing in a river. They were like mountains, like unchained melodies, like lewd sculptures from a deranged Michelangelo. I could hear the horrid woman laughing at everything the well-dressed man was saying. I glanced over and saw that they were holding hands. I considered starting a bar tab and then writing a bad check to cover it, but there was a large sign over the cash register that said NO CHECKS. I had ten dollars and change left to my name. I knew there was no whiskey at home, only a couple of cans of sardines and a few of cat food, and I wasn't down to eating that yet, just almost. My refrigerator was as empty as Hitler's heart. My daddy almost knew Hitler. He went to his house with his gun but the motherfucker wasn't home.

I felt that my daddy had been kind of like Jesus in that he'd suffered for our sins. Not our sins, maybe, just maybe our freedom. Him and about three million other guys. He hadn't been eaten by the sharks at Guadalcanal, or burned alive on the Coral Sea, but he'd had cold feet in Germany and had killed soldiers of the enemy forces and recovered pictures of their children. All that hadn't made him a happy man. He had shot a man one day and had that man's kid come up looking for his father the next day. He knew because he'd seen the picture of the kid in the man's hand the day before. He'd given the kid a piece of chocolate, and hadn't told him that his father was buried in a mass grave along with about two hundred other dead people. I think some days they just shot them like dogs. I think that most days they thought no more of them than dogs. By the time my father got to Auschwitz he was pretty pissed at the German race in particular. And I think that later in life he regretted all his anger, but what was he supposed to do about it then?

This girl, this lunatic lesbian, she leaned over and asked me if I was Leon Barlow. I admitted that I was. I kept hoping that a friend would come in, somebody I knew, somebody who might buy me a drink. I watched the door for a while but only strangers came in. I drank slowly and watched the movie. Charlton had Warren Oates shot for a deserter and then went off to chase some more Indians. Senta Berger's tits kept swaying magnificently in the background and it nearly drove me crazy. I wanted to rut with somebody like an animal, like a fuck-machine with a microchip for a brain. I was horny and I knew that if I was a woman in the right situation I could drink free all night. I knew that the terrible woman with the bad teeth was locked into a big spender who only wanted a little of her puss. I knew she'd give it gladly.

This girl next to me said: "So you're Leon Barlow, huh?"

I said: "Yeah, goddamnit, I'm him."

She said: "You want to buy me a pack of cigarettes? I ain't going to screw you."

I said: "Darlin', I don't want you to screw me. Buy your own damn pack of cigarettes."

And I turned back to my whiskey. I knew she was deranged. She had all the accoutrements of the mentally deranged: loose hair, wild shoes, paisley pants. Plus one of her buddies with very large hooters had been crotch-grabbing her. I mean you could tell that later they were going to get down. I didn't feel like I ought to have to pull out two of my hard-earned dollars and buy her some smokes.

It started raining outside and it only deepened my mood of misery and despair. I'd been down in Mexico a few weeks earlier hunting artifacts and native art and I'd been held up by mountain bandits and they'd lifted fifteen hundred American dollars off me and cut a small American flag into my stomach with a sharply pointed knife. They had laughed at me while I'd lain there bleeding, and a small boy had come up to me after they left with a wet piece of wool and bathed my wound. He had black eyes and black hair and was wearing blue shorts without underwear. His name was Pancho. He put me on a small donkey and led me to his home, and his mother had fixed me tortillas and coffee and had spread her fat thighs over me after the child had gone to sleep and whispered into my ear that she loved me and wanted to come to America. I'd gotten on a pack mule the next morning and ridden it all the way to Acapulco and bought a plane ticket home with the last of my American Express traveler's checks.

I suddenly wanted to be back in that woman's hut with the sun falling behind the mountains, drinking mescal, eyeing her heavy breasts inside her threadbare shirt, waiting for Pancho to go to sleep. I could have stayed there and married them and loved them and not been in the shape I was in. She had admitted that her brother was one of the men who had robbed me, and that if nothing happened to prevent it, Pancho would grow into a life of crime.

All of that was weighing on me pretty heavy while I sat and listened to the artificial laughter coming out of the booth behind me.

I turned around and looked again. They were smoking cigarettes and playing with each other's fingers. I knew he was suggesting things and I could see that she was ready to listen. The little road-lizard she had been running with walked back into the bar and took one look at what was happening in the booth and turned and walked back out. He knew it wasn't his day.

This chick next to me said: "You want me to read some of my poetry to you?"

I said: "Nah, I don't guess so."

So she said: "So, you're, like, Leon Barlow. Like, that's some big deal?"

I said: "It ain't no big deal to me."

She said: "My poetry's pretty goddamn good."

I said: "Good. Go blow your smoke up somebody else's ass."

She said: "Do you read stuff for people?"

I said: "I used to. I quit doing it because it got out of hand. Everybody's got the dream and the dream don't come true that often. I worked my ass off for a million years and all it got me is having to sit here and listen to somebody like you."

I usually wasn't that nasty to people, but she was starting to bother me. She had her legs spread out and her big-tittied buddy was rubbing her crotch with her elbow and leering.

I said: "Damn. Why don't y'all go off somewhere in private?"

She said: "But what's the secret, Leon? Come on, what's the secret?"

I said: "There ain't no secret. You live your life like you want to. If you want to hurt bad enough for something you can have it. That's all there is to it. Whether you write or not is up to you. I'm drinking. Now leave me alone."

I turned away from her and the band started. I got off my barstool and stood around for a while. I decided that I would take what little money I had left and go down to the liquor store before it closed and buy a bottle and get as drunk as I could on what money I had. I hadn't written anything worth a shit in seven months, and I'd worked night and day, like a maniac, filling trash cans full of sheets of paper full of words that said nothing, pure crap, not good enough to wipe my dead dog's ass with.

I walked out and got in my truck and went down the street. A cop car got in behind me and followed me for a while. They had the bad habit of hanging around my favorite bar like vultures, waiting to pick off some unlucky person who'd had one too many, who made the wrong step, who moved in an abnormal way on the way to his vehicle. I had learned to look both ways before crossing the street, like a Boy Scout. They saw that I wasn't weaving and they left me alone.

I stepped into the liquor store at two minutes before closing time. The guy eyed the clock and then sold me what I wanted, a cold bottle of Orange Driver, $2.95 a fifth. I knew I'd puke my guts out before the night was over, but I needed it for the food value. I knew it was loaded with Vitamin C.

The only good thing was that I had plenty of gas and a radio. I drove out of town, popped the top on the Driver, and started singing along with the radio. I rode through Taylor, through Tula, through Toccopola. I thought about all the decent people who were home asleep in their beds. I thought about all the lives and all the stories that were there, wonderful things, horrible things, heartbreaking things. I knew that I'd lost it and I was afraid I'd never get it back. At one time the muse would come and sit and shit on my shoulder like a pigeon and I had taken it for granted. I had thought it would always be there. Now I was just a cheap drunk, an ex-hack wearing Salvation Army shoes. I started hitting the Driver pretty hard. I smoked one cigarette after another. I ran over a polecat and had to smell it until I couldn't smell anything else. The Driver even started tasting like it. I started getting a little sick at my stomach. I stopped on the side of the road and threw up. I remember a story a nurse had told me one time, about a black guy being brought into the emergency room where she worked, with a gunshot wound in the stomach. He was screaming and puking and slinging blood everywhere, and she was trying to hold him down on a table, and he leaned his head over and puked up a big chunk of sardine right in her pocket, a chunk she said was two inches long. I puked a little more.

I wiped my mouth and staggered back into my truck, with my eyes weepy and the bile rising in my throat. I rolled the windows down and hung my head out the window like a dog while I drove, gasping in great big gulps of the night air. The smell of the polecat faded a little and I was able to take another drink of the Driver to settle my stomach. I began to feel a little better. I thought I could make it back to town.

It was late when I got back up there. I drove around the square several times thinking about everything. I was pretty drunk. I saw a bunch of kids out there, standing around, yelling at people going by, talking trash to chicks, yahooing and being young. And I thought: You boys just don't know. Never again will you have this time in your lives of carefree jubilation and you will only get your first piece once. Make it good. Run wild. Climb a mountain. Join a yacht club. Waterski. Drink plenty of beer. Learn to play a musical instrument.

I stopped driving around the square but parked near it and walked back down the alley to my home away from home. The place was nearly deserted. Two drunks, on two stools, and the bartender was the only one who didn't have his head on the bar.

I sat down and ordered a drink. I asked the bartender where everybody had gone to and he said a big party out in the county at a private lake and lakehouse. Some high roller had come in and invited the whole place out to his place, all drinks furnished, barbecue and hamburgers, swimming pool. The bartender was positive that everybody out there, most of them women, would get naked and lay in a pile.

I sat there. The bartender picked up a paperback Tom Clancy and took a powder. One of the drunks was on his way to the floor if nobody helped him pretty quick. Nobody helped him. He crashed over and laid on the floor, trying to go to sleep. It made me realize that there was a whole lot to be said for staying at home.

I kept sitting there, drinking, smoking a cigarette, looking at the guy on the floor. He might have been somebody's daddy. I felt pretty bad about everything. I got into these funks about once a year and wound up in jail or running into a deer or running off into a ditch. Once in a while I'd tie a rope around my neck and go lie down in the river and let the fish nibble on me. I'd lie there in that cold, muddy current with those slick, muddy banks all above me and think about Daddy slogging through the mud of Europe, snipers crouching in hollowed-out transformers shooting fire down on him while he talked on the radio and reported their positions, rows of telephone poles jumping off their stumps when they blew them all in line with det. cord, the big deer he killed in Germany and the cold and awful snow. How we fished when I was a child. I wanted him back and I never got over missing him and I never told any of my friends how lucky they were that their fathers were still around. I never said, Be glad, buddy, you still got him.

I ordered another drink and poured it straight down my throat. That was the last of my money. I wandered out into the street, where a light rain was falling. It fell on my cap and my camouflage jacket. I held no animosity toward the lesbians. They were only having fun with one another. I went on up the street, looking for nothing in particular. Later that night I would knock a boy one hundred feet into a river, but at that moment, as I was remembering little Pancho and thinking of my daddy, and of how I was now in bars like he used to be when I was small and confused and didn't know where he was or why he wouldn't come home, I felt him there, deep inside my forty-year-old heart, and I knew that I was made of the same stuff as him.

The girl with the bad teeth staggered up out of the bushes, her clothes in disarray, and we smiled at each other. The rest is too bad to tell.

BIG BAD LOVE
Part I

Falling Out of Love

Sheena Baby, the one that I loved, and I were walking around. It was late one evening. All the clouds had gathered up into big marshmallows and mushrooms, and it was an evening as fine as you could ask for except that we had two flat tires on our car some miles back down the road and didn't know where we were or who to ask. Besides this main emergency, I knew things weren't right. We were about ready to kill one another, and I've spoken on this subject once before.

Sheena Baby was LOVE, a sex-kitten goddess. I'd loved her for a long time, ever since I'd gotten rid of Miss Sheila, and I felt like I'd given part of myself away. Sheena Baby didn't hurt for me like I did for her. I knew it. I'd thought about shooting her first and me second, but that wouldn't have done either one of us any good. It wouldn't be nothing but a short article in some paper that strangers could read and shake their heads over, then turn to the sports. Love goes wrong. It happens every day. You don't need to kill yourself for love if you can help it but sometimes it's hard not to.

If we'd had inflated tires I could've got her off over in the woods somewhere, put some Thin Lizzy on, told her how we could work it out. Told her not only to be my baby but to be my *only* baby. Later, in the dark, we could have moved together. But she didn't love me, and I could see that finally. So I decided to be real nasty to her.

I said: "You just don't want to listen to anybody."

She said: "I've bout had it with your goddamn mouth."

"Jam it," I said.

"Kiss my ass," she said.

"Make it bare," I said, hoping she would, but she didn't, and we walked off in different directions.

I didn't know why something that started off feeling so good had to wind up feeling so bad. Love was a big word and it covered a lot of territory. You could spend your whole life chasing after it and wind up with nothing, be an old bitter guy with long nose and ear hair and no teeth, hanging out in bars looking for somebody your age, but the chances of success went down then. After a while you got too many strikes against you.

I didn't know what to do, where to go. We were miles and miles from any town, anybody who might have flat-fixer services and could perhaps send a tow truck. I could see myself walking for days, sleeping in the ditches. I knew the first man who came along would pick her up, but I doubted that the first woman who came along would pick me up. I turned around and looked at her. Sheena Baby was getting smaller in the distance with each step, and I could see that fine ass she had wobbling. I knew she'd wobble it harder when she heard something coming down the road. She wouldn't even have to stick out her thumb since she already had plenty of other stuff sticking out, and I couldn't see myself doing without her for the rest of my life. I'd finally found the one I wanted, and now she didn't want me. I knew I'd done it to myself, staying up all hours of the night playing *Assorted Golden Hits* and cooking french fries at two a.m., and letting the garbage pile up in the broom closet, not keeping my toenails cut short enough and scratching her legs with them at night in my sleep. It looked like when you first met somebody everything was just hunky-dory, and then you got to know each other. You found out that in spite of all her apparent beauty she had a little nasty-looking wart on her ass or she'd had six toes when she was born and they'd just clipped it off and then you got to wondering about genetics and progeny. You woke up in the morning before she did and leaned over and smelled her breath and said, *Jesus Christ what the hell did you eat?* Stuff like that broke the illusion, and formed opinions were changed when you really got to know somebody, when you lived with her and saw her in the morning and noticed that the backs of her thighs had little ripples of fat on them.

I wanted to run after her, though, because I loved her the way she was and I knew that nobody was perfect, especially not me, but I also knew that when a person found out how bad somebody else wanted them it automatically turned them off and they would begin to put distance between you, since the hunger one person has for another is seldom shared equally between them. It was sad, and it was messed up, but I had to figure a way out, because she was walking back the way we'd come, all the way back to Oxford, looked like, if she had to, and I needed two tubeless tires mounted and inflated pretty fast, or at least patched, and I needed a jack, and a four-way lug wrench, none of which I had. We'd gone out without those amenities, just for a short run to the beer store, and then picked up some Budweiser and things deteriorated from there. Went riding. Said fuck it. Decided to wait until later that evening to cut the grass. The *smallest* laid plans of mice and men.

An argument arose, one that had been brewing, about me talking to some chick a few nights past in a bar, somebody who'd seen some of my work. I'd warned her about that, about how I couldn't avoid that, and for a while she'd seemed to understand. She even suffered their phone calls for a while, various ladies calling at all hours of the day and night.

But then she got to saying, "*Another* call for you," handing me the phone with a tight-lipped smile, pulling up a stool to watch me while I hunkered down over the phone and spoke a soft and inquisitive hello into the mouthpiece, and listening to every word. She wanted the number changed. I didn't. She wanted it unlisted. I protested. People needed to get ahold of me for consultations, estimates, I told her. They need to get ahold of you for other stuff, too, looks like, she said. It got pretty bitter. We started fighting. We'd have to make up before we could make love, and that's always a killer. It got to killing the sensitivity between us, and once you get that eating at you, you're a prime candidate to end up chasing somebody down a road, like I wound up doing that evening.

She kept walking and I started walking after her. I was trying to get close enough to call out to her. I knew it would sound awful, and you know it would if you think about it, but I knew too that she'd probably just ignore it, keep on walking, do me like that.

It kind of reminded me of being at the Memphis Zoological Gardens one time, years before, before puberty hit me. I was walking around with a balloon on a stick in one hand, a cone of cotton candy in the other. I was just wandering, and wandered over near the bear pits, where a large group of people had gathered. They were large bears, I don't know, brown, or maybe grizzly. Something was going on, you could tell. The bears were down in a large pit with rocks and an artificial pool and an artificial cave, living out their artificial lives. People were pointing down into the pit and grinning. I pushed my way up through the crowd to see what was happening. Fathers had children sitting on their necks, holding them by their legs. There were two bears down in the pit, big fuzzy things. One of them was standing and the other one was lying on its back with its front paws up in the air, waving its head around and looking at the people. It looked a little drunk.

I looked at the bears and looked at the people and then looked at the bears again. The bear that was standing put its nose between the hind legs of the bear that was lying on its back and took a long hard sniff. The bear that was lying on its back raised its head and curled its lips out in a long tunnel and said *ROOOOOOOOOOOO!* real loud. The bear that was standing raised its head and shifted its feet and stuck its nose between the other bear's legs again and the bear on its back waved its forepaws when the other bear took a long hard sniff and said *OOOOROOOOOOO! MOOROOOOOOO! GROOOOOOOO!*

The people grinned and pointed and the bear that was standing wiggled its nose and stuck it back between the other bear's legs and took another long hard sniff and the bear on its back closed its eyes and waved its head and said *BROOOOOOOOOOOOOOOOOOOOOOOO!* Then the bear that was lying on its back got up and licked the other bear for a little bit, they both did, then they slowly turned together and went into their cave and out of sight. The crowd kept looking. I did, too. The bears didn't come back out, though. I felt, even way back then, that something strange and mysterious was going on, something we weren't going to be allowed to see. The crowd drifted away after a while, in ones and twos, then threes and fours, until I was the only one left. I kept watching the dark mouth of that cave, but there was nothing to see except the black air inside it, and shadowy forms slowly moving in there. After a while I went away, too, and left them alone.

I suddenly remembered all that, going down the road after Sheena Baby, the way you will. I was afraid for some stranger to pick up Sheena Baby, because I didn't know what he might do or try to do to her. These days, you don't want to be hitching rides with strangers. There's too much that can happen. I didn't want to see anything worse than me befall her. I was bad enough, and I knew it, and I wanted to be better to her, try and rectify things if only I could. But she seemed to be walking faster, and I wasn't getting any closer to her. My legs were hurting, and it was hot, but there was some beer in the car. She'd already passed it but I was getting closer to it. I finally reached it and stopped to take a breather beside it, and saw the cooler in the floorboard and said, Well, hell, as long as I'm here.

We'd conveniently had our two flats under a shade tree, and it wasn't bad under those large reaching limbs. It was almost cool, and the beer was cold, so I helped myself to one and sat down on the side of the road, leaning up against the car. It gave me ample time for reflection. You can figure out just about anything if you get ample time for reflection. You can sit back then and get the big picture. I opened that beer and took a long cold drink of it, then lit a cigarette, and the world didn't seem nearly as bad then. There were some other trees on the side of the road, and it was nice and shady, and there was a little ditch with some frogs sitting in it. It was kind of tranquil. I thought, Well, what if she does leave me? Is it the end of the world? No, it wasn't the end of the world. The world wasn't going to roll off its axis just because somebody had a broken heart. The sun wasn't going to stop rising. I asked myself if it would be painful. Yes, it would be painful. It would hurt for an undetermined number of days or weeks. If I was lucky it wouldn't hurt for the rest of my life, but there was no telling how long it would be until I found another one as good as her. They didn't make them like her every day. I looked up the road. She was gone.

I sat there and drank beer for a while, smoked cigarettes. It wasn't a bad way to while away the time. I didn't know what to do about the car (it was her car). I didn't want to just leave it. I didn't know but what there might be vandals about, unlawful guys who might strip off the wheels and rip off the radio/tape player, make off with the battery. I didn't want to sit around there and watch it all night, though. So I got to looking at the car. Both the flats were on the driver's side. And suddenly the idea came to me, Why don't you just drive it like it is, but *real slow?* It was such a good idea I couldn't figure out why I hadn't thought of it before. I had read somewhere that you could drive on a flat for ten miles if you drove real slow. I knew that even with two flats I could probably drive it faster than Sheena Baby could walk, and that I might eventually catch up with her. So I got in the car and put the beer between my legs. I turned the key and it cranked right up. It was just sitting a little low on my side. I knew it looked a little ridiculous, probably, and I hoped nobody would drive up behind me and start hooting at me.

I turned around slowly in the road, testing the feel of it. It felt a little bumpy. The thought came to me that I might be ruining the tires, but I just got another beer out when that thought hit me.

I tried to see how fast I was going once I got straightened out and headed after Sheena Baby, but I was still in low gear and the speedometer was just bumping up and down between 0 and 5 mph. I figured Sheena Baby was probably walking about 2 or 3 mph. I wondered:

Could I shift into second? I did. The tires went to slapping a little faster. The needle rose to nearly 10 mph. I smiled. I knew I'd overtake her before long. I turned on the radio and tried to find a little music. I put my sunglasses on. I felt like I was making some real progress.

The last time I'd been in Sheena Baby's car there'd been two or three joints in an empty Marlboro pack in the glove box. I flipped it open and the Marlboro pack was still there. I elbowed the wheel and peeked inside the pack and, sure enough, there were still two whole joints in there. I got one out and put the other one back up. Things were getting pretty groovy. It was a Sunday evening and Army Archard was counting down all the top 100 hits of 1967. I lit that joint and bumped down the road drinking my beer and keeping time on the steering wheel, holding the smoke in deep. After a while I was just shaking my head over how good it all was. I listened to Jimi Hendrix and Janis Joplin and Elvis Presley and The Doors and Cream and Grand Funk Railroad and CCR and Percy Sledge, wawa wawa wa. I got to singing out loud and moving my shoulders around and when that joint got short I took little tokes and got all I could out of it. Army was breaking in once in a while, commenting on how fine it all was and talking about how lucky we'd all been to be alive in that era. I agreed with him 100 percent. I wished I'd gone out to San Francisco and worn flowers in my hair. I wished I'd been hip instead of picking cotton. All of a sudden it didn't bother me any more that Sheena Baby was leaving me, and I saw that it had been inevitable. We were two different people. We came from different backgrounds, and our interests were not similar. It was a wonder that we'd stayed together as long as we had. Love took a lot of different forms and sometimes what appeared to be love wasn't really love at all, was just infatuation in disguise. It hurt when that happened, and it messed you up for a while, but sooner or later you got back on your feet and faced the world and saw that love was hard to find and sometimes it took some looking. Love wasn't going to just walk up and slap you in the face. It wasn't going to tackle you around the knees out on the sidewalk. Love wasn't going to leap out of a second story window on top of you.

I rode along there, slightly bumping, the needle wobbling between 7 and 10 mph. The tires went whop whop whop, and the rubber squirmed under the iron rims, and it made the car rock gently. I knew I was going to make it. I knew all this was just a temporary setback.

Army Archard kept playing those great hits from 1967. I kept drinking that beer. There was plenty more in the cooler. I had plenty of cigarettes. I saw a figure walking along the road, growing larger as I got closer, and I beat time with my hand on the steering wheel and slapped the floormat with my tennis shoe. I knew she'd feel funny when I bumped by in her car. It hit me too that I'd go home and sleep alone, that I wouldn't have her arms around me to hold me in the night, not have her arms any more forever.

Her arms, any more, forever:

I slammed on the brakes right beside her. She stopped walking and turned and looked at me. We looked at each other for about a minute. There were a lot of things I could have told her, a lot of promises I could have made and broken later, just anything to get her back in the car. But all I said was, "You want a ride?"

She didn't say anything when she got in. She shut the door and knelt on the seat across from me, with her fine thick legs folded up under her, deeply tanned, muscled as hell, a bodybuilder with fourteen trophies. I was skinny, coughed in the mornings, had a lot of gas most days. Her eyes were close to me, staring into mine, deep blue and beautiful. She came to me. She came to me and she wrapped her arms around me and squeezed me (she could bench two hundred) tight. She mashed her lips down over mine and crushed my mouth tight against hers and pushed me back against the door and I could hear her breathing hard through her nose. She was sucking all the air she could and kissing me as hard as she could. My side of the car was low and she was on top of me, trying to climb up into my lap, pawing at me and hugging me alternately, pushing me hard against the door. The door opened and I fell backwards out into the road and Sheena Baby crawled down from the car on top of me except for my feet, which were still in the car, and she laid down on top of me, kissing me, pushing the back of my head down hard on the asphalt, mashing my ears between her two hands, panting, forgiving all, covering me completely with love, blocking out the sun with it, there beside a flat tire and the rusty underside of the car on the open road where anybody driving by wanting a testament to love could ride by and see it, naked, exposed for the whole world to view.

That was when the cops pulled up, two of them, with hard faces and shiny sunglasses, and I saw with a sick feeling in my heart that our happy ending was about to take a turn for the worse.

The Apprentice

This can't be living. I drink too much Old Milwaukee and wake up in the morning and it tastes like old bread crusts in my mouth. All my underwear's dirty, I can't find my insurance policy.

Here I was thinking we had a good normal marriage. She dirtied up my car and changed the TV channels for me, and I'd bring her Butter Pecan Crunch home from Kroger's. I'd tell her to just leave the dishes until tomorrow, things like that. I didn't even say anything when her dog pissed in my chair. For better and for worse and all that. I even nursed her in sickness once.

Judy wanted to be a writer. Writewritewritewritewrite. That's all she studied. She was always writing something, and always wanting me to read it. Hell, I'd read it. Some of it. I'd tell her it was pretty good if it was. Only most of the time it wasn't. I'd try to be honest. She wrote this story one time about a man whose wife was always speeding and getting tickets. This woman would get three or four tickets a week. She'd come home and tell her husband about the tickets, and he'd raise hell with her. This went on for a while. The tickets were piling up. They owed something like sixteen hundred dollars to City Hall. So finally the guy decided he'd do something about it. He killed his wife. Blew her head off with a shotgun, and then confessed to the whole thing. When the cops found him he was wiping up her blood with the old traffic tickets. Terrific story, right? I told her I didn't think much of it, and she got pissed off. That was the thing of it. If I told her I liked one of her stories, she'd pin me down on the couch with the story in her hand and try to get me to point out every paragraph, every sentence, hell, every word I liked. And if I didn't like it, she'd sulk around the house for three or four days. There just wasn't any pleasing her.

She didn't want to have children yet. There was plenty of time, she said. Wait till I sell my novel, she said. I even took this high-paying job, working inside a nuclear reactor, so she could quit the post office and write full-time. I didn't mind. I didn't even mind having to eat TV dinners by myself sometimes. I mean, if you love somebody, you put up with them. Hell, I told her to go for it, grab all the gusto she could. But even that wasn't enough. When we first got married, we'd go to a movie every Friday night. Then on Saturday night, we'd go out somewhere with some of our friends and listen to a band, have a few drinks, do some dancing and just kick up our heels.

And then she started writing. She wrote a novel first. Blasted straight through, seven months, night and day. I'd be in there on the couch watching old Hopalong Cassidy or somebody and hear that typewriter going like an M-60 machine gun in the bedroom. That's where she writes. I'd stay in there by myself until the movie or Johnny Carson or whatever I was watching went off, and then I'd get up and open the door and ask her if she was ready to go to bed. And most of the time, she'd say she was right in the middle of a scene and had to finish it. She'd give me this sort of pained but patient expression that said clear as glass, Shut the door and leave me alone. What the hell. We had some fights about it. Anybody would. We had some knock-down-drag-outs. I busted a picture that her mother gave us over the goldfish bowl one night, and another time I kicked a hole in the bedroom door after she locked me out.

And that wasn't the worst of it. All our friends started wanting to know why we never went out with them any more. The only thing I could tell them was that she was working on her writing. I hated doing that. You tell people something like that and they look at you like you're crazy. I mean, who sits around writing fiction besides Edgar Rice Burroughs or Stephen King, or in other words, somebody who knows what the hell he's doing? I used to tell her that shit. Especially if she'd just written something I didn't particularly like. Like this one time, she wrote a short story about a woman who was a hunchback. She called it "The Hunchwoman of Cincinnati." *It wasn't worth a shit!* I didn't want to hurt her feelings, but it was boring as hell. And the whole time I was reading it, she was sitting right beside me on the couch, sipping a glass of wine, smoking one cigarette after another. She was looking over my shoulder, trying to see where I was on the page. This damn woman who was a hunchback had a son who was a cripple. The only thing he was good for, apparently, was shoveling out horse stalls. But every night he'd bring his little twopence or whatever home. I think it was supposed to be set back in olden times or something. They were trying to save up enough money for an operation. But she didn't say *who* was going to get the operation, the woman or the kid. That was the big suspense of the whole crappy story. It turned out they had this damn *dog* you didn't even know about until the last page, and the dog had some rare disease that only this veterinarian in Cincinnati could cure, for—you guessed it—the exact same amount this kid made after working for a year shoveling all this horseshit. I damn near puked when I got through reading it.

But I didn't say anything when I finished it, not right away. I got up and went into the kitchen and got a beer. I still had on my radioactive work clothes. She hadn't even given me time to eat my supper. I was trying to think of some nice way to bring her down, but hell, I didn't know what to say. She was sitting on the couch with her legs tucked underneath her, grinning. Sipping that wine, smiling like the cat that ate your sardines.

"Well?" she said. "What did you think of it?"

She leaned forward a little on the couch and held her wineglass between her hands. I told her I didn't know. I told her I thought I ought to read it again to sift out the ambiguities and decide which mode of symbolism the denouement pertained to. I took some English Lit classes in college and that was the only thing that saved my ass that night. It was like old times when we went to bed. She came twice. She said I was the greatest husband and the most understanding human on earth. I felt like a real bastard.

The next morning was Saturday, and I didn't have to go to work. I remember waking up and thinking about a little early morning love, but then I heard the typewriter pecking. I dozed off for a while because I didn't want to be by myself all day. Saturdays she wrote all day. When I got up and went into the kitchen to make coffee, it was already made. There was bacon laid out on a paper towel just as pretty as you please, hash browns and scrambled eggs on the warmer on the stove, and my plate was set with the morning paper folded right beside my cup. She had butter and biscuits and molasses on the table, just like in a restaurant. I really felt like a bastard then.

I didn't know what to do. If I said it was bad, she'd sull up or maybe cry. She cried a lot when I didn't like her stuff. And if I said it was good when it really wasn't, she'd get very encouraged and sit right down and type it up all nice and neat and send it off to *Playboy* or somewhere, and then get all broke down when it came back rejected. I used to hate mail-time on Saturdays, when I was home. About eleven o'clock, if she had a story out, she'd sit down on the couch and open the drapes on the front window, watching for the mailman. She'd sit there with a cup of coffee in her hands. She'd start doing that about three days after she'd sent a story off, I think. I guess she did it every day while it was out. I don't know. But I'm sure she did. She wouldn't even write while she was waiting for the mailman. When she was waiting for the mailman, she wouldn't do anything but look out the window. Every once in a while, she'd get up and go to the front door and open it, and look up the street to see if she could see him coming. And finally, there he'd be. She'd get up and get over to one side of the curtains, and peek out to see what he was pulling out of his bag. If it was just some small stuff, some white envelopes, or circulars from TG&Y or somewhere, she'd rush out as soon as he put the stuff in the box. But if she saw him pull a long brown manila envelope out of his bag, she'd jerk the curtains back together and sit down fast on the couch and put her face in her hands.

She'd say: "It came *back*," like she was talking about a positive test for cancer of the womb. She'd sit right there and shake her head and never lift her face from her hands.

"I don't want to go out and get it," she'd say. "Lonnie, you go out and get it."

So I'd go out and get it. What the hell, it was no big emotional experience to me. Just a piece of mail. That didn't mean I didn't know what it meant to her. I knew it hurt her to have her stuff come back. But *Playboy* is never going to publish something like "The Hunchwoman of Cincinnati." Never. Ever. Not in a million years. I'd bring it in, and she'd be sitting there. She wouldn't look at me. She would have turned on the TV by then. She'd be looking at it like she was really interested in it. We had this routine we'd go through. It was always the same thing.

"You want to open it?" I'd say.

She'd shake her head quickly, violently almost.

"*No!* You open it."

I'd always tear the damned thing opening it, and she'd scream, "Be *careful!* There might he a *note* in it!" She meant like a note from an editor.

Of course there never was. There was never a note from *Playboy* inside the envelope. Big Daddy Hugh had never taken the time to tell her he was dying to see something else she'd written.

"Open it slow," she'd say. "Look in."

I'd open it slow. I'd look in.

"Do you see anything?" she'd say.

I always said the same thing: "Yeah, I see something."

"What?"

"I don't know."

"Is it a note?"

"I don't know."

Then there'd be this small period of silence. She'd lean forward and turn down the volume on the TV. She'd look over at me like we were about to be gassed and only had a few remaining moments between us.

"Look," she'd say.

I'd reach in and pull it out. "The material enclosed has been given careful consideration and is not suitable for use in our publication at this time. Due to the volume of submissions received, we regret that we cannot offer individual criticisms. All submissions should be accompanied by a stamped, self-addressed envelope if their return is desired. Your interest in blah blah blah is most warmly appreciated. The editors."

And then she'd go off on a crying jag. She'd just get up and rush off into the bedroom and throw herself on the bed. So I didn't want another one of those scenes coming up that Saturday morning. She didn't have anything out right then; she'd sent some stuff off to *Redbook,* but they'd rejected all of it. I think she'd already gotten about fourteen rejection slips when she wrote "The Hunchwoman of Cincinnati." I was sitting there eating my breakfast when she came in. I had the story beside my plate. I'd been reading it over again, but it didn't look any better than it had the night before. As far as I could tell, the kid was a nerd, and his mother was a turd, and the only thing the dog did, even on the last page, was lie around and whine and thump "its tail weakly against the hard unforgiving gray cobblestone pavement littered with cruel gray pigeon droppings."

"Well," she said. She was grinning again. "You've slept on it." Yes I had.

"I didn't know you knew so much about literature," she said.

'Ah, I'm a closet fan of Flaubert's."

"Who's he?"

"Gustave. I like Melville, too. You ever read *Moby Dick*?"

"No, but I saw it on the late movie. Gregory Peck and all them. Did that come from a book?"

"Yes, it did, dear. A very great book."

"Well, I didn't know it was a book. What'd you think about my story?"

I knew that if I said I liked it, she'd ball my brains out. She'd shut down the typewriter, lock all the doors and pull the curtains closed, strip naked down on the floor and tell me to climb on.

"It was something else," I said. "Indescribable." She started stripping out of her clothes. "Unbelievable."

She stepped out of her panties. "I can't believe you wrote it."

She got back on the pillows of the couch and put one foot on the coffee table and said, "Come and get it, big boy."

"You're better than Jackie Collins," I said, and went to her.

OKAY, SO IT was a lousy thing to do. But it made her happy, for a while at least. Naturally she typed up a clean copy of "The Hunchwoman of Cincinnati," didn't change a word, and sent it off. I think it set some kind of record for coming back. I came home from the reactor one evening and she was drunk in the living room. She had a bottle of vodka, a pint, and she was halfway through it. She had it mixed up in some grape Kool-Aid, and she was soused. Supper wasn't fixed, and she started getting sick, and I wound up holding her head over the commode for her while she threw up.

All this happened before things got bad.

I REALLY GOT into that first novel she wrote. It was about this grizzly bear in Yellowstone National Park that had lost its fear of humans and was running around eating everybody. The story line was pretty good, even if her dialogue did suck, and she somehow knew how to make all these narrative hooks. For instance, getting one of the characters into a tight squeeze, then cutting to another chapter so that you'd rush along to see what was going to happen. And she invented all these people. That was what amazed me. She just made up all these people out of her mind. I mean people that were nothing like us. It was all about these park rangers who were trying to kill this bear. Most of them had bad marriages, but one of them, this young guy named John, was a newlywed. He was a real upright guy, loved his wife and all that, was dedicated to the Park Service. But his buddy, Jesse, had this wife who looked like Ann-Margret and was always coming on to him. Okay. Then, there was this other ranger named Walker, who'd already been dipping his wick into Jesse's wife, Glenda, and this Walker dude was sort of nuts. But he kept it carefully hidden. He was a big muscled-up mean motherfucker with a temper like a short fuse. John had this other friend, Ben, who knew what was going on between Walker and

Glenda, but he didn't say anything. (You know how that shit goes if one of your friends' wives has ever been messing around on him and you didn't want to tell him. I mean, you're sort of caught in the middle. You can tell your friend, and risk him knocking the shit out of you and calling you a liar, or keep your mouth shut and feel like a bastard for not telling him.) So that's what old Ben was going through. He had a wife, too, but she was almost nonexistent in Judy's novel. All these park rangers were running around trying to kill this man-eating bear, and the bear was killing their dogs and eating campers. They had a bunch of close encounters with the bear, missed some shots and things, and then close to the end of it, old Jesse went one-on-one with this bad Ursus Horribilus, missed his shot, and got killed. Very painfully. That was a heartbreaker. I liked old Jesse. And right after that, old Ben almost went crazy because he hadn't told Jesse that Glenda was messing around on him with Walker. And then he really went crazy. He beat the shit out of this *other* dude named Tommy, who'd been messing around with Glenda a few years before, and they kicked him off the Park Service. And see, that left John and this maniac Walker to kill the bear. I didn't know what was going to happen. I imagined all sorts of bad things happening. What I figured was going to happen was that Walker was going to rape John's wife, and John would come in and catch them in bed at the same time he found the bear going through the garbage in his backyard, and there'd be this big incredible scene of bloodshed and retribution right at the end. But the ending was so disappointing that I don't even want to talk about it.

She built me up for a big letdown. It pissed me off. But I didn't know what to say to her. I mean she came so damn *close* on her first try, and then screwed it up at the end. The ending just left me hanging. But naturally she flew into a big flurry of typing and typed it all up, didn't change a word, and sent it off to Random House. Excellent choice. One of the biggest publishing houses in the world. And guess what? It came back with a *note*. Somebody had scribbled in at the bottom of the rejection slip, *suggest you send this to a paperback house*. She freaked out. She ran around *showing* that damn note to people and calling everybody. And then she sent it off to seven other places and they all rejected it. I think it cost us about forty-seven dollars in stamps. And then she gave up on it.

"Give up on it?" I said. "What the hell for? After you spent all that time on it?"

"It's not any good," she said.

"Well, it's not the worst thing I've ever read. I think you just need to fix up the ending a little, maybe cut it some, work on the dialogue."

She just sat there with her arms crossed and her legs crossed and looked at me. I could tell what she was thinking. There I was, the non-writer, trying to tell the writer how to write.

"I used to think it was good. Now I don't."

"*Why?*"

"It's hard to explain," she said. "The more I write, and the more I read, the more I see how bad I am."

"Well hell. What's the use of keeping on, then?"

"Because. The more I write, the better I'll get."

"When?"

"In a few years."

"Years? How many years?" I wasn't sure how much more radiation my system could stand.

"I don't know. Nobody does. But I'll know it when I get there. Now run along, hon. I'm working on a new story."

"What?" I said, and I couldn't help it. "'Cinderella and the Four Flashers'?"

I didn't look at her face before I slammed the door.

I DIDN'T MEAN to be mean to her, hell. But my sex life was practically nil. Oh, sometimes we'd have a quickie, just before she went to sleep, but most of the time she was just too tired. She worked like a dog, and I started working more overtime just so I wouldn't have to sit around the house by myself. When I got home I'd smoke a joint and watch TV. I'd watch Buck Rogers, anything. I couldn't play the stereo because she said it bothered her.

Sometimes she wouldn't even eat. She'd get up in the morning and have a piece of cheese toast or something, and she'd go until supper without anything else. She started losing weight, and I bitched at her about that. That made her mad, and she'd retreat into her work. One thing caused another, and sometimes the only time we spoke to each other was during arguments.

But she was getting better. There was no denying it. Sometimes in the morning when I was getting ready for work and she was sleeping, I'd read part of what she had written the night before. You could just see the things the characters were doing, and why they did them. But she got to where she didn't like for me to read her stuff, said it wasn't good enough yet, and she'd hide it.

It wasn't just the sex. I mean, I loved going to bed with her, but more than that, I loved *her*. I wanted to *hold* her. Just kiss her. I wanted to spend time with her and talk to her, and I wanted us to be just like other married people we knew. But we weren't like them. We stayed in separate rooms and only slept together. Half the time I'd have to go to bed before her, because I had to get up. She didn't have to get up. All she had to do was write and sleep. And I guess I began to get a little bitter.

I STARTED GOING out at night. She didn't seem to care. She'd be sitting at her typewriter when I left, and most of the time she'd still be sitting there when I came back in. Or if she wasn't, she'd be in the bed asleep. I was hardly ever seeing her. I never saw anybody so obsessed. Her appearance went to shit, and she'd dress in the first thing that came to hand. Sometimes she wouldn't even get dressed, just sit there and work in her nightgown.

And then she started getting published. One story here, another one there. The first acceptance was a great event, and we were happy for a few weeks, and she wanted to throw a big party and invite all our friends. But some of them didn't show up, I guess because so many of them felt that they had been left by the wayside. I understood it. I told Judy that you couldn't keep friends like a can of worms and just open the can whenever you needed them. I said that to her after everybody had left, while we were standing in the kitchen after cleaning up the mess. She smiled a strange little smile, and went behind the closed door, and her clattering machine.

NOWADAYS I DON'T expect too much. She doesn't ask me to read her stuff any more. I get up and go to work, have a few beers with the boys afterwards. I come in and go in there and peck her on the cheek, then find my supper in the microwave and punch the button to start it. I might have a beer or two after supper, or read a little. I love her is the thing. I've tried to stop loving her, I've even tried seeing other women, but it never did feel right, so I quit it.

Sometimes she'll surprise me. She'll have a big candlelit dinner fixed, or step into the shower with me when I'm least expecting it. I don't know where this writing thing came from or what caused it, but it's a part of her now, like her arms or her face. Success for her isn't a matter of if any more. It's just a matter of when.

Once in a while, just for fun, I pull out "The Hunchwoman of Cincinnati" and read it. It's got to be the worse damn thing I've ever read. But I'm sort of beginning to like the dog.

Wild Thing

She came into a bar I was in one night and she took a stool. I noticed the tight jeans, the long brown hair, the pretty red blouse. A woman like her, you have to notice. That's what you're sitting in there for.

I noticed that she looked around to see who was in the bar. There weren't many people in there. It was early yet. So I began to wonder about her. A good-looking woman, alone in the early evening in a sort of redneck bar. I guess she felt me watching her. She turned to look at me, and she smiled for several seconds, and then she leaned over and spoke to the bartender, who soon brought her a beer.

I'd been out of things for a while. I was having trouble with my wife. One of the things that was wrong was that I was spending too many nights away from home, and it was causing fights that were hard for me to win. It's hard to win when you don't have right on your side. It's hard to win when you know that your own fucking up is causing the problem.

Boys from work, some friends I was supposed to meet, they hadn't shown up. I had a table to myself because it was more comfortable than a stool. A basketball game was on, with the sound off, lots of guys jumping around, other people like me watching it. I looked at the bar and tried to see the woman's face in the mirror behind the bottles. She didn't look old. Sometimes at first glance the bodies look young, but the faces, on closer examination, are not. This one didn't look old.

I sat there without watching what was going on on the television screen. I didn't know why I didn't just get up and go home. I could see them all in the living room, sitting in front of the television without me. My wife would be in the bed asleep when I went in, probably, if she wasn't sitting up waiting on me. There were times when I couldn't stand to stay there. Leaving the house like I did made it hard on everybody. I knew the kids asked her where I went and why I went. I didn't know what she told them. I didn't want to think about what she told them. I knew if I kept it up they would stop asking after a while. I knew that would be as bad as anything.

She kept sitting there, looking around a little, smoking a cigarette. After a while she got down off her bar stool and went to the jukebox and dug some change out of her pocket. Her jeans were so tight she had trouble getting the money out, like she'd been melted and poured into them. I watched her. She leaned over the panel of bright lights and set her beer down and held the cigarette between the fingers of her left hand, moving her head a little to what was already playing. And she turned around and looked straight at me and asked me what I liked. I smiled, told her to play E19.

"What's that?" she said, through the music. I picked up my beer and went over to her. That was the start of it.

She smiled when she looked down and saw that it was Rod Stewart and Jeff Beck on "People Get Ready." I stood beside her and pulled some quarters from my own pocket. I could smell the light fragrance of her, and I pointed to some other good ones. She took the quarters I handed her and told me how sweet I was. Her face was happy and animated, and I could feel us making a connection already. All I had to do was be halfway cool, maybe not tell any stupid jokes, ask her about herself, and let her tell me about herself, since self is everybody's favorite subject and they'll think you're a brilliant conversationalist if you get them started talking on that. We played Journey and Guns N' Roses and Randy Travis and Joan Baez and Sam Cooke. Then I told her to come on and sit down with me.

More people came in but I didn't notice them. I kept ahead of her drinking-wise so that I could keep paying, and after three I looked around and saw that the bar was full of people. I didn't tell her that I was married and she didn't ask. She kept talking to me, leaning over toward me, pushing one strand of her long brown hair back to the side. She worked in a factory somewhere in town at a desk and a computer and she had moved here recently, she said. We got closer and closer and she put her hand on my arm. We laughed and drank and listened to the music.

Later I asked her if she wanted to go for a ride and she said yes. I had some beer iced down in the trunk. They got a crazy law in this county. You can't go in a store and buy cold beer; you can only buy it hot. So you have to get a cooler and keep it in the car. You have to always be thinking ahead. We left together, her holding onto my arm, her leg brushing mine, people I knew watching.

She sat close to me in the car, her hands touching me. We left town and went out into the country and rolled the windows down. She dug in her purse and held up a twisted length of grass in a pink paper and I nodded and smiled. After that the music never sounded better. We rode nearly to the end of the county and I stopped on a bridge and got us another beer out of the trunk and she sat in the car while I stood near the rear fender taking a leak. The night was clear, all the stars out, summer on its way. I got back in the car and she was all over me, hands, mouth, I don't know how long it went on right in the middle of the bridge. Finally I pulled away and told her that we had to go someplace else. She asked me if I knew of such a place. I said yes I did.

It wasn't too for from there, up a winding old road with gravel, an old house place with just the chimney sticking up among the stars when we pulled up. I pushed the lights off. Everything was slow and clear because of the grass. When I killed the motor I could hear everything. Bullfrogs sounding in a pond down in the woods. Whippoorwills calling in the trees. The sound of cars somewhere, far off. She came to me and I held her and she put my hands on the places they wanted to be. When I kissed her she went back on the seat and pulled me down on top of her. She was more than eager. She seemed desperate. And I was the same way.

She was tight, so much that it hurt both of us for a while. I even asked her if she was a virgin but she said no. She was smooth and fine and her skin was silky and warm under my hands. Then a car drove up. I saw the lights in the tops of the trees, raised up and saw two headlights coming slowly around a curve. We had to try and find our underwear in the floorboard and our pants and the car kept coming while we jerked things on and then it stopped and just sat there with its lights shining on us. I had one sock on and no shirt. I don't know what she had on.

"I thought you said this place was safe," she said. "I thought it was. Hell. I don't know who this is."

The car sat there. I went ahead and put on my shirt and pants.

"Shit," I said. I cranked the car and turned it around and pulled up beside whoever it was. The car kept sitting there. I couldn't see anybody inside. It was like nobody was driving it. Then we went on past it and out of sight.

She didn't say anything for a while. I stopped a mile or two down the road and got us another beer from the trunk. I handed her one and she took it silently. Owls were hooting out there in the dark beside the road. She opened the beer, lit a cigarette, and just sat drinking and blowing smoke out the window.

Finally she said: "Next time we'll get us a room."

Right, I thought. Next time. Nah. There wouldn't be a next time.

THE LIGHTS WERE off at the house. She'd even cut the car-port light off. Easing in, or trying to, I bumped into things. There wasn't even a lamp on. And then suddenly there was, with her hand on it, and the quick furious anger all over her face.

"Where you been?" she said. "Riding around," I muttered. "You know what time it is?"

I was heading into the bedroom with my shirt already unbuttoned, but I stopped and looked back at her.

"No. What time is it?"

She tapped her foot on the floor and reached for her cigarettes.

"You can't keep on doing me like this," she said.

I was tired and I didn't want to hear it. All I wanted to do was close my eyes and try to sleep a little before the alarm went off.

"Okay," I said. "Okay. Now please let me go to sleep."

I left her in there, smoking, tapping her foot. I went into the dark bedroom, where my baby son was sprawled in sleep in the middle of our bed, and I took my clothes off, lay down beside him, touched his hair and the side of his face. I loved him. I knew what I was doing to him. He never moved. I thought of how horrible my life was and then I closed my eyes. Just before I drifted off to sleep I was vaguely aware of her getting into bed. She didn't speak, and the next thing I knew the alarm was going off.

I DECIDED NOT to go to work that day. I have the kind of job where I don't have to be there every day, and people working for me who can take care of things. I wanted to go fishing. I wanted to be on a boat in a lake with a pole in my hand and crickets or minnows in a bucket or a box and a cooler full of cold beer to help me think over everything I needed to think over.

Later that day I was on the lake, in the boat, a beer in my hand, fishing. I eased up to a stump where I thought a few crappie might be hiding out. I caught a little minnow from the bucket, put the hook through his back, and lowered him down to meet some of his big brothers. It kept going down, never did stop, and I pulled in one that weighed about two pounds. I had another cooler with ice just for fish and I put him in there. It looked like I was going to lay them in the shade. But after another hour, I hadn't caught another fish. I fished up, down, all around, changed minnows, squirted on Mister Fishter, did everything I knew, and still I had just that one fish in my cooler. Finally I let my cork rest and took stock of things.

I was fucking up with these other women. I wasn't spending any time with my kids. My wife and I never spoke to each other hardly unless we were arguing. I couldn't stand to stay home, and I hated myself every time I went out. Now I'd met another one, and she seemed wonderful except for the car pulling up and catching us, which hadn't been her fault. I wasn't catching any fish, and since it was only ten o'clock in the morning, I knew that if I kept drinking beer I was headed for a bad drunk sometime later that day. Possibly even a DUI conviction. For the moment I was safe. I wasn't driving anything but my boat, and they couldn't get me out there, unless it was some gung ho officer of the Mississippi game wardens, and I knew all of them. I knew I'd probably be facing another bad scene when I got home, whenever I got home. I knew I could probably make everything right by going home with a big load of fish and dressing them and cooking a good supper for my whole family, but the problem was I'd only caught one and it didn't look like I was going to catch any more now that I'd started drinking beer. There comes a time some days when you say fuck it, and I didn't know whether to say that that early in the morning or not. I hated to. I'd said it so much in the past and it hadn't ever helped anything. It looked like the whole problem was with me, looked like my wife could just keep rocking on the way she was until she was old and gray and sixty and I couldn't. It seemed like we were raising our children simply for their own benefit and not for ours. But our own lovemaking had brought that. Now it seemed we'd locked into a position that was far beyond our imaginings when we'd married, and there didn't seem to be any recourse. Be born, live, bear children in turn, get old, die. There didn't seem like there ever was anything else. And there didn't seem like there ever was anything else since man had been man, since the first primitive ape-person—was that Adam?—crawled down from the tree and found a female under another tree and hauled her away to a cave, where he ravished her. I was uneasy about a lot of things, my own mortality among them. I didn't know if when I died I was going to die forever, or maybe just for twenty years, and come back as a house cat or something. The whole universe was a secret to me, including what happened over there in Siberia in the 1920s when something hit the ground and knocked all that timber down and set all those woods on fire. I was uneasy about the Bermuda Triangle, and how long I could keep getting up and getting it up, and afraid I'd never find the best woman in the whole world for me to love. I decided I'd better just keep drinking beer and keep my hook in the water and hope for the best.

IT WAS NEARLY dark when I got home. I had three miserable fish, and all the ice I'd had on them had melted. Still, I was determined to cook fish for my family. My wife was just walking into the carport with a basketful of clothes. The kids were playing ball in the yard. Me, I was pretty drunk.

My wife came up to me and tried to kiss me and we messed around some right there in the carport and she got hot, and before I knew it we were back in the bedroom with our clothes partway off, bumping together like two minks. That was when one of my kids shot his head around the side of the window where we'd been in too big a hurry to close the blinds and said, "Hey, Dad! Want to pitch a few balls?"

He slunk away, with many looks back. I got my clothes on and got the hell away from there.

SOME MORE NIGHTS later I was in the bar again and I saw her come in again but I didn't look at her and she did her jukebox routine again without my quarters, but with glances over her shoulder at me several times. I was nursing a beer.

I'd been sitting there thinking about things for a while. I wasn't too keen on going back to work the next morning, and was pretty sure the boys could handle it for a few days without me. I knew she was going to sidle over, and pretty soon she did.

"What you got the blues about?"

"Nothing. Sit down."

"We gonna do it again tonight?"

"I don't know if we will or not."

"I wish we would. It was good the other night till them people drove up."

"I don't know if I want to or not."

"I wish we would."

"I don't know."

"Please."

"Since you put it like that."

We wound up back in the same place. I knew that lightning didn't strike twice, that I couldn't be unlucky two nights in a row. We shucked down, were moving and grooving and saying baby baby baby when the lights came around the curve. I sat up in the seat and reached under it for my pistol, told her I was getting a little tired of this shit. I had just my pants on when I stepped out of the car. I had that little hogleg down beside my leg. Somebody threw a spotlight in my face and told me to freeze, and I heard a couple of shotgun safeties snick off real soft.

"Just hold it, boy. Now turn around. Now drop that gun. Now spread out on the fender there."

I got frisked while she was putting her clothes on and she was fully dressed by the time they decided to shine their lights on her. They weren't pissed that I had the gun, they were just pissed that I'd messed up their dope surveillance, and when they went to looking through her purse I had a few bad moments, but it turned out that she'd wisely hidden her joints inside her panties, and being the Southern gentlemen they were, they weren't about to ask her to disrobe again. They told me they'd appreciate the shit out of it if I'd find someplace else to park because they were working on busting some people right there and they were sure I didn't want to be mixed up in it. I told them Nosir, Budweiser was my only vice. We booked on out of there, and I think it was like 3:47 when I got on in home, after we'd finished with a motel room we'd used for twenty-four minutes.

I GOT ON my forklift the next day and drove it all around the plant. We had to load a bunch of dishwashers and it took all day. I thought I never would get out of there. But finally the day ended and I just had enough time to get to the Little League game, where all the upstanding other fathers were standing around watching their kids swat, and there I sat, mired down in a lawn chair, digging out quarters for Cokes and popcorn, getting depressed when my own small slugger struck out or missed making a catch. It was a hard life, and I didn't know if I was going to be able to keep on living it.

My wife came over and sat down next to me and said: "What you doing?"

"Nothing."

"You want to take the kids out to eat after the game?"

"Not really."

"What you got planned?"

"Nothing."

"You don't enjoy this, do you?"

"Not really."

She looked at me. "You hate being married, don't you?"

"Why do you say that?"

She looked back at the game. "Because. I can tell."

I watched them play for a while. Mothers were yelling. Once in a while a pop fly would sail over the fence. One lad got hit in the eye and started crying and had to be replaced. They gave him a towel with some ice in it, and somebody else held his hand and bought him a snow cone.

"You want a divorce?" she said.

"Not really."

"Well," she said. "I hate you're so unhappy."

Then she got up and left me sitting there.

We happened again about a week later. I'd had two beers and she came in. She didn't even mess around with the jukebox, she just made a beeline for me and got me by the arm.

"Come on over to my house," she said.

I thought, Hell's bells. Thought, Why didn't we do this before?

We rushed on over there, to a darkened apartment, and stumbled in, pulling our clothes off and kissing in the living room. She couldn't wait for the bed, had to get down on the couch. She was moaning, and stuffing a pillow into her mouth, and that's where we were when a vehicle pulled in up front, shining lights in through the picture window, all the way through the curtains. She started making some frantic motions but I thought it was just the heat of passion. Then the lights went off. They don't have adequate parking in those places sometimes anyway, but the car door slammed so hard I thought something about it, and the next thing I knew the front door was opening and the light was on in the living room and there we were, with a big maniac with a lug wrench coming toward the couch. I jumped up and threw a pillow in his face, and he knocked the stuffing out of the couch where my leg had been. She screamed while he was calling me 900 motherfuckers, and I saw he was fixing to kill me. My dick was waving around in front of me just briefly. I didn't mess around with any diplomacy, I picked up a kitchen chair and hit him in the face with it, and the way the blood flew was awful. I called her about 900 different kinds of bitch before I got my clothes on and got out of there, but I did get out of there, hoping like hell he wasn't dead.

I didn't know what to do after that, whether to go fishing or just say no to everything. I wanted to run off. I even figured out how long I could live in another town with the money in my checking account. But he didn't know me, and I didn't know him. Of course he'd seen my face, some of it anyway. He'd be trying his best to hurt me real bad for sure if he could. Somebody busted my face with a kitchen chair, I'd be looking to return the favor.

So I stayed home. Didn't go out and hit any bars. I hung around the house and watched TV, drank coffee on the couch. Helped the kids with their homework. Played Daddy. I came in before her a couple of times and started supper and put clothes in to wash. Mopped the kitchen floor. Dusted the furniture. She got to glowing, and things were great between us in bed. But I wanted that other one again because it was different and it was dangerous now, and so the peace and tranquility only lasted about a week, nine days tops.

THE LAST TIME I saw him, he came in the bar with her. I was sitting at my table in the corner, back to the wall, watching who came in the door. They saw me about the same time I saw them. She was drunk on her ass. They went to the bar but he eyeballed me, wouldn't turn his back on me. Smart move. I saw him checking the exits. He kind of straddled a stool. They ordered drinks and the drinks came and she paid. I was wondering what to hit the son of a bitch with this time. There wasn't anything in there but cue sticks and balls. There was probably a shotgun behind the counter, but I knew I'd never make it to that. There was always the side door, but I didn't think I was quite ready for that. I wanted to see what her act was, what the game she was playing was, what I was gambling with over a small piece of nearly skinny ass.

I got up and put some money in the jukebox and sat back down. *People get ready* . . . And then Jeff Beck cut loose and filled the whole place up with his guitar. The people shooting pool moved to it. The drunks sitting around the bar wished it was them playing it. She swayed on the barstool and looked over her shoulder at me and winked, and his beer slammed down, and he was coming, and I picked up the wooden chair I was sitting in and gave it to him, this time straight across the teeth.

Nobody said a word when I walked out with her, especially not him.

WE FOUND SOME place off in the woods again, not the same place, not her house, not a motel room, just a place off in the woods. Crickets were chirping. Coon dogs or fox dogs somewhere were running. She fed the end of the joint to me and I fed it back to her and, while all that was going on in the face of what all had gone on, I wondered: what was the purpose? But I didn't want to think about things much right then. She laid those lips on me, and we moved down in the seat, and I knew that it wouldn't be but a little bit before those headlights, somebody's, would ease around the curve.

Big Bad Love

My *dog* died. I went out there in the yard and looked at him and there he was, dead as a hammer. Boy, I hated it. I knew I'd have to look around and see about a shovel. But it didn't look like he'd been dead long and there wasn't any hurry, and I was wanting a drink somewhat, so I went on out a little further into the yard to see if my truck would crank and it would, so I left. Thought I'd bury the dog later. Before Mildred got home. Figured I had plenty of time.

Birds were singing, flowers were blooming. It was just wonderful. I hated for my old dog to be dead and miss all that, but I didn't know if dogs cared about stuff like that or not. I didn't have a whole lot of gas in my truck. I didn't figure I needed to get started riding and drinking. I thought I'd just ride over and get something to drink and then ride back, sit on the porch and maybe cut my toenails until Mildred nearly got home, then start burying the dog to occupy myself.

Joe Barlow wasn't home. I sat in front of his house for three minutes and blew the horn, but nobody came out. I left there and went to U.T. Oslin's house. The whole place was boarded up, looked like nobody had lived there for three or four years. Weeds were all up in the yard and stuff. I left there and went by Manley Musgrove's, but I figured he was asleep and didn't want to wake up, so I just spurted on past his house, didn't stop.

I'd had that old dog for a long time, from way past my first marriage. I was sure going to miss him. He had a few little idiosyncratic oddities about him that didn't exactly endear him to some people, like rolling in fresh cattle droppings and then climbing up on somebody's truck seats if they left the door open. Mildred had always been after me to shoot him, but I never had. He was bad about pointing baby possums and then catching them and dragging them up into the yard and then eating them, and Mildred was always so tenderhearted she never could stand to see a thing like that. She just never had seen her cat in action, though, the one she'd let in the house to pet and sleep on the couch, get hairs all over the throw pillows. That thing had a litter of kittens last summer, and I was standing out there in the yard one day while she had them stashed under the corn crib for safekeeping. I'd been out in the vegetable garden cussing and mashing cutworms off my tomatoes. I'd cuss those little fellows and pick them off and mash each one under the heel of my tennis shoe. Those little things were green and they had green guts. That cat went out in the garden for a minute and come back carrying a little baby rabbit in her mouth. It wasn't dead. It was still kicking. What she was doing was training her babies to be killers. She laid that baby rabbit down right in the middle of those baby cats, and they didn't know what to do with it. Of course

the baby rabbit was squealing right pitiful and all and it ran off first
thing. The old mama cat ran out there in the yard after it and caught it
again. Brought it back. Set it back down in the middle of those kittens.
They started trying to bite it and stuff, growling these little bitty baby
growls. That baby rabbit jumped up and ran off again. I stood there
and watched that and thought about cats in general, and about what
that baby rabbit was going through. She caught it and brought it back
again and laid it down in the middle of her litter. They had enough
sense to bite it some then, and it squealed some more and then jumped
up and took off running out across the yard. Only it couldn't run too
good by then. She ran out there and caught it again, brought it back.
They went to gnawing on it again. It jumped up and ran off again. She
brought it back again. It was getting slower each time. I thought, Yeah,
I ought to just go in the house here and get me about four rounds of
Number 6 shot and load up my Light Twelve and clean these sadistic
creatures out from under my corn crib. The only thing was they kept
the rats away and I guess a man has to give up one or two things to get
another thing or two, but I went and got me a hammer handle and put
that baby rabbit out of its misery. I used to raise them a long time ago,
rabbits. I was pretty familiar with the rabbit family. They were so cute
when they were little. Just little balls of fur. They'd hop around there
in the cage, eating lettuce, plus I fed them Purina Rabbit Chow, and
they grew pretty fast on that, and it wouldn't be but about eight weeks
before they'd be ready to kill. They'll dress out about two pounds of
meat at that age. By then your doe's bred again and expecting some
more or maybe even having them by then, and they'll eat you out of
house and home if you don't harden your heart and take eight or ten of
them and a hammer handle out behind the corn crib and knock them
in the head. I had some neighbor kids then. They played with those
rabbits all the time. They'd hold them up beside their cheeks and just

smile and smile and rub that fur with their faces. And here I was out behind the corn crib while the kids were in school, knocking rabbits in the head and dressing them and then telling the kids they got out of the cage and ran away. It finally made me so uneasy and torn in different directions I had to quit it. I gave my doe away and turned the buck loose, I guess the coyotes ate him. I was thinking about all that while I was riding around, looking for a drink. I knew Mildred wouldn't be happy to see that dead dog in the yard. I knew she'd be happy to see it dead, only not in the yard.

I ran up on a Negro fishing by a bridge and stopped and hollered at him and asked him did he have anything to drink. It turned out it was Barthy, or Bartholemew, Pettigrew, a Negro I'd been knowing for most of my life. I had even picked some cotton with him a long time before, in my teenaged years. He didn't want to let on like he had anything to drink, but I knew he did because he always did. He was an old-timey Negro, one that wouldn't give you any sass. Of course I don't think one man ought to have to bow down to another one because of the color of his skin. But I had to get down in the creek with him and squat down talking to him before he'd even let on that he might have *anything* to drink. And what he had wasn't much. Three Old Milwaukees in some cool water that his minnows were swimming around in. We talked about cotton and cows for ten minutes and corn some, then finally I gave him a dollar and got one of his beers. He didn't know where U. T. Oslin was.

By the time I'd gone about a mile I'd finished half of that one. I knew that wasn't going to get it. I had a dog to bury, and I knew it would take more than one half-hot Old Milwaukee. I checked my billfold and I think I had four dollars. I kept driving slower and drinking slower, but the closer I got to the bottom, the hotter it got. I drank the rest of it and chunked the can out the window. I would have loved to've had about a cold six-pack iced down, and about ten dollars worth of gas in my truck. I could have rode and rode and drank then. I decided I might better get back to the house and see if I could find my checkbook.

Mildred wasn't in yet. My old dog hadn't moved any. I poked him a little with my tennis shoe toe. He just sort of moved inside his skin and came back to rest. I estimated the time before Mildred would be home. I judged it to be about forty-five minutes. That was enough time for a shower, piss on burying the dog. I figured I could do it when I come back in. I'd already taken that first drink and I wanted another one. And I told myself it wasn't every day a man's dog up and died.

I run inside and showered and shaved and slapped some shit on my hair. I drove uptown and wrote a twenty-dollar check at Kroger's, picked up a hot sixer and a one twenty-nine bag of ice. I knew Mildred would be perturbed when she saw that I was out loose again. Lord love her, she had trouble keeping me home; her puss was just not that good. And so I would have to strike out occasionally, for parts and places unknown.

There was a nice place on the other side of town that didn't look cross-eyed at country people coming in there just because they didn't have a whole lot of class. The only thing wrong with it was that sometimes the people who came in there had so little class that often they would get to arguing and begin to shoot and cut one another. They wouldn't do it when they were sober, it would just be after they were drinking. I figured it would be a good place to be sitting on a stool right about that time, before they all got to drinking heavy.

I parked my truck under a tree and went inside that establishment and it was dark and cool, like under a corn crib would be. I knew I had that six-pack to drive me all the way home. Mildred was sexually frustrated because of her overlarge organ and it just wore me out trying to apply enough friction to that thing for her to achieve internal orgasm. So, it was titillating for me to sit on a stool and talk to the young waitresses who served drinks and just generally fantasize about their young normal organs and wonder what they would be like, although it was guilty work and unsettling and morally not right.

I ordered a beer, spoke to everybody in general, lit a cigarette. I felt quite at home. I had on a clean shirt and my teeth had been brushed. I saw by my wristwatch that Mildred would be pulling into our driveway in about five more minutes. My beer arrived and I held it up high in the air and, saluting, said, "Here's to Mildred." Several people looked at me funny.

This particular bar had a lot of red velvet in it. It also had numerous mirrors that looked like they had been splattered with gold paint. It was quite classy, particularly for a place that had so many people with so little or no class come into it.

After I drank a little, I went over to the jukebox and put some money in to help pass the time and help take my mind off thoughts of Mildred. They had fourteen Tom T. Hall songs, and I played every one of them. It seemed to put everybody in a good mood. I noticed several people looking at me kindly, as if to say thanks for playing all that Tom T. I knew that, by then, Mildred had seen my dead dog. I didn't want to think about it, and I didn't know what she would think about it. I knew that she would be unhappy with me for not going ahead and burying the dog, and also for being out late drinking and riding. We had been over this thing many times before, and we weren't getting any closer to a solution. I just couldn't do anything with her big Tunnel of Love. I could hit one side at a time, but not both sides. I didn't feel like this was my fault, since I, like many other men or nearly all men, played high school basketball and football and baseball and hockey and have taken many showers with naked boys and know by

casual observance that I am adequately hung. Perhaps even well hung.
I have seen boys whose peters looked like acorns. Mildred would not
have even known one of those boys had it inserted. I would have had
to be the Moby Dick of love to adequately satisfy Mildred. But I had
sworn before God and Church to always cherish her and I supposed
I would always have to. I did not cherish my first, other wife; I threw
her over for Mildred. But it did not keep me from wanting something
a little different from the feeling of sticking my equipment out the
window and having relations with the whole world.

I got back on my stool and drank a little more and thought about
the time Mildred and I discussed corrective surgery for her deformity.
Mildred, I should point out, had the most wonderful ass. That was
the original point of interest that attracted me to her. I have seen men
pant, looking at her in a bathing suit. Mildred was always naturally
hot-sexed. I knew it had to be frustrating for her to be like that. But
she said she would be absolutely mortified to have to undergo an
operation of that nature or even discuss it with a doctor or nurse. So,
sitting there on that stool, I didn't know much other way to turn. I
knew she wasn't going to like that dead dog lying in our front yard. I
thought, Hey, baby, what about your cruel cats?

By the time I'd had my second beer, I'd thought about going home
and hauling the shotgun out and killing every cat on the place. The
last time I had counted them, there were lots of them. Rats and mice
were no longer a problem. I was sure those rodents came up on the
edge of the yard, took one look at all those cats, and said: No way, José.

Often people in bars don't speak to one another, and often this is
what happens to me. I am extremely friendly. I just don't know what
to say to people. I didn't know what to say to Mildred the first time I
met her. I met her in Destin, Florida, and saw that wonderful ass she
had. She did all the talking. I was down there recuperating from my

divorce that was almost pending. I was separated from my first wife, but divorce was not pending. It was just almost pending, and I was trying to recuperate from that and was going home to try and patch things up in a few days. When I saw Mildred, everything went out the window, good intentions, everything, the divorce became pending. Mildred represented herself as a virtuous woman with naturally hot tendencies and told me sincerely that she was technically a virgin, but on our wedding night I quickly formed the erroneous opinion that this was simply not the case. As a matter of fact, I thought on our wedding night that Mildred's puss had simply been worn out from numerous encounters over a period of many years with some enormous number of men, which caused me and Mildred to almost divorce the next day, until she broke down crying at the Continental breakfast and confessed that I was only the first and one-half person to ever penetrate her. I took that as a compliment to mean the other person had only made it in halfway.

By the time I started drinking my third beer I had thought a lot about Mildred's womb and had begun to wonder if by some lucky chance she ever got pregnant would the baby fall out prematurely. I wondered if any of the other men in that bar were facing that particular problem and didn't figure they were. What I figured was it was a unique problem but not quite out of line with the rest of my life. It seemed for some reason or another I had always been given the short end of the stick. I knew that it had nothing to do with my nature or character and was just an unlucky streak of fate, just like when I had fallen off the persimmon tree limb four feet off the ground at my grandmother's house and broken my arm and missed my own birthday party, then got back later with the cast on and there were only crumbs of cake in puddles of ice cream that flies were walking over on the picnic table, with all my little friends gone and all the toys and presents unwrapped and already played with.

By the time I started drinking my fourth beer I did not give much of a damn whether I ever got any more of Mildred's puss or not. I knew that she had been home for quite a good while by then and was probably wondering where I was. I knew that she had probably already fixed supper and had noted my dead dog in the yard and was probably sitting out on the front porch looking for me to come in. I began talking to some young women shooting pool and took up a stick myself and shot about three racks of eight ball with them, losing all three for a dollar. I was merely hustling these young ladies and trying to get a line of trash going. I thought I could lure some of them off with the promise of a cold sixer in my truck later.

By the time I started drinking my fifth beer there were several long-haired tattooed muscled young men who had come into the place and they had scabs on their arms and boots and overalls on. They didn't appear jocular and they looked like they had been out in the sun all day, working very hard. My skin was milk white and I had seven dollars left in my pocket. I knew it was about time for me to get on the road.

I went outside and got in my truck and got out of town quickly. I hated to think about my old dog lying there in the yard, unburied. I thought I might ride around for a while and think about him, and Mildred, but I didn't know what good it would do. I had considered sending off for one of these pump-up penis deals but I thought they might be dangerous or at the least would not work.

Within ten minutes I was away from town and out on a back road that didn't have lawmen patrolling it and I felt free there to open another suds I had iced down earlier. I knew that Mildred would want me in the bed beside her as soon as I got home, and I wasn't looking forward eagerly to that. I felt like all our ministrations to each other were headed to a dead end and that nobody would care fifty years in the future what we had gone through. It left me feeling a little bit depressed and fearful, and I kept drinking, faster.

I rode for quite a while. I saw some cows loose from a pasture and weaved in among them. The locusts had crawled out of the ground after thirteen long years and when I stopped to pee on a bridge I thought my truck was still running because of them. They were beyond any loudness of bugs I had ever heard.

I had put away about eight beers by that time. My blood alcohol content was probably in the .10 range or maybe a little lower or higher. It didn't actually matter. Squeezing her legs together didn't help matters any at all. It was hopeless. I didn't know what to do and I didn't want to go back home. I kept riding, drinking, riding. I thought maybe I might run into somebody. I knew I'd eventually have to bury my dog. I knew she was sitting out on the porch, waiting on me. Watching all the lights coming down the road, wondering if each one was me. I felt sad about it and bad about it. I opened another beer and realized the folly of not stopping by the liquor store while I was in town and purchasing a half pint of peach schnapps to go along with my nice cold beers. I deliberated for several minutes over this dilemma and found it was probably an oversight on my part. I did not want to go home, neither did I want to be indicted by the Mississippi Highway Safety Patrol for Driving Under the Influence of alcohol. I observed that I was driving fairly straight and I had not slurred any words yet to my knowledge. Quite the opposite, in fact, and my eyes were not red and my blood pressure did not feel elevated. I felt that a short run back to town would not have astronomical odds in favor of my being overtaken after a highspeed pursuit. I turned around at a small place on the road and began to retrace my route back to civilization.

I returned to and from town without incident and once more resumed my erratic wanderings over country roads near my home.

The evening hour had begun to wane and it was nearly dark. I knew if I stayed out much longer there would be some dramatic scene with Mildred upon my arrival home, and I wished to postpone that as much as possible. Mildred could never understand my wanderlust and my anxiety over her never-ending overtures of love and affection and requests for sexual gratification, which she constantly and at all hours of the night pressed upon me while I tried to sleep. However, I knew that however late I was, Mildred would probably only raise a token protest in lieu of the fact that I *was* home and could begin once more plunging fruitlessly into the depths of her passion. The only defense available to me was to guzzle quantities of alcoholic beverages that would allow me to arrive home in a state of lethargic consciousness in which a stupor might then be attained.

I did not know what I was going to do with Mildred or how I was ever going to be able to come to a life of harmonious tranquility where matrimonial happiness was a constant joy. The only good thing about it was it gave me a subject of regular worry that I was able to slide endlessly back and forth in my mind during my various ruminations and ramblings over blacktopped back roads. We were not social people and were never invited to parties, nor did we give parties where we invited people to them. We basically lived alone with each other on ten acres of land that was badly eroded in a house of poor quality. I was not drunk but I did not feel sober. The needle on my gas gauge was pointing toward E and had been pointing that way for quite a while. There did not seem to be anything else to do but return home and face the prospect of burying my dog/dealing with my wife. I could see her face just as well and her small ears, and I could see kissing her nose and her chin and her cheeks and the small hollow place inside her soft little elbow, and I felt like disaster was on the way, since it felt like one of those evenings that I'd already had too many of. I wanted to do all I could for her, but it didn't seem like I could do anything for her at all.

Upon entering my yard, I saw there were no lights on at my house and my dog was lying just as I had left him. Mildred's car was not in the carport, which was a most unusual sight. I was not extremely steady entering my house but stumbled around only a bit before I found the light switch and turned it on. There on the coffee table, held down by an empty beer bottle, was a note that was addressed to me. It said:

> Dear Leroy,
> I have met another man and I have gone away with him. He has the equipment to take care of my problem and we have already "roadtested" it, so to speak. Forgive me, my darling, but he is the one man I have been searching for all my adult life. I have taken the cats but of our house and property I want nothing. My attorney will be in contact with you but as for me I must bid you adieu and wish for you that you will some day find your own happiness.
>
> XXX,
> Mildred

It took a while for the words to sink in, for the reality of what I was reading to hit me. Mildred was gone, apparently, with another man with a huge penis. The reality sobered me up some, so I went out to my truck and got another beer and walked back over to my dog. He was still there, still dead, only by then he had begun to stiffen a little as rigor mortis set in. I knew I needed to get a shovel and bury him but I decided it could wait until morning. I looked at my house and I could feel the emptiness of it already. I went up on the porch and sat down. I could imagine Mildred in a hotel room somewhere with the man she had taken, and I could imagine them moving together and Mildred's happiness and total fulfillment and joy with her newfound sexual gratification. I hated that I had never been able to give her what she wanted. I knew that I would just have to try and find another wife. I didn't know where to start looking, but I decided that I would start first thing in the morning, as soon as the dog had been given a suitable burial. There were plenty of women out there, and I knew that somewhere there was one that was right for me. I hoped when I found her, I would know it. I felt like one part of my life was over but that another, just as important part, was beginning. I felt a lot of optimism, and I knew I could get another dog. But I was already beginning to feel a little lonesome, and I could feel it surrounding the house, closing in. I tried not to think about it, but I sat out there on the porch for a long time that night, doing just that. I looked around for the cats, but it was true, she had taken every last one, looked like. It would have been nice to have had maybe just one, a small one, to sit and pet and listen to it purr. I knew they could be cruel and vicious, but I knew they needed love also just like everyone else. I thought about Mildred in that other man's arms, and how fine she looked in a bathing suit. Right about then I started missing her, and the loneliness I have been speaking of really started to set in.

Gold Nuggets

It was a bar somewhere between Orange Grove and Pascagoula, one of those places where they charge you nothing to get in and then five dollars for a ten-ounce Schlitz. It was dark. Everybody had on sunglasses but me. My friend had gone off and I didn't know what had happened to him. I knew what I was, though, and I was trying to learn to live with it. I thought if I could just make it through the night, that everything would be sort of okay when the sun came up.

This place sold nude dancing. Just Ts, no As. I said, Well, bring on the dancing girls. I knew I was suffering from alcohol poisoning, and that it had settled in my brain. I could drink one beer and I'd start thinking differently, about everything. This little girl who had not even graduated from high school pranced out on the stage waving a scarf around her head and stumbling in her high heels. Her poor little titties were about a 32A.

And then like sharks two women glided in on each side of me. The one on the left had dark hair in her armpits. Tremendous titties. I checked them out and drank half of my ten ounces, then eyed the right flank. Blonde, maybe pregnant. Already stroking the inside of my thigh.

Oooooooh. Ooo and ooo and ooo. She scratched the head of it like a mosquito bite. She turned her head and yawned and came back beaming. They had nude paintings on the walls, sort of a celebration of sex, which I certainly had nothing against if I could just celebrate a little of it myself.

The little chickadee up on the stage was bent over in my face, revealing all her secrets, but I figured this kid already had two kids of her own at home and a babysitter waiting for her to show up. It made me feel slightly perverted.

"Why don't you buy me a drank?" the one on the left said.

"I'd love to have a drank."

I fumbled around for my money. She helped me peel off three ones and raised her hand. They hadn't even set it on the table when the other one leaned over and said she wanted one, too. So I bought her one. And told her to bring me another beer. I didn't care. I wanted to wake up broke and sober. I figured if I couldn't buy a drink, I couldn't get a drink. We jawed some old shit, it didn't matter what we said. We all knew the score. Their job was to rob me, my job was to pay for the robbery. All night long if possible.

I picked up the blonde's drink and tasted it when she wasn't looking. Grape Kool-Aid. Well, I thought, I don't have to put up with this shit. She got up and took her drink with her and, I don't know, poured it out or something, then came back all friendly wanting another one.

I'd gotten surly and terse. I was feeling mean. I'd had about all their shit I wanted to take. I figured there were some big dark mean motherfuckers waiting back in the shadows to break my head and roll me when I went to the bathroom. The little beaverette up on the stage had gotten down on her hands, legs spread, pumping that thing up and down. And I just shook my head.

Blonde, she leaned over, sort of stroked my neck. "You gonna buy me another drank?" she said. "Buy your own damn drink."

She looked offended. "Well, honey, if you don't buy me another one I'll have to get up and go."

I told her not to let the door hit her in the ass. Of course she got all huffy and left. Then I turned on the other one.

"And you," I said. "You can just get your ass up and go, too. Fucking grape Kool-Aid. You want me to tell you what you can do with your grape Kool-Aid?"

She didn't say anything. She just looked away, and immediately I felt like an asshole. Sometimes I feel like an asshole about ten times a day. But I didn't want to be hustled. There I was, all the way off down on the coast, didn't know how I was going to get back, my friend had gone, and I had less than I'd started out with. Shrimp money. People depending on me, already buying their crab boil and their cocktail sauce. So there was only so much leeway I had. Maybe I could haggle the guy at the boat down, maybe I couldn't. If I spent their money and then couldn't haggle, I was up Shit Creek. But at that point I wouldn't have minded legging down.

In dark places you can't see much. But on the side of this girl's face sitting next to me I saw something shining down her cheek. And I thought, Well, you asshole, you messed up again.

"Shit," I said. "I'm sorry."

She looked around and tried to smile. "It's okay," she said. "I didn't mean to be rude to you," I said.

"It's okay."

But it wasn't okay. I knew it wasn't okay and she knew it wasn't okay. Here she hadn't done anything but ask for a three-dollar drink of Kool-Aid and I'd tried to run her off.

"Let me buy you a beer," I told her.

"I can't drink a beer."

"What? You don't like beer? You got some medical problem?"

"Oh no. I like beer fine. I'd love a beer."

"Well, hell," I said. "Then drink one."

She got sort of close to me then. She leaned over to my ear, so I could look right down that Big Valley.

"They don't 'low it," she said.

"Don't 'low what?"

She jerked her head. "You know."

I looked in that direction. Then I saw the mean-ass momma watching us. Black chick, about thirty, medium fro, teeth probably filed to tiny points. Definitely not a vegetarian.

"Listen," I said. "If I want to buy you a beer, can't I buy you a beer?"

"Well, I don't know," she said. "They don't like for us to drink."

She smelled sort of bad. I was crazy and I knew it. Maybe her husband—if she had one—she probably did—was a shrimper and she shrimped with him in the daytime. Maybe she'd been down in the hot hold all day long shoveling up shrimp with a shovel. I didn't care about any of that. She was a human being. She had the right to drink a beer. Even a drunk knows that.

"Just wait a minute," I said. I got up from the table and staggered over to the momma. A hard chick. You could tell it from her eyes. No telling what she'd seen or done in her life. I wouldn't have wanted to fistfight her. She could have been pretty and might have been at one time. No more, though. All she was after was money. Money to get the hell away from that dive she'd found herself in.

"Listen," I said. "I want to buy this girl over here a beer. Do you care?"

She turned a cold pair of eyes on me. Eyes that cut me to my soul. They went up and down me, and stopped on my face. How many had she seen like me? I'd never seen such contempt.

"We don't 'low it," she said, nearly whispering. But then she leaned over. "But you can buy *me* a drink if you want to, sugar."

She didn't look bad. She had some huge ones. All I had was shrimp money. I could see the sunshine coming down on my head the next morning while I was trying to find the *Elvira Mulla* or the *Vulla Elmirea* or the *Meara Vulmira* or the *WhatEverltWas*. There had just been whispered, hurried conversations over the phone, and I didn't even like the people involved. What if the nets had holes in them or the shrimp weren't sleeping?

Well, this chick wasn't bad. She was hard. But I could see that she could be soft. Money softened her. She'd smelled money on me and right away she'd softened. Maybe she'd take me home. I didn't know. But I was so damn lonely, and horny, that I was willing to take a chance on almost anything. Plus, I was drunk.

For a minute there I sort of got the big picture. You back off from anything and get the big picture, you can figure out almost anything if you figure on it long enough. I looked at myself and I thought: Now listen, you got all this money belongs to all these people and you're supposed to take care of it. Now what the hell's gonna happen if you show up without the money or the shrimp either one? What if you just blow all the money, and don't buy the shrimp, and go back home to all those people who've already bought their crab boil and crackers and cocktail sauce? Well, you're gonna have some people pissed at you, that's what.

But, now, think about them. Think about Ed, that son of a bitch, think about him in the first place. Did that son of a bitch ask you if you wanted some shrimp last year when he went off to Pensacola and went deep-sea fishing and didn't catch shit? When he puked in a bar that Milos López once actually got thrown out of? Did that s.o.b. ask you if you wanted him to bring you some shrimp? Hell naw. Fuck *him*.

And who's the other one? Ted. That fucking Ted. That bastard. You ought to whip his ass just on general principle. Son of a bitch. Did he ever invite you over to his private bass lake when they were jerking those ten-pound lunkers out of there? Hell naw. The son of a bitch even called the law on some kids.

Now I had to consider all that stuff. I couldn't deal very well with it. She was smiling in my face and I had all that money in my pocket and I wasn't too fond of these fuckers who'd sent me down there to the Gulf to get all their shrimp for them. And all I was trying to do originally was buy a beer for a girl who shook her ass naked in a dark bar where dark people like me stalked their lusts.

"She can't drink a beer," this chick said.

"Why?" I said. "Listen, goddamnit, I'm getting pissed off at the way y'all treat these girls. What? Y'all own em?"

"Yeah, that's right," she said. "We own em. They dumb enough to come in here and work, we own em. Buy em and sell em if we get ready to."

She gave me a look so hard I said: "Wait a minute. You ain't that hard, are you? You ain't that bad, are you? Why don't you let her have a beer? What's it going to hurt?"

"It's against the rules."

"What rules?" I said. "Who makes up the rules?" I leaned over close to her and said softly: "Have you ever questioned the rules?"

"You so hot to take somebody out, why don't you take me out?" she said.

What? And maybe get my throat cut? (An anecdote to testify to this madness: The night before, I got pissed off at my friend because he was drunk and I wasn't and I was ready to go and he wasn't, I begged him five or six times too but he wouldn't hear it, he was jumping hot with this beavette, so I split. Right down the beach to our hotel room. I thought it was only a block and it was like four miles. I had to sit down and rest a few times, and I found out something. At night, that tide goes out. There's no water there. And you wouldn't believe the nasty shit that's lying down there. I mean, dead rotten fish, and Coke cups and stuff, and it doesn't look at all nice with that moonlight pouring down over that slimy sand. And I found out later that it had only been a week before when some guy got his throat cut down there, from ear to ear, on the beach, at night, late like that, probably in the same exact spot I was sitting in. Boy.) But boy I'd wanted me some of this for quite a while, just like every other white man. I almost did a double-flip hotswoon.

"Come on, baby," she said. "Take a little ride wit me."

I followed her out the door, the back door, where black guys were muttering in the dark and I couldn't tell if they were shucking oysters or not. She had it parked behind the Dumpster, where the lights didn't shine. When we walked up to that machine, it did. Brand new Henweigh, red, magnesiums on all four sides; she had the Alpine Stereo System. I was almost scared to get in the car with her. But I did.

"I got some cold cognac if you'd like some, baby," she said, when she had the little jewel purring like a kitten at its mama's titty. She sort of ran her hands up her legs and pulled the dress back.

"Hold on," she said, and I turned the cognac straight up. Brought it down immediately, wheezing and gasping and coughing, damn near choking to death. She rammed it out of the parking lot and hit second and squealed viciously on the corners until she hit a straightaway and we must have been doing seventy by then and she downshifted and braked sharply and whipped it around a curve and out onto the street, and then two streets over she pulled in behind a bread truck, and four big black guys jumped out with knives and guns and robbed my terrified ass while she hung out the window on her elbow laughing herself silly, the pee running down her leg, maybe, I guess, saying, Hoo boy, you white boys something else.

WELL, IT SCARED the shit out of me, naturally. I felt weak all over for about twelve minutes. But then I got to thinking about it and said to myself, Well, it's gone now, wasn't anything you could do, you still got your hotel room, you can charge some beer on your MasterCard and haul ass in the morning before they check. That and plus I had five one hundred dollar bills folded into a minute thing in the heel of my right sock. I'd just tell my groovy employers that they'd stripped me naked, even looked up my ass. Real killers. So I started walking back up the beach. I'd sobered up a little, what with the robbery and all. I didn't know how I'd get back into North Mississippi and my beloved pine trees. They'd specifically stated that they wanted headless shrimp. Like Captain Mike McDonald and his crew were going to sit back and shuck the fuckers. But that was just the kind of rich ignorance I was dealing with. I wanted to go out on the boat with them. I wanted to pull the nets. I wanted to see what came up from the ocean depths, what unspeakable stuff spilled out when they hoisted it up onto the deck.

But the Gold Nugget beckoned. I could see it from the beach, from the dark water, from the sucking tide sucking further south with each suck. I had to sit down to get out my money. It was good money.

A whole new shift had come on. I settled at a table, my hands trembling just a little. I knew the sister was going to come back a little later, and I didn't know what to do about it. My ass was in a crack. I tried to figure out how much they had taken off me. It was somewhere around three hundred dollars. I had two hundred dollars' worth of coolers in my pickup.

The women were still dancing, except that the junior high shift had come on. I was really starting to feel like a degenerate, and sick with what it all finally came down to. Getting robbed is kind of like getting your ass whipped, in that somebody else has beaten you. It doesn't matter that he's got a gun or a knife, you could have had a gun or a knife too and fought for your money. I decided to go armed from then on, just as soon as I could afford a gun or a knife.

I was wobbling at my table a little. I knew people could probably see it. I hated that, sort of, didn't want to be drunk in public, but didn't know what to do about it right then. There wasn't anything would fix it but another drink. I summoned somebody and somebody brought one. I was getting eyes from the bar again.

I didn't want to mess with any more of those girls. I'd already seen the fine ones, up in Memphis, where they let them go naked in front of you and then expect you to behave yourself. I knew in some men that kind of stuff caused rapes, which is why it was dangerous to offer that kind of stuff to the general public, since a lot of times the general public had a hard dick and little conscience. I decided to just sit there and nurse my beer, lick my wounds, and see if the chick walked back in.

There were guys groping chicks in the corners. I didn't know what the hour of night was. Late was all I knew. My friend wasn't anywhere around. He knew the name of the boat and I didn't. He knew the dock they docked at. But he'd probably already had his throat cut and was being eaten by fish, or the dogs and cats at the seafood plants. It didn't make me just real happy or at ease sitting there waiting for him. Maybe he'd given up on ever finding me and had just gone back home. That'd be real hucky ducky if that was the case. If he'd taken my pickup that'd be real uncool and I'd have to catch the big Hound going north emptyhanded. Rich fuckers like they were, they could get things done. They might even hire my legs broken. I knew they knew plenty of people they could sub it out to.

I ordered another beer. Some waitress brought it and I gave her some money. She popped her gum and gave me my change. I lit a smoke. Just then I noticed a guy sitting near me, almost at my elbow. He looked sort of hungry. I glanced at him, and then I didn't pay any more attention to him. All I wanted to do was just drink until something happened. I knew if I drank long enough, it would.

I got a little philosophical sitting there, surrounded by all that sin, feeling so mired down in it. I hadn't been raised to go into places like that. And there I was in one. I didn't know where the sun might find me. I just hoped it wasn't a place as dark as that one.

That guy leaned over and groped my leg. I sighed.

I'd had to deal with a thing like that once before. It had been a long time ago and I'd nearly forgotten it. A sailor had bought me a drink and then touched me in an unwelcome way in a bar. I thanked the sailor for the drink and told him to get his hand off my leg. He removed it and said he didn't mean anything by it. Then he told me about his wife and family and friends for twenty minutes. Then he bought me another drink. Then he put his hand on me in an unwelcome way again. I

remember sighing inwardly. I leaned over to the bartender and told him
I hated to get thrown out of the bar, but if that guy put his hand on
me again in an unwelcome way again I was going to have to knock the
shit out of him. Then I told the sailor exactly the same words. It made
him hot, and words were said, and I wound up choking him. It hadn't
been nice, and I knew this thing probably wasn't going to be nice either.

I turned around and looked at this guy. He had a cap shoved back
on his head, and some missing teeth, and a black eye. His hand on my
leg felt like a granite claw. I looked into his eyes. They were tinged with
yellow and red, and they looked a little wobbly.

He was a real big guy.

I sat there and held my beer, wondering what to do. For all I knew
he could have been a henchman, one of hers. I knew to operate like
she did she had to have henchmen.

I finally told him he wouldn't believe how much I'd appreciate the
shit out of it if he'd get his hand off my leg.

I thought Yeah, their goddamn shrimp. Their damn shrimpy
minds. Why do you want to put yourself in the employ of people like
that? Who have no interest in you other than what you can do for
them? I was really getting sleepy and I yawned several times. It didn't
look like my friend was going to show up and I knew somebody had
to go down to the dock the next morning and try to find that boat.
And not just any boat. *That* boat, where they were selling them for
$1.35 a pound medium jumbo, cutting out the middleman and pass-
ing the savings on to the consumer. I decided I'd be best off booking
for the local hotel, so that's what I did, like a fat man's ass.

I was hot as hell in the parking lot the next morning.
Some firemen were having a convention in the Holiday Inn, and they
had ladder trucks set up in the parking lot, and they were giving rides

to the general public. Since I was general public, I got on one. I had the fear of maybe getting up there and puking down on somebody a hundred feet below. But it was really impressive up there above the roof of the Holiday Inn. For one thing, you could see all those shrimp boats out there in the water running their nets. The sun was shining, but the sky looked smoky. It looked like they were just dredging ton after ton of little shrimps up. It made me feel a whole lot better, looking out over all that industry. I sort of got the big picture sitting up there and realized how small and unimportant my quest was, in light of the tons of available seafood already destined for restaurants all over the South. I decided to just find a shrimp boat docked with a fresh load, jew them down as much as I could, load up and haul ass.

I had a little difficulty manipulating in the traffic. There were two lanes going seventy miles per hour and the white sand beaches were loaded with women in bikinis. I wondered if any of the little beaverettes from the Gold Nugget were out there sunning but then realized they were probably in American History class reading about Benjamin Franklin. I wondered what he would have thought about all that shit, women running around nearly naked and all. I passed the Gold Nugget, which was on the ocean side of the road. It looked deserted, empty, boarded up. It was only eleven a.m., though. I started to pull in and then I said Naaaaaaa. I went on down the road until I got to the harbor, where gulls were flying, and masts were sticking up everywhere. I parked as close as I could and got out. The sun was burning down, and the beer started running out of me. I didn't know how many I'd had the night before. It must have been some kind of ungodly amount, judging from the stuff that was pouring out of me. I couldn't hardly see for the sweat in my eyes.

I started walking down the dock, checking everything out. I didn't know which section I was in. I knew I had to get to the right section, but I didn't know if I was in it or not. There were some neat sport fishermen lined up smartly along the dock with names like *Judy* and *Becca* and *Mama's Dinghy*. I kept walking and looking.

I was wanting a cold beer. I could feel the weight of all that expectation on me. I knew something bad must have happened to my friend, and I didn't feel real good about it. I didn't know how I'd be able to explain it to his wife and all. It had all started out so innocently anyway. We were just going to go down there and goof off a few days, make a shrimp run. Be back at work on Monday. There it was Monday and I didn't have shit to show for it. I knew they'd can me. The job I had wasn't worth a damn anyway, just putting washers in little holes. It wasn't anything that made me feel real fulfilled.

I was lost, and people could tell it. There were people with caps on, and old women weighing plastic baskets of shrimp, and other people with tanned skins and sunglasses watching me stumble around on the dock. Millionaires, probably, some of them, up from Orlando or Jacksonville or Destin, just taking a week off. I kept walking, and was grateful for my own shades. If the eyes were the mirror to the soul, I didn't want anybody to see inside mine. I kept walking. I knew all this was just a temporary setback. It didn't mean that I couldn't ever be saved from my life, or that I'd never find the boat I was looking for. Somewhere, somewhere there, was a connection I could make, and I knew that all I had to do was stay out there until I found it.

I staggered on down the dock, looking, sweating, among browned women in the sun, diamonds glinting, doing all I could at the time, knowing the sun would always go down, and another night would come, that our forms of salvation were ours to choose, as blessed to the misguided like me as any church.

Waiting for the Ladies

My wife came home crying from the Dumpsters, said there was some pervert over there jerked down his pants and showed her his schlong. I asked her how long this particular pecker was—I was drinking beer, not taking it half seriously—and she said it sort of resembled a half-grown snail, or slug, she said, a little hairy. It was so *disgusting*, she said, and gave off this little shiver, doing her shoulders the way she does.

Well, a sudden unreasonable anger suddenly came over me, and I slammed my beer down. I'd already slammed several down. I said by God I'd go take care of the son of a bitch. I said, If it ain't safe for women and kids to walk the roads, what'll you think'll happen when lawlessness takes over, and crime sets in, and the sick and the sexually deviated can sling their penises out in front of what might be some little kid the next time? She was just too tore up to talk about it any more. Had to go lay down and hold one forearm over her eyes. That sort of made me mad. This unknown guy getting his own personal tiny rocks off had messed up my own sexual gratification, and besides that, by God, it just wasn't right. Here I was a working man, or had been, and come to find out it ain't even safe to lay over here in your own bed and let your wife take the garbage off.

I didn't figure I'd need no gun or anything, but I did take my beer. I figured since he'd already dropped his drawers he'd be done hit the bushes, and I thought I could ride around some and listen to country music songs about drinking and cheating and losing love and finding it, since it looked like I wasn't going to be pumping any red-hot baby batter into my own favorite womb any time soon.

Riding over there, I thought about the injustice of how a few people could fuck up everything. I'd heard about these people sucking toes and stuff. I didn't want it around me. I even devised a plan. I left out a few details early on there but my wife had gone on to say that she'd seen this guy sitting there in his pickup before, when she'd been going down the road to some other place, just sitting there, not dumping any garbage or anything. Waiting on his next victim, I supposed, some innocent person he could terrorize. I said well I'd just start keeping my shotgun in my truck and ride over that way about every day, and the next time I saw that pickup (she said it was a blue Ford) I'd just stop and haul it out and peck up his paintjob a little bit until he decided to get his ass back to wherever he came from in the first place.

I got over there and of course there was nothing there. Just a bunch of trash and garbage on the ground right in front of the Dumpsters, and treetops people had dropped off, and wet magazines on the ground, and a little thin sad puppy scared of me somebody'd dropped off, so hungry he couldn't decide whether to stay or run. A son of a bitch who'll drop his pants in front of some woman he's not familiar with is the same kind of son of a bitch'll drop off a puppy like that, thinking somebody'll give him a good home. Good home, my ass. Some of these Vietnamese around here'll eat him.

I didn't know how far this perversion thing had spread, how much word of it had got around. I didn't want to sit there in my pickup thinking people driving by had already heard of the pervert and might think I was him. I tried to call up that puppy. I got down on my heels and clicked and whistled and snapped my fingers and talked nice to him, hut all he'd do was roll over with his legs up in the air and his tail between his legs, peeing on himself in little spurts. Somebody had ruined him, beat him, stomped him, him roughly the age of an eighteen-month-old baby, in dog years. I knew some Humaner would come by and capture him and take him to the pound. I should have gone on and killed him. How would the gas be any better than a knock in the head to him? That might've been Napoleon Bonaparte reincarnated running around there, sniffing coffee grounds.

I took off down the road there and rode around a while. What would have to be wrong with a guy to make him flang his thang out in front of women? It had to be some kind of guy who couldn't get any pussy, was too messed up in some way to get some from anybody, even for money, wanted some bad, and had developed this overpowering urge to gratificate himself, ergo, like the mirror is to the image, himself twinned in their eyes, what he imagined to be his big penis, his brutal, killing penis, swinging like a nine-pound hammer, suspended out there for all womanhood to draw back and gasp from, which, in his opinion, was what was happening.

I felt sort of bad for the guy. I didn't know if I needed to go talk to Daddy about it or not. I figured the guy was holloweyed, sat in a dark room with his mother watching TV all day long, eating popcorn, and waited for late evening before he started stalking his lusts. I was beginning to get a pretty good mental picture of him already. He was about fifty, with wattley skin around his neck, shaky hands, maybe a dirty cap pulled down low over his eyes and white stubbly whiskers on his jaws, weak chin, bad shoes, one of those belts about ten inches too long for him with the excess hanging loose. Yeah, he was starting to form up in my mind. He was a wimpy sumbitch from back yonder. His had not been an easy life, and he might not have all his mental faculties. He might stand in line at the welfare office every Wednesday, holding his mother's hand, and she might have cared for him like this since he was a baby. She might've had bad love, or love run off, or he might've been in the womb too long. They had some little awful house way back up in the woods around London Hill or somewhere, with tin cans out in the yard and mud on the porch, and bleak was a word they didn't understand, since that was the world as they knew it. She didn't know why he took off like that in the evenings sometimes, and she'd never recognized that he might have secret needs he was too scared to tell anybody about, or maybe she didn't even think about stuff like that.

I made one long slow circle through Potlockney and DeLay and came back up through the Crocker Woods, cut through to Paris and back through the Webb Graveyard Road, but I didn't see a blue Ford pickup parked anywhere. I knew he was back home by then, sitting on the floor in a dark room right in front of the television, his eyes blank, his hand cramming popcorn in his mouth, the lights of the "Bill Cosby Show" flickering across his face, his mother asleep on the couch behind him, unaware of the twisted needs in him, a mindless drooling idiot, someone without enough sense to turn the television off, chewing, thinking about my wife, where to try it tomorrow, a motherfucker you could crush.

LATER ON THAT night I wound up at Daddy's, drunk, as usual, when I went over there, him laying up there all by himself waiting for me, patient, never looking when you walked in like he was even expecting company. We never argued any. I always told him something or asked him something and he gave me some advice and I took it. It wasn't any different this time.

He turned his old flat gray eyes over to me real slow, his eyes as gray as his flattop, smoking one Camel after another on that old Army cot twenty years after the doctors told him lung cancer had killed him, a glass of whiskey nearby, Humphrey Bogart on the TV. *The Caine Mutiny*. One of his favorites. Laying there in his long underwear without a shave in a week, indomitable, old boxer, warrior, lover, father.

I told him somebody'd showed his dick to my wife.

He wanted to know how big a dick it was.

I told him she said it was just a small one. He paused. We watched Humphrey measure out some sand with a spoon. I felt almost out of control.

Then he looked back around to me, swung his old flat gray eyes up there on my face and said, Son, a little dick's sorta like a Volkswagen. It's all right around the house but you don't want to get out on the road with it. I didn't know what to say. He told me to bring him some whiskey sometime. I left soon after.

I'D QUIT MY job after sixteen years and drawn that state retirement money out, way over ten thousand dollars. Back in those days I thought that money would last forever. I was just laying around the house drinking beer, poking Dorothea soon as she walked in the door. I did the same thing the guy at the Dumpsters did, only behind closed doors. I had a woman who looked good, who liked to wear a garter belt and black stockings and keep the light on.

But that insult to her wore on me. I'd get in the truck to ride around and I'd get to thinking about it. I'd get to thinking about the humiliation she felt when that guy did that. I even called the sheriff's department one day and reported it, and talked to a deputy about it. They knew who it was, and I like to fell over. They knew his name. They told me his name. I said Well, if this sick son of a bitch is running around out here jerking his pants down in front of people, why in the hell don't y'all do something about it? They said he was harmless, that he'd already been arrested six times for doing it, twice in front of Kroger's uptown when ladies tried to load up their groceries. I said, You think a son of a bitch like that is harmless? They said, Believe me, he's harmless. They said, Believe me, there's a lot worse than that going on that you don't know nothing about. They said, If you did know what all was going on, you wouldn't sleep at night.

That made me uneasy and I decided to get in my truck and ride around some more. That retirement money was stacked up inside that bank account drawing 6.5 percent interest. I had beer and cigarettes unlimited. Dorothea had gotten that promotion and her boss liked her, took her out to lunch so she wouldn't have to spend her own money. She had a real future in head of her.

I put my gun in the truck. Squirrel season was open, and that meant rabbit, too, and once in a while after dark you'd see the green eyes standing out in the cut fields that meant deer. Hamburger meat was $1.89 a pound. Double-ought buckshot was thirty-three cents. Some nights I was Have Truck, Will Kill, Palladio with a scattergun.

Those nights back then out on those country roads, with that sweet music playing and that beer cold between my legs and an endless supply of cigarettes and the knowledge that Dorothea was waiting back at home with her warm pubic hairs sometimes made me prolong the sheer pleasure of getting back to it, just riding around thinking about how good it was going to be when I got back. And then there was a little son of a bitch who didn't have any, who'd never know what it was like or the heat that was in it, like a glove that fit you like a fist but better, wanner, wetter, no wonder he wanted some so bad it drove him to have one-way sex with strangers. Dorothea hadn't said, but since she'd commented on the size of it, I figured his pud was down when he did it, not up. I wondered what he'd have done if some woman had walked over and slapped the shit out of him.

I puzzled over it and puzzled over it and drove for nights on end looking for that blue pickup, but if there was one in the country I didn't see it. I took back roads and side roads and pig trails that buzzards couldn't hardly fly over when it rained, and I decided he'd done decided to take his goober-grabbing on down the road somewhere else. By then I wasn't even mad and just wanted to talk to him, tell him calmly that he couldn't run around doing stuff like that. I was sure by then that he'd been raised without a father, and I could imagine what their lives were like, him and his mother, eating their powdered eggs, and I couldn't imagine how we could spend 1.5 billion dollars on a probe to look at Jupiter and yet couldn't feed and clothe the people in our own country. I wanted a kinder, gentler world like everybody else, but I knew we couldn't get it blasting it all off in space, or not providing for people like him. Who was to say that if he got cleaned up with some fresh duds, a little education, some new Reeboks, he couldn't get a blowjob in Atlanta? Hell. Why not educate? Defumigate? Have changes we could instigate? Why couldn't everybody, the whole country, participate?

Then I saw his truck.

It was backed up between some bushes on the side of the road. A cold feeling washed over me, made me lose all compassion. I said, Here this sick son of a bitch is sitting by the side of the road waiting for some innocent woman like my wife to come along and have car trouble, and instead of helping her change her tire he's going to run out in the road flonging his dong, whipping his mule, and it gave me a bad case of the creeps. I said, I'm fixing to tell this son of a bitch a thing or two. I thought of Boo Radley, how sweet he turned out to be. But I knew this wasn't nothing like that. I went on up to the end of the road and I turned around and came back. My shotgun was loaded. I pulled it over next to me. It was warm, the stock smooth—like Shane said, a tool only as good or as bad as the man who uses it—and I wondered if I could kill that man for what he'd done to my wife.

He'd already pulled out, and you can tell when somebody wants you to pass. They'll slow down, maybe because they're drinking beer and don't want to turn one up in front of you because they don't know if you're the law or not, since all they can see is your headlights. They'll poke along and poke along, waiting for you to pass, slowing down to a crawl in the straightaways, and it's maddening if it's happening to you, if you're riding around wondering why your wife's boss keeps driving by the house and waving out the window, almost as if he's looking to see who's home, if you're riding around wondering if you're riding around a little too much.

I got right on his bumper and rode that busted set of tail-lights and watched that stiff neck and that cap pulled down low over his eyes, that head turning every five seconds to the rearview mirror for eight or nine miles, him crawling, me crawling along behind him, letting him know that somebody was onto his game and following him all the way home. I went all the way down through Yocona bottom behind him, where it's straight for three miles, nothing coming, him speeding up a little, me speeding up, too, thinking: You son of a bitch. Pull your dick out in front of her now. Swing that dick around like a billy club now.

I kept drinking and following him and he started weaving and I did, too, and we almost ran off the road a few times, but I stayed right on his ass until he got down to Twin Bridges and tried to outrun me, stayed right with him or pulled up beside him and then I eased off, thinking he might have a wreck. I didn't want to kill him. I just wanted to talk to him. I kept telling myself that. I kept drinking. Everybody wanted pussy and pussy was good. But this guy had a hell of a way of going after it. I laid in there right on his ass, and when he turned around in George Fenway's driveway, I turned right around with him and followed him almost all the way to Bobo.

I let him get a little ahead of me. I knew where he lived. Deputy sheriff had told me, and his name was on the mailbox. I knew he was trying to run, hide, I knew by then that he knew he was caught somehow. I knew there had to be a whole lot of fear going through his mind, who was after him, what'd they want, all that kind of stuff. He just hadn't thought about any of that when he flicked his Bic.

When I got to where he lived, the truck was behind the house and there wasn't a light on. I coasted by twice with the headlights off. Then I killed it by the side of the road and listened for a while. It was quiet. Some light wires were humming. That was it. Dorothea and her boss had taken some awful long lunches. I got out with the shotgun and a beer and closed the door. The law wasn't there, and I was the law. *Vigilante Justice.* Patrick Swayze and somebody else. *Dirty Dancing.* But he never flashed his trash.

The yard was mud, the house almost dark. I could just see that one little light inside that was Johnny Carson saying goodnight. I knew he might have a gun, and might be scared enough to use it. In my state I thought I could holler self-defense in his front yard.

I hope I didn't ruin their lives.

The door was open, and the knob turned under my hand. The barrel of the gun slanted down from under my arm, and I tracked their mud on their floor. He didn't have his cap on, and his hair wasn't like what I'd imagined. It was gray, but neatly combed, and his mother was sobbing silently on the couch and feeding a pillow into her mouth.

He said one thing, quietly: "Are you fixing to kill us?"

Their eyes got me.

I sat down, asking first if I could. That's when I started telling both of them what my life then was like.

Old Soldiers

for Lisa

I used to spend a lot of time with Mr. Aaron. He had a bench you could pass out on behind the stove and that's where I was one day. We'd been after some antlerless deer that morning, or just whatever happened to run across the road in front of the dogs, but it was so cold their noses couldn't smell anything. We'd resorted to whiskey. It was only one o'clock but I was messed up, I won't deny it. My truck was parked at the store, and they dropped me off there at my request. I told them I'd be okay. They didn't want to leave me, they were my friends, I'd made an impossible shot at 340 yards the day before on a running eight-point buck. We'd already eaten him. I told them to leave me, that I was in good hands.

Mr. Aaron was quietly benevolent. He never said anything. You as a stranger could say hi to him and he'd just grunt. He was my kind of people. I got a small green glass Coke for my whiskey toddy, and I settled on the bench. I had part of a pint in my game bag. Before long he brought around a hot Budweiser and we toasted each other silently. He despised all the needless words that people said. It was his store and he didn't like loudmouths. Our darker brothers he especially turned a deaf ear on. Once I saw a darker woman pull up outside and want her air checked. He checked it. But it took him about thirty minutes. When she left, all four tires were very low.

He had a Mitsubishi TV we were watching with the sound turned off. My boots were thawing out beside the stove and water was puddling on the floor. Mr. Aaron brought a mop and swabbed and never said a word about the mess. He kept his beer in the candy case, hot. If kids came in giving him any shit he ran their asses off. I was almost swooning with delight. I knew he was ready with a war story.

"By God, I miss your daddy," he said.

I was on my back, flat, drink on my belly. I didn't even have to coax him sometimes. It was warm in there and I took off my coat. Here was a man who never turned down a drink of whiskey.

"By God, it was rough, too. Your daddy knowed how it was. I seen him in Germany one time he was riding on a tank with a machine gun in his lap. Stopped the tank and he had a bottle of brandy and we got drunk. Run that tank through some woman's wash line and through a post office. Course that was after the worst fighting was over. In France them French girls run to meet us holding their dresses up, was so glad to see American soldiers instead of German. They was probably not a one of them over twelve years old had not been raped by Germans at one time or another."

I felt like getting the crying jags over my father and him. But the whiskey will make you want to cry after it makes you want to laugh. I could have stayed with that old man forever. He had seventeen hundred silver dollars. He had two cars but he never went anywhere, and he ate Vienna sausage off the shelf. Had done it for thirty years.

"How's your leg?" I said. I always asked him about his leg. Most people who carried on their commerce there didn't even know about his leg. I did. All the shrapnel had gone into the bone where they wouldn't cut for it. There was a perfect circle of scar tissue on his calf that looked to me like a grenade ring.

He waved the question away with his hand. "It's all right," he said. "They'd might near have to cut my whole leg off to get rid of it. It's pitiful what the world's going to now."

Somebody stopped beside the gas pump and waited five minutes for him to come out.

"I ain't getting up again," he said, then got up immediately for another beer from the candy case. He brought me back a pack of pig-skins and threw them in my lap. The car pulled away.

"Damn niggers," he said. "Think you ought to wait on em hand and foot. But you look at all this shit. Reason the government ain't got no money right now is cause they shooting it all up in space. What damn good's it do to beat the Russians to the moon? I ain't going to the moon. Ain't nobody in his right mind would even want to go to the moon. I don't even think they been up there. I think they just took a buncha pictures over in Africa or somewhere."

I was standing outside the Kream Kup in Oxford the Sunday after-noon Neil Armstrong walked on the moon. We all looked up there. That was before I'd ever had any nooky. But by that afternoon in Mr. Aaron's store, I'd had plenty.

I must have fallen asleep. There was a long period when nothing was said. I tried to raise up and I couldn't raise up. I heard a rhythmic noise. The front door was shut and the lights were off. In my socked feet I could sneak. From behind the curtain behind the counter came the rhythmic noises. They stopped. I peeked.

Mr. Aaron was pulling a big one out of a lady who lived down the road. It looked like he might have hurt her with it the way she was taking on. I was back on the bench conked seemingly out when Miss Gladys Watson came through adjusting her white Dixie Delite uniform. Soon as the door slammed shut I raised up and said: "Who's that?"

Let me tell you something else Mr. Aaron did one time. He had this old dog named Bobo, whose whole body was crooked from being run over so many times. Mr. Aaron fed him potato chips. He'd go out once a day and dump a bag of pigskins or something on the ground and then go back in. As children we'd all sit around in front of the store, on upended Coke cases and such, and wait for a dogfight to occur. This was in the days before pit bulls, when a dog could get his ass whipped and just go on home. One day Mr. Mavis Edwards, an old man who lived across the road, had been sitting out there with us. But then he went off to the post office to get his mail and left a whole pound of baloney on top of a Coke case. Bobo grabbed it. And was chomping on it when Mr. Mavis came back. Mr. Mavis had been in the war, too, the First World War. He carried a cane and wore a Fu Manchu of snuff spittle. Of course he was incensed. Went to whipping Bobo about the ears and head with his cane. But you could see that the dog was ready to kill for that comparatively juicy snack. I mean, after a steady diet of potato chips, he was eating the waxed paper along with the baloney. Mr. Aaron heard the commotion going on outside. Some other people were fixing flats. The bros who had pulled up beside the gas pumps were afraid Mr. Aaron would shoot them if they tried to pump their own. And we didn't know but what Mr. Aaron might out with his 9MM and bum Mr. Mavis down. Mr.

Mavis had sprayed everybody with snuff juice during his exhortations. Mr. Aaron came back to the door and thrust another paper sack at him. "Here!" he said to Mr. Mavis. Then he reared back and kicked the hell out of the dog.

Mr. Mavis took the new baloney and said, "Why, hell, Aaron." He never darkened the door again.

One time I was up at the store after doing my tour in the service. He always had a soft spot in his heart for the men who toted the guns. I was going to town and asked him if he wanted me to bring him anything back and he said yes, whiskey. I bought it and returned. Miss Gladys came in, ostensibly to buy some flour, and fumblefucked around on the shelves for five minutes after she saw me sitting there. She left in a huff without making a purchase.

He came around there where I was and sat down beside me.

"Listen," he said. "Don't be like me. Get old and you won't have nobody to take care of you."

"Did you not ever want to get married?" I said.

"Nah, hell, wasn't that. They's all married off when I got back."

I knew better. War had hurt him. He never got the bullets and the bombs out of his head. I know he shot men. He once saw a dog-fight over the African desert, with all the action at five thousand feet. He said the American plane that went down left a solid black trail of smoke all the way to the ground, and the whole company sat down in the sand and cried. Then they went out that night and killed a bunch of people. He told me that.

He was drunk by the time he'd told it, and that time I left him asleep on the floor. I locked the door before I left. He wouldn't have let me help him across the road to his house.

The other thing I'm fixing to tell you has a lot to do with what I just told you.

THIS WAS YEARS LATER. Uptown in a bar one night. It was raining so hard I had to make a mad dash from my car to the door, raining so hard you could hardly see how to drive with the wipers going full speed. But I got in there and took my coat off and was glad to be in out of the rain. I was between women, living alone for a while again, and I didn't know how or when I'd find another one. The beer I ordered came and I paid.

There was nothing much going on. A few guys shooting pool and a few older women sitting at tables talking. Then I saw Squirrel at about the same time he saw me. I could tell he was drunk. He got up and started making his way over to me. I sat there and waited for him.

He's a good man. He's worked hard all his life laying brick, but he's had his troubles with the bottle. He's somewhere in his fifties, maybe sixties, I don't know now.

He sat down beside me and we talked for a while. Or he did. With drunks you know you just mostly agree and nod your head a lot. You don't have to worry about carrying the conversation, they'll do it. Squirrel was pissed off. He was ready to go home and he didn't have any wheels, because he'd left his wheels at home and come to town with two of the old guys shooting pool. He was ready to go and they weren't. I didn't want to think about what he was working his way up to. I was in out of that rain, I wanted to stay in out of it for a while.

This boy I knew walked in and asked me what in the hell I was doing in there when they had nickel beer up at Abbey's Irish Rose from 7:30 to 9:30 after you paid a two-dollar cover charge upstairs. I told him I didn't know anything about it. Squirrel leaned over right fast and in close to me and said, "Can you take me home?"

There it is a lot of times. You go out somewhere, just planning on drinking a few beers, and you run into some drunk you've known all your life who doesn't have a way home. You either have to take him home, refuse to, or tell him a lie. Usually I tell a lie. I told Squirrel I wasn't planning on going on home for a while, which was the truth. He said he understood and wouldn't think of imposing on me. I felt guilty, and I hated for him to make me feel guilty, but I hadn't brought him up there and poured any whiskey down him. And he lived way back up in the woods on a mud road the mailman has to use a Jeep on when it rains. In four-wheel drive. With Buckshot Mudders.

I finished my first beer and got another one, and Squirrel bummed a cigarette off me. I lit it for him, and he started telling me how he'd lost all his money. I wasn't listening that close, but it was something about them driving down to Batesville and unloading some two-by-fours and him asking the man he was working for to loan him a hundred dollars. The guy gave him five twenties, and when they got back to town, Squirrel paid for two fifths of whiskey. I know they were drinking when they went down there, he didn't have to tell me that. He said that left him about eighty dollars, but he said he didn't have it now and it was making him sick. And he wanted to go home.

"Sumbitches drug me off up here and got me drunk and now they don't want to go home," was what he said.

I hated to hear of his troubles, but I didn't want to drive him all the way back to Old Dallas on those muddy roads in my Chevelle and more than likely slide off into a ditch. He said he wouldn't think of imposing on me. His head was starting to droop. And I was wishing I'd never gone in there. There was no way I could leave without him. He only lived six miles from me.

I always think I'm going to find something when I go out at night, I don't know why. I always think that, and I never do. I always think I'll find a woman. But if you go out in sadness, that's all you're going to find. It was too quiet in there with him sitting next to me drooping his head, so I got up and put some change into the jukebox. I just had sat down and picked up my beer again when he leaned over and said, "Take me home, Leo. Please, please."

There wasn't anything else I could do. I couldn't sit there and drink beer with gas in my tank and him saying please to me. All he wanted was to get home and get up the next morning in time to go to work. I knew the other guys would stay until last call, and I knew they had his money. I stared at them but they wouldn't even look at us. I picked up my coat and put it on and I led him to the door. I had to help him down the stairs so he wouldn't fall, and then I had to help him into the car. I had some beer on the back seat, and I gave him one after we got up on the bypass.

Squirrel always talked through his nose. I guess he had a birth defect, a partial palate or something like that, but it wasn't hard to understand him. I think it was easier to understand him when he was drunk. I guess he talked slower then. I know I do.

"How many times you ever seen me drunk, Leo?" he said.

"I don't know, Squirrel. Not many."

"You ain't never seen me drunk, have you?"

"Not too many times," I said. "I think I saw you drunk about six months ago, out there one night."

"How bout opening this beer for me? I can't get this god-damn thing open."

I opened the beer for him and then gave him another cigarette. It was still raining and I was dreading that drive up that muddy road like an asswhipping. I knew with my luck, I'd get about five miles up in the woods before I slid off into a ditch, then I'd have to walk all the way out and wake up somebody who had a tractor while Squirrel slept it off in the car. I wasn't just real damn happy thinking about it.

"I been ready to go home for the last three hours, and them sorry sumbitches wouldn't even take me home," he said.

I told him it was hell to get off with some sorry sonofabitches who wouldn't even take you home.

"I don't mean to impo on you, Leo. You know that. Please, please."

I didn't feel like talking. Even if I got him home without getting stuck, it would be too late to turn around and go back to town. And there wasn't even anything *in* town. There was no sense in going up there looking for it. The people who were in the bars were just as lost as I was.

"If you just get me to Aaron's. You know Aaron, don't you?"

Well, I knew Aaron. I didn't know what Mr. Aaron would think about me dumping Squirrel on him.

"Yeah, I know Aaron. I imagine he's in the bed asleep by now."

"You just get me to Aaron's and I'll be all right. I wouldn't think of impoin on you, please, please."

I told him not to sweat it, that I'd been off with drunks who didn't want to go home, that he was in good hands now. He talked some more about losing his eighty dollars. He said it made him sick. A dollar was so hard to come by, he said. I clamped my lip shut and drove.

"I was on the front lines at Korea," he said. I looked sideways at him.

"I didn't know that," I said. "Hell yes."

I listened then, because moments like that are rare, when you get to hear about these things that have shattered men's lives. I knew my daddy never got the war out of his head. When he got to drinking that's what he'd talk about. Mama said when they first got married he'd wake himself up screaming from a nightmare of hand-to-hand combat, knives and bayonets and gun stocks. With sweat all over him like he'd just stepped from water. I listened to Squirrel.

"First night out, they was fifty of our boys got killed. Just cut em all to pieces with machine guns. Half of em my friends. I mean friends like you and me. They wadn't nothing nobody could do. I can't forget about it. I thought about it all my life. Please, please."

There wasn't much I could do but listen.

"They was this one boy with me in a foxhole one night. He was my old buddy. Been knowing him ever since basic training, Fort Campbell, Kentucky. But then he got away from me and a machine gun cut loose up on top of a hill. He was screaming for me, Help me, Help me, all night long. Them goddamn bullets like to cut him half in two. Wasn't nothing I could do. You know that. I thought about it all my life. Please, please. Next morning he was dead."

There wasn't anything I could say.

"I come back off the front lines for the first time in three months. I walked in a tent there and saw this captain standing there. I had a fifth of whiskey in my hand, and he asked me what I wanted. I told him I wasn't looking for nothing but a smile and a kind word. Sumbitch just cussed me and told me to get the hell out. I laid down and cried all night long. I've cried many a night all night long, Leo. Just get me to Aaron's and I'll be all right."

And Daddy had seen the same things, had marched all the way across Europe, freezing, getting shot at every day, seeing all those people he knew die. Fighting the Germans hand to hand. And waking up yelling, thinking he was back in it with them again. Bayonets and knives.

"Just get me to Aaron's and I'll be all right. Please. I don't want to impo on you. I ain't got no money to pay you, but I'll have some later. I can go home and in five minutes I can have a hunnerd dollars. A hunnerd dollars to me don't mean what it used to. You boys just don't know."

"You don't want me to take you home?"

"Naw. Just take me to Aaron's. I'll get one of his cars and go home."

"You don't think he'll get pissed off?"

"Naw. He won't get pissed off. Aaron don't care."

We pulled into Mr. Aaron's place and I parked in his yard. Squirrel looked at me before he opened the door.

"I got to see if Aaron will let me in. You won't leave me, will you?"

"Naw, Squirrel," I said. "I ain't gonna leave you. I'll take you home if Aaron won't let you have a car. I'm gonna get out and take a piss, though. I'll be right here."

I got out and stood in the rain while Squirrel staggered up to Mr. Aaron's window and knocked on the glass. I could hear him talking.

"Aaron? Aaron. Squirrel. Can I come in? Squirrel. Can I come in?"

Standing there watching him in the rain, I felt bad. He was old and withered and drunk and all he wanted was to get home so he could go to work the next day. Forget all this. Try to forget all this. But he wouldn't. He'd be back up there within a few nights. And I probably would be, too.

The light came on finally, and I saw Mr. Aaron coming to the front, his hair puffed up like wings on each side of his head. The rain fell on me. He didn't have his glasses on and he looked confused. I hollered and told Squirrel that he was coming to the front. He walked through a mud puddle and Aaron opened the door. I stepped up there and said, "I'll take him home if you don't want to mess with him, Mr. Aaron."

Squirrel stepped up beside me. "Can I come in, Aaron?" he said. "I'm trying to get home."

"Hell yeah, you can come on in," Mr. Aaron told him. He looked different without his glasses and with sleep in his eyes. He was still confused. He didn't know what was going on yet. When I was a child he treated me with kindness always. He wouldn't talk to you if he didn't know you, but he told me a lot of war stories. Squirrel walked across the boards laid on the ground that were all the porch Mr. Aaron had and stuck his hand out. We shook.

"Thanks, Leo," he said. "I'll be all right now."

They went on inside, already talking, already forgetting about me, and I watched them for a moment before I ducked out of the rain and back into my car. I thought about things while I drove home alone. I thought about being old, and alone, and drunk and needing help. I knew I might be like that one day. I thought about having to turn to somebody for help. I hoped it would be there.

WE BURIED AARON TODAY. We stood up in the church and smelled the flowers, and sang those beautiful songs over him, and the preacher said his words. I helped carry the coffin; I was one of the chosen six. It turned out that he had picked out his resting place thirty years ago. It's on high ground, in the shade, and from there you can stand and see the green hills folding away, all the way to the horizon.

I'm drinking beer now and a little into my cups, thinking about Aaron, and Squirrel, and Daddy, and about all the conversations they probably had about war. I know now that they suffered like all soldiers do, and I know they saw things that affected them for the rest of their lives.

And I just realized something. Squirrel didn't want to go home that night. He had no intention of going home. He wanted to be with somebody who knew him. And if there was anybody that night who knew what he was feeling, and what it meant, Aaron did. Aaron did for sure.

So long, old buddy. God bless you and keep you. Me, I need some sleep myself.

Sleep

My wife hears the noises and she wakes me in the night. The dream I've been having is not a good one. There is a huge black cow with long white horns chasing me, its breath right on my neck. I don't know what it means, but I'm frightened when I awake. Her hand is gripping my arm. She is holding her breath, almost.

Sometimes I sleep well and sometimes I don't. My wife hardly ever sleeps at all. Oh, she takes little naps in the daytime, but you can stand back and watch her, and you'll see what she goes through. She moans, and twists, and shakes her head no no no.

Long ago we'd go on picnics, take Sunday drives in the car. Long before that, we parked in cars and moved our hands over each other. Now all we do is try to sleep, seems like.

It's dark in the room, but I can see a little. I move my arm and my elbow makes a tiny pop. I'm thinking coffee, orange juice, two over easy. But I'm a long way away from that. And then I know she's hearing the noises once more.

"They're down there again," she says.

I don't even nod my head. I don't want to get up. It's useless anyway, and I just do it for her, and I never get through doing it. I'm warm under the covers, and the world apart from the two of us under here is cold. I think maybe if I pretend to be asleep, she'll give it up. So I lie quietly for a few moments, breathing in and out. I gave us a new electric blanket for our anniversary. The thermostat clicks on and off, with a small reassuring sound, keeping us warm. I think about hash browns, and toast, and shit on a shingle. I think about cold places I've been in. It's wonderful to do that, and then feel the warm spaces between my toes.

"Get up," she says.

Once I was trapped in a blizzard in Kansas. I was traveling, and a snowstorm came through, and the snow was so furious I drove my car right off the road into a deep ditch. I couldn't even see the highway from where I was, and I foolishly decided to stay in the car, run the heater, and wait for help. I had almost a full tank of gas. The snow started covering my vehicle. I had no overshoes, no gloves. All I had was a car coat. The windshield was like the inside of an igloo, except for a small hole where I ran the defroster. I ran out of gas after nine hours of idling. Then the cold closed in. I think about that time, and feel my nice warm pajamas.

"You getting up?" she says.

I'm playing that I'm still asleep, that I haven't heard her wake me. I'm drifting back off, scrambling eggs, warming up the leftover T-bone in the microwave, looking for the sugar bowl and the milk. The dog has the paper in his mouth.

"Did you hear me?" she says.

I hear her. She knows I hear her. I hear her every night, and it never fails to discourage me. Sometimes this getting up and down seems to go on forever. I've even considered separate beds. But so far we've just gone on like we nearly always have.

I suppose there's nothing to do but get up. But if only she knew how bad I don't want to.

"*Louis.* For God's sake. Will you get up?"

Another time I was stationed at a small base on the North Carolina coast. We had to pull guard duty at night. After a four-hour shift my feet would be blocks of ice. It would take two hours of rubbing them with my socks off, and drinking coffee, to get them back to normal. The wind came off the ocean in the winter, and it cut right through your clothes. I had that once, and now I have this. The thermostat clicks. It's doing its small, steady job, regulating the temperature of two human bodies. What a wonderful invention. I'm mixing batter and pouring it on the griddle. Bacon is sizzling in its own grease, shrinking, turning brown, bubbling all along the edges. What lovely bacon, what pretty pancakes. I'll eat and eat.

"Are you going to get up or not?"

I sigh. I think that if I was her and she was me, I wouldn't make her do this. But I don't know that for a fact. How did we know years ago we'd turn out like this? We sleep about a third of our lives and look what all we miss. But sometimes the things we see in our sleep are more horrible and magical than anything we can imagine. People come after you and try to kill you, cars go backward down the highway at seventy miles an hour with you inside and you're standing up on the brake. Sometimes you even get a little.

I lie still in the darkness and, without looking around, can see the mound of covers next to me with a gray lump of hair sticking out. She is still, too. I think maybe she's forgotten about the things downstairs. I think maybe if I just keep quiet she'll drift back off to sleep. I try that for a while. The gas heater is throwing the shadow of its grille onto the ceiling and it's leaping around. Through the black window I can see the cold stars in the sky. People are probably getting up somewhere, putting on their housecoats, yawning in their fists, plugging in their Mr. Coffees.

Once I was in the army with a boy from Montana and he got me to go home with him. His parents had a large ranch in the mountains, and they took me in like another son. I'd never seen country like that Big Sky country. Everywhere you looked, all you could see was sky and mountains, and in the winter it snowed. We fed his father's cows out of a truck, throwing hay out in the snow, and boy those cows were glad to get it. They'd come running up as soon as they heard the truck. But I felt sorry for them, having to live outside in the snow and all, like deer. Once in a while we'd find a little calf that had frozen to death, frozen actually to the ground. I would be sad when that happened, thinking about it not ever getting to see the springtime.

I lie still under the covers in my warm bed and wonder what ever became of that boy.

Then she begins. It's always soft, and she never raises her voice. But she's dogcussing me, really putting some venom into it, the same old awful words over and over, until it hurts my ears to hear them. I know she won't stop until I get up, but I hate to feel that cold floor on my feet. She's moved my house shoes again, and I don't want to crawl under the bed looking for them. Spiders are under there, and balls of dust, and maybe even traps set for mice. I don't ever look under there, because I don't want to see what I might.

I tell myself that it's just like diving into cold water. I'll only feel the shock for a second, and that the way to do it is all at once. So I throw the covers back and I stand up. She stops talking to me. I find the flashlight on the stand beside the bed, where I leave it every night. Who needs a broken leg going down the stairs?

It's cold in the hall. I shine the flashlight on the rug, and on my gun cabinet, and for a moment I think I'll go and make coffee in the kitchen, and sit there listening to it brew, and drink a cup of it and smoke a few cigarettes. But it seems an odd time of the night to do a thing like that. The thought passes, and I go down the stairs.

I open the door to the kitchen. Of course there's nothing in there. I shut the door hard so she can hear it. I cross the dining room, lighting my way, looking at her china in the cabinet, at the white tablecloth on the table and the dust on it, and I open the door to the living room. There's nothing in there but furniture, the fireplace, some candy in a dish. I slam the door so she can hear that, too. I'm thinking of all the dreams I could be having right now, uninterrupted. It's too late for Carson, too late for Letterman, too late for Arsenio. They've all gone to bed by now.

I stand downstairs and listen to my house. I cut the light off to hear better. The silence has a noise of its own that it makes. I move to the window and push the curtains aside, but nobody's out there on the streets. It's cold out there. I'm glad I'm in here, and not out there. Still.

I sit in a chair for a little while, tapping the flashlight gently on my knee. I find my cigarettes in the pocket of my robe, and I smoke one. I don't want it, it's just a habit. It kills three or four minutes. And after that, it's been long enough. I find an ashtray with my flashlight, and put out the cigarette. I'm still thinking about that coffee. I even look in the direction of the kitchen. But finally I go ahead and climb the stairs.

I put my hand over the bulb of the flashlight when I get near the bed. I move in my own little circle of light with quiet feet. I keep my hand over it when I move it near her face. I don't want to wake her up if she's asleep. My hand looks red in the light, and my skin looks thin. I don't know how we got so old.

Her eyes are closed. She has her hands folded together, palms flat, like a child with her head resting on them. I don't know what to do with her any more. Maybe tomorrow night she won't hear the things downstairs. Maybe tomorrow night they'll be up in the attic. It's hard to tell.

I turn the flashlight off and set it back on the table beside the bed. I might need it again before the night's over. I don't want to be up stumbling around in the dark.

"Mama had three kittens," she says, and I listen. Her voice is soft, remarkably clear, like a person reciting a poem. I wait for the rest of it, but it never comes. I'm lucky, this time, I guess.

I sit on the side of the bed. I don't want to get under the covers just yet. I want to hear the house quiet again, and the silence is so loud that it's almost overpowering. Finally I lie down and pull the covers up over my head. The warmth is still there. I move toward her, looking for I don't know what. I think of a trip I took to Alaska a long time ago, when I was a young man. There were sled dogs, and plenty of snow, and polar bears fishing among cakes of ice for seals. I wonder how they can live in that cold water. But I figure it's just what you get used to. I close my eyes, and I wait.

BIG BAD LOVE
Part II

Discipline

Please tell the court again, Mr. Lawrence.

We were tortured in pairs, singly, that is, individually, but only on Saturdays, or in groups of not more than four.

Let me see if I have this straight. Now, you said you were only tortured on Saturdays, is that right?

No. You misunderstood me. What I said was that we were only tortured individually on Saturdays.

And why do you suppose that was? I have no idea.

[*Turns, facing the room, head shaking in mock wonderment, small malicious smile of feigned chagrin or imagined bond of friendship obvious*] You have no idea. I see. Well then, let me ask you something else. [*Referring to notes*] You said that on the evening of March twelfth, yourself and a man named Varrick? I believe? were taken from your quarters and allowed intercourse, blindfolded, with two obese women?

Well, that's partly correct. . . .

And where do you suppose—no wait. *Who* do you suppose these two women were?

I told you we were blindfolded.

Ah, yes.

And we weren't al*lowed*. We were forced. That's all in my deposition. I don't see any need to—

Just answer yes or no, please. How well did you know this Mr. Varrick? Was he a close friend?

Well. [*Perhaps hedging here?*] No. I wouldn't say he was a close friend, no. I mean we ate lunch together a few times. We read a few of each other's stories.

And you took a few showers together, too, didn't you? Yes. Did you at any time of your last period of incarceration engage in a sexual act with Mr. Varrick?

I did not.

You're under oath here, sir. Need I remind you?

Never.

Did you ever catch Mr. Varrick watching you in the shower? While you were in there together? Naked?

I never noticed.

Never noticed. I'm constantly amazed at how much you didn't notice over a period of—what was it? Five?

Four. Four years.

Four years, five years, whatever. All right. Now back to Mr. Varrick. How long did you know him?

Let's see. Let me think. I think it was . . . four, no, three years. Yes, three years. [*Nodding vigorously, hands clasped in lap*]

I think we've already established your capacity for not noticing things, but during the time you knew Mr. Varrick, did you ever happen to notice what his first name was?

I be*lieve* it was Howard.

You believe it was Howard.

Yes.

Under the contention of cruel and unusual punishment, the defense would like for us to believe that this alleged torture actually took place without due cause. Without being deserved, in other words. All right, Mr. Lawrence. Doyle Huey, isn't it? [*Titters from crowd; judge's gavel rapped lightly, perfunctorily*] You have already stated, under oath, that you and Mr. Varrick had sex with these two unidentified women.

I would like for you to explain to the jury and to this court exactly how you knew this act was being consummated while you were blindfolded and, apparently, engaged simultaneously in the same alleged action.

What do you mean? I don't know what you mean.

Forgive me. Let me make it simple enough for you to understand it. I mean, how did you know Mr. Varrick made love to this woman while you were blindfolded? I believe in your deposition you also stated that you were equipped with earplugs? And nose plugs? Is that correct?

That's correct. We . . . we had to breathe through our mouths. So there was no kissing. Involuntary sex, well, for involuntary sex that's required. It was just one of the rules.

And you always followed the rules.

Always tried to, yes. I mean, we were at the mercy of these people. Every time we tried to—

Let's not go off on that particular tangent again, please. Please. Just. Answer the question. How do you know Mr. Varrick had sex with this woman?

Well. I could just tell.

You could just tell. That's interesting. A prisoner for four years doesn't know why he was individually tortured only on Saturdays, doesn't know a close friend was a homosexual—

That hasn't been proved.

—isn't sure what that friend's first name was; in short, doesn't notice a whole lot about what is going on immediately around him for four years. Not very good recommendations for a writer, are they? Right?

[*Silence*]

I said, Isn't that RIGHT!

Yes. Yes. That's right.

Yet you knew without the shadow of a doubt what was going on in a cot twenty feet away, *clear across the room*, while you were blindfolded and literally deprived of any other sensory perception. Is that what you're saying?

Yes.

You're a liar. Aren't you? No.

You *are* a liar. You've been a liar all your life, haven't you?

No.

Isn't it true that you were classified as a pathological liar by the United States Navy as early as 1966? Didn't you lie about your age to get into the Writers' Institute? Didn't you lie about the mileage on a 1963 Chevrolet Impala that you traded in Shreveport, Louisiana, for a Dodge Dart?

I . . . I don't—

Remember? Let me refresh your memory. Didn't you also take a Delco twelve-volt battery in good condition from that same Impala and replace it with a battery that actually had two dead cells, that you had been using with a trolling motor for three years?

Yes. [*With head hung*]

All *right*. Now we're getting somewhere. [*Speaking to jury*] Look at him, ladies and gentlemen! How'd you like to curl up on Christmas Eve with a good novel by him? [*Taking twenty seconds to stroll back to desk, pour glass of water, sip, reflect, study notes carefully, walk back to front*] Mr. Lawrence. Let's go back to the day you and Mr. Varrick were taken from your quarters. Why don't you just tell us about it?

Which part? You mean when we went over there? I mean, which part do you want to know about?

Why were you and Mr. Varrick selected for this alleged 'involuntary sex'? Was it because of something you had done?

I'm not sure. They never told us.

Was anybody else ever forced to perform involuntary sex with obese women? Did they just pick people out at random? Did they walk down the line and say, "Well, let's get him today"?

I don't know. We were kept isolated.

How did you and Mr. Varrick manage to read each other's stories and eat lunch a few times if you were isolated? How did you and Mr. Varrick manage to take showers together?

We had visitation. Everybody did.

Well, which was it?

Which was what?

Was it isolation or was it visitation? Why do you keep changing your story?

I'm not changing my story! I'm trying to tell the truth!

I don't think you are. I think you're lying. I think you've been lying since the first day of this hearing. You'd do anything to get paroled. Wouldn't you?

No.

Yes you would. You'd perjure yourself to save your own neck, wouldn't you?

I'm telling you the truth!

I don't think so.

You weren't there! You didn't have to live through it! You don't know what they made us do! [*Rising from chair halfway, hands gripping armrests*]

Control yourself, Mr. Lawrence. Just tell us. Go on.

[*Easing back. A little flustered, confused. Slight licking of lips*] Well. I guess it was about—about four o'clock in the afternoon. I was working on some revisions in my study. I remember it was almost time for beer call and I was trying to get through my revisions.

What kind of revisions are we discussing here?

Several different kinds. Some poetry. And I think, ah. Some short stories. Yes. I believe that's what it was. Well anyway. It was fifteen till four or something, and I was trying to hurry up and get through so I could turn in my revisions. We had so many each week we had to turn in for grading. But they turned on the siren ten minutes early. So, I just scooped everything up, boxed it up, then locked my study and went out to the yard.

Was Mr. Varrick in the yard when you got there?

Yes, he was.

Did you know the reason Mr. Varrick was in the camp?

Yes. [*Uneasy look. Shifting around in chair: Unable to find a comfortable position*] I did.

Would you like to tell us why Mr. Varrick was in the camp?

[*Extremely uneasy. Rubbing palms together, averting his face, appearing to be searching for something at his feet*] Well. It was common knowledge, I suppose. He was in for plagiarism. Like seventy-five percent of the other inmates.

Was this a first offense for Mr. Varrick?

I'm . . . I'm not sure. [*Obviously lying*]

Right. Not sure. Can't remember. Didn't notice. Isn't it true that Mr. Varrick had in fact had his probation revoked for plagiarism?

Well . . . yes. But it wasn't the same author.

Oh? Your memory seems to be improving. I don't suppose you'd remember who he plagiarized the first time, would you?

I believe it was Flannery O'Connor. I think it was a line out of "A Good Man Is Hard to Find."

A line? Is that right? One line?

I believe so. Yes. I'm sure that's what it was.

[*Shaking his head. Wry humor touched with pity*] Mr. Lawrence. Didn't Mr. Varrick actually copy, verbatim, every single word from the time the grandmother's family went into The Tower, until they had the wreck? And turn it into *Playboy* as his own?

[*Shaken badly now*] I don't know. I—didn't know it was that bad.

Bad? You don't think it's bad to steal from a dead woman? Pilfer words from a sick, dying writer, who barely had the strength to work three hours a day? Who had more guts and talent in one little finger than you and your buddy Varrick have in your whole bodies?

I didn't mean that! I meant I didn't know he stole that much!

Stole! That's the right word. Robbed. [*With vigor*] Extorted. That's a better word. But even that. Even *that* wasn't as bad as what he did later. Was it? It wasn't as bad as what got him thrown in hacks' prison for five years, was it?

No. [*Almost whispering*] It wasn't.

Well. You're telling it. Your memory's coming back now, isn't it? Why don't you just tell us what he did do? After he was already on probation for the same crime?

I told you. It was plagiarism. Why do I have to say all this? You know it already. You know what he did!

Didn't it ever strike you that Mr. Varrick might have been just a little bit stupid?

Well. I suppose so.

You suppose so? Is that all you can say? You suppose so?

All right. It was stupid.

Who did he plagiarize the next time, Mr. Lawrence? The five-year sentence. And please don't tell me what you believe.

[*Grim, fatalistic conviction of lethargic hopelessness*] It was Cormac McCarthy.

Well, well. Now we're getting somewhere again. Now we're talking about *living* writers. Now we're getting up to a new level of theft. We're getting up into grant country now. Now we're talking about the American Academy of Arts and Letters. The big time.

Yes. [*Whispered*]

You're telling it so good I think I'll just let you go on. Why don't you just tell us what Mr. Varrick did to Mr. McCarthy?

[*Studying fingernails*] He stole different passages from three of his novels.

And?

And submitted—

Wait, wait. First—

First he put them into his own novel.

It was actually a novella, wasn't it?

I don't know. I never read it.

You never read it because it was never published. It was never published because it was submitted to the same house that originally published those same three novels. Ladies and gentlemen, the act of a stupid man. He stole ten thousand words, whole, uncut scenes, dialogue, ripped them up a little, tore them up some, and mixed them with ten thousand of his own miserable words and called it his own. Didn't he?

Yes. Yes, he did.

And he got caught.

Yes.

Just like you got caught.

Yes.

In a blatant, vicious act of plagiarism. Literary theft. And it got him five years.

Yes.

Did Mr. Varrick ever confide in you? Did he ever tell you any of his secrets?

Secrets? [*Shrugs shoulders, still studying nails*] We talked. Some.

Did he ever say to you that he thought his sentence was unfair?

[*Looking up*] Yes. He did.

What exactly did he say?

He said . . . he said he thought it was too long. And he said he thought the regimen was too strict. He said he thought we should have more beer and more recreational reading. More contemporary reading.

Like what?

Oh, you know. More new stuff. He thought we should have been allowed to read what was on the best-seller lists.

In short, he didn't want to have to read the classics, correct? He just wanted to skip Melville and Twain and Tolstoy, didn't he?

Essentially, yes. That's correct.

He thought they were a bunch of old geezers, didn't he?

Well. Not in so many words. I guess you could put it like that.

Didn't he actually say that once, though? Didn't he once, in the presence of two other prisoners, call Sophocles 'a dried-up old fart'?

I . . .

You don't remember.

No.

Your memory just comes and goes, doesn't it? Well, why don't you just see if you can remember what happened on the afternoon you met Mr. Varrick in the yard, before you were taken in for involuntary sex? I'm sure everybody would just love to hear that.

It may take a while.

I've got all day.

[*Deep breath, gathering will*] Well. Like I said, we thought it was beer call. I mean, it was almost four o'clock. We just thought they were a little early.

Were they ever early for a beer call?

Not usually, no.

Up until that time, had you ever seen an early beer call?

No.

Wasn't everything timed to a very strict schedule, right up to the minute?

Yes. Well anyway. I saw How—Mr. Varrick, standing in line on the yellow footprints, and I went over to him. We talked for a minute. He'd been writing some poetry—

Whose? Raymond Carver's?

and he said he thought something funny was going on. He said they'd been heavy on his grading. He said all his papers were coming back with red marks on them, and they'd caught him with three comma splices in one week. And he'd lost his thesaurus. He was worried.

Under oath, Mr. Lawrence. Did he mention anything to you at that time about involuntary sex?

He said . . . he said he thought we were in for it. Those were his words.

He didn't specifically mention involuntary sex?

No. Not in so many words. I just told you what he said.

But you knew. You knew what was coming.

We didn't know for sure. They hadn't told us anything.

You knew it wasn't beer call yet. Didn't you?

Well, everybody else was beginning to line up. They all had their papers. We hadn't been given any reason to suspect. We . . . we thought they'd let us slide. At least, I did.

And why was that? Had they ever let anybody slide before?

[*Ghastly smile, horrific remembrance, flood of emotions rapidly flickering across face*] No. They never had.

Then why did you think this time would be any different? Why did you think they weren't going to take you out and torture you? Were you friendly with any of the guards?

No. Certainly not. They were all former editors. That was one of the requirements.

I'm well aware of the requirements. This court is not questioning the integrity of the guards.

It should! If you call yourselves lawmakers! This hearing is a farce! Howard Varrick was a humorist! If he'd been published he'd have been one of the greatest writers of this century! He was on his way! He was making some real progress until he was tortured! I read his drafts! I laughed!

[*General confusion, buzzing from peanut gallery, rapping of gavel, uneasy order quickly restored. Small gaping faces at door swiftly pushed outside*] Thank you. [*Turning, pausing, acknowledging appreciation to judge*] If we can proceed. . . . Tell us about that afternoon. Tell us what happened after you and Mr. Varrick discussed your problems.

We had to turn our papers in. That came first. Dr. Evans was the personal guard and senior editor.

Did Dr. Evans review your revisions in the exercise yard?

Yes. He did. But that was common practice. We had to get the initial okay from him before we could go to beer call.

And how long did that usually take?

[*Ruminating, chin in hand*] Not long, usually. He'd just give it a quick glance. He wouldn't read all the way through.

How long would you say? Ten minutes? Five? Probably about five. Maybe a little less.

And how many words of copy are we talking about here?

Well. It varied.

How much?

It depended. On what we were revising.

How many words would you say, on the day in question?

Between us?

Yes, Between you.

Oh. Probably. About six thousand. Somewhere around that.

He was a fast reader, wasn't he?

Fairly quick, I suppose. I'm sure he'd had a lot of practice.

But you didn't go to beer call that day. Did you?

No. We didn't.

What did it, Mr. Lawrence?

I don't understand.

Whose work was it that caused Dr. Evans to cancel your beer break and send you in for involuntary sex instead?

[*Mad panic now, sudden, furious, eyes searching the court, hands gripping chair arms wildly*] What?

I said whose work was it?

I don't have to answer that question! Answer it.

No.

Answer it!

Damn you! Damn you and your court. I'm not saying anything else. I want to see my lawyer.

Well, there he is. Sitting right there at that table.

[*Unable to decide. Fear. Horror. Mouth chewing knuckle*] I . . .

Answer the question. Wasn't it in fact *your* work that got Mr. Varrick sent in for involuntary sex along with you? Hadn't he been cribbing your notes? Didn't you drag him down with you? Weren't you still secretly copying Faulkner, at *night*, under the covers, with a flashlight?

Eee . . . yes! Damn you! Yes!

Weren't you laboring along, in the 'great southern gothic tradition,' using heavy, frightening imagery?

Yes! [*Beaten. Whipped. Chastised. Chastened. Cowed. Diminished. Uncertain. Afraid. Tentative. Sick*]

Ignoring punctuation, running whole pages of narrative together, incorporating colons, semicolons, hyphens, making your characters talk like Beeder Mackey on LSD?

[*Softly*] Yes.

All right. What happened after Dr. Evans finished reading your . . . *work*?

[*Trying to regain composure*] He became irrational.

Irrational? Was it irrational for him to show displeasure over unacceptable work?

No.

Was it irrational for him to have little patience. with two longtime inmates who refused to be rehabilitated? Repeaters?

No.

Then why did you say he became irrational?

He . . . [*shifting in chair, crossing legs, uncrossing legs*] he started taking the paper clips off the papers. He was shouting.

What was he shouting?

Obscenities.

Were these obscenities pertaining to the work at hand?

Yes.

Did he tell you he was about to take you in for involuntary sex?

No. He didn't. He just told us to wait, that we weren't going to beer call with the rest.

What happened then?

Well. We waited. We waited in the yard.

Did everybody else take a beer break?

Yes. They did. We could hear them. They sounded like they were having a good time.

Really whooping it up, eh?

Yes.

And that really bothered you. Didn't it?

Yes. It did.

You thought you weren't being treated fairly, didn't you? You thought even a convicted copycat should have rights, didn't you?

Yes. I do. I mean I did.

When did you first realize that you were about to be taken in for involuntary sex?

When they brought the blindfolds out.

Were the earplugs and the nose plugs applied at this time, also?

Yes. They were. [*Eyes downcast*] We knew, then.

Were you afraid?

I . . . [*Ashamed*] I was very afraid. I'd never had to do anything like that before in my life.

But you'd been given plenty of warning.

Yes.

You'd been told to pick up the level of your writing. Both of you.

Yes.

Were you blindfolded before you were taken inside?

No, they—made us look at them first. For several minutes.

And then.

[*A whisper*] Then they blindfolded us. [*Whole court straining forward to catch words, reporters scribbling furiously*] I tried to hold Howard's hand but I couldn't find it. I told him . . . I told him to be brave. He was crying. I was, too. We were both . . . at the lowest point of our lives. They'd reduced us to animals.

What happened then?

[*Eyes closed. Huge gulp*] Someone touched me. She said—she said she was a member of a book club. And a poetry society. She put her arms around me. They were big arms. Huge.

Were you scared?

I was terrified.

Can you describe it?

Describe *what*? Do you want to hear about the *act*? Oh, you filthy animal. You dirty, dirty man. You want to hear about it? I'll tell you about it. I'll tell you all you want to hear. If it'll keep one person from going through what I went through. She was fat, okay? She was big, and fat, and heavy, and she sweated, all right? [*Rising from chair, face heated, turning red, carotid artery protuberant, teeth gritted*] She couldn't have sat down in two chairs, okay? She didn't have any teeth. She was covered with tattoos and she was hairy, and she had bad breath. Now. You want to hear some more?

Bailiff?

No! She got on top of me! They'd told her I was famous! She was mashing me! I was trying to get out from under her but she was too big! It was horrible, do you hear me? Horrible! I can't forget about it! I wake up in the night screaming from it, screaming from it, screaming huh huh huh . . . [*Complete breakdown, hands over face, gradual grading off to racking sobs loud in hushed awe of courtroom*]

All right, Mr. Lawrence. [*Going back to table for manuscript pages, waving them in the air*] The state has one more piece of evidence to present in this parole hearing. [*Approaching witness stand, thrusting papers rudely forward*] Read this. Out loud.

[*Looking up, face still contorted, eyes wet, nose snuffling*] What?

[*Shaking pages belligerently*] You wrote it. I should think you'd be proud to get a chance to read it in public. I want this court to hear the real reason your parole should be denied. Go on, read it.

[*Taking papers slowly, recognizing them*] Oh. God, no. [*Head shaking, papers trembling slightly in fingers*] You can't mean . . . I don't want to read this. Please. It isn't fair to make me read this. If you have one shred of decency . . .

Read it.

This . . . this is just a rough draft.

I thought you'd revised it, Mr. Lawrence.

I was drunk when I wrote this.

Wasn't beer call yet, Mr. Lawrence. Remember? Read it.

You. You got this out of my files somehow. This was locked up in my study. [*Looking up, amazed*] You won't stop, will you? It's never going to end, is it? You want to keep me in there forever, don't you? You don't really believe in rehabilitation. It's just a way to keep us out of print. [*Soft, unbelievable horror. Pause. Bitter resignation. Determination*] All right, I'll read it. I'll read every damn word of it. It may be the only time I'll get to. [*Bracing himself, adjusting tie, one hand on knee, beginning . . .*] And it was with a timorous expression of the wide upturned Afro-American nostrils that, arched and slightly hissing, Otis McQuay paused and turned toward his eating, sitting, brother, the twin, the Aquarius, the one with whom he had shared the dark bloody nacreous unlighted cavern of his mother's womb, and sniffed, hesitantly, not blatantly or in open astonishment or anything so challenging as that, at the malodorous gases drifting cloudlike and thick as turtle soup down the rough unplaned splintered wobbly table to where he sat eating his butter beans and cornbread, his stance like that of a bluetick on a mess of birds. For it was not in his nature to be challenging. Then he heard it, the slight thin whistle like steam escaping, and his eyes shifted quickly in their sockets, huge and white and rolling. Trapped, with him now, his own supper but half eaten, frozen in that indecision or flight or willingness to endure, to stand, the muscles of his legs coiled tight as screen-door springs, his hands on either side of his plate like dead or wounded or dying blackbirds, while all around him the fumes grew stronger and more malodorous, more pungent. The air grew rank, grew right funky. There came a long ragged sound like paper tearing and it was chopped off short, immeasurably loud in the close silence. Then like two toots on a bugle came the next two toots: toot, toot. But it was not the brass mouth of a trumpet, not an instrument of music that played that sorry scale. It was something deeper, more sinister—

I think that will do.

a sound born not of clean air and lungs but a fecund, a ripe smell, like burning shoes . . .

Your Honor, I think we've proved our point. . . . Bailiff, would you show this man to his seat?

. . . like dead rattlesnakes, like soured slops, like contaminated sheepdip—

Could we get the bailiffs to perform their duties, please?

[*Bailiffs surging forward, babble of voices rising from courtroom, judge rapping gavel*]

Like moldy mattress stuffings! Like bad cheese!

Your Honor! Could we have order restored! Please!

[*Judge rapping gavel louder, bailiffs grappling with defendant on witness stand, now wild-eyed, smiling! Defiant! Eyes ablaze!*] Like putrid prairie dog meat! Wait! There's more! Do you hear me! Just listen!

BIG BAD LOVE
Part III

92 Days

for buk

1

Monroe came over to see me one day, shortly after I divorced. He had some beer. I was glad to see him. I was especially glad to see his beer.

"How you taking it?" he said.

"Pretty good, I guess."

"Have a beer."

"Thanks."

"Women," he said. "Jesus Christ."

"Right."

We sat there and drank his beer. I was almost out of money. I was too upset to write anything. I'd tried it a few times, and wound up just gnawing my knuckles. I was afraid I'd lost it for good. I was almost out of food, too.

"When you gonna get a job?"

"I don't know. I need one. I need some money."

"I can let you paint houses for me a few days."

"Thanks, Monroe."

I started that afternoon. It went pretty well. It was soothing, mind-less work, and I didn't have to think. I thought plenty, but not about what I was doing. What I had decided to do was just live hand to mouth. Work a few days and then quit and live off the money and write until the money was gone. Then work a few more days, and so on. It was a spur-of-the-moment plan, and as soon as I planned that, I promised myself I'd never plan anything else as long as I lived.

At the end of three days Monroe gave me a hundred and eighty dollars. I bought some food and some beer. That was all I needed. Well, two cartons of Marlboros. I had a place to stay. I had a bed, a chair, some books and records.

The first night I just sat there looking at a blank sheet of paper.

Next night, same thing. Nothing would come. I knew I'd lost it. I'd have to be a house painter for the rest of my life.

The third night I typed one paragraph and threw it away. The fourth night I started a new story.

2

I got a letter back in the mail along with a manuscript of one of my novels from an agent in New York. I read the letter while I drank a beer and smoked a cigarette. It said (along with Dear Mr. Barlow):

> We are returning your novel not because it is not publish-able, but because the market at this time is not amenable to novels about drunk pulpwood haulers and rednecks and deer hunting. Our comments relate more to its marketability than

to its publishability, and even though this novel is hilarious in many places and extremely well-written with a good plot, real characters, refreshing dialogue, beautiful descriptions and no typographical or spelling errors, we don't feel confident that we could place it for you. We would, however, be delighted to read anything else you have written or will write in the future.

It was signed by some asshole. I didn't read his name. I rolled a piece of paper into the machine and wrote my own letter. It said:

You, sir, are an ignorant man. How the fuck do you know it won't sell if you don't try to sell it? And do you think I can just shit another one on five minutes' notice? I worked on this cocksucker for two years. You got any idea what that takes out of a man? You like to play God with all of us out here, is that it? You kept my manuscript for three months and didn't even send it around. Here I was thinking the whole time that maybe somebody was thinking about buying it. I wish I had you down here. I'd whip your ass. I'd stomp a mud hole in your ass and walk it dry. You turd head. I hope you lose your job. You're not worth a fuck at it anyway. I hope your wife gives you the clap. I wish I had your job and you had mine. How'd you like to paint a few houses while it's a hundred degrees? I can tell you it's not any fun. I hope you get run over by a taxi cab on your way home. And then die after about a month of agonizing pain.

I rolled the letter up and read it. I thought it was pretty good. It expressed my feelings exactly. It made me feel a whole lot better. I read it twice and then I took it out of the machine and tore it up and threw it away. Then I started working on my story.

At four a.m. I was still working on it. I liked working in the middle of the night. There wasn't any noise anywhere. You didn't have to think about anything but what you had right in front of you.

I finished the story, read it, then addressed an envelope and stuck a few stamps on it and put the story inside it and carried it out the door, down the driveway to the mailbox. I knew it would go off for a while and then probably come back with a marvelous note on the rejection slip.

I was knocking, had been knocking for years, but it was taking a long time for them to let me in.

I went back inside, turned off the lights, and went to bed. Alone.

3

Lots of friends came by to see me. One of them was Raoul. Raoul had been in the crop-duster business and had made a fortune by flying in a load of marijuana to Jackson, Tennessee, one night. He had cousins in Caracas. He had plenty of money, and now he was trying to write. He wrote poetry mostly, and wanted me to read it. The night he came over he had three or four poems. He also had a lot of beer with him. I was glad to see him. I wasn't so glad to see his poems.

"Hey, Barlow, I've got some new poems," he said.

He'd caught me at the typewriter, in the act itself, which, of course, was almost sacred to me.

"I'm kind of busy, Raoul. I'm trying to write."

"Oh, come on, man, I brought you some beer. Sit down and read these poems."

I hated to have to mess with him, but I was almost out of beer.

"The only way I'll read them is if you leave me some beer, Raoul. I'm trying to write."

"Hey, man, take all the beer you want. You understand this shit, Barlow. Read these poems. Tell me what you think about them."

Raoul sat on the couch and I started looking at his poems.

"I've got some women we can pick up later, Barlow."

"Great, Raoul."

The first poem was about a bullfighter. There was a lot of blood and sand in it. There was a lot of death in the afternoon. The bull-fighter was a candyass, though; he couldn't face the bulls. Finally he ran from one and got a horn rammed up his ass and had to have a colectomy. And then he just stayed on a cot in a cantina for the rest of his life, sucking on a tequila bottle.

"This poem sucks, Raoul." I laid it aside and picked up the next one. "I think it'd be a lot better if you tried to make a short story out of it."

"I know, man, I know. I don't know the *prose,* though, man, I don't know the prose."

The next poem was about a garbageman who tried to smell the roses in life every day. And as bad as it was, Raoul had his finger on something. He was touching the hurt in people, trying to. For that I gave him an A.

"Listen, Raoul, you're a good guy. You've got some humanity in you even if you did put a lot of dope on the streets of Jackson, Tennessee."

"It was just a one-time thing, man."

"Listen, Raoul, none of that shit matters. If you want to write, you've got to shut yourself up in a room and write."

"I've been thinking about doing that, man."

I got one of his beers and looked at the next poem. It was called "Viva Vanetti." It was about a Mafia hit man who weighed four hundred pounds and was nicknamed the "Salsa Sausage." He went around killing people by submerging their heads in vats of pizza dough.

"This one sucks, too, Raoul." "Read the next one, man."

"How can you write good stuff one minute and such crappy stuff the next?"

"I don't know, man. It just comes to me."

I swore for a little bit and then picked up the last poem. It started off hot. The narrator was screaming things about lost pussy, and alley-cats rutting behind garbage cans. It had the heat of a summer night in the city in it. It had people on dope, switchblades, and cops who slapped the hell out of people and screamed in their faces. It had people trapped on fire escapes and gorillas loose from the zoo. It had everything in it. I was a little pissed that I hadn't written it. It was A-OK.

"It's great, Raoul. Son of a bitch is great. It'll be published."

I didn't tell him that might take ten or fifteen years.

"No shit, man? No *shit*?"

"I don't know how you did it," I said. "You ought to try writing some stories."

Raoul got up and started walking around the room.

"Wow, man," he said. "Wow!"

"Let's go get the women, Raoul," I said. I was ready for the women.

"Oh, shit, man, we can't go get the women now! I've got to go home and type up a clean copy of that poem. I've got to get that poem in the mail, man!"

Then he rushed right out the door. Then he rushed right back in and snatched the poem out of my hands.

"Thanks a million, Barlow! I'll never forget you for this!"

I drank four or five more of his beers and thought about the unfairness of everything. A guy like Raoul could make one big score and have it dicked for the rest of his life. But poetry was a hobby for him. It wasn't life and death for him. All he wanted was to see his name in a magazine. He wouldn't starve for his art. I was down to thirty-two dollars, and about to starve for mine.

I started writing another story.

4

My *mother* came to see me. I'd had about four beers that afternoon. I knew she was going to lay a lot of stuff on me that I didn't want to hear.

"How are you doing?" she said.

"I'm doing all right."

"Have you seen the children?"

"Not lately."

"Well, what are you going to *do*?"

I wanted to reach for a beer but I'd been raised not to drink in front of my mother.

"What else? I'm going to keep writing."

"After all it's cost you."

"Right."

"After you've lost your whole family over it."

"Wouldn't make a whole lot of sense to stop now, would it?"

She started crying. I knew she would. I went ahead and got the beer. She was probably thinking How did I ever raise this cold-blooded child?

I sat down with her.

"Look, Mama, I can't help it that I want to do this. It's not even a matter of wanting to. I *have* to. I can't live without it." "Well, how are you going to live? You don't even have a job."

I looked out the window.

"I work when I need the money. I paint a house once in a while. I work for a while and then I write for a while. I'm okay. Don't worry about me."

"It's my grandchildren I worry about. How are you going to pay your child support? When are you going to get to see them?"

"I guess I'll see them when she lets me. Have you seen them?"

"Yes."

"What did they say?"

"They wanted to know when you were coming home." Then she started crying again.

5

I hadn't made love in about sixty-four days, which is not an easy thing after you've been married and used to getting it whenever you want it. I didn't know many women and had great difficulty communicating with them. Most of the women I did know were friends of my ex-wife or wives of my friends. I was never able to tell women just exactly what I thought about womanhood in general, what wonderful things I thought women were. I had composed several poems about women that I had not submitted to any of the literary quarterlies, but basically they sang the praises of legs and breasts and long hair and painted toenails, red lips and nipples. Once in a while I would take these poems out and read them and then put them away again.

I missed my children. They were big holes torn out of my life. I knew that I had torn a big hole out of their lives. I hoped that their mother would have the good sense to marry a good man who would take care of them and give them a home, educations, food, love. I knew there'd never be a reconciliation. Their mother didn't want it, and I didn't want it. Our children and our parents were probably the only ones who wanted it. I only had one life, and I'd be damned if I'd live it in a way that would make me unhappy and please somebody else. I had already lived that kind of life, too much of it already.

6

The money ran out and I knew I'd have to go back to work. I knew also that my ex-wife's lawyer would soon be dunning me for an alimony payment which I didn't have. I considered full-time employment for about fifteen seconds, and then realized that since I had made the choice to be sorry, I wanted to be sorry full-time.

I went back to painting houses. I painted houses in Oxford, in Taylor, in Toccopola, in Dogtown. I wore paint-spattered clothes and let my hair and beard grow out. I wrote at night, with beer in the cooler on the floor next to the desk. All of my stories came back in. I bought a small postage scale and weighed my own envelopes to the penny and mailed them back out. Nothing, nothing. Nobody wanted my work. Sometimes I wrote all night and staggered out the door the next morning to paint houses. I painted houses for twenty-three days straight and then took the money and retired again. I hit the grocery store first. Forty pounds of leg quarters that I could fry and keep cold in the fridge. Salami and baloney. Cheese. Chili and hot dogs. I got a few brown steaks that were already frozen, perfectly good cheap meat. The rest of the cart I filled up with beer and cigarettes.

They were good days. I slept late and got up and read the newspaper and made coffee and breakfast, then sat down and started writing. Stories, nothing but stories. The last novel had taken me two years, and I wasn't ready to commit to that kind of time again right away. I could write a story in two days, revise it in a couple of hours, and be ready to start another one. I wrote through the afternoons, stopped for a while to fix something for supper, then went back to writing again. There was nothing I could do but keep going. I had already made all my decisions.

. . .

7

I thought she looked bad when I saw her. She was coming into a bar with some other people just as I was going out. She saw me and she stopped, so I had to stop, too. The people with her spoke briefly, friends of ours, friends of hers, ex-friends of mine, evidently. People who had been to our house and eaten with us and shared our wine and music. Or maybe they just wanted to get out of the way. I didn't blame them. The end hadn't been nice. The end had been nasty. Nasty people and nasty words and phrases and nastiness to make you go puke in the gutter. Me, her: both of us.

I didn't ask where the kids were. I didn't want to seem accusatory. I didn't want to seem drunk, but I was. I'd been in there for four hours. I was on my way to try and weave my key into the ignition. Everything that might be said would be forgotten the next morning. Just a black hole with her somewhere standing in it, a picture of her face to rock to sleep against your pillow.

"Hey," she said.

"Hey."

"You leaving?"

"Me? Well, yeah, I think so. What you up to?"

"Oh, nothing. Just out here looking for somebody to fuck. Right?"

"I don't know."

"Well, I am. Fucking everybody I can. You know how that goes, trying to fuck everybody you can."

I didn't say anything, so she went on by herself.

"Yeah, I'm trying to get enough together to have a gangbang about midnight if I can. If I can find enough of them still sober enough to fuck. A lot of men have that problem, you know. Start drinking beer about nine o'clock in the morning and drink all day and then have a bad case of the limpdick about dark."

"You doing okay?" I said.

"Nah. Ain't getting enough dick. This one of your hangouts, huh?"

"I come here sometimes."

"I bet there's some real sluts in here. It must be."

"You seem to be in here."

"Yeah, I just got here, though."

"Where's the kids?"

"None of your fucking business. Where's my money?"

"What money?"

"Oh. You ain't got my letter from my lawyer yet?"

"No."

"You'll get it tomorrow, probably. He mailed it yesterday. I hope you're ready to fork over your alimony payment of three hundred and twenty-five dollars."

"Three twenty-five? I thought it was one seventy-five."

"You get to pay the lawyer fees. He don't like waiting on his money. You're paying him a hundred and fifty for five months. Then you can go back to one seventy-five but after that I'm going to ask the judge to raise it back to three twenty-five since I ain't getting enough with two kids to feed and a house payment to make. You fucked anybody in here tonight?"

I just looked at her for a minute.

"Why does there have to be all this ugliness? Why do you have to act like this? Do you hate me that bad?"

"You goddamn right I do. And I'm gonna make you pay for every night I have to stay by myself."

"I don't have that kind of money."

"You better shit it then. Your mama said you'd been painting houses."

"Well. Some."

"Well, the kids ain't asked about you. I told them you left us. You better paint plenty of houses is all I can say."

"I'm not working that much. I'm trying to write, too."

"Ha! You better forget that shit. You're not gonna divorce me and then think you're gonna get to do what you want to. Uh uh, honey. Me and these kids come first. You brought em into this world and you're gonna take care of em till they're twenty-one. And if that don't leave you enough time for your life, tough shit."

"Why do you have to make me so mad? Why do you have to make me want to bust your face open for you?"

"I just wish you'd try it. I'd have your ass stuck in that jail so fast it'd make your head swim."

"When do I get the kids?"

"When I get ready."

"That's not what the judge said."

"Well, you just let me know when you want em. They can be sick sometimes, you know. They *can* be out of town."

All she wanted was for me to fall on my knees and grab her leg and beg to be taken back, so she'd have the enjoyment of turning me down. All she wanted was to be filled with hatred and bitterness for the rest of her life, and to turn her life into a secret and twisted and perverted thing that would torment her as badly as it would me. You read about these killings in the paper, between men and women, husbands and wives, ex-Adams and Eves? This is how they happen.

8

If I killed anybody that night, I didn't know anything about it the next morning. I woke hot, sweating, dizzy with the heat. I pulled down all the windows and blinds, turned on the air conditioner, and made some coffee. While it was perking I picked up a clock and looked at it.

11:30. The mail had already run, surely. I put on a pair of blue jeans and slipped my feet into my house shoes and went down the driveway. There were three manila envelopes inside the mailbox. I went back to the house with the little mothers tucked under my arm.

I poured myself a cup of coffee and stirred some sugar into it, didn't have any milk. I lit my first cigarette. I was almost out of beer again, but I hoped Monroe would leave me alone.

The news was bad, but it was news I was used to. I sat down on the couch with my coffee and my cigarettes and an ashtray and the three stories. All I could remember was her being nasty to me, and something about a pine tree being hung under my wheel on the way home. I looked at my tennis shoes on the floor. They had mud and pine needles on them. I opened the first envelope.

It was a plain rejection slip from *Spanish Fly*. On it was scrawled: *Nice, try again*. And some scribbled initials. What? Nice but not nice enough to publish? Nice enough to publish but you've got two years' worth of stories already accepted? Explain yourself here. Somebody might be getting ready to hang himself over this shit. What about Breece D'J Pancake? What about John Kennedy Toole? *Nice, try again* might have driven them over the edge.

I was silently weeping. I had anger. I tore open the second envelope. I knew it would be more of the same. There was a long, neatly typed letter from the assistant editor of *Ivory Towers* that said (along with Dear Leon):

This story came so close to being accepted. Majority rules and many people who read it misinterpreted it. We have had an argument for two weeks here over it. "White Girls with Black Asses," do you think you could tone that down a little bit, maybe change it to something else? Because the story doesn't really fit the title. And although it works wonderfully, what is the reason that Cleve beats his wife? He is always remorseful after he does it, enough to where he lashes himself to the tree in the lightning storm. Some people were revulsed by it. I must say it's one of the strongest things I've seen in a while. I would never tell you how to write. But maybe if you changed the title another magazine might be interested in it. We would love to see anything else you would care to send us.

Please keep writing. Don't let this be disappointing to you. You have great talent, and with material like this you will need great stamina.

All warmest wishes,
Betti DeLoreo

The next question was, what did Betti DeLoreo, Betti Del Oreo, look like? Was she married? Was she seventy years old? Would she be willing to meet with me and give me some of her nooky on the strength of my work? They were uncertain questions, and my hands were shaking just to think that a letter might come back one day minus the story I'd sent off. I opened the third envelope. It contained a story that had been going around for two years. There was a rejection slip from *Blue Lace* attached to it. It seemed that my material was not right for them; however, it was no reflection on the work itself, and they were sorry they were unable to make individual comments on each story because of their small staff, et cetera.

9

I went to town to get some more beer. I hadn't been answering my phone, even though it had rung several times. I knew it might be the lawyer, and I knew it might be Monroe, wanting me to go back to work. I had enough money to tide me over for a little while, and I didn't want to go back to painting houses until I had to. I knew the alimony payment would have to be reckoned with before long, and that was making me nervous, and I needed something to drink while I worked. It seemed like the harder I tried, the worse things became. I wondered how other people dealt with it. I tried to bury myself in my work, forget my feelings and my shortcomings and my fears and the sick weak hangovers that accompanied a night of writing and drinking. In winter it would be too cold to paint houses and what would I do then for money? I could work for the rest of the summer and try to save a little, but there wouldn't be any way I could save enough to pay the alimony. If I couldn't pay it, she'd have me put in jail. But maybe I'd be able to write in jail. I hoped I would.

I went into a grocery store to get the beer. Usually I went to wherever it was the cheapest. I got beer, barbecued pigskins, Slim Jims to munch on while writing. Sometimes when the muse wouldn't hit I had to have something to do and sometimes chewing worked. I had to have a cart to hold everything. When I got to the checkout I had to wait in line. I saw people looking at the things in my basket. I ignored them and looked instead at the covers of *Cosmopolitan* and *The National Enquirer*. Religious freaks had made them hide the *Playboy*s and *Penthouse*s under the counters several years before. The whole world seemed to be trying to be decent, and I seemed an indecent thing in it. I wanted titties, lots of them. I wanted to hear ZZ Top play "Legs." I wanted to live in a house on a hill with a swimming pool and a cool back porch where my friends could listen to music after I mixed them drinks. I looked at what I wanted and then I looked at what I had. There was a great gulf between the two of them. My clothes were stained with paint, and my fingernails were dirty. I wanted my children somehow without their mother. The woman rang up my purchases and they came to $29.42, including tax.

10

I knew I hadn't exhausted the possibilities in New York, but they had nearly exhausted me. I knew that publishers were men and women like men and women here, that they breathed, ate, read, got bored, watched TV. My novel had been to so many offices it had become dog-eared, but I didn't want to retype it. That would have been about a two-week job, possibly for nothing.

I sat there looking at it. It was just a stack of typed paper an inch and a half thick. But I knew there was nothing wrong with it. I knew that all it would take would be for the right person to see it. So far that hadn't happened.

I opened my copy of *Writer's Market* to the section that lists commercial publishers and closed my eyes. I flipped pages this way and that, flipped some more, flipped some backwards, then forward again. I stabbed a page with my finger, and then opened my eyes. I located a name, an address, and copied them onto a large manila envelope. I mailed it without hope or dread, without a covering letter, without retyping it. I just mailed it.

11

The letter from the lawyer came in the mail. It said (along with Dear Mr. Leon Barlow):

> My fees for handling your divorce trial and proceedings amount to $750.00. I would like to be paid as soon as possible, of course, but Mrs. Barlow has informed me that you are in a state of near penury. Therefore we have worked out a schedule of payments by figuring $150/month along with your alimony payment. This will be deducted by me before turning over the remainder to Mrs. Barlow each month. Your first payment is

due immediately and four more payments thereafter on the 1st of each month. Please remit your payment by return mail.

It was signed by that lawyer, I didn't read his name. I had forty-seven dollars to my name. I wondered if the jail still fed only twice a day. The only time I had been a weekend guest of that establishment, they had.

12

My uncle came by to see me. He was the brother of my mother, the only one who seemed to understand what I was trying to do. He had no love of reading or even movies except westerns, but he admired will and determination in a person no matter the odds, and he liked to see a man try to rise above his station in life.

"What are you doing?" he said.

"Nothing. Drinking a beer. You want one?"

"I might drink one. You're not writing anything?"

"Yessir, I'm writing. I'm writing every day. I'm just not publishing anything."

"Why not?"

"I don't know."

"Is it good enough to publish?"

"Yes. It is."

"How do you know?"

"Because I read the other stuff they publish."

"You think it's politics?"

"I don't know what it is."

"How you fixed for money?"

"Pretty bad. I've got to get out and find some work."

"You want me to give you a cow? I can give you a couple of cows if it would help you."

"What good's a couple of cows gonna do me?"

"Hell, dumb butt. Carry em to the sale and sell em. They're worth five or six hundred apiece."

"I hate to take anything from you. Marilyn's trying to wring my balls dry with alimony, though."

"I know it. She'll do it, too. Any time a man gets divorced in Missippi he's gonna pay through the nose. She letting you see the kids?"

"No. I haven't seen them a time."

"Take her back to court."

"I'd owe a lawyer some more money then."

"She's fucking over you, though. You just gonna lay here and take it?"

"I don't seem to have much choice."

My uncle got up and snorted. "There's always a choice." He drained his beer and tossed the can into the trash. "Come over to the house tomorrow and we'll catch those cows, load em up, haul em to the sale. They ought to bring eleven or twelve hundred anyway."

"What time?"

"Early. We need to be at New Albany by two."

"I'll be there. Thanks, Uncle Lou."

"Don't mention it."

13

My uncle had so many cows he didn't know exactly how many he had. He had cows he'd never even seen before. He was forever trying to catch them and put tags in their ears. He had started with two cows in 1949 and now he had around four or five hundred head, and they intermingled and bred unchecked and ran more or less wild on his place, through woods and pastures and a river bottom.

I showed up at his house wearing cowboy boots, jeans, and a long-sleeved shirt. My uncle had learned to rope and ride cutting horses after the war and he had taught me how. He had a brown gelding named Thunderbolt, who was aptly named. Riding him was like riding a fifteen-hundred-pound jackrabbit. He could start so fast that he could slide you backwards out of the saddle and then make a turn and bounce you off his hip as he was leaving. I had learned to ride him at first by holding onto the horn with both hands. And then I had learned to move with the horse. He was worth $18,000.

My uncle came out of the house. Thunderbolt and another horse were standing saddled in the yard.

"Why don't you write a western?" he said. "I bet you could sell a western."

"I don't want to write westerns."

"I bet you could sell one, though."

He pointed to Thunderbolt and I climbed up on him. He got on the other horse and we left through the gate. We kicked them a little and then cantered down through the pasture with the wind in our hair. The cows that had been standing in the bottom suddenly raised their tails like deer and took off running. The horses' hooves drummed in the earth. Clods of black dirt and grass were torn loose and kicked into the air behind us. Uncle Lou started swinging his rope. Most of the cows had horns, and some had Brahma blood. All of them were heavy and muscular and mean-tempered. What I would have given for my little boy to be in the saddle with me.

We cut a couple of cows out from the main group and raced along beside them. We gradually singled one out, a long lean gray cow with sharp tapering horns. I had to make a loop wide enough to settle over her head. I stood in the stirrups with the running end of the rope in my teeth and whirled the loop over my head and leaned forward and dropped it over her horns. I snubbed it tight on the saddle horn and Thunderbolt put on the brakes. When the cow hit the end of the rope, she went tail over head and hit the ground flat on her back, all the wind knocked out of her. Uncle Lou roped a hind foot and we got off the horses while they stood with their backs arched and holding her tight, and we wrapped two of her feet together with a pigging string. We took the ropes off her horns and the hind foot, and left her on the ground, bawling, with her eyes rolled up white in her head with anger. Then we coiled our ropes and took off after another one.

My uncle had been with a boy from Montana in the war. He had become close friends with this boy and after the war was over the boy invited him to come and stay with him and his family for a while. My uncle wasn't married, and didn't have anything at home to hold him or draw him back with any immediacy, so he went. The boy's family had a ranch high in the mountains, and they had been punching cows for four generations. My uncle didn't know which end of a horse was which, but they taught him. They taught him how to rope and brand and bulldog and bullride and even cook. They taught him how to hunt elk and how to rig packsaddles. They took him in like another son, fed him and washed his clothes. My uncle in turn had showed me some of these things. The thing unsaid that was hurting him the most was knowing that now he might not get to do it for my kids.

We didn't talk while we worked. We flushed the cows from the woods like coveys of quail, and then he pointed to a brutish-looking cow that was trotting away rapidly through some sage grass, watching us over her shoulder. She had some truly wicked horns. I wouldn't have gone after her. Uncle Lou rode straight for her. I let Thunderbolt get too close. He put his shoulder against her rump, and she whirled and opened a five-inch cut in his shoulder with her horn. Uncle Lou snatched a 30.30 Marlin from a scabbard on his saddle and shot the cow dead between the eyes and hollered that he'd dress the mother-fucker later. Blood poured down Thunderbolt's leg. The lips of the wound were flapping, open and loose. I could see the muscle beneath it bunching and working. These were the things I had done to my uncle with the circumstances of my own life, my divorce, my writing. I had cost him money and pain in a way that was no fault of his whatsoever. We kept riding. Thunderbolt bore it silently. We roped another cow. I kept working somehow. The day was long and I knew that other days would be long, and I knew that men sometimes had to be close to other men to help them through the hard times. Because that's what these times were.

14

We stood outside in the dust of the New Albany stockyard. The smell of shit was overpowering. Nobody was being murdered yet, they were just now getting sold. It made me a little sick, but how else could I enjoy my juicy T-bones if not some cattle took the big one in the brain? I tried not to think about them being hoisted, throats cut, skinned, sawed up. Ground up. Once in a while a little piece of rebellious bone from a long-dead cow would rise up in my mouth from the hamburger meat at Kroger's and threaten to chip a tooth. *Revenge of the Cows*. Let's don't make a movie out of it.

Lots of guys around there had cowboy boots on. Some had barrel chests and bellies and checkered shirts. I felt somehow inferior and unmanly in the midst of them, even though plenty of shit was smeared on my own boots. I leaned, if not physically, at least spiritually in the direction of my uncle, who was at peace there, at one with his own kind. Which I certainly didn't have anything against.

We had our cow tickets and we perched up on the corral above the
auction ring.

Obba deebe mobba beebe forty mouth a poe,
Six potater sebm potater fo potater moe,
I'm a tater you a tater kick him out the doe.
Hummmbabe who gonna gimme ten gimme ten ten
    gimme Rin Tin Tin;
Humbabe well you wanna watch this cow on the flo,
Hooma jimmy homma fimmy moe.

It went on like that for a while. I admired the auctioneers. They
wore straw hats and were good old boys. They had big, round voices. I
hated it that I had a scratchy, raspy voice, the kind of voice that made
me sick when I taped it along with "Top Forty Hits" and listened to it
late at night, singing songs like "Puff the Magic Dragon" and "Blowin'
in the Wind." I had a small cheap guitar I tried to play when I couldn't
write, with twangy strings, but I only knew four chords, G, C, D, and
G7. I had once made the mistake of making a tape of myself playing
and singing George Jones's "Yabba Dabba Do, The King Is Gone, And
So Are You," and leaving it lying around. Marilyn had played part of
it, much to the amusement of some guests at a party at our house one
night, while I was in the kitchen mixing drinks and boiling shrimp,
and it hadn't endeared her to me to walk in and realize what was going
on, people sniggering, and so on.
    First thing they did was run two shoat pigs out into the ring. First
thing one of the pigs did was leap through the pipe bars and shit in
a man's lap. The man was trying to get up out of his chair, and he
was holding the pig while it was shitting on him. Later on the man
bought the pig, I was sure just so he could kill it. But the pig wouldn't

understand. I've heard that pigs are very smart. Pigs learn how to hunt truffles. A pig in Arkansas was trained to point birds once. I believe pigs contributed to Ulysses' downfall. I've eaten a lot of pork chops myself. Imagine the pigs that have to die for us. These pigs go valiantly not even to their graves; they don't even have any graves, when you think about it. You ever seen a pig graveyard? What would you put on his tombstone?

Here lies no pig;

Don't dig.

Ain't no bones,

Just leave em alone.

Some horses ran through, got sold pretty fast. I had eyes for a Mexican-looking señorita who was selling sandwiches. I ate two pork barbecues and then realized that the pigs had probably come through the ring a few weeks before, pigs without a future, pigs without a life insurance plan. Pigs who'd never been set down around the supper table and oinked to. Pigs who just didn't know how good they'd had it, plenty of mud and corn to wallow among, happy days over with now.

She seemed to be a señorita, but I didn't know for sure. I was still thinking about Betti Del Oreo. I decided I would write her a real nice letter.

15

Dear Miss DeLoreo,

Thanks for taking so much time to tell me why the story was rejected. Most editors wouldn't do that. It's pretty lonely out here, you know, writing all these things and not getting anybody to pay any attention to them. I appreciate you taking the time, though. I'm gonna try to write something better for you. Something that'll make you stand up and put the gloves on with them.

Best wishes,
Leon Barlow

I was nervous as hell when I mailed the letter. I don't know why. I didn't even know her. And maybe she was seventy years old, retired from Florida or something, with skinny knees. But why couldn't she be some *goddess*, kneeling in the streets of New York for the right prophet to come along? With the rain in her face, black hair beautiful, screaming for me?

I licked it shut and sent it. I'd enclosed a story, also.

I was waiting for the check from my uncle for the two cows he'd given me that we'd subsequently sold. The other cow, the one he'd shot for goring Thunderbolt, was probably down in the pasture still, stinking, covered with flies, coyotes eating on it, but I didn't want to go check. There were some things I didn't want to be around and rotting putrid meat was one of them.

16

I smoked some marijuana and drank a lot of beer one day and then wrote this:

HONED

Honed's daddy had a good reason for changing his name early. But he was almost too late with the thought. He had Honed up in his arms, wrapped in a nice soft blanket Honed's mother had spent about eight

and a half months knitting, with little flowers and soft bunny rabbits
hopping around on it in fields of green clover—real nice stuff for a kid
they'd just gotten to know—just pure damn love for the little guy—
and he'd been kissing around on Honed's head and telling his koochie-
poo that MomMom was right behind them in a wheelchair and so
he was going to warm his bottles and stuff for him for a while, since
MomMom had had her puss stretched inside out. But Honed didn't
have any idea what was happening. They'd had to calm him down anyway. He was upset big time. He'd been rudely expulsed from the warm
dark saltwater sea of his mother's belly, where he'd begun to think he'd
always be, into the hard red hands of a grinning bald-headed guy with
big white teeth (Like fangs! Shit! Honed thought) who hit him on the
ass four or five times. And then a whole bunch of people he didn't even
know had been dressing him and undressing him and they even messed
with his goober for a while one day—there was still something going
on down there but he was scared to look (I've got to figure out what
the hell's going on, he thought)—so he was just mainly trying to sleep
and hide from it all he could. He knew that he was helpless and at their
mercy. He couldn't walk, couldn't talk, couldn't do anything but shit
and cry. And they were all a lot bigger than he was.

Honed's daddy named him Ned originally. And it occurred to him
just as he was going down the hall with Honed in his arms, getting
ready to take him home, that people would be saying Hi to Ned a lot
in his life (which he hoped would run about a hundred wonderful
years) and where they were going home to, they wouldn't necessarily
say Hi. They might say Hey. But a bunch of them would probably
say Ho. Ho Ned. Whassup, main? And then when Ned came up in
his world and put his legs into his britches like men do, he'd be out
in it seeing people. If they said Hi they'd say Hined and if they said
Ho they'd say Honed. (He was a little whacky, Honed's daddy. But he

didn't live long after Honed was born anyway. And he was a good guy. He could have done a lot for Honed. He was a millionaire playboy/ professor with two published novels, and the MacArthur Foundation was getting ready to give him about $60,000 a year for five years when he got killed. It actually happened in a freight elevator. It was very ironical. It was at the very top of the Empire State Building, when it was still the tallest. Honed's daddy was the kind of brilliant person who is severely dumb in other ways. He mistook the freight elevator for the one people were supposed to ride. He rode it all right. He punched floor seven, and what they thought happened was all the relays that controlled the up cables blew, and the damn thing just took off, straight up, flying. Honed's daddy peed all over himself. It was a horrible death. And he knew he was going to die. That was the thing. He did have enough sense to know that it was going up way too fast, the floors just flashing by on the lights. But he was calm even in the face of that. He allowed himself three-quarters of a second of all-out, mindless mute screaming-ass terror, and then dropped his briefcase and started punching elevator buttons. Nothing happened. A bunch of mechanical things that the elevator people *should have been maintaining a little more closely* gave way at the same time. Oh, they had a big lawsuit, and Honed's mother got richer than she already was, but it didn't bring Honed's daddy back. The elevator car hit the top of its channel with so much force that it threw Honed's daddy up against the ceiling of the car and broke open a big place in his head. One cable snapped on impact, and the motor downstairs started freewheeling without belts because they had snapped, too, and the other cable was strong enough almost to hold the car all those hundreds and hundreds of feet above the floor of New York City. But then it snapped, too. Honed's daddy was on the floor, stretched out, his eyes closed, his fingers trying to dig. The downward rush was so great that Honed's daddy's body was actually floating about an inch above the floor of the car a millisecond before it hit the basement.) What Honed's daddy thought, standing just short of the doors of the hospital with Honed in his arms, was that he would save all those people the trouble of saying Ho, comma, Ned, and call him Honed. And in that way be kind of like a tribute to Honed for someone to say his name. That kind of thinking may be crazy, but that's the kind of thinking Honed's daddy did.

I NEVER FINISHED that one, either.

17

The check from my uncle came in the mail. It was $1143.68, and it was made out to me. I booked. Salad tomatoes, some movies, couple of cassettes, shrimp, some oysters, couple of sirloins, beer, whiskey, some blue jeans, a belt, two shirts, some underwear, some Collins mix, garbage bags, a broom, Spic 'n' Span, a cigarette lighter, *The Sound and the Fury*, *Hot Water Music*, *Jujitsu for Christ*, *Child of God*, *The Complete Stories of Flannery O'Connor*, *The Old Man and the Sea*, some barbecue bread, socks, a *TV Guide*, fourteen typewriter ribbons, some of those little chocolate-covered cherries, some kids' clothes, a little blue squeeze giraffe that squeaked when you squeezed it, a little baseball and bat and glove, some rubbers, some toothpaste, some English Leather, some fingernail clippers, some shampoo, Slim Jims, barbecued pigskins, some Jimmy Dean smoked sausage, catfish, some seafood sauce, two reams of paper, some correction film, four dozen manila envelopes, some ink pens, a new *Writer's Market*, a new band for my wristwatch, some rolling papers, a fanbelt, some brake shoes, a sending unit for my oil pressure gauge, G and A guitar strings, and some charcoal.

It was kind of like Christmas.

I hauled all that home, called my ex-wife and told her I had some stuff for the kids she could pick up at my mother's, told her I was fixing to write her lawyer a check for two months' alimony, hung up, sat down, wrote the check, addressed an envelope, considered writing him a letter, didn't, licked it shut, put a stamp on it that I steamed off one of my returned envelopes that the postal employees had let edge through the cancelling machine, and walked down the driveway whistling and put it in the mailbox.

When I stepped back in the house there was still some of the money left. Provisions had been laid in. I was ready for the siege. I opened a beer, took a swig, put on Johann Pachelbel's Kanon and listened. My uncle had caused all this. And he was out three cows over it. Later that night I called him and thanked him, and tried to explain the enormity of what he had done for me, how he had given me at least sixty days of freedom and time to write, but all he said was don't mention it.

18

Couple of days later it was her on the phone. I asked her if she'd gotten her mon.

"Yeah, I got it. Where'd you get it?"

"That's all right where I got it. You don't need to call over here and get nasty with me just because I made your alimony payment on time."

"I ain't being nasty with you. I know where you got it anyway."

"You don't neither."

"I bet I do."

"No, you don't."

"Yes, I do."

"Don't do it."

"Do too."

"Well, where'd I get it, then, you know so much?"

"Your uncle gave it to you. He sold two cows and gave you the money."

"Who told you that?"

"Your mother."

"Goddamn it."

"She tells me everything."

"I bet by God she won't after I get through talking to her."

"What you so pissed about? I got a right to know what you're doing."

"Not any more you don't."

"Did you make it home all right that night?"

"What night?"

"That night I talked to you. I don't guess you remember it, you's so drunk. Couldn't hardly walk. You gonna have a car wreck and kill yourself one night. Or fuck some old haint and get AIDS all over you. Then what's your kids gonna do for a daddy?"

"I wasn't aware that they had one now other than biologically speaking."

"Other than biologically speaking? You are so full of shit, Leon, do you know that?"

"Are you through bending my ear? Cause if you ain't, tough shit. I'm through talking to you. I got your damn alimony paid so I don't want to hear another word out of you for two months. You got that?"

"Sure. Less one of the kids gets sick or something."

"Yeah. Well, call me if that happens. I want to know if they're sick."

"I mean to pay the bills. You got to pay the doctor bills, too, you know."

"*I know*, Marilyn. Now anything else? No? Bye!"

Fuck you. Goddamn couldn't write while I was married to you and now I'm having to listen to you while I'm divorced, trying to work over here. Shit. Get me so goddamn upset I can't even do anything for thinking about all the shit you get me upset about. Call over here and mess up a whole day's work because of you. Didn't even mention the stuff I got the kids. Just wanted to worry the hell out of me for a while. Probably told them you bought it yourself. Be just like you.

19

I wondered if the great Betti DeLoreo would write me back. I wondered how high up she was. It was entirely possible that she might be fat, fifty-eight, and gap-toothed. She was probably married and had grown children. She might be bulimic, or lesbian, or have no legs. What did I mean imagining these things about people I didn't even know? I did it, though. I imagined what she looked like. I imagined her flying down from New York and pulling up outside in a white stretch limo and getting out, flashing a lot of leg, telling the driver to wait, coming in, Leon? Yes, Leon darling, yes, and then pulling off her fur and having this cleavage like Jayne Mansfield. I actually sat at the typewriter and did that. I did that a lot. Usually while I was under the influence of Uncle Bud.

20

I got drunk one night. Actually several nights in a row and it scared me. When I came to, I believed I had been on a "running drunk" for two days. It was the first time that had ever happened to me, and I'd always said it never would. Now I had done it, and it hadn't seemed that hard.

I curled up there in my bed the next morning and thought about it. This is what brought it on. You've got your art and you've got your precious life and where does that leave room for them? I rolled over, closed my eyes, mashed my face into that pillow. Trying to keep that old sickening straight truth from pushing in. If you's worth a shit you'd act right. Stay home two or *three* nights a week anyway. You just love to run drunk. Ain't nothing going to help it. You can fix it for a while and then it's all going to come back. Sooner or later. You can straighten up for a while till things get better and then gradually you'll get off into it again. Why she left you. Look how long she stayed. And you just threw it all away. Think about those fat little faces. That little one cutting teeth, crawling, whatever. You a sorry son of a bitch. Probably don't even know how old they are. Yeah . . . Alisha's . . . twenty-one months . . . Alan's four years three months.

I sat up in the bed. Had the sheet up over my legs, like I was going to get up with it wrapped around me like guys you see in these TV movies or even real movies where they don't want their dicks to be seen, but it's really ironical when you think about it, like two people who have been slamming each other's bodies naked for two hours are suddenly going to get up and wrap sheets around them.

Yeah, I was sorry. Sorry as hell. Sorriest sumbitch ever shit behind a pair of shoes. But one thing in my favor was that I wouldn't rather climb a tree and tell you a lie than stand on the ground and tell you the truth. No sir, you could trust me to do what I said. I had a lot of things wrong with me, but lying wasn't one of them.

That old sunshine was burning in on my head. I had a bunch of pimples on my legs, or maybe not pimples, just these little red irritated spots from wearing long pants all my life. Man wasn't meant to wear long pants, but my legs are so skinny I can hardly bear it.

It was hot as hell. Again. My head was hurting, and I had about two truckloads of guilt on me. They'd already backed up and dumped. Right on my head.

The day didn't seem worth getting dressed for. So I flopped again.

21

It was hotter than before when I woke. Sweat had matted the hair on the side of my head. The pillow was damp with it. It seemed to be about two o'clock in the afternoon. I knew the mail had run.

I lay there and thought about it. What good would it do to get up and go see? The motherfuckers weren't going to publish any of it.

I got up and showered. I looked out the window. My neighbor's corn in the field next door was being burnt, parched, withered. He was having a rough time of it, too.

I went down and checked the mail. Water bill, light bill, phone bill, and somebody wanting to give me an AM/FM radio worth $39.95 if I bought a quarter acre of land in some resort area in Arkansas for $6800. Nothing from Betti DeLoreo. But at least nothing had come back. Yet. I had fourteen stories on their way to or back from various editorial offices across America.

I went back to the house, opened a beer, and sat down at the machine. I sat there all afternoon waiting for it to say something to me, and it never did.

22

I wanted to write a story about love one morning. I liked love and could hardly do without it, but I didn't really want to write a love story. I mean not a bodice-ripper. So I started writing a story about a lady whose husband had died and left her with two children. He had been killed in a tragic pulpwood-cutting accident, mashed flat by a falling pine tree, and now he was dead and gone, fresh dirt heaped over his grave. The lady, whose name was suddenly Marie, couldn't even afford to buy him a headstone. He, the lately deceased husband, who didn't need a name, had not taken out a large life insurance policy to provide for his family's future in the event of a sudden and unexpected death. As a matter of fact, one night after a long day of pulpwood cutting only two weeks before, he had told an insurance salesman who had come by to see him that he didn't have time to listen to that shit, and would he get the fuck out the door. Two weeks later, pow. Flat as a pancake. The kids were grabbing hold of the door-knobs hollering Biscuit, Daddy, biscuit. Marie didn't have any skills, couldn't read. Plus she had a nervous condition that made her head shake very slightly. She didn't know what she was going to do, how she was going to provide for these two children, who needed Pampers and other things.

She tried go-go dancing for three nights, locking her sleeping children in the car in the parking lot. But it was no good. She couldn't concentrate on her rhythm, thinking about the kids outside, whether they were awake or not, crying, thinking they had been abandoned. So she had to turn in her G-string. She drove home through the night, gripping the steering wheel "so tightly her knuckles whitened," wondering what she was going to do. The kids continued to sleep in the back seat, secure in the knowledge that their mother would take care of them.

Marie rode around for a while, wondering why her husband hadn't had enough sense to buy life insurance. She didn't even have dog food for their dog.

At this point I realized I couldn't help them, realized I wasn't a writer, and threw it away, which scared the shit out of me.

23

I was sitting on the porch drinking a beer about sundown. Nothing was good. My life was rotten. My ex-wife would have a yoke around my neck for the rest of my life, and if I happened to remarry one day, her hate would be doubled. I didn't know if I could take double hate. Nothing I could ever do would be able to repair the feelings that had been stomped on. I had promised before God in His church to cherish her always and I had not honored that promise.

I heard a car turning in the driveway, saw headlamps coming up even though it was too early for them. It was Monroe. The evening gloam was upon us. It was gloaming time. We would be Gloamriders in the Sky.

He shut off the motor and got out with a beer, stuck his arm back in and turned off the lights. He got up on the porch and sat down beside me in a chair.

"What's up, man?" he said.

"Not much. Just sitting here watching it get dark."

"You want a beer?"

"I've got one. You need one?"

"I've got one. You want to go ride around?"

"Suits me. Let me get some more beer."

"I've got plenty. Just come on and get in."

I got in. We rode down the road.

"What do you hear from your old lady?" he said.

"That she hates my guts."

"That's nothing new, is it?"

"No."

We rode for a while. Drank a while. He had some Thin Lizzy and he plugged old Philip Lynott in and the evening gloam began to turn purple and be immersed with beautiful gray-lit white clouds that rolled high up in the heavens and began to slowly unfold like gigantic marshmallows or mushrooms until the beauty of it just made me shake my head. I was alive, he was alive, the snakes were in the ditches, the deer were beginning to ease out of the woods, the beer was cold, he was free from his old lady, I was free from my old lady, both of us were just free as birds. We'd both been through the woman trouble and we knew what it was. It was a heartsick and a fuckup and nobody could warn you from one to the next. Lose one, get another one. One day loves you and then another day years apart hates you. You bastard. You sorry son of a bitch. Oh yes, baby, do it make me *come*. All them words out of the same mouth. Tsk, tsk. Be my *only* baby. Get up and fix it yourself.

"We in the gloam, old buddy," he said. "We definitely right in the middle of it."

It was true. James Street had given us the phraseology. The wind was sweeping our hair. We had the windows rolled down, arms stuck out. It was warm. Life was alive, and real, and we were not putting a whole lot of poisonous emissions into the air. I felt about as good as I'd felt in a while.

"It's a gloaming, all right," I said.

He kind of snickered over there at the steering wheel.

"Let's go fuck up. You want to?"

"Fuck up? Where at?"

"Ah hell, we can just go fuck up uptown if you want to. I don't care. Just anywhere."

I lit me a cigarette. I'd been cutting down.

"Ah hell. I don't guess I better go fuck up. I think we fucked up a lot the last two nights, didn't we?"

"In a row, buddy roe. In a row. That's why I want to get out so bad and fuck up tonight. See if we can't make it three in a row."

"Boy, I was fucked up last night."

"I know it. I was, too. Do you remember us even going home?"

"Naw, man. I was too fucked up."

We rode some more. The stars couldn't make it out yet, not yet, but they'd be peeking before long. Night was going to cover the land. Everything that slept in the woods would wake up then, the coons from their lairs and the rabbits that feared everything. I could almost see the beavers' heads cutting the ripples up Potlockney Creek. I wanted womanflesh. I mean, as good as that was, I wanted long hair in my hands, and breasts on my chest. And I was aching, awful, didn't want him to see. So I said: "Yeah. All right. Let's go fuck up."

24

We woke up hot. Out in the middle of the woods. Why we do these things I don't know. It seems so easy when you first start out. Couple of cold beers, little smoke. Ain't going to hurt nothing or nobody. Just going to pass off an enjoyable evening. And wind up almost dying before you get home.

He wasn't in the car. He was out on the ground. Lying in a patch of sunlight with ticks crawling all over him. It was nine o'clock. He was fucked for work. And would have to call in.

Bark and stuff were stuck to his face when I woke him up. He couldn't believe where we were. We'd had no nooky, neither of us. The nooky was all at home asleep. We had some vomit dried on us, real regular pickup guys. Swinging Singles. We were as bad a fuckup as a screen door in a submarine.

He didn't want to get up. Wanted to just stay there on the ground and sleep. Said he could make it if I just moved him into the shade.

25

I was sitting on the back porch the next evening not doing a damn thing. Drinking a beer. I'd said fuck it for the day. I'd hammered some stuff out, but I didn't know for sure how good it was. It felt good, but I wasn't certain. The world at large had a pretty narrow-minded conception of everything. Some rootintooter from Chillicothe might get ahold of my stuff, and not have on his favorite pair of crotchless panties that day, and that might cause him to reject my work. I didn't know. I knew editors had to be human, but I also knew that some of them had to be square, uncool, unreceptive to cool new work. I also knew that plenty of them were actively looking for the next new voice. I just didn't know how to find them. They didn't have names that I knew, and the names they had, I didn't know how to find.

It looked like a bat uprising out there. Like all the bats in all the caves of hell had decided to come out and fly around my house. I grew tired of it pretty quickly. I got my shotgun and started shucking and pumping. Pow! Blow your little ass out of the sky. Blam! Leave a hole for the moon to look through.

Well, I harried them away from the dusk, finally. Blew a couple of holes in a few flocks. How could they hang upside down and sleep? I didn't care, because I wasn't with Marilyn any more, and Betti DeLoreo hadn't answered, and I had about four beers in me, which seems to be the break point for me, when I make the decision to fuck up or not. Usually I do, but to my credit, there have been a few times when I have not.

26

Same evening, a little later, I'd moved the speakers out onto the back porch and I was communing with nature a little. I loved nature and I felt like nature loved me. Why else would they send those fireflies, and doves, and geese that honked like a pack of wild dogs howling down the sky?

Dark was fine with me. That was when the women moved. They were sort of like snakes, or owls, looking to see what they could latch onto in the night. I loved them for that, thought it was a fine way to be. That was the way I was, and I didn't figure anything was going to change it.

I heard him slowing down on the highway before he got close to the driveway. The distant roaring grew slighter; he was giving himself plenty of room to slow down, taking it easy on his brake shoes. I looked out across the trees and the river and the grass. Catfish were swimming down there in the water. Old turtles that were there when Lee surrendered. I'd seen them, monsters with moss on their heads, pulled up from the depths and clawing against the boat. If you sit down there in a boat still enough, the beavers will come out and sit on the banks and wash their hands and faces.

Yeah, it looked like a night for women. He kept slowing down, coming nearer, and I cranked it up just a little on Thin Lizzy's "Cowboy Song." I hated it that Philip was dead, and it had only been a couple of weeks since Roy Orbison had died. My heroes had fallen all around me, had been falling for years. Hendrix and Morrison and Joplin and Croce and Chapin and Redding, Elvis and Sam Cooke, he was dead, too, Lennon and Mama Cass, I didn't even want to think about the rest of them.

I heard the gravel crunching under his wheels. Coming to take me away. Lights lanced around the side of the house. I heard his alternator protesting a loose belt, and all fell to naught. I sipped my beer. I'd been sipping beer for a couple of hours, waiting on him.

27

The girl looked dead. Damn, she's dead, I thought, looking at her. But then I looked at Monroe and thought, Surely to God he's not dead, too. Finally I could see their chests rising and falling. His pants were halfway on, hers were halfway off. The sun was on us again. We were sort of like superstrong vampires who just got sickened by the sun. It wasn't going to kill us or anything. But it sure didn't make us feel good at certain times.

They were on the back seat. I was on the front. Somebody was plowing a field on a tractor right across the road from us. It was pretty unwonderful there, and to wonder who else might ought to be with us and where we might have left them and what stages of jail/bail we might have left them in, since I vaguely remembered us having some running mates with us at some point the night before.

I woke them up. Monroe seemed to think that a couple of them might be in the Pontotoc County jail and need our renderings, slim as they were.

We booked, naturally, to the Pontotoc County jail. A large man with red cheeks presented himself at the front door.

"Hep y'all?"

"Yessir, we think we got some friends in jail over here maybe."

"Name?"

"What's their names, Monroe?"

She spoke up. "Jerome and Kerwood White." She was looking sort of anxious, since they were her little brothers.

"White? White. I don't believe I've got them names on my list. Now I believe we had two Whites killed in a car wreck last night. Here it is. Yeah. That them? Jerome and Kerwood? One subjeck twenty-seven, one twenty-five. Dead on impact. Tractor trailer over here on Highway 6. Cut one of em's head off, I believe. Y'all some kin to the family?"

28

The funeral of those boys was not a good place to be. It was raining, and muddy, and people were beating each other with fists of grief and screaming and blaming the whole thing on God. It was ironic since they'd all come to Him for comfort on this particular day. I saw some lady bust her ass on the church steps, had black bikini panties on, showed it to the whole world. I had several cuts on my head that nobody could explain.

The place where they buried them was down under a hill with white oak trees. It was very muddy. You could see it sticking to the heels of the ladies' shoes. It was that red clay that lifts out two shoe sizes when you raise your foot. But what made me sadder than anything was all the old wreaths and styrofoam green spray-painted crosses from old monuments and tributes to love piled up against a rusty barbed-wire fence, forlorn and all, wet, funky. Funky funky love. I realized right that moment how different were the different types of love. Love between man and woman, husband and wife, was much different from, say, between son and father, or father and daughter, or brother and sister, or brother and brother, and father-in-law to second cousin. Love for the right person could make you do anything, give up your own life. I knew there was love that strong. I felt it for my children. I looked next to me and saw Jerome and Kerwood White's mama and daddy holding each other up, staring at those two coffins, and I thought of times in diapers and even before, dates and weddings and visits on the front porch, the first kiss, a little house to start with until some kids came along. What they had on their faces was horror.

I was afraid I knew how it would go. He'd start drinking more, and she'd age quickly. From her loneliness and grief. There'd be a hole in her that nobody'd be able to fill up. Sex at their age was probably not much of a consideration any more. But maybe it was, between them. I hoped it was. I hoped it was an intimate thing between them that would hold them together, his wrinkled old body naked up against her old wrinkled naked body, bodies they remembered from forty years ago. But if it didn't . . . if that couldn't hold them together . . . if there were late nights home from the bars . . . her knitting in the living room, so quiet . . . what purpose to their lives any more. Two of the things they had centered on for so long. From diapers to death. And probably drunk when they died.

I went over to them and held them. I cried with them. They didn't know me. They cried with me anyway.

29

I saw Raoul's poem. It appeared in the spring issue of *Rabbe Mabbe*. They'd edited it a little, toned it down, taken some or most of the guts out of it, but Raoul didn't want to talk about it. He was writing a novel. I said Go for it, motherfucker.

30

I got the kids one weekend and she went off to spend it with somebody, I don't know if it was male or female. At that point I wouldn't have put anything past her. I just hoped she wasn't doing anything adverse around the kids.

Alisha shit on me a couple of times. Alan and I built a big fire in the backyard out of wood crates and things and roasted twenty-seven hot dogs and a pack of marshmallows. We pitched our old tent and carried quilts out of the house and pillows and camped out in the backyard the whole weekend except for TV-watching inside in the daytime. Alisha liked it. We didn't know if she was retarded or not. There was a chance, they said, but we didn't know yet. She seemed slow. Slow to focus her eyes, slow to understand words. Slow to learn to use the pot.

At night in the tent I held her to my chest and felt her heart beating under her skin, felt the silk of her hair brushing against my face. You deserve better parents than us, kiddo, I thought. She would try to talk but the words would never come. I must have said Daddy to her five hundred times that weekend, just trying to get her to say it. She never would. But she knew who Daddy was. That was the main thing. She might not have had that word in her head. But she knew who Daddy was.

Alan did, too. He was my cowboy. I wanted him on Thunderbolt with me and I told myself I'd call Uncle Lou about it. We all slept in one sleeping bag because I wanted them close to me, I wanted their little faces and their little hands on me and I wanted to breathe their little sweet untainted exhalations all night long. I did that. And on Sunday evening at five o'clock I gave them back to their mother and tried not to cry when they went down the driveway, waving back to me through the glass and the dust.

31

Monroe blamed himself for those boys' deaths. That girl was their sister, but I hadn't known that earlier. What they'd done was drive their car at ninety miles an hour under a tractor-trailer that was crossing the highway. One skid mark was ninety feet long. The Highway Patrol said that meant they had one brake shoe working. They went 302 feet out the other side of it before coasting to a rest. The entire top was one small pinched thing like a steel suitcase.

I had to go over to the junkyard with them and look at it. Their sister cried softly on Monroe's shoulder the whole time. I didn't know what had happened, didn't know that we'd met them and gotten in with them briefly and rode around with them for a while, and then gone back to our cars and let them go on to their deaths. She seemed to think somehow that it was all my fault. I hadn't even been driving.

I told them I'd see them later.

32

Marilyn called me again. Betti DeLoreo hadn't answered yet. I was getting pretty impatient. I wanted to know the news whether it was good or bad. I didn't mind screwing around with uncertainty, it was dead flat failure I had a problem with.

"Lisha's got ticks all over her."

"We had her out in the tent. Put some nail polish on em. What are they? Those little bitty ticks?"

"Yeah. Them little tiny ones. You can't hardly see em."

"They don't carry tick fever. That's the Spotted Brown Dog Tick."

"What are you doing?"

"Nothing. Trying to write. Enjoying knowing you can't even think about trying to wring my balls for thirty-eight more days."

"Well. I'm getting to be pretty good friends with Judge Johnson. He bought me a milkshake down at Burger King the other day."

"He sounds like a real groovy guy."

"Oh, he is, he is. He thinks it's a shame how divorced women get treated in Missippi."

"What is he, a liberal?"

"I think he's horny."

"He probably is. I guess you been shaking your ass at him."

"Nah."

"Don't tell me. You let him look down your shirt."

"I think I'm fixing to change jobs."

"Oh yeah?"

"Yeah."

"I heard about a good job the other day."

"You did?"

"Yeah."

"Where is it?"

"Up at a woodworking mill in Memphis. They need somebody to eat sawdust and shit two-by-fours. You interested?"

"I'm gonna have you begging for mercy."

"Not me, baby."

"You wait and see. You going out with anybody?"

"I wouldn't tell you if I was."

"What, she some great old big fat thing with great big titties?"

"Wouldn't you like to know?"

"Well. I been dating a guy that's *real* nice. And for your information, he thought *Blue Velvet* was a sick movie."

"Shit. What'd you do, rent it just so you could see if he thought it was a sick movie?"

"No."

"Boy. I bet David Lynch is just losing his lunch right now because you and your boyfriend thought his movie was sick. You dilbert-head."

"Well, that wasn't the only thing you were crazy over. Anybody who'd buy a red hunting hat and turn it around backwards on his head, and wear it like that, get up in the bathroom and tap dance . . ."

"Look. We've been over this time and time again. He wasn't crazy."

"Then why'd they put him in that place?"

"Because they *thought* he was crazy."

"Aha! See there!"

"Look, goddamnit. For the last time. His little brother died. This kid he knew jumped out a window and killed himself. And he was just a kid himself. Now if you don't think that would fuck somebody up . . ."

"But it was just a book!" I paused.

"Right, right," I said, and eased the receiver gently onto the cradle.

33

Some more stories came back in. Some had marvelous rejection slips. Nobody promised their body to me over any of them. I knew that would come later. But I wished they'd hurry up. I still hadn't legged down with anybody and I knew that my sperm was backed up pretty deep. I didn't want the heartbreak of prostate trouble.

I tried to write all I could. I tried to put balls and heart and blood into it like a good writer had once told me to do. Sometimes it wasted me, just laid me out. I knew that at least some of what I was writing was good, but I just hadn't found anybody to share my vision yet. Nobody with any power. Nobody who could say yes or no to publication. I knew about the pecking order, and jealousy, and inter-departmental office memos and the little notes that were jotted with a quick hand. They didn't know about the careers they were advancing or retarding with their little papers, the numbers of us who lived and died with a stroke of their pens. They didn't have any idea of the power they wielded. We were a vast unfaced effluvium of authors with unproven work, and there was so much bad that it was hard to find the good in all of it. Maybe they became jaded with it, their eyes turned to stone by the shit that fell before them. Maybe so much bad work had convinced them that it all looked alike, that nothing was going to come from the shit pile, that the quest was already over and they weren't going to discover the next Hemingway. I felt these things strongly. I couldn't prove them, but I felt them.

I wondered if the great Betti DeLoreo was somewhere in her high ivory tower, her fingernails painted red, her black mane of hair drawn to one side, reading manuscripts, one load of shit after another. I wondered if she was thinking of me. I knew the chance was small. There were many of us and only one of her. And she was only one cog in a big machine. It seemed almost hopeless sometimes, but I knew I had to keep going on. I had chosen my own path. Nothing could turn me from it.

34

I was in a bar one night and I had been drinking before I got there. I knew I was treading on shaky ground, drinking at night in town and then having to drive myself home. The state troopers nailed people with regularity. It helped to take secondary roads, to be responsible. I had good intentions that were often spoiled by drinking.

The evenings began it. The two or three beers in the late evening, then the false sense of security when night fell. To be driving on the backroads, the cooler in the floorboard. Little music playing. The road just slowly going by at thirty-five miles an hour. But sometimes the road wound to town.

Sometimes you see somebody you don't like and you know when you look at him that the feeling is mutual. Your eyes meet briefly and then part, like two dogs sizing each other up. And any time later that night when you look at him, he'll be looking at you. You only have to wait for the liquor to do its work to get your surprise. Your mouthful of fist, if it comes.

That was what I happened to be facing that night. Some fucker with a freaky face. I guess he was jealous of my handsome one, or relatively unmarked one anyway, which was the main difference between us. First off, somebody'd kicked both his front teeth out. And then bit off half of one of his ears. Then they, like, tried to *gouge* his right eye out with a class ring or something, really grinding it deep into the tissue of his eyelid, so that it hung down halfway over the eye and gave him this . . . freaky look. Man has a problem. You understand it immediately. He won't go to a plastic surgeon. Whatever in his life led him to his altered state won't let him repair himself. He'd rather take it out on unscarred people like you, try to make you look more like him. It's the kind of thing that makes you want to turn your back and finish your beer and find another place to drink in that night. Because after he's given you that pit bull look, you know you won't go unchallenged.

I knew a few people down there shooting pool. They had some peeled cedar posts propping the ceiling up. Playmates were plastered over the same ceiling. You could look up and see titties of the most delectable types. Small rounded asses reclining over velvet couches, their elegant legs stretched out. Where do they find these women? They're not out here in the world. I've never seen them. They don't hang out in this particular bar, anyway.

I just moseyed around for a while. It was really pretty dull. I should have been at home writing. But I'd written so much I was temporarily tired of it. And I was hoping I might find some disreputable woman or some cast-off woman disreputable enough to take me in for the night. I knew I had no line of chatter, none. I just couldn't open up. I knew they thought I was unfriendly, that I had no rap. But it really wasn't that way at all. What did you say after you said Hi? You from around here? Why did they look so snotty when you tried to talk to them? Weren't they lonely, too? Didn't they want some warm flesh to press up against? I didn't know any of the answers. I'd met my wife on a blind double date. We'd gotten pretty well acquainted in the back seat before we ever got out of her daddy's driveway.

The young lady who was barmaiding smiled when she came over to pick up my empty.

"Another Bud, please."

She stuck the empty in a cardboard case and bent over the cooler for a fresh one.

"Here you go. Dollar fifty."

I paid and waved away the change. What was wrong with me? No rap at all. My ex-wife was probably getting all the good loving she needed. I couldn't understand why the male had to court the female. Was what she had better to him than what he had was to her? I didn't think so. I thought it was an equal thing. And then of course there was the question of homosexuality and lesbianism. Whips and chains, foot fetishes, all that other kinky stuff you read about.

I saw a boy I sometimes painted houses with, and went over and stood by him. Like me he wasn't much of a talker.

"Hey."

"Hey."

"How's it going?" '

"All right. You?"

"Pretty good. You need a beer?"

"Nah."

We watched some people shoot pool for a while. I didn't even know why I was up there. I always expected something to happen and it never did. It wasn't going to, not to me. I turned to leave and the guy I'd seen earlier was in my face. I've had it happen before.

"I don't like your face."

"Oh yeah? Tough shit."

He swung. I ducked. He swung again. I ducked again.

"Hey, man. You're drunk. Why don't you fuck off?"

He swung again. This time he hit one of the cedar posts with his fist. I heard his hand break. It took the starch out of him right away. I saw then that he wasn't some badass who could kick the shit out of anybody he wanted to. He was just a wimp with a broken hand.

He went down on his knees and did quite a bit of howling, holding his hand. I could have kicked him as hard as I wanted to, right on the side of his head, or on the back of his neck. I just stood there and watched him, and enjoyed it, which is one of the negative traits of my character, I suppose.

35

I was up there another night and some old guy was collapsed over the bar, mumbling and muttering to himself. I bought a beer and stood close to him. If you tuned out the television and the guys shooting pool and the stereo and the MTV you could hear what he was saying. He looked about seventy, ragged coat, untrimmed hair, disreputable shoes. Just about what I knew I'd look like in thirty more years if I kept going the way I was going. Have none of my work published and be an old wasted guy, bitter at the world. It wasn't a very pretty picture.

"Nineteen sixty-six," he said. He shook his head viciously and stared at his beer bottle with murder in his eyes. "You. Her. Everybody. The whole world. Yeah. The whole world knows. And what good did it do to try? Huh? Three goddamn weeks. Only time when you was little it did any good to try and talk to you. Just one right after another. Keep on hoping and hoping and it don't do no good. It ain't no way. Never will be. Grow their hair and smoke cigarettes and run off away from home and get in trouble and call wanting money. Or sell your ass in the street. Just make more like you. Don't even know how many. Gather em up and send em off to China or Africa or somewhere don't nobody know you."

I leaned against the bar next to him. "Emptiness," I said. "That hollow feeling. The empathy of the whole world or the uncaring glance of a businessman in a car. Trying to sell newspapers with gum stuck on your shoe. Raining. Cold hard snow ice sleet falling from the sky. A biscuit and no jelly to put in it."

I looked at him. He looked at me. He looked back at his beer.

"She had geraniums," he said. "Little black notebooks crammed full of em. You couldn't tell how many." He shook his head. "I started counting one day at eleven forty-five p.m. and got up to three hundred and seventy-two and the doorbell rang. I went to the door, I was thinking, three seventy-two, three seventy-two, three seventy-two. Guy with a delivery van out there. Had fourteen chrysanthemums for Mrs. Rose Dale Bourdeaux. Small guy, black, little pencil moustache. Sneaky eyes, trying to see all in the house behind me."

"Drunk," I said. "That's where I've been. Night after night after night. When even the whole world don't want to wake up and look at you. And why? Because they don't like it. Not in their house, not in their car, not in their church. Throw you in the garbage. Pick you up the next morning. Wipe you off and set you down and say, Boy, walk straight, now. Walk the straight and narrow. Walk the straight and narrow arrow."

"Shoot em all," he said. "Just line em up against the wall and line their goddamn drivers up too and give em forty whacks. What they did to that guy out there in Utah. Made him feel better. It let all that poison out of him. He had that poison in him and it wasn't no way for it to get out except when he went to the bathroom and then just a little bit at a time. His body was making more poison than it could get rid of. It was making about two quarts a day and this was in the wintertime."

"They should have bottled it and sold it," I said. "What?"

"His poison."

"Oh no. No no. No no no no no. There ain't a container made that'll hold it. It won't ride in a truck. First thing you know it'll have done fell off and rolled down the hill and busted open. Then where would you be? Little kids running around stepping in it. No, you best not bottle it," he said.

I shut up. He wasn't looking at me any more. He had said his last sentence with a finality that left no room for discussion. I didn't try to engage him in any more conversation, and after a while, after looking around the whole room fearfully for a while, he hurried out.

36

I started having wet dreams at night and sometimes in the daytime. I'd have these tremendous ejaculations that felt like lumps of lava flowing down my urethra. And it would always be on the verge of putting it in. I never got to put it in. The sight of her titties or something, maybe just her puss, would make me skeet off. Wake up with wet underwear and just moan and turn over. But I often had fantasies about women while I was awake. I would imagine a whole elaborate scene with dirty dialogue, just construct a short erotic film in my head.

I wasn't hearing anything from my work. I had plenty of money, but not much desire. I was drinking more and writing less. I read the reviews of books in the local papers and noted what was on the best-seller list each week. I dreamed dreams of having my stories published in magazines and having my name on the covers of books, things the people I was raised around had never thought of. I knew people who were illiterate or nearly so and drank with them. One day I rode across the river with a boy who lived near me to get some beer. He was a pulp-wood hauler but he knew that I wrote, somehow. He wore a T-shirt thick with sawdust and the cooler in the floor of his truck was full of beer already, but it was Friday and he'd been paid for two loads that day and he just came by the house and asked me to ride over there with him. It turned out he wrote poetry and wanted me to read some of it. The more I talked to him, the more I found out about him. He wasn't from around here. He'd been educated at Washington University and he had a degree in neurobiology but had decided suddenly that he didn't want to do that. Now he was cutting pulpwood, risking his life and neck every day for pine logs, and writing poetry at night. His name was Thomas Slade, and he told me he was ready to start writing a novel.

Once we were in the road, he gave me a beer, and I smoked cigarettes and started reading his poems. They had a strange meter and rhyme and his words were good. We didn't talk while I read them. We drank beer and enjoyed the sunshine and the feeling that maybe two kindred souls were about to come together. The first poem was about his father, who was an alcoholic, and it had some vivid images. It was strong and I told him so. The next one was about a family of children whose father ran over a squirrel in the road, and they all screamed until he stopped. The guts were squashed out of it but it was still alive. The father had to stop and back over it a couple of times to kill it. It was a really good poem and I told him so. He smiled shyly, but I could tell that he was pleased. We had a Stihl 041 Farm Boss chainsaw on the seat between us. Jugs of oil and gasoline were on the floorboard. I was really starting to enjoy myself.

We got pulled over two miles this side of the beer joint by a state trooper. We'd been listening to Patsy Cline on his tape player. It was just sort of hammered into the dash with wires hanging everywhere, but it played, and he had some excellent speakers hung from the roof of the cab with coat hangers. We'd been moving and grooving and wailing with Patsy, God bless her soul, slammed into the side of a mountain so many years ago. My driver had had several beers, which the trooper smelled after he noticed that Thomas had no lights of any kind on his truck. He didn't have an inspection sticker either. His tires were like soft shit. I knew we wouldn't get off lightly.

I stayed in the truck while he talked to the man. While he walked the line. While he closed his eyes and leaned his head back and walked a line backwards down the side of the road. While he did ten push-ups and clapped his hands together under his chest each time he came up. After all that the man let us go. Told us to "get them fuckin lights fixed." Seemed disgruntled that he couldn't carry us to jail. Well, he had his job, and we had ours.

We made it on over to the beer joint in good time, considering we'd been messed with by the Troopers of Control, the most motivated, energetic, dead-set-on-catching-folks-like-me highway boys ever farted in a cruiser. There were lots of other folks over there. I latched or tried to latch onto what appeared to be a woman but turned out to be a fourteen-year-old girl and got told right quick by her brother, who was large, that she was underage. He was like seventeen himself. It made me feel old.

I wandered around for a while. I started having a sinking spell. It helped to hold onto posts and stuff. And a whole lot of stuff happened that I don't remember. People kept handing me beers. I guess old Thomas Slade was paying for them, but I don't remember. I never did find out, though, since that was the last time I talked to him. While passed out on the seat, late that night, going home, I woke up, saw some lights, heard something hit, and then we flipped over about eight times. I kept rolling around from the seat to the floor. Things were flying and hitting me in the head. I guess some of them were old Thomas Slade's Patsy Cline tapes. He had about nine of them.

I woke up again as some firemen were pulling the truck apart with the Jaws of Life. There was a long wrapped white bundle on the ground that was Thomas Slade. I, miraculously, was not injured much. Five-inch cut on my wrist, three-inch cut on my forehead. Thomas had his spine broken and his head crushed, and I saw that he wouldn't be cutting any more pine trees, or writing any more beautiful poetry.

37

I was getting pretty sick of death. It canceled a lot of checks. It snuck up on people who thought they didn't have time for it, laid families to waste who had just bought a new house. It caused problems miles down the road for children and everybody else. I didn't know what I was worrying about it for. It was going to get me one day, and there wasn't anything I could do about it. Death was going to put the bite on everybody, even if it did sometimes bite before its time. It got Raymond, and I knew he wasn't ready to go. It made me sick for it to

get Gardner, just cruising on his Harley before his marriage. It made
me sick, death did. I'd buried lots of my own. I was afraid I might
have to bury Alisha. I was afraid they might have to bury me. I didn't
want Alan to see that. I wanted him to go out to Uncle Lou's and stay
a few weeks, learn to rope and ride, trim the horses' feet, how to brush
their hair so it's most pleasing to them. I had a whole lot of faith, but
I hadn't been to church in a while. God probably didn't recognize me
because He hadn't seen me in so long in His house. I felt sort of slime
ball, sort of scuz bag, sort of piss-complected puke. I felt like I'd make
almost anybody barf. So I skipped town for a few days.

38

It wasn't any better down the road. This place I checked into charged
thirty dollars a week rent. But I thought I might really get into the
underside of life there and find something to write about. I was sort
of undercover. There was a small wading pool out back where guests
could sit around in their lawn chairs and drink beer. I did this several
evenings. Most of the people there were old, like they didn't have anywhere else to go, or maybe it was just a decrepit nursing home. I didn't
know what I was doing there with them. I had a home of my own, so
why was I sitting around drinking beer with a bunch of old people?
Looking at leaves in a wading pool? I knew I needed to go home and
check my mail. But I could hardly bear to go back to my loud empty
rooms.

After I'd been there two days I saw a fight. Two old guys who
couldn't do much, just pushing and shoving at first. But they were
cussing plenty. If they could have fought as well as they could cuss
they'd have both wound up in the hospital or the morgue. They were
filling the air with oaths that reeked of filth and vulgarity. It nearly
embarrassed me myself.

One of the old guys shoved the other old guy down and that ended the physical part of the fight. I looked at the loser. He was sitting on the ground, trying to get up. The victor was walking away. He was swaggering a little. You could tell he thought he was hot shit on toast. I didn't know what they'd been fighting over. I didn't want to know. I just wanted the old guy who'd been pushed down to stop cussing so much. He was slinging one motherfucker after another one to the point where it went past ugly. I knew God was up there hearing it. I put my sunglasses on.

After a while the old guy on the ground got up and went inside. I kept sitting there drinking my beer, looking at the leaves in the pool. It needed cleaning really badly, but nobody seemed to want to do it. I damn sure didn't want to do it.

I vacated the place a few hours later, wondering when things would come to some kind of end. I was restless and couldn't stay still. I wasn't happy at home and I wasn't happy away from home. It looked like there was nothing to do but go home. So that's where I went, a little reluctantly.

39

I stayed drunk for a few days and didn't really notice a lot of what was happening around me. The phone rang a few times, usually while I was in bed. People would try to talk to me and I would try to talk to them, but we couldn't understand each other, so I'd hang up. I lost track of the days. I didn't know if a particular day was Sunday or Saturday, or Tuesday. I went to the refrigerator once to see if there was anything there to eat, but there was nothing there, so I crawled back to bed. I left beer in the freezer compartment and it froze and burst and ran down the front of the refrigerator. I put more beer in, overslept, and it froze and burst. I knew I'd have to sober up sometime and clean it up, but I wasn't ready to yet. I wanted to get that drunk over with and let things go back to normal if they could.

I tried to write a poem about Thomas Slade while I was drunk. The poem was no good. I tried to write two other poems, about Jerome and Kerwood White, while I was drunk, but they were no good either. I rode around drunk, walked around drunk, slept and woke up drunk. I wrote drunk, ate drunk, washed my hair drunk. I watched television drunk as a boiled owl. I went over to Monroe's house drunk one day to see him while he was at work and his mother didn't appreciate it worth a damn. I knew better. It was just that drunk had done me in. I considered going to see my mother drunk but I knew that wouldn't do, either. I thought about going to see Marilyn drunk, but I knew that would just reinforce her belief that I was nothing but a drunk. And I thought about going to see my uncle drunk, but I wasn't too drunk to know that he'd probably haul off and knock the hell out of me, things being what they were and sacrifices being as valuable as they were, and all the shit I'd blown to him about blah blah blah. I wound up just going back home drunk, drinking some more, and going to bed.

I had a nightmare that night. I was drunk in the nightmare, with a whole lot of other people who were drunk in a large log pen. There were hogs walking around. They had caught all of us out on the highways drunk. The hogs had been in the trailer of a drunk truck driver. All of us had been sentenced to death. Society was going to be rid of this problem with no qualms. We were being killed one at a time, and the whole world was watching. Some were shot, some were hanged, some were stabbed with long sharp knives. Two guys in front of me got it with axes. There were bodies left and right. Whoever was in charge of the thing was selling beer in there, too, just to see what would happen, I guess. Everybody was sober by then, and the beer stand wasn't getting much business.

They had a huge slave chained to a tree stump in the line I was in. The people went forward one at a time, after handcuffs were put on them. The slave rested on his axe handle until their necks were across the stump. Then he swung it and grunted and the bloody head of the axe flashed through the air and there was a loud *THWACK!*

They led me to the stump. My toes were squishing in blood. They handcuffed me and forced me down on the bloody wood. Splinters dug into my throat. I tried to move but they held me down. I turned my head sideways toward the slave. His feet moved, and he grunted, and bloody mud splashed from between his toes.

40

I woke at daybreak. Nighthawks were calling softly in the stillness, and it was cool. I got up. There was one can of frozen orange juice in the freezer compartment, frozen beer all over it. I ran the water in the sink until it got hot and then I thawed the orange juice out partway, holding it under the running water. I found a pitcher, opened the can, and put the yellow lump into it. I took a steak knife and tried to chop it up into smaller pieces. I measured out three cans of hot water and poured them in and stirred it, my tongue so dry I couldn't lick my lips, or bear to. There were some ice cubes in the trays. I filled a glass with cubes and poured the orange juice over it and got my cigarettes and lighter and went out to the front porch in my underwear and sat in a chair.

Fog was lifting off the river. Crows were rising from the fog. Cars with their headlights on were going down the highway. The trees were mantled with mist, standing dark with their heavy rafts of leaves. I drank some of the orange juice, and it was like a parched man two days in the desert being offered a drink from a well. It was that good. I lit a cigarette, and the smoke hurt my lungs. The things I did to myself were stupid, and without reason, or for reasons that I only imagined, slights I imagined had been done by the world, never my own fault. I knew the kids were sleeping somewhere, their eyes closed, their breathing shallow. In sleep their long lashes were easy to see, faces I'd kissed again and again.

I put my face in my hand, and I cried, and promised myself that I would try to do better, for me, for everybody, for the kids especially. I hoped the promise would last.

41

The money started running low again, due to drinking and smoking too much and being a generous guy with drinks for drunks who had no money. There were people I knew who could make their way to a bar with no money, but sit there and drink by careful and calculated cunning. I couldn't do it, but I knew plenty of people who did. I decided to write interesting stories about them, stay home, drink less. But when I got to writing all those drinking stories, it made me want to get drunk myself while I was writing them. So what I wound up doing was writing them in the *bar*, with my pencils and notebook and papers all spread out everywhere. And I'd sit there and smoke and have cigarette ashes thumped all over everything, be smoking like a fiend, scribbling all these words. They knew I was trying to put out some good stuff and nobody messed with me. They were proud of having me write in their bar. They didn't know any published authors. But they knew one unpublished author.

There was a little chickadee who started working in there. My heart sank the first time I saw her, because I knew I could never have her. She was just too good for me. She had long brown hair and she had on a jogging suit bottom with a red striped T-shirt over the top. She had a shy way of smiling when she talked to the other guys around the bar. Her beauty broke my heart.

I was deep into some things about two guys fresh out of the penitentiary and some other guys moose-hunting with secret dopers in the Great Pacific Northwest and another little thing about dead children who got up and walked at night, when she came over and asked me what I was writing. This was after she had seen me do this for a couple of nights in a row.

"I, uh, I'm writing some stories," I said, and shielded my work with my hand. "Could I get another beer?"

She smiled her shy little smile and got the beer for me, smiling while she was reaching in the cooler, smiling when she put it up on the bar in front of me. I laid two dollars on the bar. She took one and pushed the other one back.

"Happy Hour," she said, and I looked and it was four o'clock.

"Thanks," I said. I folded the other dollar and put it in her jar.

For the next thirty minutes I wrote. I heard a couple of carpenter types come in a few times and wonder aloud what that motherfucker was doing over there in the corner, but I didn't pay any attention to that because it was to be expected. I'd paid for my space and I figured I could use it like I wanted to, as long as I wasn't dealing dope or selling insurance. I was trying to decide whether or not to let a story have an ambiguous ending, and also fretting over tone and symbolism in one particular piece, when she came back over.

"You're Leon Barlow, aren't you?" she said.

I just barely looked up. I knew I couldn't get over with her. "Yeah, I'm him," I said, and looked back down at my papers.

"You know Monroe, don't you?"

"Yeah."

"He's the one told me you wrote. He was talking to me the other night about you. He said you were a real good writer."

I didn't say, Well, the world's out to fuck me. I said: "Well, I haven't had anything published."

"I'd sure like to read some of your stuff sometime. I love to read."

I looked at her. That sweet little mouth. Fine little ass. Smooth skin I knew like my hand had never felt. Marilyn's was lumpy and had scabs on it, stretch marks and cellulite and pones on her feet, plus she stunk up the bathroom something terrible. I figured this dainty thing didn't even have to shit but just farted little fragrant poots when she had to. I didn't know what a real dick would do to her. Probably kill her. I looked back down at my work.

"I don't let nobody look at my stuff except Monroe," I muttered.

42

Alisha died right after that. They said it was crib death, SIDS, but I don't think that's what it was. I thought it was punishment to me for giving up my wife and my family and all the wrath of God howling after me all the days of my life to the ends of the earth. I wanted to go out into the forest and live like a madman with leaves for clothes and live in a hole in the ground and throw rocks at anybody who came near.

My whole family was there. I was stunned with all the marijuana and liquor I could stuff into myself and still remain standing. I signed papers, made promises, heard prayers and screaming and gnashing of teeth. Cried till my eyes were sore. I took on a pain that would never leave me, never let me rest until years had passed, and then it would always remain like lead that had settled in the bottom of my heart, a little sad face smiling up, reminding me always, even when I lay on my deathbed, Alisha, born wrong, Alisha, child of God, Alisha a soul wafting out across space with her tiny hands clapping.

43

I got drunk and thrown in jail. They let me out, I got drunk again, they threw me in again. I had ample time to reflect upon my situation. It hadn't been DUI, just public drunk, and then it wouldn't have happened if I hadn't happened to smart off to the arresting officers. They got me going down the street the first time and then coming up the street the second time. Same street.

There were quite a few jailbirds in there, people doing long time. Everybody had the option of doing community service and reducing their sentences by half, but hardly anybody wanted to. I guess they were sorry, plus they had two squares a day and television, game shows mostly. I put up with it for two days, and then I told them to let me go pick up some trash or something.

They put me to helping an old lady cook food for the prisoners in a kitchen halfway across town. She seemed suspicious of me at first, but I kept my nails clean and washed my hands a lot and said ma'am to her, and before long she was smiling and laughing and telling me about her grown kids. We talked a lot. I told her about Alisha. She let me eat all the time, and there was good stuff in there she fixed for me that the prisoners in the jail never saw. Ham, steaks, catfish. I washed pots and pans and wore a white apron and sat on the back steps sometimes, smoking cigarettes while the free people walked down the sidewalk next to the bank.

There was a bar just down the alley that happened to be mine, and I'd sit out there watching the people going in and out, free as birds. I could see the exact spot where they'd nabbed me. There was a large Dempsey Dumpster that the cops hid behind and leaped out and grabbed drunks from, guys just trying to make their way back to their cars and sleep it off. It was the same method they'd used on me. She saw me sitting out there one afternoon and asked me what I was looking at.

"I'm just watching those people," I said.

I could feel her standing behind me. Her husband had died of a heart attack the year before, the year before he'd been going to retire. They'd been planning on opening a small cafe together in their retirement years. They'd had it planned for over ten years. Now she was cooking two meals a day for the county.

"Why don't you go down there and drink you a beer?" she said. "Might help you get rid of the blues. If they come check on you I'll tell them I sent you to the store for me."

"I ain't got any money. They took it all away from me in the jail."

A five-dollar bill slid down over my left shoulder and stopped right in front of my pocket. I twisted my head around and looked at her. She was smiling down on me like an extra grandmother. I put my fingers on the money and held her hand for a moment.

"My baby died, too," she said. "Forty years ago. I can handle it for a couple of hours."

I wanted to cry because I felt so damn good that there was such kindness in the world. Instead I got up and took off my apron. I hung it on the nail where I always hung it and looked at her. She was stirring stuff on the stove, and the steam was rising off her pots and pans.

I went to her and hugged her shoulders. She shook her head, patted me on the hand. I went out the door and down the alley, looking both ways for cars, looking all ways for cops from the jail. I'd found out that once they got after you, they tended to stay after you, and I didn't want them after me any more.

The Happy Hour light was on. Beer was a dollar. If I drank fast I could get five down in a couple of hours. On the other hand, if I was obviously drunk when I went back to the jail, I'd probably get the nice old lady in trouble, might even cause her to lose her meal contract with the county. It was a dilemma, and I hated dilemmas. I sat down on a bar stool and waited for somebody to wait on me.

There weren't many people in there. A couple of guys in business suits, a couple more in carpenter's overalls. Two middle-aged women with sunglasses who pulled them down and looked over the tops of them at me when I sat down. I wondered if it would be possible for me to make a break for it while I was out on my own like that. I only had three more days to serve, which actually meant a day and a half if I stayed in the kitchen with the sweet old lady. I was tired of listening to all the shit in the jail every night, though, lying there on that one-inch mattress and looking up at the ceiling. There were also some homosexual things going on in there at night that I didn't particularly like to hear.

Sweet thing popped up from behind the counter. She grinned real big when she saw me.

"Well, hey," she said. She came over and laced her fingers together on the bar. "Where you been so long?"

"Jail. Can I get a Bud?"

She got the bottle for me and gave me four back from my five.

"Monroe told me you were in jail but I didn't believe him. I thought he was just playing with me. What'd you do?"

"Walked down the street. Had a little too much to drink. Got smart with a fucking officer of the law."

I was looking everywhere but at her, and she was steady watching me. I didn't know why. I knew I looked awful. I hadn't had a shave in about nine days and I knew my teeth were beyond funky. I knew

I had to get my shit together pretty soon because this wasn't getting it, no sir.

"So how much longer you got to go?"

"Couple of days. Three, I think. Can I get another beer?"

I shouldn't have been drinking that fast, but I was. At that rate I could make Happy Hour live up to its name. She got the beer and pushed away the dollar. I said to myself,

Hmmmm.

She went back behind the counter and started doing some other stuff. I had some generic cigarettes and I lit one of them. It tasted like a selected blend of dried horse turds. I didn't want to go back to jail. I didn't see how I could. I thought again about making a break. It would have been easy. All I had to do was walk out of town and stick out my thumb. But I knew they'd finally get me back, and it would probably be worse when they did. I sat there drinking. I drank two more. The little sweet thing kept smiling at me, but I've always somehow had this look on my face that makes people stay away. I don't mean for it to be there. I don't even know it's there. But people have told me they've seen it before, and that it doesn't look friendly. If I knew how to get rid of it I would.

Finally I went on back to my kitchen. I had one dollar left. I gave it to her. She just smiled and patted my hand.

44

I laid on my rack at the jail that night and looked at the ceiling some more. People had written things all over it with either cigarette lighters or matches. Ugly things, sexual things, the ugliest things you could imagine and some you couldn't. They never turned the lights off in there, let them stay on twenty-four hours a day. It made it very hard to sleep.

I didn't feel like a criminal, but here I was in with criminals. Some had stolen, some had killed or nearly killed people, some like me had just been caught publicly drunk. I would have written something if I'd had anything to write on, but finally I just went to sleep.

45

They let me out a couple of days later. I felt about as shabby as I'd felt in a while, unshaven, dirty, shamed. Nobody told me not to come back any more. I knew they were memorizing my face so they could nab me again the next time I even thought about fucking up.

I walked outside. It was hot. I'd neglected to ask them if they'd towed my car, so I decided to walk back to the parking lot and see if it was still there.

It was a long way over there on foot. I almost got run over a few times. Everybody seemed to be going somewhere in a hurry. It was dangerous to step off the curb that day.

My old car was sitting all by itself in the middle of the parking lot. The tires were low. Somebody'd ripped off the radio antenna. It looked sort of sad and forlorn. I was just hoping it would crank.

I opened the door and got in and sat down. The seats were burning hot. I put the key in and turned it over, and it went waw, awaw, waw. I let it rest a minute. Both of us had been through a lot. I was afraid I'd have to be jumped off, but I didn't have any cables, and there didn't seem to be anybody familiar around with a fresh hot battery. I said Lord, please.

I turned it over again and it coughed and farted and finally ran. I sat there revving it up. The bar across the street was closed. I wondered if the little sweet thing would be there that night. I wondered if I went home and cleaned up and showered and shaved and cut my fingernails and brushed my teeth, if it would be possible for me to get over with her. Then I looked at myself and said Naaaaaaa.

I looked at the gas gauge. It was damn near on empty, and I only had two dollars on me. However, I still had some of Uncle Lou's money stashed.

I limped out of town, almost whipped, my head hanging, and my hopes not too high. I wasn't completely beaten. I just needed a breather in between rounds.

46

My house hadn't burned down or anything while I'd been gone. There were a few notes from Monroe tacked on the front door. One of them said WHERE YOU AT? I'VE BEEN BY HERE THREE TIMES ALREADY. LET'S GO DRINK A BEER ONE NIGHT, MONROE. Another one said, I HEARD YOU WERE IN JAIL. I AIN'T GOT ANY MONEY OR I'D COME GET YOU OUT, MONROE. The last one said, LYNN SAID SHE SAW YOU THE OTHER DAY AND SHE SAID YOU SAID YOU WERE IN JAIL. IF YOU DON'T GET OUT PRETTY SOON I'LL SEE IF I CAN BORROW SOME MONEY FROM MAMA AND COME GET YOU OUT, MONROE. P.S. IF YOU WERE IN JAIL HOW COME THEY LET YOU GO DRINK BEER?

I threw the notes in the trash and looked in the refrigerator. There just happened to be a couple of cold ones in there. I wondered who Lynn was and then realized she must have been the sweet little thing I wanted to murder with my dick. I got one of the beers and sat down on the couch and pulled my boots off. Just as soon as I did that, I realized that I had about nine days' worth of mail stacked up in my mailbox. I left my beer on the coffee table and went down the driveway, my feet tender on the gravel, saying Ouch, damn, shit. The mailbox was crammed full of shit, a lot of it manila envelopes of my own fiction that had found its way home. There were letters from my ex-wife's lawyer, letters from the funeral home, letters from the tombstone people. There was even a letter from the jail that had beat me home. I scooped it all out, didn't examine it too closely, and carried it all back to the house, hot-footing it over the gravel, saying Oh, fuck, oo. My feet were too tender. I never did spend enough time going barefooted. Marilyn used to, though. Her feet were tough as hell. She could walk over nails, gravel, anything. She could lay a fucking on you, too. She really knew how to do it. She really knew how to get pregnant, too. She was about six and a half months gone when we finally got married. Her daddy wanted to shoot somebody, I think. On the other hand, I guess he was just glad to have somebody finally claim her.

I got back to the house and collapsed on the couch with my mail, sucked down a big drink of the beer, and tossed out everything that didn't pertain to my writing. The first thing I noticed was a manila envelope that I had sent off with a story inside that had come back without the story inside, which I knew meant something. I didn't know if it meant what I was hoping it meant. It might not have meant anything at all. But it just happened to be from *Ivory Towers*, home of the great or maybe not-so-great Betti DeLoreo. I was in a quandary as to opening it. I was scared to open it and scared not to open it. I had self-addressed the thing, true, and the great et cetera had sent it back to me minus my story. I could tell the story wasn't inside it. I held it up to the light, but I couldn't see a thing through the manila. What did it mean? Had she taken my story? Was everything fixing to be worth it? Had I broken through? Or had they just lost my story and were writing to apologize for it? It was hard to stand the pressure. I ripped the envelope open. There, inside, in Betti DeLoreo's own handwriting, was a note to me:

Dear Leon,

I like your story a lot up here but I'm having trouble convincing the senior editor that we ought to publish it. I know this is very unorthodox to do this, but I want to keep it around here a while and nag him every chance I get. The only thing is, if I nag him too much, he'll get pissed off and reject the story. I have to work on him real slowly and bring it up gradually. He's trying to write his master's thesis right now and things are very bad for him. However, your story, "Raping the Dead," is a big favorite around here and a lot of people who don't have the power to accept or reject a story like it. If I owned this magazine we'd publish it. Please have some patience. Your work is difficult and complex and everybody doesn't understand it. I think it scared some people and some people are jealous of it too and some are failed writers or struggling writers and it's just very hard to explain. I don't like seeing the infighting that goes on here, and I hate to see good work by an unknown author rejected in favor of bad work by an established one. I want to give you all the encouragement I can. You're too good a writer to remain unknown forever. You have to hang in there and if this tale does get rejected then you just have to send it out to somebody else. Write me, please. Or send something else. If this one doesn't make it, maybe another one will. Please don't give up.

All *very* warmest wishes,
Betti DeLoreo

Well, well well well well well. Shit.

47

The sun went down late that evening like it always does. I was sitting out on the front porch marveling at the way it lit up the sky. It was pretty beautiful, and I didn't know what I'd done to deserve it. Just sitting at the right time in the right place, I guess.

I saw Monroe coming down the highway, and I saw him turn into the driveway. I knew he probably had a trunk full of cold beer. That was all right with me. He pulled up and stopped beside the house and hung his head out the window, and he was drunk as a by God.

"Mone get in," he said. "Ride you aroun a while."

"You got anything to drink? You look like you done drank it all up."

He nodded his head and almost went to sleep hanging out the window. I knew better than to get in with him.

"Get ya drank, bro. Mone. Ride you roun a while. Get you drank a while."

He was waving a beer can around the whole time he was saying that, sloshing beer out.

I got in with him. We just sat there in the car for five minutes. Finally he spoke.

"Wanna tell you summin. Made me mad, them mufuggers put my bro in jail. Ain't right. Din have nobody ride aroun with. Rode aroun by myself. Talk myself."

"You feeling all right, man?" I said.

"What? Kme? Lin. Em mufuggers put you in jail, again, you caw me. I'll come up and get in jail too. Keep you compny. Play cards. Yona beer?"

"I got one," I said.

"Good." He pulled the shift lever down into reverse. "We gone ride aroun some."

"Can you drive, man?"

"Drive fine. Lin. Mufuggers give you shit, you caw me. I got a ungle, Ungle Dick! Ungle Dick has been messin with them sumbitches years. Stick at money in back pocket, see. Rest you, ain't shit."

He'd backed over a couple of discarded bicycles by then, but I didn't say anything. I reached over and put my foot on the brake, stopped the car, and pulled it down into drive.

"Thain you. We gone ride aroun while. Got date later. Cain't stay long, gotta picker up at six. Ain't stay long. What time it?"

I looked at my watch. It was six-thirty and the gloam hadn't even started yet. I had about half of a hot beer.

"You got any cold beer?"

We'd started rolling down the driveway, but he slammed on the brakes and we slid in the gravel. He ratcheted the shift lever back and forth for a while until he got it into reverse. He started backing up the driveway. I reached over and stepped on the brake.

"You got any beer?"

"What?"

"You got any cold beer?"

He opened the door and fell out. I stepped on the brake a little harder and put it up in park. He was crawling in the gravel, heading for the trunk, muttering something.

I got out and asked him why didn't he just let me drive, but he didn't answer me. I had to help him back into the car. It wasn't even dark yet. I got him onto the back seat and stretched him out. About the cold beer I'd been right. The trunk was full of it.

I got one and got into the driver's seat.

"Who's your date with, man?"

"Wha?"

"Who's your date with?"

"Vemma. You know Vemma?"

"Velma? Velma White?"

"Yeah. Less go pick up Vemma."

He had his eyes closed talking to me. I didn't know why he'd chosen to get so fucked up right before a date. I was hoping he wasn't supposed to meet her parents.

"Tell you what, man. Why don't you give me her number? I'll call her and tell her you can't make it."

"Naw. Naw. Naw. Just dry me on over to Vemma's house. Vemma's gossum good pussy. Vemma's in love a me. Vemma thinks you a good-lookin summitch. We'll double date. Go on over Vemma's."

I started driving. I didn't figure it mattered where I drove to. I was sober anyway. I had a joint that I'd rolled up earlier, and I pulled it out of my pocket and lit it. I had all that cold beer to drink, and I figured I could handle it for a few hours. That would be about enough time for him to sleep it off. I didn't want to interfere with his love life, but I remembered where Velma lived. I decided to go in a roundabout way over there.

Monroe had some good tapes, and as quick as the buzz hit me, I started playing them. I felt good about taking care of him in the back seat.

Night closed in. It came slowly, and we rode down by the river and I looked at the hawks perched on the high limbs in the trees and saw a huge owl come out of the woods and find a single light wire with his talons and sit there swiveling his head after me as we drove by. Life seemed pretty fine. I didn't have a woman like he did, but I could at least enjoy riding around. Marilyn had always questioned it. We never had been able to get along. It always seemed that she thought what I was doing was nothing, that it would never amount to anything, and so far it hadn't. I hadn't sold anything, hadn't published one word. Maybe I never would, but Betti DeLoreo didn't seem to think so. I got to thinking about her again. I knew I didn't need to, because I knew that if I really knew what she really looked like, I'd probably be disappointed. She'd probably have tartar on her teeth or something. I decided we'd better ride by Velma's house at least and see if the light was on. I'd entertained the idea of stopping and explaining things to her, let her see him in the back seat so she'd know I wasn't lying.

We rode by there four times. The light was on each time. I knew she was probably pissed.

"Hey, man," I said. "You awake?"

Silence from the back seat.

"Hey, man! You awake?"

He wasn't doing anything but sleeping, and I knew it wouldn't go over well with her. I decided to stop anyway. I whipped it around in the middle of the road and went back to her house. I pulled up in front like I belonged there—after all, I did—and sat down on the horn. Nothing happened for about two minutes. Then somebody came to the front door and peeked out. Then another person came and peeked out. I figured the second one was probably her daddy with a gun. I let off the horn.

I already had it in reverse when she came out the door. She had on white pants and a black blouse, and she had a purse with her. I hated I'd even stopped.

"Hey, Velma," I said. "I'm Leon. Remember me?"

She poked her head in the car. I turned on the interior light so she could see him.

"What's the matter with him?" she said. She looked at her watch. "He's two hours late."

"I believe he's having a little sinking spell. I'm surprised you waited this long."

"What'd you do? Take him off and get him drunk?"

I thought about it. I remembered how nasty she'd been when her brothers got killed, but that had been understandable. On the other hand, I didn't know why Monroe was messing around with her, even though he'd said that her nooky was excellent. That was probably true, based on the fact that the worst I've ever had was wonderful.

"Yeah," I said. "I tied him down and taped a funnel on his mouth and then poured ten Old Milwaukees down him. Then I poured four shots of peppermint schnapps down him. Then I poured two shots of whiskey down him. Then I poured a snifter of brandy down him. Then I poured two martinis down him. Then he puked. But I kept pouring it down him. Then I opened a bottle of tequila."

"Oh bullshit," she said. She went around to the passenger side and got in. "Just drive me uptown," she said. "I'll get him sobered up after awhile. You got a beer in here?"

"Trunk's full of it."

"Well, how about getting me one out?"

"That your daddy looking out the window?"

"Yeah. He watches me like a hawk now. Where's that beer?"

The ice broke after she got one down her. I had a little of the joint left and we shared that. By the time we got to town we were laughing and talking and singing along with Monroe's tapes. I felt a little guilty, but he was still sleeping on the back seat. When we got to the bar he was still asleep, and she had wormed her way over next to me in the seat. When we pulled up and stopped, she said she didn't really want to go in, and could we ride around a little longer? I said sure.

I can't remember anything that happened after that. I know a lot of things happened, but I can't remember what they were.

48

We were in a ditch when we woke up. It was muddy, and we had mud all over us. Mud was all over the seats. It had caked on the dash, on our clothes, on the headliner. We were way up in the woods somewhere, as usual. The sun was shining. It was nine o'clock in the morning. My mouth felt like a wad of cotton, and mosquitoes had feasted on us all night long. He was still asleep on the back seat. I woke him up and we flipped a coin to see who'd walk out to the road and flag somebody down to come pull us out. He won. Or lost.

49

I slept for about two days and then I went back to work on my work. I thought about painting a few houses just to keep my hand in and help tide me over when winter came but I could hardly bring myself to do it. It was hard to turn loose some of that freedom. That old freedom was nice.

Raoul came by to see me one day but I wouldn't let him in. He could see me, and I could see him, but I just kept sitting at my type-writer, pecking words out, and he started knocking and it went on for a long time. He shouted something, several things, but I didn't listen. I'd about decided not to listen to anybody for the rest of my life. He kept knocking, and I got up and went over to the stereo and put Johnny Winter on and ignored him. He kept knocking. I started writing a story about a woman and a man with a little child going down a sidewalk late at night, the little girl in a long white dress and having to run to keep up with her mother and father, who were running from something beyond bad. I saw that it was on a dark street somewhere in New Jersey with the rain falling and I wondered what was going through the little girl's head. She was running to keep up, her mother barely holding her hand, her bare feet flying over the wet sidewalks, up and down over the curbs as they crossed the alleys. Her hair was long, brown, and her arm was stretched out in front of her as she held onto her mother's hand, and her feet were flying. I kept that image with me, desperation, flight, fear, until the knocking stopped and Raoul went away, I knew sadly. I went to the refrigerator and got a beer. I sat back down at my machine. I had to find out what they were running from. I had to find out if the little girl was going to be safe. I didn't know if she would be or not. But whatever it was she was running from, I knew I had to save her from it, and that I was the only one who could do it. They were running, running, the cars going by, and I could see the slippery sidewalks, and the lights in the stores, and I could see my mother and my father looking back over their shoulders at whatever was chasing us, and I ran as fast as I could, terrified, not knowing how it would end, knowing I had to know.

A Roadside Resurrection

Story opens, Mr. Redding is coughing in a café by the Yocona River, really whamming it out between his knees. He's got on penny loafers with pennies in them, yellow socks, madras shorts, a reversible hat, and a shirt that's faded from being washed too many times. His wife, Flenco, or Flenc, as he calls her, is slapping him on the back and alternately sucking her chocolate milkshake through a straw and looking around to see who's watching. She's got a big fat face, rollers in her hair, and she's wearing what may well be her nightgown and robe. Fingernails: bright red.

"Damn!" Mr. Redding coughs. "Godamighty . . . damn!"

Flenco hits him on the back and winces at his language, sucking hard on her straw and glancing around. Mr. Redding goes into a bad fit of coughing, kneels down on the floor heaving, tongue out and curled, veins distended on his skinny forearms, hacking, strangling, and the children of the diners are starting to look around in disgust.

"Oh," he coughs. "Oh shit. Oh damn."

Mr. Redding craws back up in the booth and reaches into his shirt pocket for a Pall Mall 100, lights it, takes one suck, then repeats the entire scenario above. This goes on three times in thirty minutes.

Customers go in and out and people order beers and drink them at the counter on stools, but Mr. Redding lies back in the booth while his wife mops his feverish forehead with wetted paper towels brought by a waitress from the kitchen, along with another milkshake just like the last one. The hair on Mr. Redding's forearms is dark and scattered, like hair on a mangy dog just recovering, and his sideburns sticking out from under the reversible cap are gray. Twenty years ago he could do a pretty good imitation of Elvis. Now he's washed up.

"Oh crap," he said. "Oh shit. Oh hell."

Flenco mops him and sops up his sweat and sucks her big round mouth around the straw and looks at people and pats him on the back. Truckers come in with their names on their belts and eat eggs and ham and wash down pills with coffee and put their cigarettes out in their plates, stagger back outside and climb into their sleepers. Flenco looks down the road and wonders what road she'll be on before long.

"Oh shit," Mr. Redding wheezes.

MILES AWAY DOWN the road, a legendary young healer is ready to raise the roof on a tent gathering. Sawdust is on the floor and the lights are bright and a crippled boy in a wheelchair has been brought forward to feel his healing hands. The boy lies in his chair drooling up at the lights, hands trembling, the crowd watching on all sides, spectators all piled up along the back and sides and others peeking in the opened opening, some lying on the ground with their heads stuck up between the tent pegs. The crippled child waits, the mother trembling also, nearby, hands clasped breastwise to the Holy Father. Sweet Mary Mother of Saints heal my child who was wrong from the womb Amen. The lights flicker. The healer is imbued with the Spirit of God which has come down at the edge of this cotton field and put into his fingers the strength of His love and healing fire. Outside bright blades of lightning arch and thunderclouds rumble in the turbulent sky as the healer goes into his trance. His fine dark hair is sleek on the sides of his head and he cries out: "Heeeeeal! Heal this boy, Lord! Heal him! Dear sweet merciful God if You ever felt it in Your heart to heal somebody heal this boy! This boy! This one right here, Lord! I know there's a bunch of 'em over there in darkest Africa need healing too Lord but they ain't down on their knees to You right now like we are!"

The healer sinks to his knees with these words, hands locked and upflung before him. Ushers are moving slowly through the crowd with their plates out, but nobody's putting much into the plates yet because they haven't seen the boy get up and walk.

"Lord what about Gethsemane? Lord what about Calvary's cross? Lord what about Your merciful love that we're here to lay on this child? There's his mama, Lord. I guess his daddy's in here, too. Maybe all his brothers and sisters."

"He's a only child," the mama whispers, but nobody seems to notice. The rain has started and everybody's trying to crowd inside.

"Neighbors? I don't believe there's much faith in this house tonight. I believe we've done run into a bunch of doubting Thomases, folks who want to play before they pay. Maybe they think this ain't nothing but a sideshow. Maybe they think this boy works for me. Because I don't believe they're putting in any money to further our work."

The ushers make another pass through the crowd and collect six dollars and fifty-two cents. The boy lies in the wheelchair, legs dangling.

This child has never walked before. The mother has told the healer his history. He was born with spinal meningitis, his heart outside his body, and she said God only gave him one kidney. She said on the day she goes to her grave she will still owe hospital bills on him. The healer can see that the congregation thinks nothing is going to happen. He can almost read their faces, can almost read in their countenances the unsaid accusations: *Ha! Unclean! Prove yourself! Make him walk!*

The healer comes down from the podium. The fire of God is still in him. The wheels of the wheelchair are mired in the sawdust. The mother has already begun to feel what has come inside the tent. She faints, falls over. An uncle stands up. The healer lays his hands on.

"Now I said *heal!* I don't give a damn! About what's happening over there in Saudi Arabia! I don't care what else You got on Your mind! You got to heal this boy! Either heal him or take him right now! Heal him! Or take him! We don't care! He's with You either way!"

The child wobbles in the wheelchair. The healer digs his fingers down deep into the flesh. More people stand up to see. The mother wakes up, moans, and faints again. The lightning cracks overhead and the lights go out and then come back on dim. The ushers are moving more quickly through the crowd. An aura of Presence moves inside the tent to where everybody feels it. The child grips the armrests of his chair. His feet dig for purchase in the sawdust. He cries out with eyes closed in a racked and silent scream.

"Yeah!" the healer shouts. "Didn't believe! Look at him! Watch him walk!"

The boy struggles up out of the chair. People have come to his mother's side with wet handkerchiefs and they revive her in time to witness him make his stand. He rises up on his wasted legs, the healer's hands octopused on his head.

"Heal! Heal! Heal! Heal! Heal! Heal! Heal!

The boy shoves the hands away. The mother looks up at her son from the dirt. He takes a step. His spine is straight. He takes another step. People are falling to their knees in the sawdust. They are reaching for their purses and wallets.

MR. REDDING HAS to be taken outside because he is bothering the other customers. Flenco lets him lie on the seat of the truck for a while and fans him with a Merle Haggard album.

"Oh shit," Mr. Redding says. "Oh *arrrrgh*."

"It's gonna be all right, baby," Flenco says.

Mr. Redding is almost beyond talking, but he gasps out: "What do . . . you mean . . . it's . . . gonna . . . be . . . all right?"

"Oh, baby, I heard he'd be through here by nine o'clock. And they say he can really heal."

"I don't . . . believe . . . none of that . . . *bull*shit!"

Mr. Redding says that, and goes into great whoops of coughing.

A lot of money in the plates tonight. The mission can go on. But some helpers have wives back home, trailer payments have to be met, others want satellite dishes. The healer requires nothing but a meal that will last him until the next meal. He gives them all the money except for the price of steak and eggs at a Waffle House and heads for the car. The road is mud. The tent is being taken down in the storm. The memory of the woman is on him and he doesn't feel very close to God.

"OH SHIT," Mr. Redding says. "Oh damn oh hell oh shit."

"Baby?" Flenco says. "Don't you think you ought not be cussing so bad when you're like this?"

"Li . . . iii . . . iiike what?" Mr. Redding spews out.

"When you're coughing so bad and all. I bet if you'd quit smoking them cigarettes you wouldn't cough so bad."

She pats him on the back like she saw the respiratory therapist do and feels she knows a little about medicine.

"Oh crap," Mr. Redding says. "Oh *shit!*"

Flenco mops his sweaty head and fans hot air with her hand. She has heard that the healer drives a long black Caddy. They say he refuses to appear on network television and will not endorse products. They say he comes speeding out of the dusty fields in his dusty black car and they say the wind his machine brings whips the trousers of the state troopers before they can get into their cruisers and take pursuit. They say he lives only to heal and that he stops on the roadsides where crippled children have been set up and where their mothers stand behind them holding up cardboard placards painstaking printed HEALER HEAL MY CHILD. They say that if the state troopers catch up with him while he is performing some miracle of mercy on one of God's bent lambs, the people pull their cars out into the road and block the highway, taking the keys out of the ignitions, locking the doors. It's said that in Georgia last year a blockade of the faithful ran interference for him through a web of parked police cars outside Waycross and allowed him to pass unmolested, such is the strength of his fame. Flenco hasn't a placard. She has rented a billboard beside the café, letters six feet tall proclaiming HEALER HEAL MY HUSBAND. Telephone reports from her sister-in-law in Bruce confirm the rumor that he has left Water Valley and is heading their way. Flenco imagines him coming down out of the hilly country, barreling down the secondary roads and blasting toward the very spot where she sits fanning Mr. Redding's feverish frame.

"Oh shit," Mr. Redding says. "Oh God . . . dang!"

"Just rest easy now, honey," Flenco says. "You want me to go get you some Co-Coler?"

"Hell naw, I don't want no goddamn Co-Coler," Mr. Redding says. "I want some . . . want some goddamn . . . I want some . . . shit! Just carry me . . . back home and . . . goddamn . . . let me die. I'm . . . god-damn . . . burning up out here."

Flenco hugs his skinny body tight and feels one of his emaciated wrists. Hands that used to hold a silver microphone hang limply from his cadaverous arms, all speckled with liver spots. She wants him to hold on a little longer because she doesn't know if the healer has worked his way up to raising the dead yet. She knows a little of his scanty history. Born to Christian Seminoles and submerged for thirty-seven minutes in the frigid waters of Lake Huron at the age of fourteen, he was found by divers and revived with little hope of ultimate survival by firefighters on a snow-covered bank. He allegedly lay at death's door in a coma for nine weeks, then suddenly got out of his bed, ripping the IV tubes out, muttering without cursing, walked down the hall to the intensive care unit where a family of four held a death vigil over their ninety-year-old grandmother fatally afflicted with a ruptured duodenum, and laid his hands on her. The legend goes that within two minutes the old lady was sitting up in the bed demanding fudge ripple on a sugar cone and a pack of Lucky Strikes. Fame soon followed and the boy's yard became littered with the sick and the crippled, and the knees of his jeans became permanently grass-stained from kneeling. The walking canes piled up in a corner of the yard as a testament to his powers. A man brought a truck once a week to collect the empty wheelchairs. He made the blind see, the mute speak. A worldwide team of doctors watched him cure a case of wet leprosy. The president had him summoned to the White House, but he could not go; the street in front of his house was blocked solid with the bodies of the needing-to-be-healed. People clamored after him, and women for his seed. The supermarket tabloids proclaim that he will not break the vow he gave to God in the last few frantic moments before sinking below the waters of Lake Huron: if God would bring him back from a watery death, he would remain pure and virginal in order to do His work. And now he has come south like a hunted animal to seek out the legions of believers with their sad and twisted limbs.

"Flenc," Mr. Redding coughs out, "How many goddamn times I told you . . . oh shit . . . not to . . . aw hell, *ahhhhh*."

THE TENT IS DOWN, the rain has ceased. The footsteps of many are printed in the mud. He's had to sign autographs this time, and fighting the women off is never easy. They are convinced the child they'd bear would be an Albert Einstein, an Arnold Schwarzenegger, a Tom Selleck with the brain of Renoir. Some tell him they only want him for a few moments to look at something in the back seat of their car, but he knows they are offering their legs and their breasts and their mouths. He can't resist them any more. He's thinking about getting out of the business. The promise has already been broken anyway, and the first time was the hardest.

His bodyguards and henchmen push with arms spread against the surging crowd, and his feet suck in the mud as he picks his way to his Caddy. All around sit cars and pickup trucks parked or stuck spinning in the mud as the weak sun tries to smile down between the parting clouds.

He gets into the car and inserts the ignition key and the engine barks instantly into life with the merest flick of the key. The engine is as finely tuned as a Swiss watchmaker's watch and it hums with a low and throaty purring that emanates from glasspack mufflers topped off with six feet of chrome. He tromps on the gas pedal and the motor rumbles, cammed up so high it will barely take off.

He hits the gas harder and the Caddy squats in the mud, fishtailing like an injured snake through the quagmire of goop. The crowd rushes the bodyguards, pushing their burly bodies back and down and trampling them underfoot, stepping on their fingers, surging forward to lay their once withered hands on the dusty flanks of the healer's automobile. Faces gather around the windows outside and the healer steers his machine through the swampy mess of the pasture and over to a faint trail of gravel that leads to the highway. Many hands push and when he guns the big car mud balls thwack hollowly and flatten on the pants and shirts of the faithful left gawking after him in his wake. They wave, beat their chests to see him go. Liberated children turn handsprings in the mud and perform impromptu fencing matches with their useless crutches and these images recede quickly through the back window as the car lurches toward the road.

The healer looks both ways before pulling out on the highway. Cars are lined on both sides all the way to the curves that lie in the distance. Horns blare behind him and he turns the car north and smashes the gas pedal flat against the floorboard. The big vehicle takes the road under its wheels and rockets past the lines of automobiles. Small hands wave from the back seats as he accelerates rapidly past them.

The needle on the speedometer rises quickly. He eyes the gas gauge's red wedge of metal edges toward FULL. He finds K.D. Lang on the radio and fishes beneath the seat for the flask of vodka his bodyguards have secreted there. The prearranged destination is Marion, Arkansas, where droves of helpless are rumored to be gathered in a field outside the town.

He takes one hit, two hits, three hits of vodka and pops the top on the hot Coke while reaching for his smokes. His shoes are slathered with mud and his shirt is dirty, but fresh clothes await him somewhere up ahead. Everything is provided. Every bathroom in the South is open to him. The Fuzzbuster on the dash ticks and he hits the brakes just in time to cruise by a cruiser hidden in a nest of honeysuckle. At fifty-seven mph.

He feels weak and ashamed for breaking his vow, but the women won't let him alone. They seem to know the weakness of his flesh. A new issue of *Penthouse* is under the seat. He reaches over and takes his eyes off the road for a moment, pulls the magazine out. He flips it open and the pictures are there, with nothing left to the imagination, the long legs, the tawny hair, the full and pouting lips. With a sharp stab of guilt he closes it up and shoves it back under the seat. He can't go on like this. A decision has to be made. There are too many who believe in him and he is the vessel of their faith. He knows he's unworthy of that trust now. It's going to be embarrassing if God decides to let him down one night in front of a hundred and fifty people. The crowd might even turn ugly and lynch him if he's suddenly unable to heal. They've come to expect it. They have every right to expect it. But they don't know about his needs. They don't know what it's like to be denied the one thing that everybody else can have: the intimate touch of another.

He lights the cigarette and cracks the vent as a smattering of raindrops splatters across the windshield. He turns the wipers on and passes through a curtain of rain as perpendicular as a wall, crosses over onto a shiny darkened highway with tiny white explosions of water pinging up on its surface. He tromps on the gas pedal and the Caddy's tires sing their high-speeded whine. Small heads on front porches turn like tennis spectators as a black flash shoots down the road. He waves.

MR. REDDING LIES near comatose under the shade tree Flenco has dragged him to, and people coming out of the café now are giving him queasy looks. Flenco knows that some good citizen might have an ambulance called.

"Just hold on now, baby," Flenco says. "I feel it in my heart he's coming any minute now."

"I don't give a . . . give a good . . . a good . . . a good goddamn . . . I don't give a shit who's coming," Mr. Redding hacks out. His lips are slimy with a splotching of pink foam and his breath rattles in his chest like dry peas in a pod. He quivers and shakes and licks his lips and groans. Flenco cradles his graying head in her ample lap and rubs the top of his hat with her tremendous sagging breasts. Her rose-tipped nipples miss the passion that used to be in Mr. Redding's tongue. Flenco deeply feels this loss of sexual desire and sighs in her sleep at night on the couch while Mr. Redding hacks and coughs and curses in the bedroom and gets up to read detective magazines or rolls all over the bed. She's ashamed of her blatant overtures and attempts at enticement, the parted robe, the naked toweling off beside the open bathroom door, the changing of her underwear in the middle of the day. Mr. Redding appears not to notice, only lights one Pall Mall after another and swears.

She has sent a wide-eyed little boy inside for another chocolate milkshake and he brings it out to her under the tree where she holds the gasping wheezebag who used to belt out one Elvis song after another in his white jumpsuit with the silver zippers. He'd been nabbed for bad checks in Texas, was on the run from a Mann Act in Alabama, but Flenco fell in love with his roguey smile and twinkling eyes the first time she saw him do "You Ain't Nothin' but a Hound Dog" at the junior-senior prom. His battered travel trailer had a cubbyhole with a stained mattress that held the scented remnants of other nights of lust. But Flenco, pressed hard against the striped ticking with her head in a corner, found in his wild and enthusiastic gymnastics a kind of secret delight. Shunned by her schoolmates, sent to the office for passing explicit notes to boys, downtrodden by the depression caused by her steady eating, Flenco was hopelessly smitten in the first few minutes with this hunk of "Burning Love."

Now her lover lies wasted in her lap, his true age finally showing, his wrinkled neck corded with skin like an old lizard's as he sags against her and drools. She's not asking for immortality; she's not asking for the Fountain of Youth; she's only asking for a little more time. The hope that burns in her heart is a cradle lit to the memory of physical love. She wipes his hot face tenderly with a wadded napkin soaked in the cold sweat from the milkshake cup. Mr. Redding turns and digs his head deeper into her belly. People at the tables in the café are staring openly through the windows now, and Flenco knows it's only a matter of time before somebody calls the lawdogs.

"Can I do anything for you, baby?" she says.

Mr. Redding turns his eyes up to her and the pain buried in them is like a dying fire.

"Hell yeah you can . . . do . . . something . . . goddamn . . . do something . . . oh shit . . . for me. You can . . . goddamn . . . oh shit . . . you can . . . just . . . hell . . . by God . . . shoot me."

"Oh baby, don't talk like that," Flenco says. Her eyes mist up and she covers his face with her breasts until he reaches up with both hands and tries to push the weighty mass of her mammary monsters up out of the way.

"Goddam, what you . . . what you trying to . . . trying to . . . I didn't say . . . smother me," Mr. Redding says.

Flenco doesn't answer. She closes her eyes and feels the former flicks of his tongue across her breastworks in a memory as real as their truck.

THE ROAD IS STRAIGHT, the cotton young and strong, and the Caddy is a speeding bullet across the flat highway. The needle is buried to the hilt at 120 and the car is floating at the very limit of adhesion, weightless, almost, drifting slightly side to side like a ship lightly tacking on the ocean in the stiff edges of a breeze. The blue pulses of light winking far behind him in the sun are like annoying toys, no more.

The healer dips handful after handful of roofing tacks out of the sack beside him and flings them out the open window, scattering them like bad seeds. The blue lights fade, are gone, left far behind. Others of like bent are waiting probably somewhere ahead, but he'll deal with them when the time comes.

Fruit and vegetable stands flash by the open windows of the car, junk peddlers, mobile homes, stacked firewood corded up on the sides of the road for sale, waving people, fans. It is these people he heals, these people crushed and maimed by the falling trees, by the falling house trailers, by the falling cars and junk. These innocents carving a life out of the wilderness with their hands, these with so much faith that he is merely an instrument, a transmitter to funnel the energy required to make them stand and throw away their braces. He thinks of the promise he made going down reaching for the surface of Lake Huron. He gets another drink of the vodka and lights another cigarette and shakes his head as the hubcaps glitter in the sun.

"Lord God I wouldn't have touched her if I was the Pope!" he suddenly screams out into the car, beating his fist on the seat. He turns his head and shouts out the open window? "Why didn't you let me die and then bring me back as the Pope? Huh? You want to answer that one, Lord?"

He takes another quick suck of the hot vodka. His shoulders shiver, and he caps it.

"I cain't cure everbody in the whole world!"

He slows down and rolls to about fifteen mph and shouts to a God maybe lurking behind a dilapidated cotton pen and guarded by a pink Edsel with the hood on the roof.

"You ought not made it so tough on me! I ain't like Jesus, I'm human! I can't do it no more, they's too many of 'em! They's too many women! I take back my promise, I quit!"

The long, low surprised face of a farmer in a 1953 Chevrolet pickup with a goat in the back passes by him in slow motion, his head hanging out the window, a woman looking over his shoulder, seeing, figuring the black car and the haranguing finger poking out at a telephone pole, gathering her wits, her thoughts, her breath, to point back, inhale, scream: "It's HIM! PRAISE WONDERFUL GOD IT'S HIIIIIIM!"

The healer looks. He sees the old black pickup grind to a halt, the one brake light coming on, the woman hopping out the door, arms waving, the farmer leaning out the window waving. For the first time ever the healer is tempted to burn rubber and leave them smelling his getaway fumes, leave behind him unheard the story of their huge drooling son, prisoner of the basement, chained in the garage at the family reunions. But the faces of these two parents are lit like rays of sunshine with the knowledge that a modern messiah has chosen the road that borders their alfalfa patch as the place to receive His divine instructions.

The woman runs up to the side of the car and lays her hands on the fender as if she'd hold it to keep the car from leaving. Her beady eyes and panting breath and hopeless, eternal, hope-filled face tell the healer this woman has a task of such insurmountable proportions she's scarce shared the secret of her problem with minister or preacher or parson, that this one's so bad she can't quit now. Holy cow. What pining cripple on his bed of moldy quilts with his palsied arms shaking lies waiting nearly forever for his release? What afflicted lamb has lain behind a curtain to be hidden from company all these years? Here, he sees, are the mother and the father, the suffering parents, here with their pain and their hope and their alfalfa patch and cows and fish ponds, their world struck askew by the birth or the affliction or the accident that befell their fallen one, with neither hope of redemption or cure available for what might be eating mothballs or masturbating in old dirty underwear and hiding it under his mother's mattress to be discovered when the springs need turning, might be roaming the pastures by night creeping stealthily upon the female livestock.

"Healer," the woman asks, "will you heal my child?"

HE'S NOT COMING, Flenco suddenly decides. In a burst of thought process too deep for her to understand, a mere scab on the broad scar of telepathy which man's mind forgot to remember eons ago, she knows somehow that another emergency has detained him. She knows, too, that they must therefore go find him. She gets up and catches Mr. Redding under the armpits and drags him through the dust toward the truck, where now in large numbers on the other side of the café windows people stand gathered to track the proceedings and place wagers on the estimated time of arrival of Mr. Redding's demise.

"Oh hope, there's hope," she chants and pants. His heels make two trails of dust through the parking lot, but his loafers stay on like a miracle or a magic trick. Flenco gets him next to the running board and stoops to release the precious burden of him, opens the door, gives a hefty grunt, and hauls him up into the seat. Mr. Redding falls over against the horn of the truck and it begins to blow as Flenco shuts the door and runs around to the other side. She yanks open the door and pushes him erect in the seat and reaches across him and locks the door so he won't fall out and hurt himself any worse. Those cigarettes have a hold on him that keeps him from eating, from gaining weight, from not wheezing in the early morning hours when she awakens beside him and lies in the dark staring at his face and twirling the tufts of gray hair on his chest around her fingers. But maybe the healer can even cure him of his addiction, drive the blackness from his lungs, the platelets from his aorta, flush the tiny capillaries in their encrusted fingers of flesh. She belts him in.

Mr. Redding sits in a perfect and abject state of apathy, his head keened back on his neck and his closed eyes seeing nothing. Not even coughing.

"Hold on, baby," Flenco says, and cranks the truth. Truckers and patrons stand gawking at the rooster tail of dust and gravel kicked up by the spinning wheel of the truck, then it slews badly, hits the road sliding, and is gone in a final suck of sound.

WITH STABBING MOTIONS of her arm and hand, index finger extended, the mother directs the healer into the yard. A white picket fence with blooming daffodils belies the nature of the thing inside.

"Please, he's a baby, harmless really, come in here, behind, I just know you, please, my mother she, my brother too they," she gasps.

The healer turns in and sees the black pickup coming behind him, the goat peeking around the cab as if directing its movement, this Nubian. Before he can fully stop the car, the woman is tugging on his arm, saying, "In here, you, oh, my husband, like a child, really."

He opens the door and starts out as the truck slides to a stop beside him, dust rising to drift over them. The healer waves his hand and coughs and the woman pulls on his arm. The farmer jogs around the hood on his gimpy leg and they each take an arm and lead him up the steps, across the porch, both of them talking in either ear a mix of latent complaints, untold griefs, and shared blames for the years this child born wrong and then injured in the brain has visited on this house. The healer is dragged into a living room with white doilies under lamps and a flowerful rug spread over polished wood and a potbellied stove in one corner where a dead squirrel sits eating a varnished walnut.

"Back here, in here, he," the woman rants.

"You know, he, by golly, our field," the farmer raves.

The healer is afraid they're going to smell his breath and he turns his face from side to side as he's dragged with feet sliding to the back room, inside the closet, down hidden stairs revealed by a trapdoor. The farmer unlocks a door in the dark, hits a switch. A light comes on. Gray walls of drabness lie sweating faintly deep in the earth's damp, and they're hung with old mattresses, brown with spots. The furniture in the room is soft with rot, green with mold. A large naked, drooling hairy man sits playing with a ball of his own shit in the center of the room, his splayed feet and fuzzy toes black with dirt and his sloped forehead furrowed in concentration. He says, "*Huuuuuuuurrrrrnnn . . .*"

The healer recoils. The hairy man sits happily in the center of the floor amongst plates of old food and the little pies he has made, but looks up and eyes his parents and the paling youth between and instantly his piglike eyes darken with total ignorance or, like the darkest of animals, an unveiled hostile threat.

"*Hurrrrr,*" he says, and swivels on his buttocks to face them.

"Sweet Lord Jesus Christ," the healer whispers. "Get me out of here."

"Not so fast, young fella," the farmer says, and unlimbers from a back pocket a hogleg of Dirty Harry proportions, backs to the door behind him, locks it, pockets the key deep in his overalls.

It doesn't smell nice at all in this dungeon and the thing before him begins to try to get up on its knees and makes sounds of wet rumbling wanting deep in its throat. The eyebrows knit up and down and together and apart, and the healer draws back with his hands up because the man is sniffing now, trying like a blind calf to scent his mother, maybe remembering milk.

MR. REDDING LIES back in the seat not even harrumphing but merely jackknifed into the position his wife has seated him in, like a form set in concrete, while the truck roars down the road. Flenco slurps the sediment of her shake through the straw and flings the used container out the window into a passing mass of sunflowers' bright yellow faces. Her right hand is clenched upon the wheel and her foot is pressed hard on the gas.

"Hold on, baby," she says. "I don't know where he's at but we're going to find him." Her mouth is grim.

Mr. Redding doesn't answer. He sits mute and unmoving with his head canted back and lolling limply on his neck, the squashed knot of his reversible fishing hat pulled down over his ears. He seems uninterested in the green countryside flashing by, the happy farms of cows grazing contentedly on the lush pasture grass, the wooded creeks and planted fields within the industry of American agriculture thriving peacefully beside the road.

Flenco reaches over and gets one of his cigarettes from his pocket and grabs a box of matches off the dash. She doesn't usually smoke but the situation is making her nervous. Afraid that his rancid lips might never again maul her fallow flesh, she scratches the match on the box and touches the whipping flame to the tip of the Pall Mall 100. Deluged with the desperation of despair, she draws the smoke deep and then worries her forehead with the cigarette held between her fingers. Her eyes scan the fertile fields and unpainted barns for a gathering of cripples miraculously assembled somewhere to seek out the ultimate truth. Somewhere between the borders of three counties a black Caddy runs speeding to another destination and she must intercept it or find its location. The rotting fruit of her romance lies hanging in the balance. The sad wreck of her lover must be rejuvenated. All is lost if not.

Flenco remembers the early years with Mr. Redding. Through him the ghost of Elvis not only lived but sang and whirled his pumping hips to dirges engraved on the brains of fans like grooves in records. He could get down on one knee and bring five or six of them screaming to their feet and rushing to the edge of the stage, the nostalgic, the overweight, the faded dyed ever faithful. Now this sad, wasted figure lays his head back on the seat with his lips slightly parted, his tongue drying.

Flenco smokes the cigarette furiously, stabs the scenery with her eyes, roars down the left fork of the road where a sign says HILLTOP 10 MILES. Dust hurtles up behind the pickup as it barrels down the hill. Flenco has the blind faith of love but she panics when she thinks that she might not find the healer, that he might be out of reach already, that he might have taken an alternate road and be somewhere else in the county, doing his work, healing the minions who seek him out, laying his hands on other unfortunates whose despair has eclipsed hers. But as long as there is gas in the truck, as long as Mr. Redding draws breath, she will drive until the wheels fall off the truck, until the cows come home, until they piss on the fire and call the dogs. Until hope, however much is left, is smashed, kicked around, stomped on, or gone. Until Mr. Redding is dead.

Flenco eyes him and feels uneasy over his stillness. She's never known him to be this quiet before. She smashes harder on the gas and her beloved sways in the curves.

"Hold on, baby," she whispers.

THE HEALER STANDS unmoving with the hard round mouth of the pistol in his back. The man on the floor is growling low and grinding his tartared teeth. His hairy arms are encrusted with a nasty crap.

"*Aaaarrrrr*," he says.

"Yes, darling," the mother coos. "The nice man has come to help us. You like the nice man, don't you, dear?"

"He likes to play," the farmer says. "He plays down here all the time, don't you, son?" the farmer says. "We just keep him down here so he won't scare people," he explains.

The parents see no need to recite the list of stray dogs and hapless cats caught and torn limb from limb, dripping joints of furred meat thrust mouthward without mayonnaise. The six-year-old girl still missing from last year is best not spoken of. The farmer now makes use of a pneumatic tranquilizer gun before laying on the chains and padlocks at night. Deliver at home beside his stillborn twin like Elvis, the hairy one has a headstone over his undug grave.

The warped and wavy line of his dented skull is thick with a rancid growth where small insect life traverses the stalks of his matted hair. He sways and utters his guttural verbs and fixes the healer's face with his bated malevolence and grunts his soft equations into the dusty air.

"He wants to play," the mother says. "Ain't that cute."

"Cute as a bug," the farmer says, without loosening his grip on the pistol.

"I can't heal him," the healer says.

"What did you say?" the farmer says.

"Did he say what I think he said?" the mother says.

"I think you better say that again," the farmer says.

"I can't heal him. I can't heal anything like this."

"What are you saying?" the mother says.

"You heard what he said," the farmer says. "Says he can't heal him."

"Can't?" the mother says.

"I can't," the healer says, as the man on the floor drools a rope of drool and moans a secret rhyme and moves his shoulders to and fro and never takes his eyes off the healer's face.

"I bet you'd like to know what happened to him," the mother says.

"Horse kicked him," the farmer says.

"Right in the head," the mother says.

"Turned him ass over teakettle," the farmer says. "Kicked him clean over a fence."

"Like to kicked half his head off," the mother says. "But you've cured worse than this. That little girl over in Alabama last year with that arm growed out of her stomach and that old man in the Delta who had two and a half eyes. You can heal him. Now heal him."

"We done read all about you," the farmer says. "We been trying to find you for months."

"And then he just come driving right by the place," the mother says. "Will wonders never cease."

The man on the floor is trying to form the rude impulses necessary to gather his legs beneath himself and put his feet flat on the floor. He wants to stand and will stand in a moment, and the farmer reaches quickly behind him for a coiled whip on a nail.

"Easy now, son," he says.

A low, uneasy moaning begins at sight of the bullwhip, and the bared teeth alternate with that in a singsong incantation as he totters up onto his knees and rests his folded knuckles flat on the floor. The hair is long on his back and arms and legs. His face is transfixed with an ignorance as old as time, yet a small light burns in his eyes, and he has a little tail six inches in length extending from the coccyx bone with a tufted tip of bristles. He slides forward a few inches closer to the healer. Old bones lie piled in corners for safekeeping with their scraps of blackened flesh.

"You might as well go on and heal him," the farmer says. "We ain't letting you out of here till you do."

"He's been like this a long time," the mother says.

"You don't understand," the healer says. "I've never dealt with anything like this."

"You cured cancer," the farmer says.

"Raised the dead, I've heard," the mother says.

"No ma'am. Ain't nobody ever raised the dead but Jesus Himself," the healer says, as the thing begins to look as if it would like to grab his leg. He tries to retreat, but the gun is in his back like a hard finger.

"What you think, mama?" the farmer says.

"I think he's trying to pull our leg," she says.

"You think he's a false prophet?"

"Might be. Or maybe he's used up all his power?"

"I known it was him when I seen that black car," she says.

"Lots of people have black cars," the healer says dully, unable to take his own eyes off those dully glinting ones before him. What lies inside there will not do to look at, it won't be altered by human hands, probably should have been drowned when it was little. "Don't let him hurt me," he says.

"Hurt you? Why he ain't going to hurt you," the mother says. "He just wants to play with you a little bit. We come down here and play with him all the time, don't we, daddy."

"That's right," the farmer says. "Hopfrog and leap-scotch and like that. Go on and lay your hands on him. He won't bite or nothing, I promise."

"He's real good most of the time," she says. "We just keep him penned up so he won't hurt hisself."

"I can't . . . I can't . . ." the healer begins.

"Can't what?" the farmer says.

"Can't what?" the mother says.

"*Touch* him," the healer breathes.

"Uh oh," says the farmer. "I's afraid of that, mama."

"You people have got to let me out of here," the healer says. "I'm on my way to Arkansas."

"Wrong answer, mister," the farmer says.

"Definitely the wrong answer," the mother says.

Their boy moves closer and his snarling mouth seems to smile.

FLENCO STANDS IN her nightgown and robe and curlers, pumping gas into the neck of the fuel tank located in the left rear quarter panel of the truck. Years ago Mr. Redding took a hammer and screwdriver to it so that it would readily accept a leaded gasoline nozzle. Flenco pumps five dollars worth into it and hands the money to the attendant who wiped no windshield and checked no oil but stood gawking at the rigid figure of Mr. Redding displayed in the seat like a large sack of potatoes. The attendant takes the five and looks thoughtfully at Flenco, then opens his mouth to ask:

"Lady, is this guy all right?"

Flenco starts to go around and get behind the wheel and then, when she sees the beer signs hung in the windows of the gas station, thinks of the twenty-dollar bill wadded in the pocket of her robe like used facial tissue.

"Well he's been sick," she says, hurrying toward the door of the building.

"I don't believe he's feeling real good right now," he says to her disappearing back. When she goes inside, he watches her heading for the beer coolers at the back of the store and steps closer to the open window of the truck. He studies Mr. Redding from a vantage point of ten inches and notices that his lips are blue and his face is devoid of any color, sort of like, a *lot* like, an uncle of his who was laid out in a coffin in the comfort of his own home some two weeks before.

"Mister," he says. "Hey, mister!"

Mr. Redding has nothing to say. Flenco comes rushing back out the door with three quart bottles of cold Busch in a big grocery sack and a small package of cups for whenever Mr. Redding feels like waking up and partaking of a cool, refreshing drink. She eyes the attendant suspiciously and gets in the truck and sets the beer on the seat between them, pausing first to open the bottle and set it between her

massive thighs. She leans up and cranks the truck and looks at the
attendant who steps back and holds up one hand and says, "Don't
mind me, lady, it's a free country." Then she pulls it down into D and
roars out onto the road.

Flenco gooses it up to about sixty and reaches over briefly to touch
Mr. Redding's hand. The hand is cool and limp and she's glad the fever
has passed. He'll feel better now and he's had a nap, maybe, not be so
irritable. Maybe she can talk to him reasonably. His temper's never
been good even when he was sober which hasn't been much these last
twenty years. Flenco wonders where all those years went to and then
realizes that one day just built onto another one like with a mason
stacking bricks. All those nights in all those beer joints with all that
singing and stomping and screaming and women shouting out declara-
tions of desire for the frenzied figure that was him just past his prime
blend together in her mind and spin like carousel horses in a fun-house
ride. They billed him as Uncle Elvis, and he's told Flenco a little about
his one trip up the river and how they'd hit you in the head with something if you didn't act right, but those days are long gone and what does
it matter now since the cars he stole were transient things and even now
probably lie stripped and rusted out in some junkyard bog, a hulking
garden of flowers adorning their machine-gunned sides?

Flenco feels guilty for feeling her faith sag a little when she thinks
of all the miles of roads the healer could be on and how easy it will be
to miss him. She wonders if it was smart to abandon her big billboard
sign by the side of the road and take off like this, but she was feeling
the grip of a helpless sudden hopeless inertia and there was nothing to
do but put some road under her wheels.

Flenco glances at Mr. Redding who is still oblivious to everything
with the wind sailing up his nostrils. She takes a hefty slug of the beer
between her legs. She nudges him.

"You want some of this beer, baby? You still asleep? Well you just go on and take you a nap, get rested. Maybe you'll feel better when you wake up."

Flenco hopes that's so. She hopes for a clue, a sign somehow, maybe that gathering of the crippled in a field like she's heard happens sometimes. If she can find him, she'll deliver Mr. Redding into the healer's healing hands herself. But if she can't, she doesn't know what she's going to do. She feels like the eleventh hour is fast approaching, and her beloved sits on the seat beside her in stony silence, his mouth open, his head canted back, the wind gently riffling his thin gray hair now that his reversible cap has blown off.

"I THINK MAYBE they need a little time to get to know one another, mama, what do you think?" the farmer says.

"That might be a good idear," the mother says. "Leave 'em alone together awhile and maybe they can play."

The healer looks for a place to run but there are no windows in the airless chamber of what his good work has brought him to and no door but the one the farmer guards with the point of a gun.

"You can't leave me down here with him," the healer says, and he searches for some shred of sanity in the seamed faces of the farmer and his wife. His playmate edges closer.

"You could even eat supper with us if you wanted to after you heal him," the mother says. "Be right nice if we could all set down at the table together."

"He makes too big a mess for him to eat with us very much," the farmer says, a little apologetically, gesturing with the gun. "Throws his food everywhere and what not."

The farmer turns with the key in his pocket and fumbles down deep in there for it. He takes the key out and has to almost turn his back on the healer to get it in the lock, but he said, "I wouldn't try nothing funny if I was you."

"If you're scared of him biting you we'll hold him and not let him bite you," the mother says.

The key clicks in the lock and the farmer says, "I just don't believe he's much of a mind to heal him, mama. We can go up here and take us a nap and when we come back down they liable to be discussing philosophy or something, you cain't never tell."

"You people don't understand," the healer says. "He's beyond help. There's nothing I can do for him. I don't deal with the mind. I deal with the body."

"Ain't nothing wrong with his body," the mother says. "We just had to slow him down a little."

"His body's in good shape," the farmer says. "He's strong as a ox. Why I've seen him pull cows out of mud holes before. I don't believe he knows how strong he is."

"We'll be back after a while," the mother says, and out the door she goes.

"Come on, daddy," she says back. The farmer backs out the door holding the gun on the healer and then the door closes. There are sounds of the other lock being affixed on the other side. The healer backs hard into the corner and eyes the mumbling being in front of him.

"Jesus would heal him if He was here!" the farmer hollers through the thick door. "I done read all about what He done in the Bible! What They've done, They've done laid this burden on us to test our faith? Ain't that right, mama!"

"That's right, daddy!" the mother shouts through the door.

"We been tested!" the farmer screams. "We been tested hard and we ain't been found wanting! Have we, mama!"

"You got that right, daddy! Lot of folks couldn't put up with what we've put up with!"

"Just don't make him mad!" the farmer shrieks. "Don't try to take nothing away from him if he's playing with it! He don't like that! He's a little spoiled!"

"He likes to rassle but don't get in a rasslin' match with him 'cause he gets mad sometimes! Don't get him mad! We'll be back in about a hour! Talk to him! He likes that!"

A rapid clump of footsteps climbing up the stairs fades away to a slammed door above. The healer flattens himself in the corner with his arms bracing up the walls.

"Don't touch me, please," he says, then adds, "I'm not going to hurt you."

The prisoner has made himself a bed of soiled quilts and assorted bedding and he pillows his head with a discarded tire. His nest is knotted with hairs and his lair is infested with lice. The farmer has snipped his hamstrings and Achilles tendon on alternate legs and cauterized the severed sinews while the mother kept the head restrained and the howling muffled with towels rolled and stuffed over his mouth one midnight scene years ago. He moves toward the healer slowly, hard. The healer watches the painful stance, the shifting feet, the arms outspread for balance, and he walks like a man on a tightrope as he makes his way across. Perhaps to kiss? His dangling thangling is large and hairy, swaying there like a big, brown anesthetized mole.

The healer watches him come. On the edges of the wasted fields of the South and stuck back in the roadless reaches of timber where people have trails like animals, the unseen, faceless sum of mankind's lesser genes quietly disassemble cars and squat underneath trees talking, and back of them lie small dwellings of rotted wood and sagging floors where strange children sit rapt for hours on end slavering mutely and uttering no words from their stunned mouths. Pictures of porches full of them all shy and embarrassed or smiling in delight turn up now and again here and there, but no visitor but the documenter of the far less fortunate comes to visit again. It is not that they are not God's children, but that mankind shuns them, bad reminders of rotted teeth and mismatched eyes, uncontrollable sexual desire turned loose in the woods to procreate a new race of the drooling mindless, eating where they shit. He is like them, but even they would not accept him. An old midwife who knew anything would not allow the question. In the first few desperate moments the hand would smother the mouth, pinch the nostrils, still the heaving chest trying to draw in the first tiny breath. The brother and sister above know this. They have known it for years.

The thing comes closer and the healer looks into its depthless eyes, eyes like a fish that lives so deep in the dark black of the ocean and has no need to see. He thinks of the woman's legs in the back seat of the car parked behind a Walgreens in Sumter and the strength of the promise to God. He thinks not of retribution or outrage, and not even fear anymore. He thinks of mercy, and lambs, and he brings his hands out from his sides to suffer to him this outcast. His fingers reach and they touch and he clamps them down hard over the ears. Dust motes turn in the air. They stand in stillness, hardly breathing, locked by the touch of another hand. Their eyes close. The healer fills his chest with air. He prepares to command him to heal.

FLENCO SITS SOBBING beside the road in a grove of trees with a cool breeze wafting through, gently moving the hair on Mr. Redding's head. It's a nice afternoon for a nap, but Flenco has no thoughts of sleep. The search is over and he is cold like a slice of bologna, an egg from the refrigerator. The state troopers cluster behind her and slap their ticket books along their legs, heads shaking in utter solemnity or undisguised amazement. The ambulance crew waits, their equipment useless, their Ambu bags and cardiopulmonary cases still scattered over the gravelly grass. The sun is going down and the legendary speeder has not appeared, and the roadblock will soon be broken up, the blue-and-white cruisers sent out to other destinations like prowling animals simply to prowl the roads.

But an interesting phenomenon has briefly materialized to break the boredom of an otherwise routine afternoon, a fat woman drunk and hauling the dead corpse of her husband down the road at ninety, sobbing and screaming and yelling out loud to God, and they wait now only for the coroner to place his seal of approval so that the body can be moved. One trooper leans against a tree chewing a stem of grass and remarks to nobody in particular: "I been to three country fairs, two goat-ropin's and one horse-fuckin', and I ain't never seen nothing like that."

Some chuckle, others shake their heads, as if to allow that the world is a strange place and in it lie things of another nature, a bent order, and beyond a certain point there are no rules to make man mind.

A wrecker is moving slowly with its red light down the road. Doves cry in the trees. And down the road in a field stand three giant wooden crosses, their colors rising in the falling sunlight, yellow, and blue, and tan.